For Flora

THE ROMANCE OF A SHOP

Amy Levy

edited by Susan David Bernstein

broadview editions

Library and Archives Canada Cataloguing in Publication

Levy, Amy, 1861–1889.
    The romance of a shop / Amy Levy ; edited by Susan David Bernstein.

(Broadview editions)
Includes bibliographical references.
ISBN 1-55111-566-2

    1. Women—Employment—England—London—Fiction. 2. Middle class women—England—London—Fiction. 3. London (England)—Fiction. I. Bernstein, Susan David II. Title. III. Series.

PR4886.L25R64 2006   823'.8   C2006-900633-4

Broadview Editions

The Broadview Editions series represents the ever-changing canon of literature in English by bringing together texts long regarded as classics with valuable lesser-known works.

Advisory editor for this volume: Rebecca Conolly

Broadview Press is an independent, international publishing house, incorporated in 1985. Broadview believes in shared ownership, both with its employees and with the general public; since the year 2000 Broadview shares have traded publicly on the Toronto Venture Exchange under the symbol BDP.

We welcome comments and suggestions regarding any aspect of our publications—please feel free to contact us at the addresses below or at broadview@broadviewpress.com.

North America
Post Office Box 1243, Peterborough, Ontario, Canada K9J 7H5
3576 California Road, Post Office Box 1015, Orchard Park, NY, USA 14127
Tel: (705) 743-8990; Fax: (705) 743-8353;
email: customerservice@broadviewpress.com

UK, Ireland, and continental Europe
NBN International, Estover Road, Plymouth PL6 7PY UK
Tel: 44 (0) 1752 202300 Fax: 44 (0) 1752 202330
email: enquiries@nbninternational.com

Australia and New Zealand
UNIREPS, University of New South Wales
Sydney, NSW, 2052 Australia
Tel: 61 2 9664 0999; Fax: 61 2 9664 5420
email: info.press@unsw.edu.au

www.broadviewpress.com

Typesetting and assembly: True to Type Inc., Mississauga, Canada.

PRINTED IN CANADA

Contents

Acknowledgements

I am indebted to the growing legions of Levy scholars, many of whom I met at the colloquium on Amy Levy held at the University of Southampton in July 2002, especially Linda Hunt Beckman, Naomi Hetherington, Ana Parejo Vadillo, and Nadia Valman. Linda and Ana shared their research on Levy and the London literary culture in which she moved. I am also grateful to Christine Pullen for similar generosity and stimulating advice. This edition has benefited from comments provided by Michael Galchinsky and Cynthia Scheinberg. My appreciation as well goes to Julia Gaunce at Broadview Press.

My gratitude extends to Camellia Plc, now part of Linton Park Plc in Kent, which owns Levy's unpublished manuscripts, letters, diaries, scrapbooks, and sketches. The present curator, Mary Ann Prior, assisted me in my two research visits to Linton Park. I appreciate permission from Malcolm Perkins, chair of Camellia, to quote from Levy's unpublished notes taken in the Reading Room of the British Museum. Evelyn Haselgrove and Sheila Morris provided information and access to the archives of the University Women's Club in London, where Levy was an early member. Anne Thomson, librarian at the Newnham College Archive, facilitated my research on Levy at Cambridge, including the photograph of her as a student at Newnham reproduced in this edition.

The University of Wisconsin Graduate School supported me with research grants that funded my work on this edition, especially my fabulous project assistants. Elizabeth Evans hunted down many bibliographic details for the footnotes, and gathered assorted documents from late-Victorian magazines on modern women in London. Julia Chavez discovered material to illuminate stubbornly arcane references, and she assembled in digital form the map of Levy's London in this edition. With the support of the Department of English at the University of Wisconsin, Catherine Price accomplished the sometimes frustrating task of converting the novel into electronic format, and Karin Heffel scrupulously formatted, edited, and proofread the novel and the appendix items. Trevor Coe provided assistance in the last stages of this work.

I am also grateful to colleagues at the University of Wisconsin, including Nancy Rose Marshall for her ready knowledge on matters pertaining to Victorian painting and photography, Laura

McClure for her Greek translations, and Carole Newlands for her advice on Levy's Latin sources. My appreciation goes to Emily Auerbach, who co-hosted my interview on Levy for the downloadable episode of University of the Air on Wisconsin Public Radio on 5 October 2003. Beyond Madison, a wide community of scholars supported this project. The Victoria discussion list provided a convenient forum of specialists for several queries, with valuable replies from Jack Kolb, Keith Ramsey, and Charles Sligh. I thank my friend Rebecca Stott for her comments on the Introduction.

Melvyn New's 1993 edition *The Complete Novels and Selected Writings of Amy Levy, 1861-1889* has made available the work of this Victorian writer to a broad audience today. Levy's writings that I have selected for this volume include a few not collected in New's edition, namely her essays on Christina Rossetti and on the Reading Room of the British Museum, her short story "Eldorado at Islington," and a few of her poems.

My family, Flora Claire Berklein and Daniel Lee Kleinman, have made my work thrive in more ways than I have space to convey.

Introduction

A Snapshot

In his obituary of Amy Levy, Oscar Wilde described *The Romance of a Shop* (1888) as "a bright and clever story, full of sparkling touches," while Richard Garnett, in his entry on Levy in *The Dictionary of National Biography*, barely mentioned the novel as "a minor work of fiction."[1] Recent scholarship has tended to concur with Levy's contemporaries in appraising her second novel, *Reuben Sachs*, on Jewish life in West End London, as the more complex and superior achievement. Yet this "faint praise," as Levy herself regarded the reception of her first novel, does not convey the innovations of the portrayal of modern urban women in this story of four sisters who establish a photography business in the center of London. *The Romance of a Shop* opens up a representational landscape for Victorian feminism when middle-class women's lives were expanding far beyond the confines of the domestic drawing-room to universities, into the streets of the city, the public resources of libraries and women's clubs, and into the workaday world of the shop. The very title of the novel—linking the "romance" of imaginative possibilities for young women with the everyday "shop" of social realism—showcases the kind of border-crossing Levy's writing and indeed her life encompassed. More than the Lorimers' line of business, photography operates as a motif for nineteenth-century debates around art and technology, while the camera lens brings attention to the sisters' "intensely modern young eyes" (chap. I) and the gendered dynamics of the gaze upon young women working and living independently in late-Victorian London. On the cusp of literary modernism, Levy's writing reflects a shifting consciousness, a mode of representation hovering between romance and realism, between idealized visions of remodeled lives for women and men, and the mundane hazards of such social change.

As a middle-class Jewish woman, Levy inhabited both Jewish and gentile cultures, exemplified by *Reuben Sachs*, *The Romance of a Shop*, and her frequent publications in two magazines, *The*

---

1   Garnett's entry is in volume 33 of *The Dictionary of National Biography* (London: Smith, Elder & Co., 1892).

Jewish Chronicle and *The Woman's World*. Levy was the first Jewish student at Newnham College, Cambridge University, in the first decade of both women and Jews at Cambridge. In her brief literary career, cut short by suicide at the age of 27, Levy published three collections of poetry, three novels, numerous short stories and essays, as well as translations of poetry and prose. Her writing, as did her life, suggests the pleasures and perils of a young woman in late-Victorian London, caught between new and old, between opportunities and social disabilities, between privileged and outsider status. Highlighting this structure of in-betweenness, Levy's depictions of London public spaces capture this sense of temporal, spatial, and social discontinuities as the fluctuating edge between tradition and modernity.

Although her writing has only recently been brought back into print, in her day Levy's fiction, poetry, and essays were known to and valued by men and women prominent in literature and the arts, and Levy's calendar of 1889 places her at the center of the London literary scene. Her daily schedule reveals an immersion in the varied opportunities of urban life, an illuminating parallel to *The Romance of a Shop* about middle-class working women inhabiting the multiple dimensions of the modern city. Some highlights of Levy's London life[1] include regular visits to "the Club" (the University Club for Ladies, established in New Bond Street in 1887)[2] and to the British Museum's Reading Room, where Levy regularly researched and met a lively literary network of colleagues, including Olive Schreiner, Eleanor Marx, and Dollie Radford.[3] She attended "at-homes" of the Fabian Society and salon events where she encountered such literary luminaries as Thomas Hardy, Oscar Wilde, George Bernard Shaw, and William Butler Yeats, and an astonishing group of women writers and artists, including Graham Tomson, A. Mary F. Robinson, Alice Meynell, Mona Caird, and Marie Bashkirtseff.[4] Levy's London calendar also records several meetings with Grant Allen, the writer

---

1 See Appendix F for a map of landmarks in Levy's London and *The Romance of a Shop*.

2 See Appendix B2.

3 See Appendix B3 and Appendix C5. For information on Levy's 1889 calendar, see Linda Hunt Beckman, *Amy Levy: Her Life and Letters* (Athens: Ohio UP, 2000) 175-79.

4 For an analysis of the salon culture of London women poets including Levy, see Ana Parejo I. Vadillo, "New Woman Poets and the Culture of the *salon* at the *fin de siècle*," *Women: A Cultural Review* 10.1 (London: Routledge, 1999): 22-34.

whose eugenicist views are captured in his novel *The Woman Who Did* (1895) and in his essays "Plain Words on the Woman Question" and "The Girl of the Future."[1] Levy viewed art exhibits at the Grosvenor Gallery and saw the first London production of *A Doll's House*, a translation of Henrik Ibsen's play by her friend William Archer. Levy's daily life also included visits to the office of the Women's Protective and Provident League, later renamed the Women's Trade Union League, whose secretary Clementina Black appears to have been Levy's closest friend. Like the young female Londoners in *The Romance of a Shop*, *Reuben Sachs*, and in her short fiction, Levy circulated across the metropolis using the public transportation system of omnibuses and trains. In "Ballade of an Omnibus," Levy offers a lyrical account of the passions of modern urban spectatorship from the top of a moving vehicle: "The city pageant, early and late / Unfolds itself, rolls by, to be / A pleasure deep and delicate. / An omnibus suffices me." The vehicle that Levy celebrates offered an open-air platform on top for viewing the "city pageant," a delight enjoyed by Gertrude Lorimer who mounts "boldly to the top of an Atlas omnibus" from where she surveys "regions where the pulses of the great city could be felt distinctly as they beat and throbbed" (80). Both the poem and Gertrude's London travels in *The Romance of a Shop* illuminate the powerful "pleasure" of this moving vantage point of a modern female gaze, a defining element in Levy's aesthetics. Her diurnal calendar also details Levy's ongoing work as an author, since she recorded what, where, and when during the day she wrote, meetings with publishers, and account of payments for her various publications. Thus we gain a snapshot of Levy's bustling and intellectually vibrant activities in the months before her death in September 1889.

Biographical Context

Amy Judith Levy was born on 10 November 1861 into a London middle-class Jewish home. Her parents, Isabelle and Lewis Levy, were cousins, and both her paternal and maternal ancestors had arrived from Central and Eastern Europe in the eighteenth century. Levy herself was the second of seven children—three daughters and four sons. Amy and her older sister Katie wrote plays together and produced a children's magazine, *The Poplar*

---

1 See Appendix D1.

Club Journal, to which many family members contributed. The family belonged to the West London Synagogue of British Jews, located conveniently near their Sussex Place residence. This synagogue was at the forefront of the reform movement in England to bring religious services in line with the acculturated character of modern diasporic Jewry.[1] Little is known about Levy's own religious instruction, although both *Reuben Sachs* and her essays published in *The Jewish Chronicle*, as well as some remarks in her letters to her sister and mother, make evident that she possessed at least a basic knowledge of Jewish traditions.

Consistent with their modern religious practices, Isabelle and Lewis Levy were in the vanguard with respect to female education. In 1876 Levy enrolled at Brighton High School for Girls, as part of the Girls' Public Day School Company, a program of rigorous academic training for secondary schoolgirls founded in 1871 by feminists Emily and Maria Shirreff. Edith Creak, the head of Brighton High School at that time, was herself a member of the very first class of five students at Newnham College, which opened its doors as one of two women's colleges at Cambridge University in 1871.[2] This progressive academic training included a course of study in classical Greek and Latin. It was during her education at Brighton that Levy wrote "Xantippe," about Socrates's wife characterized in a Latin florilegium (a text which may have been available to Levy at Brighton) as "ill-tempered and quarrelsome ... with a constant flood of feminine tantrums and annoyances."[3] Levy's dramatic monologue voices a different perspective, however, through Xantippe's persona:

---

1 Two of these reforms include abbreviated services and sermons delivered in English rather than Hebrew. See Peter Renton, *The Lost Synagogues of London* (London: Tymsder Publishing, 2000).

2 See Ann Phillips, ed., *A Newnham Anthology* (Cambridge UP, 1979) 1-4.

3 Aulus Gellius, *Attic Nights of Aulus Gellius*, trans. John C. Rolfe, vol. 1 (Cambridge, Mass.: Harvard UP, 1961) 85. A note in the text indicates that an English translation of Gellius's florilegium first appeared in the eighteenth century. James Thomson's 1866 essay "A Word for Xantippe" assails the portrayal of the "conjugal life of Saint Socrates and shrew Xantippe." See Karen Weisman, "Playing with Figures: Amy Levy and the forms of Cancellation," *Criticism* 42.1 (Winter 2001): 59-79.

'Twas only that the high philosopher,
Pregnant with noble theories and great thoughts,
Deigned not to stoop to touch so slight a thing
As the fine fabric of a woman's brain—
So subtle as a passionate woman's soul.
I think, if he had stooped a little, and cared,
I might have risen nearer to his height,
And not lain shattered, neither fit for use
As goodly household vessel, nor for that
Far finer thing which I had hoped to be.... [1]

Echoing Elizabeth Barrett Browning's verse-novel *Aurora Leigh* (1856) with its acute delineation of a woman's ravenous appetite and aptitude for classical intellectual study, Levy's Xantippe links patriarchal privileges of the past with current debates about women's higher education. That the question of what she calls here "the fine fabric of a woman's brain" made university education a controversial subject emerges in Levy's depictions of women at Cambridge in a few published stories, including "Between Two Stools." Her unpublished story "Lallie: A Cambridge Sketch" describes Rhoda Chodmonley—a "Newton girl"—as "a modern production—the offspring of a period of social and intellectual transition;—and as such, was it to be wondered at if she bore the marks of acute psychical pain?" [2]

While her Brighton education surely fostered Levy's feminist ideals, she also encountered anti-Semitism from a Brighton classmate whose religious family "did not like to visit Jews, no Orthodox persons *did*." [3] How she fared as the first Jewish student at Newnham College, where she continued her formal education in 1879 upon graduating from Brighton High School for Girls,

---

1 "Xantippe," lines 113-25. This poem is included in Melvyn New, ed., *The Complete Novels and Selected Writings of Amy Levy, 1861-1889* (Gainesville: UP of Florida, 1993) 357-65.

2 Quoted in Linda Hunt Beckman, *Amy Levy: Her Life and Letters* (Athens: Ohio UP, 2000) 43. Levy's poems, such as "Cambridge in the Long" and "Alma Mater," both included in New's collection (see previous note), capture impressions of Cambridge.

3 Quoted in Linda Hunt Beckman, *Amy Levy: Her Life and Letters* (Athens: Ohio UP, 2000) 225.

might be surmised from her 1889 short story, "Cohen of Trinity," about a Jewish male student's "unfortunate University experience" at Cambridge and its aftermath. The irony of the title that alludes to the Cambridge men's college, also forecasts the narrative structure in which the portrayal of Cohen belongs to the perspective of the non-Jewish and implicitly Christian narrator of the story who describes the physical anomaly of a Jew at Cambridge: "A curious figure: slight, ungainly, shoulders in the ears; an awkward, rapid gait, half slouch, half hobble."[1] Just as women's appearance as Cambridge students was a recent phenomenon, so too was the admission of Jewish students only possible with the University Tests Act of 1871, abolishing a religious test of faith for graduates and faculty. Since Oxford and Cambridge universities traditionally were training grounds for the Anglican ministry, both schools were defined by Christian culture, which explains why Jewish students remained a very small minority—only up to a dozen undergraduates—well into the twentieth century.[2]

Following a course of study in classical and modern languages, Levy's literary production at Cambridge was considerable, including her first collection of poems, *Xantippe and Other Verse*, in 1881. After two years at Newnham, Levy left. To be a Jewish woman at Cambridge around 1880 meant a doubly marginalized position, while in the more varied and populous urban setting of London, such social disabilities would be less apparent.[3] The remaining eight years of Levy's too short life were filled with travels on the European continent and an extraordinary involvement with the literary and intellectual culture of 1880s London.

Levy and the "New Woman"

Levy's literary significance in recent scholarship has been bifurcated into two constituencies: those interested in Levy as an Anglo-Jewish Victorian writer and those interested in Levy as a "new woman" author. Edward Wagenknecht's 1983 *Daughters of*

---

1 Amy Levy, "Cohen at Trinity," *The Gentleman's Magazine* 266 (1889): 417-23. Reprinted in *Reuben Sachs*, ed. Susan David Bernstein (Peterborough ON: Broadview Press, 2006).

2 See Todd M. Endelman, *Radical Assimilation in English Jewish History 1656-1945* (Bloomington: Indiana UP, 1990) 77-80.

3 By 1900, women comprised only 15 per cent of students at British universities, according to Carol Dyhouse, *No Distinction of Sex? Women in British Universities 1870-1939* (London: UCL Press, 1996) 7.

the Covenant: Portraits of Six Jewish Women Writers introduced Levy to an audience interested in Jewish literature, while Deborah Epstein Nord's 1990 essay on "Female Community in Late Nineteenth-Century London" brought *The Romance of a Shop* to the attention of academic feminists.[1] Scholars interested in Levy's engagement with gender and sexuality have focused primarily on her poetry, such as "Xantippe" and "Magdalen," the latter a dramatic monologue challenging traditional representations of the biblical "fallen" woman. Moreover, Levy evocatively imagines the complexities of same-sex desire in several lyric poems, such as "London in July," "The Dream," and "In the Mile End Road."[2] While lesbian sexuality does not figure explicitly in *The Romance of a Shop*, the novel does portray a self-sufficient community of young women who establish and maintain a home together, support themselves through their photography business, and relish the pleasures of London: "Life, indeed, was opening up for them in more ways than one. The calling which they pursued brought them into contact with all sorts and conditions of men, among them, people in many ways more congenial to them than the mass of their former acquaintance; intercourse with the latter having come about in most cases through 'juxtaposition' rather than 'affinity'" (135). Levy's wording suggests an additional freedom to choose companions by "affinity" rather than by prescribed social positions. This widening sphere of middle-class women engendered through alternatives to the tradition of marriage and domesticity becomes the chief subject of a plethora of English and American novels published in the last two decades of the nineteenth century.

Ann Ardis estimates that around a hundred novels were written about the "new woman" between 1883 and 1900.[3] Although the moniker "new woman" is credited to Sarah Grand's 1894 essay, "The New Aspect of the Woman Question," depictions of modern young women challenging conventional femininity became increasingly frequent in the decade of Levy's literary career. Published in 1883, *The Story of an African Farm* by Olive Schreiner, who became a close friend of Levy's, presents

---

1 Deborah Epstein Nord, "'Neither Pairs Nor Odd': Female Community in Late Nineteenth-Century London" *Signs: Journal of Women in Culture and Society* 15.41 (Summer 1990): 733-54.

2 See Appendix B4.

3 Ann Ardis, *New Women, New Novels: Feminism and Early Modernism* (New Brunswick, NJ and London: Rutgers UP, 1990) 4.

gender-bending characters, including an impassioned feminist, in a colonial African setting. In contrast, London furnishes a crucial scenery of urban mobility and professional opportunities for modern women in fiction, from *The Romance of a Shop* to George Gissing's *The Odd Women* (1893) and Ella Hepworth Dixon's *The Story of a Modern Woman* (1894). New woman fiction, as literary scholars have grouped these novels of *fin-de-siècle* England, questions traditional gender roles through critiques of marriage, domesticity, and motherhood, by attributing to women sexual passions for men and between women, and by imagining aspiring young women with careers in the public sphere. Like some of her "new woman" counterparts, Levy pursued a university education, traveled independently and with women friends both on the European Continent and in England, smoked cigarettes, and participated in literary salons and the new women's or mixed-gender club culture of 1880s London.

A facet of the new woman is "free unions," or sex expression outside of marriage, a topic often portrayed pessimistically, such as in *The Story of an African Farm, The Woman Who Did*, and in Thomas Hardy's *Jude the Obscure* (1895). In *The Romance of a Shop* the youngest Lorimer sister, Phyllis, embarks on a sexual affair with a married painter, and Levy's treatment of this relationship transposes the naïve female victim of the seduction plot into a knowing and willing partner. However, it is lyric poetry that best captures the new female sexuality of Levy's day. Sappho, the Greek seventh-century BCE poet from Lesbos, was regarded as a classical model of the female wandering bard of love. According to popular legend, Sappho drowned herself over her unrequited love for a boatman named Phaon, presumed to be the focus of desire in Sappho's verse. Significant for Levy's own poetics, the Sapphic tradition was reoriented by two late-Victorian publications: Henry Thornton Wharton's 1885 translation of Sappho and Michael Field's 1889 *Long Ago*. Wharton's translation restored for the first time in English the original feminine pronouns as the object of Sappho's love, and Michael Field's poems in *Long Ago* rearticulated Sappho's story through lesbian sensuality.[1] Sapphic desire also functioned as a counterpart to

---

1 See Appendix C4. "Michael Field" was the pen name of two women, Katherine Bradley (1846-1914) and Edith Cooper (1862-1913), who were aunt and niece, collaborators in verse, prose, and drama, and lived together as lovers. While Levy did not know them, they shared many women poet friends, including Dollie Radford and Vernon Lee.

the new Hellenism, the tradition of "Greek-love" between men derived from ancient Greece that formed a backdrop for male aestheticism and decadence, most famously, though not exclusively, in the work of Oscar Wilde.

In her *Woman's World* essay on Christina Rossetti, Levy situates her subject in this newly accented Sapphic tradition: "A woman poet of the first rank is among those things which the world has yet to produce. Even the broken, beautiful strains which float up to us from Lesbos, tell of a singer whose lyre had few strings; whose voice, exquisite as it must have been, but few notes."[1] For Levy and her contemporaries, Sappho inspired fresh currents in women's poetry, as this "lyre" of female erotic poetics gained more varied forms of expression. In this context of a new Sapphic voice, many of Levy's lyrical poems address a feminine lover, such as "London in July," where the speaker yearns for "My love, she dwells in London town." In some poems, neither the lyrical voice nor the object of love is clearly gendered, an ambiguity that encourages a reading of same-sex desire. In Levy's day emerged an articulated discourse of homoeroticism.[2] Although "homosexuality" did not become the favored term until well into the twentieth century, sexologists Edward Carpenter and Havelock Ellis, and poet John Addington Symonds did introduce concepts, including "the intermediate sex," "sexual inversion," and "uranians," to describe passionate love between women and between men. Among Levy's circle of women writers, Vernon Lee and A. Mary F. Robinson were lovers; Levy knew them both, and possibly was herself in love with Lee.[3] Whether free love, Greek love, or the intermediate sex, the language of sexual liberation permeated Levy's literary London.

Like Levy's life, this late-nineteenth century literature of new womanhood does not uniformly depict a gloriously empowering world for modern middle-class women. New woman fiction of the 1880s and 1890s sketches a decidedly mixed image of exhilarating freedom and overwhelming obstacles as the turbulent condition of this social vanguard in gender transformations. Several novels attest to the costliness of change, such as Mona Caird's *The*

---

1   See Appendix B1.

2   Edward Carpenter's theory of homogenic love was published as *Love's Coming of Age* by T. Fisher Unwin, also the publisher of *The Romance of a Shop*.

3   See Linda Hunt Beckman, *Amy Levy: Her Life and Letters* (Athens: Ohio UP, 2000) 119-22.

Daughters of Danaus (1894) in which two women commit suicide. A new woman character, Hadria, leaves her unsatisfying marriage and her child to pursue a career as a musical composer, only to return home again after encountering myriad barriers. The novel is rife with commentary on the psychological, social, and physical consequences of a feminist movement of young women going against the grain of gender roles. As Hadria reflects, "But I was born ten years too early for the faith of this generation."[1]

While the common explanation of her suicide by her contemporaries attributes this act to an inherently melancholy disposition, Levy's death by charcoal asphyxiation might also be approached in this context of gender pathbreakers, uneasily suspended between change and the tenacious hold of tradition. As Mary Robinson's poem "Will" puts it, "Alone in the kingdom of space I stand / With Hell and Heaven in either hand."[2] It is difficult to fully comprehend the dissonance between the excitement of emancipation and the pressures of custom in Levy's day, but we see this vacillation between hope and despair in much of her writing, from some of her lyrics such as "A Minor Poet," "The Two Terrors," and "Contradictions," to short fiction like "Between Two Stools" and "Eldorado at Islington," and to the wild vacillations of fortune and mood especially tuned to the characters of Phyllis and Gertrude in *The Romance of a Shop*. A few years after Levy's death, E.K. Chambers described Levy as suffering from "this modern disease of pessimism," which he understood as the bleak underside of "a passionate idealist,"[3] an assessment correlative to the doubleness of "romance" and "shop" elements in her novel.

Levy's own sardonic views of social progress convey a profound ambivalence about the set of her era. In "Wise in Her Generation" (1890), Levy portrays a woman who chooses to decline marriage proposals from a wealthy man she does not love, while at the same time recognizing that "there is only one way of success open to a woman: the way of marriage."[4] As this charac-

---

1 Mona Caird, *The Daughters of Danaus* (New York: The Feminist Press, 1989) 451.
2 See Appendix C3.
3 E.K. Chambers, "Poetry and Pessimism," *Westminster Review* 138 (1892): 372, 370.
4 "Wise in Her Generation," *The Woman's World* 3 (1890): 20-23. Reprinted in *The Complete Novels and Selected Writings of Amy Levy, 1861-1889*, ed. Melvyn New (Gainesville: UP of Florida, 1993) 493.

ter puts it, invoking evolutionary language as she meditates on her refusal, "Better be unfit and perish, than survive at such a cost." In a poem privately printed twenty-six years after Levy's death, "A Ballad of Religion and Marriage,"[1] the speaker, speculating on the future of matrimony, chafes against the stubborn perpetuation of traditional femininity:

Monogamous, still at our post,
  Reluctantly we undergo
Domestic round of boiled and roast,
  Yet deem the whole proceeding slow.
Daily the secret murmurs grow;
  We are no more content to plod
Along the beaten paths—and so
  Marriage must go the way of God.

The monotony of "monogamous" domesticity provokes a gathering discontent with "the beaten paths" of the status quo. This leaden pace of dreary daily life "at our post" is accentuated in the final stanza:

Grant, in a million years at most,
  Folks shall be neither pairs nor odd—
Alas! we sha'n't be there to boast
  "Marriage has gone the way of God!"

Readers have variously interpreted the line "Folks shall be neither pairs nor odd—" as envisioning a future society that does not classify people by marital status or sexual orientation. However, the irregular form "Grant" rather than "Granted" might suggest an oblique address to Grant Allen, whose eugenicist views on gender and sexuality were familiar to Levy.[2] A remark in her 1889 calendar suggests an intriguing context for this stanza. On the occasion of a visit to Grant Allen's home, Levy commented about the after-dinner conversation on the Woman Question: "G.A. thinks marriage not permanent."[3] This verse implies that social change is an infinitesimally slow process along the order of Darwinian evolution, with the wry observation that such a schedule necessitates the extinction of the "we" currently craving progress.

---

1 See Appendix B5.
2 See Ana Parejo Vadillo, *Women Poets and Urban Aestheticism* (London: Palgrave, 2005) 211, note 21.
3 Quoted in Linda Hunt Beckman, *Amy Levy: Her Life and Letters* (Athens: Ohio UP, 2000) 177.

Allen inserted his opinion of Levy's suicide into his 1890 essay, "The Girl of the Future," in which he construed higher education for women as deleterious in his eugenic vision of English society: "A few hundred pallid Amy Levys sacrificed on the way are as nothing before the face of our fashionable Juggernaut. Newnham has slain its thousands, and Girton its tens of thousands; the dark places of the earth are full of cruelty."[1] This depiction of Levy's suicide as a senseless martyrdom is but one illustration of the controversy surrounding the new woman and her emancipation from traditional roles through sex expression, through academic training and careers, and through a more extensive presence in the public sphere outside the home. In Levy's poetry and fiction, London provides an exemplary environment for these diverse experiences, and for the hazards hovering over the horizons of change.

A Cultural Cameo of Levy's London

Women working, living, and traveling throughout London without male chaperones are crucial aspects of the urban world Levy inhabited. *The Romance of a Shop* functions as a narrative guide to the modern city, with frequent references to addresses, public establishments, and itineraries. For instance, details of the novel disclose which omnibus line Gertrude uses to travel from Baker Street Station to the British Museum, where she takes "a course in photographic reading." The Reading Room of the British Museum provided a pivotal public space as an educational alternative to the restrictions of Oxbridge universities, and it also offered intellectual comradeship for young women writers. In November 1882, Levy registered as a reader at the Reading Room of the British Museum.[2] Her sister Katie had likewise registered as a reader in March 1881 when she came into her majority, as had several writers and friends, including Clementina Black, Oscar Wilde, and Eleanor Marx. Olive Schreiner registered the following June. This public space, open on a regular basis weekdays and Saturdays, with hours extended into evenings once electric lights were installed in 1879, became an around-

---

1 See Appendix D1.
2 15 November 1882, a few days after Levy turned 21, the minimum age of readers typically admitted to the Reading Room. Information is in the British Museum Archives, "Alphabetical List of Ticket Holders, 1880-1888, L-R." Other dates are from the same source.

the-clock and calendar arena for intellectual pursuits and social exchange. Levy used the Reading Room not only as a networking station, but also as a place for research and writing. Her "British Museum Notes"[1] notebook, probably written in early 1888, includes reading notes on Christina Rossetti, drafts of poems, and five handwritten pages of her short story "Eldorado at Islington." On the back cover is a sketch of a bride in profile with the words "St. George's Hanover Square," mentioned in *The Romance of a Shop*. Later that year, Levy published "The Poetry of Christina Rossetti," and the short story drafted in this notebook appeared in 1889.[2] In the essay, Levy sketches for her readers a female literary tradition by directing them to Rossetti's first collection of verse as "a modest little volume, which may be seen by the curious in the Large Room of the British Museum."

In addition, the Reading Room forms the chief locale in a short story, "The Recent Telepathic Occurrence at the British Museum," and again in an essay, "Readers at the British Museum."[3] Levy's image of this space as a "general workshop," the library of record of the modern industrial state, recalls the history of one of its most prominent readers, Karl Marx, who wrote *Das Kapital* within its circular walls. Levy's conceit of the Reading Room as a "workshop" was taken up after her death by two other frequenters of this space. George Gissing in *New Grub Street* (1891) describes this community of museum readers as "toilers" subject to the environmental hazard of "the Reading-room cough."[4] In *A Room of One's Own* (1929), Virginia Woolf writes, "London was a workshop. London was like a machine. We were all being shot backwards and forwards on this plain foundation to make some pattern. The British Museum was another department of the factory ..."[5]

Levy's own research notebook and her publications furnish a sense of working conditions for women writers in this London

---

1   The unpublished "British Museum Notes" is part of the Amy Levy Archive, Camellia Plc.
2   See Appendix B for the complete text of both the essay and short story.
3   "The Recent Telepathic Occurrence at the British Museum," *The Woman's World* 1 (1888): 31-32. See Appendix B3 for "Readers at the British Museum."
4   George Gissing, *New Grub Street* (New York: Oxford UP, 1998) 106, 83.
5   Virginia Woolf, *A Room of One's Own* (New York and London: Harcourt Brace & Company, 1981) 26.

landmark where women appeared in unprecedented numbers as reported in several magazines of the 1880s.[1] In "Readers at the British Museum" Levy offers an inviting image of the Reading Room to the young female readership of *Atalanta: Every Girl's Magazine*, as she paints a picture of a "vast, circular apartment" with the "lavender-white light of the electric lamps," where "desks and tables are models of comfort and convenience" and where the ventilation system produces an atmosphere likened to "a cool and shady dell" of summertime. Transforming for her audience a heterogeneous public space under "the great dome— almost the largest in the world," Levy inscribes a factory in a drawing-room, thus melding together public and private spheres of labor and domesticity into one realm that itself traverses social boundaries of class and gender. Most significant, Levy fashions the Reading Room as an egalitarian venue with "wonderful accessibility" to a wide spectrum of visitors: "For some it is a workshop, for others a lounge ... in many cases it serves as a shelter,—a refuge, in more senses than one, for the destitute." Here Levy implies the intellectual hunger of many middle-class women still deprived of the benefits of a university education, as the essay repeatedly praises the democratic impulse of a room that "attracts to itself in ever-increasing numbers all sorts and conditions of men and women."

The gender-inclusive phrasing of "all sorts and conditions of men and women" expands upon the title of Walter Besant's novel, *All Sorts and Conditions of Men* (1882), a story of an idealistic wealthy Newnham graduate who disguises her identity and takes up lodgings in East End London in order to help the impoverished by establishing a "People's Palace" in Mile End Road. Social reform occupied the energies of many of Levy's London friends, including Beatrice Potter Webb, Eleanor Marx, and Constance and Clementina Black. In 1887 Constance Black became the librarian for the People's Palace, the establishment inspired by Besant's novel; during her tenure, Black compiled its general catalogue following the principles employed by Richard Garnett when he undertook this endeavor for the library of the British Museum.[2] Garnett's role as a literary mentor to many women working at the British Museum, including Levy, Clementina

---

1 See "Ladies in Libraries," *The Saturday Review* 62 (August 14, 1886): 212-13.

2 Richard Garnett, *Constance Garnett: A Heroic Life* (London: Sinclair-Stevenson, 1991) 57-58.

Black, Mathilde Blind, and Olive Schreiner, affords yet another aperture into the extensive constellation of professional connections that London afforded Levy. Yet the British Museum Reading Room was only one of many landmarks in Levy's everyday London itinerary.

Another venue for cultural exchange between women in these years was the University Club for Ladies, which officially opened in New Bond Street in January 1887. As an early member, Levy frequented this new institution for women with the unusual training of a university or medical education where members might congregate to use the library, attend lectures, enjoy refreshments, or socialize. Levy's essay, "Women and Club Life," considers women's clubs as an established fact of the contemporary cityscape, and as a meeting-ground for old and young, intellectual and fashionable, traditional and modern women.[1] Like her view of the Reading Room of the British Museum as a "refuge," Levy suggests that feminine club life satisfies "the desire among women for a corporate life, for a wider human fellowship, a richer social opportunity." Acknowledging a desire for intercourse beyond the confines of middle-class domesticity, Levy accentuates the importance of this hybrid space for women pursuing careers: "But it is to the professional woman ... that the club offers the most substantial advantages. What woman engaged in art, in literature, in science, has not felt the drawbacks of her isolated position? ... She has to fight her way unknown and single-handed; to compete with a guild of craftsmen all more or less known to one another, bound together by innumerable links of acquaintance and intercourse." The passage makes evident the enormous benefits men have reaped for generations through an extensive and seasoned networking system of clubs. In *The Romance of a Shop*, Levy depicts the effects of this isolation on the Lorimer sisters, who struggle to establish their photographic business clutching whatever threads of social or professional connection that might bolster their reputation. Offering a contemporary London context for this novel, Levy's essay on women's clubs focuses on challenges facing the modern working woman.

In essays and in fiction, Levy addresses the changing conditions for London middle-class women, but she was well aware of the plight of working-class women through her close friend Clementina Black, who advocated for employment reforms on behalf of East End lower-class women who held menial jobs as

1   See Appendix B2.

laundresses and needleworkers. Radical clubs such as the Fabian Society and the Socialist League were also part of Levy's London, frequented by many of her friends, including Webb, the Black sisters, Marx, and Radford. Linda Hunt Beckman's biography maintains that Levy herself did not share her friends' "interest in left-wing politics" and qualifies some scholars' constructions of Levy as a radical social reformer as inaccurate.[1] In "Wise in Her Generation," Levy's narrator construes such activism as a fashionable trend where one character "is very strong on all the social questions. He is also an Agnostic, and a Socialist of an advanced type."[2] If Levy questioned the sincerity of some reformers through her fiction, she knew well the political work of her close friend Clementina Black. Levy's 1889 calendar entries show her repeated presence at "the office" of the Women's Protective and Provident League where Black worked, an address in Levy's immediate Bloomsbury neighborhood. Although Levy herself did not write about the employment struggles of poor women, her name was on the donation lists of the league, and a brief review of her last novel, *Miss Meredith*, relates that profits from Levy's posthumous publications were to be applied to the "philanthropic work of Miss Clementina Black."[3]

Although we can only speculate about the influence on Levy of her friend's commitment to the rights of poor women laborers, *The Romance of a Shop* does underscore the difficulties faced by working women in its many references to the Lorimers' financial struggles, as well as the monetary problems of their neighbours, including the dressmaker who cannot pay her bills. The sisters' ambiguous status as middle-class women employed both inside and outside the home is another way in which the novel takes up a frontier space between firmly entrenched notions of position based on occupation, wealth, and family. Other narratives Levy wrote also reflect the social and economic challenges of working women, whether within or beyond the domestic sphere. Twice Levy retells the governess's story. A tale about a young Irish woman whose family is forced to leave Ireland due to economic

---

1   Linda Hunt Beckman, *Amy Levy: Her Life and Letters* (Athens: Ohio UP, 2000) 3-4, 83.

2   "Wise in Her Generation," *The Woman's World* 3 (1890): 22. Reprinted in *The Complete Novels and Selected Writings of Amy Levy, 1861-1889* (Gainesville: UP of Florida, 1993) 491.

3   "A Story by Amy Levy," *The Jewish Chronicle* 6 December 1889: 16. See Black's essay about organizing working-class women in London in Appendix D2.

hardship, "Griselda" (1888) explores this familiar form of women's employment in Victorian novels with crisp allusions throughout to Charlotte Brontë's *Jane Eyre* (1847). In *Miss Meredith* (1889), Levy relocates the governess's story to Italy as a cross-cultural romance plot between a salaried Englishwoman and the son of her Italian employer. Even the marriage of one of the Lorimer sisters to a lord whom she first meets while employed as his photographer glances ironically at the plot staple of class-crossing romance in the governess's story.

Like *The Romance of a Shop*, Levy's unpublished writing explores women's work beyond the governess's job. "The Doctor" pits a woman doctor's knowledge and insight about a sick child against a traditional mother's bias for male doctors, and "Miss C's Secretary" reverses the typical gender arrangement in this story of a frail and impressionable young man working as an assistant to a school headmistress on whom he develops a crush.[1] Levy's social realism also registers the stress and dreariness of struggling middle-class characters whose London does not encompass the tony addresses of Kensington and Regent's Park. In "Eldorado at Islington" Levy unfolds the cramped life and dashed dreams of Eleanor Lloyd and her family. At the same time, the Lloyds refuse the "Eldorado" of an uncle's inheritance because to do so would be at the expense of others in worse material conditions: "the money was the fruit of cruelty and extortion: it was wrung from the starving poor."[2]

When Levy turned to the fortunes of women photographers in *The Romance of a Shop*, she modeled the Lorimers on her friends the Black sisters. While Levy and Constance Black were class-mates at Newnham, Black's sisters Clementina, Grace, and Emma shared a flat on Fitzroy Street, London in 1879, a time when young middle-class women taking up residence on their own was a dubious novelty. The Black sisters were unconventional as well in their interior design: out of material necessity, they converted one space into a combined kitchen and sitting-room with writing tables and a floor painted red.[3] Like the Lorimer sisters, the Blacks moved from posh Campden Hill to a shop-lined street in central London near Regent's Park. In the

---

1 See Linda Hunt Beckman, *Amy Levy: Her Life and Letters* (Athens: Ohio UP, 2000) 66-69, 32-33.
2 See Appendix B4.
3 Liselotte Glage, *Clementina Black: A Study in Social History and Literature* (Heidelberg: Carl Winter, 1981) 20.

early chapters of *The Romance of a Shop*, Levy conveys the thrill of this relocation to the heart of the city: "Indeed, for Gertrude, the humours of the town had always possessed a curious fascination. She contemplated the familiar London pageant with an interest that had something of passion in it; and, for her part, was never inclined to quarrel with the fate which had transported her from the comparative tameness of Campden Hill" (80). Where the Black sisters redecorated their modest home, the Lorimer sisters and friends "laid down the carpets and hung up the curtains" and outfitted the flat with shelves. In a letter to Vernon Lee, Levy comments on the Black sisters' apartment on the top floor of a house in which "they do their own housework," a clear departure from the middle-class luxury of hired domestic service.[1]

Photography, Working Women, and Victorian Visual Culture

Levy's representations of London life suggest the field of vision of a *flâneuse*, the feminine version of the *flâneur*, an urban wanderer who observes the varieties of urban culture from a distance. The nineteenth-century Parisian poet Charles Baudelaire first introduced the idea of *flânerie*, while James Thomson's *The City of Dreadful Night* (1874) is often regarded as the quintessential epic of the *flâneur* of Victorian London.[2] Levy herself invoked the image of the *flâneuse* in her essay "Women and Club Life." Deborah Parsons names Levy as one of the first women writers to represent across different genres the female gaze on the modern metropolis.[3] What better piece of technology to place in the hands of a "new woman" observing the city than a camera? Affording a protected spectatorship for women poised between public and private spheres, the camera figures as the Victorian eye for documenting urban life, both exterior and interior scenes.

Similar to the Lorimer sisters' "Photographic Studio," photography businesses flourished in Levy's London, given that the pho-

---

1 Quoted in Linda Hunt Beckman, *Amy Levy: Her Life and Letters* (Athens: Ohio UP, 2000) 255.

2 Levy published an essay, "James Thomson: A Minor Poet" in 1883. Her second volume of poetry, *A Minor Poet and Other Verse* (1884), highlights Levy's fascination with this modern bard of London in the title poem.

3 Deborah L. Parsons, *Streetwalking the Metropolis: Women, the City, and Modernity* (Oxford: Oxford UP, 2000) 86-98. Parsons extends Deborah Nord's work on Levy and the figure of the *flâneuse*.

tograph was well established with multiple uses for personal portraiture, journalism, and the fine arts. By the 1860s, photography supplied a domestic pastime, one that a few notable women transformed into celebrated careers. Julia Margaret Cameron's married daughter gave her a camera as a birthday present in 1864, and Cameron recounts how she adapted her country home to her hobby: "I turned my coal-house into my dark room, and a glazed fowl-house I had given to my children became my glass house!"[1] Within a few years Cameron had produced many illustrious portrait photographs, including a series of her niece Julia Jackson (who would become Virginia Woolf's mother), and images of notable men, including Alfred Tennyson, Thomas Carlyle, and Charles Darwin. Another Victorian woman photographer, Lady Clementina Hawarden, converted the first floor of her Kensington London home into a studio where she focused her camera on her daughters, with the cityscape as a backdrop beyond the balcony.[2] As experiments with the female gaze, Hawarden's photographs feature young women, sometimes staring from a window, other times with mirror reflections, to generate intriguingly ambiguous effects. Besides these art photographers whose work was exhibited in Levy's lifetime, many women worked in photographic shops throughout London in the late-nineteenth century.

Michael Pritchard's research into Victorian London photography designates this city as "the most prolific producer of studio photographs, notably *carte de visites*," the small portraits mounted on cardboard that were widely distributed by middle-class people, much like personal business cards.[3] In the 1880s, there were nearly 300 photographic studios in London, with many in the vicinity of Levy's family home in Sussex Place, Regent's Park, bearing addresses near or at 20B Upper Baker Street, where Levy sets the Lorimers' shop. This particular location has a literary echo in 221B Baker Street, the home of Sherlock Holmes and Dr. Watson, first published in Arthur Conan Doyle's 1887 *A Study in Scarlet*.[4] Whether it is mere coincidence that Levy chose

---

1 "Mrs. Julia Margaret Cameron's 'Annals of My Glass House," *The Photographic Journal* (July 1927): 298.
2 See the cover photograph of this edition, "Clementina Maude, 5 Princes Garden" (1862).
3 Michael Pritchard, *A Directory of London Photographers 1841-1908* (Bushey: ALLM Books, 1986) 19.
4 Doyle's Sherlock Holmes story, "A Scandal in Bohemia," appearing in *The Strand Magazine* in July 1891, centers on an incriminating photograph of a woman who outwits Holmes.

this particular address the following year when she wrote *The Romance of a Shop*, it is noteworthy that her story gives the Lorimers as photographers professional license to wield the power of the gaze, a feminine counterpart to Doyle's celebrated private eye detective. Echoing actual businesses of the 1880s like "The New Photographic Studio" at 20 Upper Baker Street is "G. & L. Lorimer: The Photographic Studio," the sisters' shop sign in gold letters over the street door (79). Names of these establishments, whether fictional or not, often do not reveal the gender of the proprietor. By the same token, the novel's epilogue capitalizes on the gender neutrality of "photographer" as an occupation open to women and men to suggest that the Lorimers' successor is either a woman working alone or a man with savvy as an interior decorator: "The Photographic Studio is let to an enterprising young photographer, who has enlarged and beautified it beyond recognition" (194). Perhaps unlike other entrepreneurs of Upper Baker Street studios, the Lorimers also make their home at this address.

The novel provides considerable detail about the placement of the shop in London and its juxtaposition with the Lorimers' living quarters. When cautioned about the abundance of photographers in this region of the city, Gertrude remarks, "I am told it is the right thing for people of the same trade to congregate together; they combine, as it were, to make a centre, which comes to be regarded as the emporium of their particular wares" (75). The studio itself almost assumes the prominence of a character, with its unique structure jutting out between the ground and first floors, sandwiched between a pharmaceutical chemist's shop below, and a French dressmaker's shop above it. On the top two floors are the Lorimers' kitchen and sitting room underneath their three bedrooms. This architecture removes the photography shop from street-level direct access. At the same time, the French dressmaker, who attempts suicide because she cannot pay her rent, inscribes both a literal wedge between the sisters' studio and their residential spaces, as well as a melodramatic flourish that offsets the realism of shop life. With this blueprint, Levy poses her enterprising women photographers across various boundary lines, between public and private, between business and domesticity. The irregularities of both the shop's bulging physical structure and the Lorimers' nearby domicile mimic the eccentricity of their social position as "four beautiful, fallen princesses, who kept a photography-shop" (90). Scrutinized by the public as curiosities, Gertrude defends their work,

"But we are photographers, not mountebanks!" (90). As part of the novel's realism, Levy even details the Lorimers as subject to gender discrimination where their customers "seemed to think the sex of the photographers a ground for greater cheapness in the photographs" (85).

Photography shopkeepers occupied an equivocal status much like the Lorimers as working middle-class women. In this sense, Levy reveals the contradictions of class through a comment in the novel about Mr. Russel, who mentors Lucy: "He carried on a large and world-famed business as a photographer in the north of England; to the disgust of a family that had starved respectably on scholarship for several generations" (66). The mixed class implications of the professional photographer is another way in which the novel assumes a frontier space between ranked social positions based on occupation, wealth, education, and family. Two sisters manage the bulk of the business, with Gertrude taking the lead as bookkeeper and public relations director, and Lucy developing an expertise in the technical aspects of photography. Thus Levy remodels the modern image of the working-class "shop girl" into a middle-class career woman with money-making skills. As a writer of fiction and dramatic literature, Gertrude's character unites imaginative work with practical shop business. And while she experiences frustration with publishing, and applies herself to the fledgling family firm for much of the novel, Gertrude eventually receives "a handsome cheque" for a story that has made "various journeys to editorial offices" (190). The eldest and most conventional sister Fanny—described as a "superannuated baby"—maintains the household, and the youngest sister, Phyllis, assists on occasion, sometimes helping Lucy retouch photographs, or Gertrude with on-site assignments.

As a manual of instruction for aspiring young women, *The Romance of a Shop* surveys the multiple forms of photography in Victorian culture. The very opening of the novel before the Lorimers resettle in the center of London introduces photography as a family hobby where "the great glass structure" of the conservatory contained not the expected "palms and orchids," but "was fitted up as a photographer's studio" (52). Once the sisters make the conversion from amateurs to professionals, their work entails postmortem photography, photographic studies for artists, slides for scientific lectures, and studio portraiture, all frequent commercial uses of the photograph in Victorian England. Levy also anticipates the outbreak of photojournalism with Frank

Jermyn's job on *The Woodcut*, a fictitious magazine much like the popular *Illustrated London News,* which mingled photographs, sketches, and engravings in its heavily pictorial content. The Lorimers' occupation primarily involves studio portraiture, work the sisters can accomplish without leaving their 20B Upper Baker Street premises, while other photography assignments take them into the city streets and the private homes and studios of men. In these forays as professionals employed in the public sphere, the narrative envisions—almost as a cautionary tale—the compromised situations entrepreneurial women may encounter, best exemplified by Phyllis's affair with a married artist. Yet the novel suggests that such risks are unavoidable for the Lorimers to make their venture a success. When Gertrude tells her sisters that they have been engaged for a postmortem photography assignment of Lord Watergate's wife, she tries to assure them that such work is "quite usual" and that in any case they can hardly afford to refuse it.

Both within and outside Levy's novel, photography signifies a boundary genre in aesthetic debates about mechanical versus artistic representation. *The Romance of a Shop* reorients the conventional opposition between romance and realism, between imagining artistic resolutions that transcend the prosaic limitations of everyday life on the one hand, and an insistence on the gritty liabilities of social, economic, and physical survival on the other. The form of literary realism associated with Levy's titular "shop" means more than the attention to such details of the photography business of women working in late-Victorian London. Photography in *The Romance of a Shop* offers a theoretical framework for exploring questions of representation and genre. In *Fiction in the Age of Photography,* Nancy Armstrong argues that nineteenth-century photography and realism are collaborators in a "cultural project" that fosters a desire to see the real world beyond mediation, that is, to calculate representation to appear as if an accurate or truthful account of what is referenced in that depiction.[1]

During the Victorian era, as photography became an established medium, a sustained debate arose about whether it constituted an art form or merely a mechanical practice. Lady Elizabeth Eastlake's 1857 essay "Photography" addresses this question as she proposes "to investigate the connexion of pho-

---

1   Nancy Armstrong, *Fiction in the Age of Photography: The Legacy of British Realism* (Cambridge: Harvard UP, 1999) 26.

tography with art—to decide how far the sun may be considered an artist, and to what branch of imitation his powers are best adapted."[1] Herself a practitioner of photography and a cultural critic of art and literature, Eastlake fashions photography as crucial technology for "unravelling ... other secrets in natural science," but at the same time figures photography as "Ariel-like"[2] in its unpredictablities. Eastlake concludes that the photograph can "give artistic pleasure of a very high kind" but only as a facilitating agent: "Photography *is* intended to supersede much that art has hitherto done.... but though hitherto the freewoman has done the work of the bondwoman, there is no fear that the position should be in future reversed." This metaphor of "the bondwoman" accentuates a view of photography as enslaved to a mechanical reproduction of nature, the perfunctory recorder of "literal, unreasoning imitation" for which women were deemed qualified to pursue in contrast to the more esteemed creative arts. Before writing *The Romance of a Shop*, Levy uses photography as a trope for clumsy and methodical representations in an 1884 essay, "The New School of American Fiction," as she compares a selection of recent novels to photographs "where no artistic hand has grouped the figures, only posed them very stiffly before the lens." Yet if this metaphor for recent American fiction focuses on artificiality, Levy also observes the uncanniness of the photographic gaze in contemporary novels: "We are like and yet strangely unlike ourselves."[3]

Just as Levy diversifies the significance of photography in her novel, Eastlake complicates the notion of the photograph as mere documentation by underscoring its mercurial, "Ariel-like" attributes. This capriciousness is exemplified by the use of diffused focus, an outstanding feature of Cameron's art photography which was widely exhibited, especially after her death in 1879. On the occasion of an 1888 exhibition, a reviewer praised Cameron's work for "a daring fashion of her own, forfeiting the sharpness of definition which ordinary photographers strive for."[4] This modulated focus transposes the mechanics of the lens

---

1 See Appendix E1.

2 Ariel is the spirit who performs acts of magic for his master Prospero in Shakespeare's *The Tempest*.

3 Amy Levy, "The New School of American Fiction," *Temple Bar* 70 (March 1884): 386.

4 Talbot Archer, "A Famous Lady Photographer," *Anthony's Photographic Bulletin* (22 September 1888): 565.

into an artistic gaze. In "The Work of Art in the Age of Mechanical Reproduction," Walter Benjamin grants the photograph a salient position in his Marxist account of the commodification of visual and verbal imagery: "For the first time in the process of pictorial reproduction, photography freed the hand of the most important artistic functions which henceforth devolved only upon the eye looking into a lens. Since the eye perceives more swiftly than the hand can draw, the process of pictorial reproduction was accelerated so enormously that it could keep pace with speech."[1] This shift from hand to eye equates the efficiency of seeing with speaking, activities that obscure the labors of drawing and writing in visual or verbal reproduction. Most significantly, photography elevates the gaze, and Levy's narrative of women photographers heightens this concentration on ocular power.

Visuality offers a mode for experimenting with the novel form for other late-Victorian writers who found traditional realism too restrictive. In Olive Schreiner's 1883 preface to the second edition of *The Story of an African Farm*, the author uses a visual metaphor to propose a different style of representation: "Human life may be painted according to two methods."[2] The first she likens to the stock stage performance in which "each character is duly marshalled at first, and ticketed," so that the "immutable certainty" of these roles means that "when the curtain falls, all will stand before it bowing." But Schreiner goes on to identify a different narrative of uncertainty, where "nothing can be prophesied" and "when the curtain falls no one is ready. When the footlights are brightest they are blown out; and what the name of the play is no one knows. If there sits a spectator who knows, he sits so high that the players in the gaslight cannot hear him breathing." Like the diffused focus of Cameron's art photography, Schreiner recommends "grey pigments" rather than bold colors. Visual art becomes the critical trope for reforming literary representation in fiction for new women writers like Schreiner and Levy.

Henrik Ibsen also employs a photography studio as the main setting for his play *The Wild Duck* (1884). Ibsen's *A Doll's House*,

---

1   Walter Benjamin, "The Work of Art in the Age of Mechanical Reproduction," *Illuminations*, ed. Hannah Arendt (New York: Schocken Books, 1969) 219.

2   Olive Schreiner, *The Story of an African Farm*, ed. Patricia O'Neill (Peterborough, ON: Broadview Press, 2003) 41.

the drama of a woman who eventually leaves her husband and young children, became a flashpoint in new woman critiques of marriage, domesticity, and conventional gender roles. Levy's 1889 calendar not only reveals that she attended the London performance of this play with Olive Schreiner, but also that Ibsen's English translator William Archer and his wife were part of her social circle, so it is likely that she knew about *A Wild Duck* even if it had yet to be translated from Norwegian and performed in London. In the story, the wife and daughter run a photography business; they advertise their services, arrange and conduct client sittings, and develop and retouch the photographs. Where the women immerse themselves in the "shop" aspects of photography, the husband, Hjalmar, devotes himself to inventing a device that will upgrade photography from simply a mechanical skill: "I viewed that if I was going to dedicate my powers to this calling, I would raise it so high that it would become both a science and an art."[1] By the end of the play, Hjalmar's idealism, figured by the vagueness of his incomplete and off-stage photographic invention, is overcast by bleak psychological realities. In this way, Ibsen utilizes photography as a genre to comment on romance and realism.

Romancing Realism and the Gendered Gaze in *The Romance of the Shop*

Where Eastlake uses photography to examine demarcations between the imaginative and the methodical, and Ibsen to pose the betrayal of idealism by everyday life, *The Romance of a Shop* explores romance and realism as mutually constitutive forms of representation. As Gillian Beer notes, ideal worlds amplify the possibilities in everyday worlds.[2] Yet in the novel's initial reception in 1888, reviewers objected to this wedding of the visionary with the ordinary. One critic complained about the title of the novel as an instance of this conflation and took issue with Levy putting "vulgar slang" in the mouths of her female characters.[3] By pushing at the boundaries of what was considered appropriate behavior for a middle-class lady, Levy infuses her fantasy of the Lorimers managing a business and a home of their own with quo-

---

1 Henrik Ibsen, *The Wild Duck*, trans. Dounia B. Christiani (New York: W.W. Norton and Company Inc., 1968) 39.

2 Gillian Beer, *The Romance* (London: Methuen, 1970) 9.

3 See Appendix A2.

tidian details, including "such sordid matters as shabby clothes and the comparative dearness of railway tickets" (91). Not simply an inspiring romance of the Lorimers' achievements, *The Romance of a Shop* keeps within its scope another view of London life, as in the following passage, where Gertrude reflects upon the value of "the grosser realities" of the wider world: "Fenced in as she had hitherto been from the grosser realities of life, she was only beginning to realise the meaning of life. Only a plank—a plank between them and the pitiless, fathomless ocean on which they had set out with such unknowing fearlessness; into whose boiling depths hundreds sank daily and disappeared, never to rise again" (95). Yet Levy's initial readers criticized this mingling of realism with romance. A reviewer in *The Woman's World* objects to "the sudden introduction of a tragedy" as "violent and unnecessary" in a "mundane book.... so brightly and pleasantly written," a comment highlighting the novel's literary dissonance.[1]

Like Schreiner and Levy, several late nineteenth-century writers sought a new relationship between aesthetics and realism in the contemporary novel, and the metropolis figured in this equation. Advocating the principles of the aesthetic movement in the arts, John Ruskin's 1881 essay "Fiction—Fair and Foul" deplores the popularity of modern urban life in recent fiction where "the personages are picked up from behind the counter and out of the gutter; and the landscape, by excursion train to Gravesend, with return ticket for the City-road."[2] Contending that such streetwise ugliness of new novels is a symptom of the morbidity of modern culture, Ruskin trains his criticism of social realism on George Eliot's *The Mill on the Floss* (1860) by comparing its characters to "the sweepings-out of a Pentonville omnibus." Ruskin's choice of a figure of speech for the "foul" realism in fiction is surprising given that the rural scenes of *The Mill on the Floss* never approach the environs of modern London, condensed in this image of the Pentonville omnibus.[3] A review of Eliot's novel credits the author with descriptions of "the

---

1 "Literary and Other Notes," *The Woman's World* 2 (February 1889): 224.
2 See Appendix C1.
3 This London transport as a sign of the decline in modern fiction also emerges in Levy's 1884 essay, "The New School of American Fiction": "In an article published some time ago ... Mr. Ruskin complained that the persons of George Eliot's novels suggested nothing so much as the sweepings of a Pentonville omnibus. What would he have said of a literature which, if the expression be allowed us, occupies itself so largely with the Pentonville omnibus of the soul?"

sordid scenes of Dorlcote Mill" as an alloy of "photographic truth and minute manner-painting worthy of Miss Austen."[1] Levy's hybrid of romance and realism approximates the kind of stylistic medley attributed here to Eliot.

Eight years after Ruskin's assessment of Eliot's realism as refuse from a city vehicle, Oscar Wilde recaptures this metaphor in his seminal statement on the new aestheticism, "The Decay of Lying." Wilde too assails current literature as journalistic reporting on "the doings of the lower orders" with the imperative of "going directly to life for everything."[2] Like Ruskin, Wilde recommends the elevation in art of the imaginative as "lying" over the everyday "truth" of realism. Following on Ruskin's criticism and Walter Pater's insistence on "the love of art for art's sake," Wilde's manifesto for aestheticism extols the self-sufficiency of art for its own enjoyment apart from social, political, and moral considerations. Levy and her women colleagues, including Schreiner, entered this debate from a different angle, given their acute attention to the relationship between gender, class, and artistic privilege.

Highlighting sight and visuality in *The Romance of a Shop*, Levy demonstrates that art and work can never be disaggregated from social and political considerations. As middle-class "public women" with a photography shop, the Lorimers' eyes on the modern city convert the masculine flâneur's gaze into the urban viewing of the flâneuse. Rather than the direct, roving eyes of the male gazer in streets, parks, and arcades, these sisters cast their eyes on public London through a veil, whether the protected spaces of the window pane or the camera lens. Not only is vision formalized through the business of photography, the novel accentuates the act of seeing. Indeed, *The Woman's World* commends the novel for a style "full of quick observation" and "keen vision." As the narrative commences, Gertrude gathers her sisters together in the glasshouse that serves as the family photography studio so that she can unveil her plan that they start their own business, and she quips: "Now that we are all grouped...there is nothing left but for Lucy to focus us" (53). Like the profession the sisters

---

1 "The Mill on the Floss," *Spectator* 7 April 1860, quoted in George Eliot, *The Mill on the Floss*, ed. Carol T. Christ (New York and London: W.W. Norton & Co., 1994) 443. "Miss Austen" refers to Jane Austen (1775-1817).

2 See Appendix C2.

practice, the gaze sets this scene, and in turn, the course of the narrative itself. Levy plays with this idea of focus by rendering appearances sometimes as ghostly shadows, much like the diffused focus of Cameron's art photography, and other times as sharply delineated. Thus the narrator describes Gertrude entering Darrell's studio to encounter the already married artist and Phyllis on the verge of elopement: "The flames leapt, the logs crackled pleasantly...then suddenly into that bright scene glided a black and rigid figure" (172).

The gaze also qualifies the set of characters. Gertrude is the visionary in the family, the one who first imagines the possibilities of a photography shop to support themselves independently in the center of London. At the same time, Gertrude readily frames what she encounters as a "picture." But Gertrude's progressive vantage point is also beset by her actual short-sightedness and by masculine glares. The gendered power dynamics between Sidney Darrell, the aesthete Royal Academician painter whose "studio is quite a museum of trophies of the chase" (104), and Gertrude is orchestrated through an exchange of gazes. When Gertrude first arrives to photograph Darrell's artwork, she is acutely conscious of being measured by his eyes: "Gertrude, looking up and meeting the cold, grey glance, became suddenly conscious that her hat was shabby, that her boots were patched and clumsy, that the wind had blown the wisps of her hair about her face. What was there in this man's gaze that made her, all at once, feel old and awkward, ridiculous and dowdy; that made her long to snatch up her heavy camera and flee from his presence, never to return?" (107). In such instances, *The Romance of a Shop* transposes into a battle of gendered gazes the struggles of modern women venturing into the public working world. After Darrell informs the Lorimers of his wish to use Phyllis as a model for his painting, Gertrude "glanced up as she spoke, and met, almost with open defiance, the heavy grey eyes of the man opposite" (131).

Of the four sisters, Phyllis and Gertrude come closest to the flâneuse, a woman who views with delight the spectacle of city life from an interior and stationary vantage point. Gertrude frequently delights in watching urban scenes while riding an omnibus or from her window. At the same time, Phyllis "long-sighted" (79) eyes viewing Baker Street are often noted. Where Lucy's and Gertrude's eyes are behind a camera lens, Phyllis surveys the streets through a window pane: "Phyllis went over to the window, drew up the blind, and amused herself, as was her frequent custom, by looking into the street" (105). However, as

Lucy cautions Phyllis, for women gazing can be dangerously reciprocal: "I wish you wouldn't do that ... any one can see right into the room." The female gaze from inside the home becomes embodied as an object of a passerby's eyes, as Levy conveys that the power of urban spectatorship for women comes with a price. This fear that Phyllis's watchfulness from a sitting-room window makes the sisters vulnerably visible inside their home again reveals the complexities of gendered gazing in the novel. The scene concludes with Phyllis noting the limitations of her interior perch: "It is a little dull ... to look at life from a top-floor window" (106).

The character of Phyllis also unites both the "romance" and "shop" aspects of the novel. More than her sisters, this youngest Lorimer uneasily straddles boundaries between tradition and modernity, between the private sphere of home and the public station of a shop girl, and Levy uses the language of visuality to impart this as well. Through Levy's revision of the standard seduction plot, Phyllis conveys the hazards of modern women working outside the home who assume the dubious social position of "public women" aligned with streetwalkers and working-class wage earners. As the beauty of the Lorimer family, Phyllis represents the aesthetic ideal of femininity, while her moral and physical vulnerability signify the dangers of modern women transgressing the boundaries of prescribed femininity. Like her resemblance to the flâneuse, Phyllis suggests a female aesthete, "the spoilt child" with a fondness for luxury and pleasure, along with *fin-de-siècle* ennui, her languidness and sardonic wit anticipating features of the Wildean aesthete in *The Picture of Dorian Gray* (1890). But as with her restricted gaze on the city, Phyllis' similarity to the aesthete dandy assumes a gendered dimension. Condemning this one character in the novel, reviewers especially took issue with her sexual fall as a consequence of boredom: "The easy and flippant way in which she falls from virtue, not from passionate love, but because she was dull, is, it may be hoped, untrue to Nature. Surely there must be a series of downward steps before a girl sinks into a gulf like that."[1] With this intricate character, Levy considers the liabilities not only of working women, but also of women on the margins watching the pageant of London life.

How else does *The Romance of a Shop* push on the boundaries

---

1 See Appendix A3.

of gendered conventions in middle-class Victorian culture? Again blurring oppositions, Levy's treatments of Fanny and Phyllis challenge the binary of "the angel in the house" and the fallen woman to offer more mixed portraits of modern femininity. Fanny's revived romance reverses the plot staple of the disappointed and dejected old maid who, in Levy's revision, unexpectedly becomes a new bride. Yet even before her suitor resurfaces, Fan is enlivened through the experimental lifestyle she shares with her sisters. With Phyllis as well, Levy challenges the typical fallen woman of Victorian fiction by refusing to frame her character as either innocent female victim or knowing temptress.

Recent scholars have appreciated *The Romance of a Shop* as a borderland fiction, inscribing a space between traditional and progressive representations of women. For Deborah Epstein Nord, Levy anticipates George Gissing's *The Odd Women* (1893), with its attention to the distress and exhilaration of independent women working in London in the 1880s.[1] Impressed with the "self-consciously female urbanism" of much of the novel, Nord faults the latter chapters for devolving into "a shoddy *Pride and Prejudice* with all four sisters searching for an appropriate mate," and consequently judges the closure a "failure." Deborah Parsons concurs that "Levy backs down from the implied female radicalism by concluding the girls' stories with the conventional endings of marriage or fall and death."[2] Yet what other Victorian novel imagines an outcome where women inhabit successfully both domestic and professional roles? At the end of the novel, one sister has a husband, children, and an award-winning photography career; as the narrator proclaims, "The photography, however, has not been crowded out by domestic duties" (193).

This culminating vision of a balance between domesticity and work signifies the harmonious yoking together of "romance" and "shop," an ideal vision of social change that casts a glance of hope on the concluding passages about the vacant rooms to be let and another "enterprising young photographer" installed in the Upper Baker Street studio. As a progressive story of middle-class women entering the public sphere as London entrepreneurs, *The Romance of a Shop* envisions prospects beyond the "domestic round of boiled and roast," as Levy's poem, "The Ballad of Reli-

---

1 Deborah Epstein Nord, *Walking the Victorian Streets: Women, Representation, and the City* (Ithaca: Cornell UP, 1995) 200-02.

2 Deborah L. Parsons, *Streetwalking the Metropolis: Women, the City, and Modernity* (Oxford: Oxford UP, 2000) 93.

gion and Marriage" has it, for its intended readership of young women. The novel's sustained fascination with the varied gazes of and upon modern women in London looks forward to the style and subject matter of modernism, including Virginia Woolf's novels, *Night and Day* (1919) and *Mrs. Dalloway* (1925). The narratorial eye of *The Romance of a Shop* celebrates this scene of new women: "Often, before business hours, Gertrude might be seen walking round Regent's Park at a swinging pace" (119). Levy intensifies this narrative gaze upon women in the public sphere of modern London by giving the Lorimers a profession that insists that they travel through the streets and into homes and studios, and that requires that they record and sell the products of this gaze. In this way Levy allows her central characters to be both subjects and objects of scopic power. With our early twenty-first-century literary attention to in-betweenness and border-crossings, Levy's exploration of the transitional status of young urban women on the verge of the twentieth century finds contemporary resonance as well.

Amy Levy: A Brief Chronology

1861 Amy Judith Levy is born on 10 November at 16 Percy Place, Clapham, the second of seven children, to Isabelle Levin Levy and Lewis Levy.

1872 Levy family moves to Regent's Park. Levy and her siblings produce a family magazine, *The Poplar Club Journal* with articles, short stories, and sketches.

1875 Levy wins junior prize in *Kind Words Magazine for Boys and Girls* for essay on Elizabeth Barrett Browning's *Aurora Leigh*. Levy's first published poem, "The Ballad of Ida Grey (A Story of a Woman's Sacrifice)," appears in *The Pelican*, a feminist magazine.

1876 Levy enrolls at the new High School for Girls at Brighton, under headmistress Edith Creak, one of the original students at Newnham College, Cambridge.

1879 In February, Levy's letter to *The Jewish Chronicle* is printed under the heading, "Jewish Women and 'Women's Rights.'" Her poem "Run to Death: A True Incident of Pre-Revolutionary France" appears in the July issue of *Victoria Magazine*. Levy enrolls at Newnham College, Cambridge, in October.

1880 Levy publishes two short stories: "Euphemia" in *Victoria Magazine* and "Mrs. Pierrepoint" in *Temple Bar*. Female students at Cambridge granted admission to university examinations, although women are denied degrees.

1881 Levy publishes on daily life at Newnham College. *Xantippe and Other Verse* published. Levy leaves Cambridge, and travels on the European Continent.

1882 Levy returns to London from Germany and Switzerland. She joins a discussion club for women and men intellectuals and artists, including Karl Pearson, Dollie Radford, Mary Robinson, and Eleanor Marx; the club disbands in 1885. In November she obtains admission to the Reading Room of the British Museum. She publishes translations of poems by Heinrich Heine and Nikolaus Lenau.

1883 "Between Two Stools" appears in *Temple Bar*. "The Diary of a Plain Girl" is published in September in *London Society*; this is the first of a series, many in epistolary or diary form, appearing in *London Society* in 1883-86, featuring "Melissa."

1884 Levy travels to Germany and Switzerland. "Sokratics in the Strand" is published in *The Cambridge Review*, and "The New School of American Fiction" appears in *Temple Bar*. In June, T. Fisher Unwin publishes *A Minor Poet and Other Verse*.

1885 Levy moves with her family to 7 Endsleigh Gardens, Bloomsbury. Several stories are published in *London Society*, including "Easter-Tide at Tunbridge Wells" and "Revenge."

1886 Levy spends a few months in Florence with Clementina Black at the Casa Guidi, where she meets Vernon Lee (Violet Paget). She returns to London and publishes five essays in *The Jewish Chronicle*: "The Ghetto in Florence," "The Jew in Fiction," "Jewish Children," "Jewish Humour," and "Middle-Class Jewish Women of To-Day."

1887 The University Club for Ladies opens in New Bond Street. Two of Levy's sonnets appear in Elizabeth Sharp's *Women's Voices: An Anthology of the Most Characteristic Poems by English, Scottish, and Irish Women*.

1888 Levy begins publishing in *The Woman's World* with a short story, "The Recent Telepathic Occurrence at the British Museum," in the first issue, followed by "The Poetry of Christina Rossetti" and "Women and Club Life." *The Romance of a Shop* is published by T. Fisher Unwin in October. Levy submits the manuscript of *Reuben Sachs* to Macmillan and travels to Florence.

1889 *Reuben Sachs: A Sketch* is published by Macmillan in January, when Levy returns from Florence. In May, *Miss Meredith* appears in the *British Weekly* and then in volume form. "Readers at the British Musem" is published in *Atalanta*, "Cohen of Trinity" is published in *The Gentleman's Magazine*, and several publications appear in *The Woman's World*. On 10 September, alone at her family's home in London, Levy commits suicide by charcoal asphyxiation after correcting proofs for *A London Plane-Tree, and Other Verse*, later published in the Cameo Series of T. Fisher Unwin. Her body is cremated and her ashes buried at Balls Pond Cemetery under the auspices of the West London Synagogue for British Jews on 15 September 1889. Clementina Black's notice about Levy's death appears in *The Athenaeum* in October.

1890   Oscar Wilde's essay on Levy appears in *The Woman's World*. Also in this magazine are four poems by Levy and her short story, "Wise in Her Generation."

1915   Levy's undated poem, "A Ballad of Religion and Marriage," is privately printed and circulated.

A Note on the Text

The text of *The Romance of a Shop* is based on the first American edition under the imprint "The Algonquin Press," published in 1889 by Cupples and Hurd of Boston. I have corrected only inconsistencies in spelling and punctuation, and the rare but clear typographical error. The original London edition, on which the American version is based, was published as a single volume by T. Fisher Unwin in October 1888.

Amy Levy's original notes have been retained in the text and are identified by asterisks.

The Romance of a Shop

CHAPTER I

In the Beginning

Turn, Fortune, turn thy wheel and lower the proud;
Turn thy wild wheel through sunshine, storm, and cloud;
Thy wheel and thee we neither love nor hate.

Tennyson[1]

There stood on Campden Hill[2] a large, dun-coloured house, enclosed by a walled-in garden of several acres in extent. It belonged to no particular order of architecture, and was more suggestive of comfort than of splendour, with its great windows, and rambling, nondescript proportions. On one side, built out from the house itself, was a big glass structure, originally designed for a conservatory. On the April morning of which I write, the whole place wore a dejected and dismantled appearance; while in the windows and on the outer wall of the garden were fixed black and white posters, announcing a sale of effects to take place on that day week.

The air of desolation which hung about the house had communicated itself in some vague manner to the garden, where the trees were bright with blossom, or misty with the tender green of the young leaves. Perhaps the effect of sadness was produced, or at least heightened, by the pathetic figure that paced slowly up and down the gravel path immediately before the house; the figure of a young woman, slight, not tall, bare-headed, and clothed in deep mourning.

She paused at last in her walk, and stood a moment in a listening attitude, her face uplifted to the sky.

Gertrude Lorimer was not a beautiful woman, and such good looks as she possessed varied from day to day, almost from hour to hour; but a certain air of character and distinction clung to her through all her varying moods, and redeemed her from a possible charge of plainness.

She had an arching, unfashionable forehead, like those of Lionardo da Vinci's women, short-sighted eyes, and an expressive

---

1 Alfred, Lord Tennyson (1809-92), "Idylls of the King: Song from the Marriage of Geraint" (1859), lines 347-49.
2 In South Kensington, near Holland Park and west of central London.

mouth and chin. As she stood in the full light of the spring sun-shine, her face pale and worn with recent sorrow, she looked, perhaps, older than her twenty-three years.

Pushing back from her forehead the hair, which, though not cut into a "fringe," had a tendency to stray about her face, and passing her hand across her eyes, with a movement expressive of mingled anxiety and resolve, she walked quickly to the door of the conservatory, opened it, and went inside.

The interior of the great glass structure would have presented a surprise to the stranger expectant of palms and orchids. It was fitted up as a photographer's studio.

Several cameras, each of a different size, stood about the room. In one corner was a great screen of white-painted canvas; there were blinds to the roof adapted for admitting or excluding the light; and paste-pots, bottles, printing-frames, photographs in various stages of finish—a nondescript heap of professional litter—were scattered about the place from end to end.

Standing among these properties was a young girl of about twenty years of age; fair, slight, upright as a dart, with a glance at once alert and serene.

The two young creatures in their black dresses advanced to each other, then stood a moment, clinging to one another in silence.

It was the first time that either had been in the studio since the day when their unforeseen calamity had overtaken them; a calamity which seemed to them so mysterious, so unnatural, so past all belief, and yet which was common-place enough—a sudden loss of fortune, immediately followed by the sudden death of the father, crushed by the cruel blow which had fallen on him.

"Lucy," said the elder girl at last, "is it only a fortnight ago?"

"I don't know," answered Lucy, looking round the room, whose familiar details stared at her with a hideous unfamiliarity; "I don't know if it is a hundred years or yesterday since I put that portrait of Phyllis in the printing-frame! Have you told Phyllis?"

"No, but I wish to do so at once; and Fanny. But here they come."

Two other black-gowned figures entered by the door which led from the house, and helped to form a sad little group in the middle of the room.

Frances Lorimer, the eldest of them all, and half-sister to the other three, was a stout, fair woman of thirty, presenting some-what the appearance of a large and superannuated baby. She had a big face, with small, meaningless features, and faint, surprised-looking eyebrows. Her complexion had once been charmingly pink and white, but the tints had hardened, and a coarse red colour clung to the wide cheeks. At the present moment, her little, light eyes red with weeping, her eyebrows arched higher than ever, she looked the picture of impotent distress. She had come in, hand in hand with Phyllis, the youngest, tallest, and prettiest of the sisters; a slender, delicate-looking creature of seventeen, who had outgrown her strength; the spoiled child of the family by virtue of her youth, her weakness, and her personal charms.

Gertrude was the first to speak.

"Now that we are all together," she said, "it is a good opportunity for talking over our plans. There are a great many things to be considered, as you know. Phyllis, you had better not stand."

Phyllis cast her long, supple frame into the lounge which was regarded as her special property, and Fanny sat down on a chair, wiping her eyes with her black-bordered pocket-handkerchief. Gertrude put her hands behind her and leaned her head against the wall.

Phyllis' wide, grey eyes, with their half-wistful, half-humorous expression, glanced slowly from one to the other.

"Now that we are all grouped," she said, "there is nothing left but for Lucy to focus us."

It was a very small joke indeed, but they all laughed, even Fanny. No one had laughed for a fortnight, and at this reassertion of youth and health their spirits rose with unexpected rapidity.

"Now, Gertrude, unfold your plans," said Lucy, in her clear tones and with her air of calm resolve.

Gertrude played nervously with a copy of the *British Journal of Photography*[1] which she held, and began to speak with hesitation, almost with apology, as one who deprecates any undue assumption of authority.

"You know that Mr. Grimshaw, our father's lawyer, was here last night," she said; "and that he and I had a long talk together about business. (He was sorry you were too ill to come down,

---

1 Leading journal of photography issued weekly from 1865. An 1861 notice reads: "official organ … of all Photographic Societies and pre-eminently the Recognised Organ of Photographers—Professional and Amateur."

Fanny.) He told me all about our affairs. We are quite, quite poor. When everything is settled, when the furniture is sold, he thinks there will be about £500 among us, perhaps more, perhaps less."

Fanny's thin, feminine tones broke in on her sister's words—

"There is my £50 a-year that my mama left me; I am sure you are all welcome to that."

"Yes, dear, yes," said Lucy, patting her shoulder; while Gertrude bit her lip and went on—

"We cannot live for long on £500, as you must know. We must work. People have been very kind. Uncle Sebastian has telegraphed for two of us to go out to India; Mrs. Devonshire offers another two of us a home for as long as we like. But I think we would all rather not accept these kind offers?"

"Of course not!" cried Lucy and Phyllis in chorus, while Fanny maintained a meek, consenting silence.

"The question remains," continued the speaker; "what can we do? There is teaching, of course. We might find places as governesses; but we should be at a great disadvantage without certificates or training of any sort. And we should be separated."

"Oh, Gertrude," cried Fanny, "you might write! You write so beautifully! I am sure you could make your fortune at it."

Gertrude's face flushed, but she controlled all other signs of the irritation which poor hapless Fan was so wont to excite in her.

"I have thought about that, Fanny," she said; "but I cannot afford to wait and hammer away at the publishers' doors with a crowd of people more experienced and better trained than myself. No, I have another plan to propose to you all. There is one thing, at least, that we can all do."

"We can all make photographs, except Fan," said Phyllis, in a doubtful voice.

"Exactly!" cried Gertrude, growing excited, and walking across to the middle of the room; "we can make photographs! We have had this studio, with every proper arrangement for light and other things, so that we are not mere amateurs. Why not turn to account the only thing we can do, and start as professional photographers? We should all keep together. It would be a risk, but if we failed we should be very little worse off than before. I know what Lucy thinks of it, already. What have you others to say to it?"

"Oh, Gertrude, need it come to that—to open a shop?" cried Fanny, aghast.

"Fanny, you are behind the age," said Lucy, hastily. "Don't you know that it is quite distinguished to keep a shop? That poets sell wall-papers,[1] and first-class honour men sell lamps? That Girton[2] students make bonnets, and are thought none the worse of for doing so?"

"*I* think it a perfectly splendid idea," cried Phyllis, sitting up; "we shall be like that good young man in *Le Nabab*."[3]

"Indeed, I hope we shall not be like André," said Gertrude, sitting down by Phyllis on the couch and putting her arm round her, "especially as none of us are likely to write successful tragedies by way of compensation."

"You two people are getting frivolous," remarked Lucy, severely, "and there are so many things to consider."

"First of all," answered Gertrude, "I want to convince Fanny. Think of all the dull little ways by which women, ladies, are generally reduced to earning their living! But a business—that is so different. It is progressive; a creature capable of growth; the very qualities in which women's work is dreadfully lacking."

"We have thought out a good many of the details," went on Lucy, who was possessed of less imagination than her sister, but had a clearer perception of what arguments would best appeal to Fanny's understanding. "It would not absorb all our capital, we have so many properties already. We thought of buying some nice little business, such as are advertised every week in *The British Journal*. But of course we should do nothing rashly, nor without consulting Mr. Grimshaw."

"Not for his advice," put in Gertrude, "but to arrange any transaction for us."

"Gertrude and I," went on Lucy, "would do the work, and you, Fanny, if you would, should be our housekeeper."

"And I," cried Phyllis, her great eyes shining, "I would walk up and down outside, like that man in the High Street, who tells me every day what a beautiful picture I should make!"

"Our photographs would be so good and our manners so charming that our fame would travel from one end of the earth to the other!" added Lucy, with a sudden abandonment of her grave and didactic manner.

"We would have afternoon tea in the studio on Sunday, to

1 Probably an allusion to William Morris (1834-96).
2 Girton was the first college at Cambridge University for women; it first opened at Hitchen in 1869, and then established in Cambridge in 1872. Newnham College, Cambridge, where Levy studied from 1879 to 1881, was founded in 1871.
3 1877 novel by French author Alphonse Daudet (1840-97).

which everybody should flock; duchesses, cabinet ministers, and Mr. Irving.[1] We should become the fashion, make colossal fortunes, and ultimately marry dukes!" finished off Gertrude.

Fanny looked up, helpless but unconvinced. The enthusiasm of these young creatures had failed to communicate itself to her. Their outburst of spirits at such a time seemed to her simply shocking.

As Lucy had said, Frances Lorimer was behind the age. She was an anachronism, belonging by rights to the period when young ladies played the harp, wore ringlets, and went into hysterics.

Living, moving, and having her being well within the vision of three pairs of searching and intensely modern young eyes, poor Fan could permit herself neither these nor any kindred indulgences; but went her way with a vague, inarticulate sense of injury—a round, sentimental peg in the square, scientific hole of the latter half of the nineteenth century.

Now, when the little tumult had in some degree subsided, she ventured once more to address the meeting.

That was the worst of Fan; there was no standing up in fair fight and having it out with her; you might as soon fight a featherbed. Convinced, to all appearances, one moment; the next, she would go back to the very point from which she had started, with that mild but terrible obstinacy of the weak.

"I suppose you know," she said, having once more recourse to the black-bordered pocket-handkerchief, "what every one will think?"

"Every one will be dead against it. We know that, of course," said Lucy, with the calm confidence of untried strength.

Fortunately the discussion was interrupted at this juncture, by the loud voice of the gong announcing luncheon.

Fanny rushed off to bathe her eyes. Gertrude ran upstairs to wash her hands, and the two younger girls lingered together a few moments in the studio.

"I wonder," said Phyllis, with the complete and unconscious cynicism of youth, "why Fan has never married; she has just the sort of qualities that men seem to think desirable in a wife and a mother!"

"Poor Fanny, don't you know?" answered Lucy. "There was a person once, ages ago, but he was poor and had to go away, and

---

1 Henry Irving (1835-98) was the most prominent actor of the Victorian stage.

Fan would have no one else."

This was Lucy's version of that far away, uninteresting little romance; Fanny's "disappointment," to which the heroine of it was fond of making vaguely pathetic allusion. Fan would have no one else, her sister had said; but perhaps another cause lay at the root of her constancy (and of much feminine constancy besides); but if Lucy did not say no one else would have Fan, Phyllis, who was younger and more merciless, chose to accept the statement in its inverted form; which, by the by, neither she, nor I, nor you, reader, have authentic grounds for doing.

"Oh, I had heard about *that* before, naturally," she answered; but further conversation on the subject was cut short by the appearance of Fanny herself, come to summon them to the dining-room, where lunch was set out on the great table.

Old Kettle, the butler, waited on them as usual, and there was nothing in the nature of the viands to bring home to them the fact of their altered circumstances; but it was a dismal meal, crowned with a sorrow's crown of sorrow, the remembrance of happier things. In the vacant place they all seemed to see the dead father, as he had been wont to sit among them; charming, gay, *debonnair*, the life of the party; delighting no less in the light-hearted sallies of his daughters, than in his own neatly-polished epigrams; a man as brilliant as he had been unsatisfactory; as little able to cope with the hard facts of existence as he had been reckless in attacking them.

"Oh, girls," said Fanny, when the door had finally closed upon Kettle; "Oh, girls, I have been thinking. If only circumstances had been otherwise, if only—things had happened a little differently, I might have had a home to offer you, a home to which you might all have come!"

Overcome by this vision of possibilities, this resuscitation of her dead and buried might-have-been, Miss Lorimer began to sob quietly; and the poor eyes, which she had been at such pains to bathe, overflowed, deluging the streaky expanses of newly-washed cheeks.

"Oh, I can't help it, I can't help it," moaned this shuttlecock of fate, appealing to the stern young judges who sat silent around her; an appeal which, if duly considered, will seem to be even more piteous than the outbreak of emotion of which it was the cause.

Gertrude got up from her chair and went from the room; Phyllis sat staring, with beautiful, unmoved, accustomed eyes; only Lucy, laying a cool hand on her half-sister's burning fingers, spoke words of comfort and of common sense.

CHAPTER II

Friends in Need

And never say "no," when the world says "ay,"
For that is fatal.
E.B. Browning[1]

When Gertrude reached her room she flung herself on the bed, and lay there passive, with face buried from the light.

She was worn out, poor girl, with the strain of the recent weeks; a period into which a lifetime of events, thoughts, and experience seemed to have crowded themselves.

Action, or thoughts concerned with plans of action, had become for the moment impossible to her.

She realised, with a secret thrill of horror, that the moment had at length come when she must look full in the face the lurking anguish of which none but herself knew the existence; and which, in the press of more immediate miseries, she had hitherto contrived to keep well in the background of her thoughts. Only, she had known dimly throughout, that face it she must, sooner or later; and now her hour had come.

There was some one, bound to her by every tie but the tie of words, who had let the days of her trouble go by and had made no sign; a fair-weather friend, who had fled before the storm.

In these few words are summed up the whole of Gertrude's commonplace story.

Only to natures as proud and as passionate as hers, can the words convey their full meaning.

She was not a woman easily won; not till after long siege had come surrender; but surrender, complete, unquestioning, as only such a woman can give.

Now, her being seemed shaken at the foundations, hurt at the

---

1   Elizabeth Barrett Browning (1806-61), *Aurora Leigh* (1857), book 1, lines 437-38. These lines, from Barrett Browning's verse-novel about a woman poet, come from Aurora's meditations on the social limitations placed on women. At age 13, Levy won a school prize for her review of *Aurora Leigh* in which she observes that the writer's "learned allusions" should be excused "because it is only natural that she should wish to display what public opinion denies her sex—a classical education."

vital roots. As a passionate woman will, she thought: "If it had been his misfortune, not mine!"

In the hall lay a bit of pasteboard with "sincere condolence" inscribed on it; and Gertrude had not failed to learn, from various sources, of the presence at half a dozen balls of the owner of the card, and his projected visit to India.

Gertrude rose from the bed with a choked sound, which was scarcely a cry, in her throat. She had looked her trouble fairly in the eyes; had not, as some women would have done, attempted to save her pride by refusing to acknowledge its existence; but from the depths of her humiliation, had called upon it by its name. Now for ever and ever she turned from it, cast it forth from her; cast forth other things, perhaps, round which it had twined itself; but stood there, at least, a free woman, ready for action.

Thank God for action; for the decree which made her to some extent the arbiter of other destinies, the prop and stay of other lives. For the moment she caught to her breast and held as a friend that weight of responsibility which before had seemed—and how often afterwards was to seem—too heavy and too cruel a burden for her young strength.

"And now," she said, setting her lips, "for a clearance."

Soon the floor was strewn with a heap of papers, chiefly manuscripts, whose dusty and battered air would have suggested to an experienced eye frequent and fruitless visits to the region of Paternoster Row.[1]

Gertrude, kneeling on the floor, bent over them with anxious face, setting some aside, consigning others ruthlessly to the wastepaper basket. One, larger and more travel-worn than the rest, she held some time in her hand, as though weighing it in the balance. It was labelled: *Charlotte Corday;*[2] *a tragedy in five acts;* and for a time its fate seemed uncertain; but it found its way ultimately to the basket.

A smart tap at the door roused Gertrude from her somewhat melancholy occupation.

"Come in!" she cried, pushing back the straying locks from the ample arch of her forehead, but retaining her seat among the manuscripts.

---

1 Considered the heart of the publishing trade, an area in the City of London near St. Paul's Cathedral where several wholesale booksellers and publishers were situated.

2 Charlotte Corday (1768-93), a heroine of the French Revolution who was guillotined for murdering Jean-Paul Marat, leader of the Paris Commune and Jacobin Party.

The handle turned briskly, and a blooming young woman, dressed in the height of fashion, entered the room.

"My dear Gertrude, what's this? Rachel weeping among her children?"[1]

She spoke in high tones, but with an exaggeration of buoyancy which bespoke nervousness. When last these friends had met, it had been in the chamber of death itself; it was a little difficult, after that solemn moment, to renew the every-day relations of life without shock or jar.

"Come in, Conny, and if you must quote the Bible, don't misquote it."

Constance Devonshire, heedless of her magnificent attire, cast herself down by the side of her friend, and put her arms caressingly round her. Her quick blue eye fell upon the basket with its overflowing papers.

"Gerty, what is the meaning of this massacre of the innocents?"

"'Vanity of vanities, saith the preacher,'[2] since you seem bent on Scriptural allusion, Conny."

"But, Gerty, all your tales and things! I should have thought"—she blushed as she made the suggestion—"that you might have sold them. And *Charlotte Corday*, too!"

"Poor Charlotte, she has been to market so often that I cannot bear the sight of her; and now I have given her her quietus as the Republic gave it to her original. As for the other victims, they are not worth a tear, and we will not discuss them."

She gathered up the remaining manuscripts, and put them in a drawer; then, turning to her friend with a smile, demanded from her an account of herself.

Miss Devonshire's presence, alien as it was to her present mood, acted with a stimulating effect on Gertrude. To Conny she knew herself to be a very tower of strength; and such knowledge is apt to make us strong, at least for the time being.

---

1 Jeremiah 31.15. Conny misquotes the biblical line, as Gertrude points out.

> A cry is heard in Ramah—
> Wailing, bitter weeping—
> Rachel weeping for her children.
> She refuses to be comforted
> For her children, who are gone.

2 Ecclesiastes 1.2.

"Oh, there's nothing new about me!" answered Conny, wrinkling her handsome, discontented face. "Gerty, why won't you come to us, you and Lucy, and let the others go to India?"

Gertrude laughed at this summary disposal of the family.

"Of course I knew you wouldn't come," said Conny, in an injured voice; "but, seriously, Gerty, what are you going to do?"

In a few words Gertrude sketched the plan which she had propounded to her sisters that morning.

"I don't believe it is possible," said Miss Devonshire, with great promptness; "but it sounds very nice," she added with a sigh, and thought, perhaps, of her own prosperous boredom.

The bell rang for tea, and Gertrude began brushing her hair. Constance endeavoured to seize the brush from her hands.

"You are not coming down, my dear, indeed you are not! You are going to lie down, while I go and fetch your tea."

"I had much rather not, Conny. I am quite well."

"You look as pale as a ghost. But you always have your own way. By the by, Fred is downstairs; he walked over with me from Queen's Gate.[1] He's the only person who is decently civil in the house, just at present."

Tea had been carried into the studio, where the two girls found the rest of the party assembled. Fan, with an air of elegance, as though conscious of performing an essentially womanly function, and with much action of the little finger, was engaged in pouring out tea. In the middle of the room stood a group of three people: Lucy, Phyllis, and Fred Devonshire, a tall, heavy young man, elaborately and correctly dressed, with a fatuous, good-natured, pink and white face.

"Oh, come now, Miss Lucy," he was heard to say, as Gertrude entered with his sister; "that really is too much for one to swallow!"

"He won't believe it!" cried Phyllis, clasping her hands, and turning her charming face to the new-comers; "it's quite true, isn't it, Gerty?"

"Have you been telling tales out of school?"

"Lucy and I have been explaining *the plan* to Fred, and he won't believe it."

Gertrude felt a little vexed at this lack of reticence on their part; but then, she reflected, if the plan was to be carried out, it could remain no secret, especially to the Devonshires. Assured

---

1 Area of London adjacent to Kensington Gardens and near the Royal Albert Hall.

that there really was some truth in what he had been told, Fred relapsed into an amazed silence, broken by an occasional chuckle, which he hastened, each time, to subdue, considering it out of place in a house of mourning.

He had long regarded the Lorimer girls as quite the most astonishing productions of the age, but this last freak of theirs, as he called it, fairly took away his breath. He was a soft-hearted youth, moreover, and the pathetic aspect of the case presented itself to him with great force in the intervals of his amusement.

Constance had brought a note from her mother, and having delivered it, and had tea, she rose to go. Fred remained lost in abstraction, muttering, "By Jove!" below his breath at intervals, the chuckling having subsided.

"Come on, Fred!" cried his sister.

He sprang to his feet.

"Are you slowly recovering from the shock we have given you?" asked Lucy, demurely, as she held out her hand.

"Miss Lucy," he said, solemnly, looking at her with all his foolish eyes, "I'll come every day of the week to be photographed, if I may, and so shall all the fellows at our office!"

He was a little hurt and disconcerted, though he joined in the laugh himself, when every one burst out laughing; even Lucy, to whom he had addressed himself as the least puzzling and most reliable of the Miss Lorimers.

Gertrude walked down the drive with the brother and sister, a colourless, dusky, wind-blown figure beside their radiant smartness, and let them out herself at the big gate. Here she lingered a moment, while the wind lifted her hair, and fanned her face, bringing a faint tinge of red to its paleness.

Phyllis and Lucy opened the door of the studio which led to the garden, and stood there arm-in-arm, soothed no less than Gertrude by the chill sweetness of the April afternoon. The sound of carriage wheels roused them from the reverie into which both of them had fallen, and in another moment a brougham, drawn by two horses, was seen to round the curve of the drive and make its way to the house.

The two girls retreated rapidly, shutting the door behind them.

"Great heavens, Aunt Caroline!" said Lucy, in dismay.

"She must have passed Gertrude at the gate; Fanny, do you hear who has come?"

"Kettle must take the tea into the drawing-room," said Fanny, in some agitation. "You know Mrs. Pratt does not like the studio."

Phyllis was peeping through the panes of the door, which afforded a view of the entrance of the house.

"She is getting out now; the footman has opened the carriage door, and Kettle is on the steps. Oh, Lucy, if Aunt Caroline had been a horse, what a hard mouth she would have had!"

In another moment a great swish of garments and the sound of a metallic voice were heard in the drawing-room, which adjoined the conservatory; and Kettle, appearing at the entrance which divided the two rooms, announced lugubriously: "Mrs. Septimus Pratt!"

A tall, angular woman, heavily draped in the crispest, most aggressive of mourning garments, was sitting upright on a sofa when the girls entered the drawing-room. She was a handsome person of her age, notwithstanding a slightly equine cast of countenance, and the absence of anything worthy the adjectives graceful or *sympathique* from her individuality.

Mrs. Septimus Pratt belonged to that mischievous class of the community whose will and energy are very far ahead of their intellect and perceptions. She had a vulgar soul and a narrow mind, and unbounded confidence in her own judgments; but she was not bad-hearted, and was animated, at the present moment, by a sincere desire to benefit her nieces.

"How do you do, girls?" she said, speaking in that loud, authoritative key which many benevolent persons of her sex think right to employ when visiting their poorer neighbours. "Yes, please, Fanny, a cup of tea and some bread-and-butter. Cake? No, thank you. I didn't expect to find cake!"

This last sentence, uttered with a sort of ponderous archness, as though to take off the edge of the implied rebuke, was received in unsmiling silence; even Fanny choking down in time a protest which rose to her lips.

With a sinking of the heart, Lucy heard the handle of the door turn, and saw Gertrude enter, pale, severe, and distant.

"How do you do, Gerty?" cried Aunt Caroline, "though this is not our first meeting. How came you to be standing at the gate, without your hat, and in that shabby gown?"

For Gertrude happened to be wearing an old black dress, having taken off the new mourning garment before clearing out the dusty papers.

"I beg your pardon, Aunt Caroline?"

The opposition between these two women may be said to have dated from the cradle of one of them.

"You ought to know at your age, Gertrude," went on Mrs.

Pratt, "that now, of all times, you must be careful in your conduct; and among other things, you can none of you afford to be seen looking shabby."

Mrs. Septimus spoke, it must be owned, with considerable unction. She really meant well by her nieces, as I have said before, but at the same time she was very human; and that circumstances should, as she imagined, have restored to her the right of speaking authoritatively to those independent maidens, was a chance not to be despised. Gertrude, once discussing her, had said that she was a person without respect, and, indeed, a reverence for humanity, as such, could not be reckoned among her virtues.

There was a pause after her last remark, and then, to the surprise and consternation of every one, Fanny flung herself into the breach.

"Mrs. Pratt," she said, vehemently, "we are poor, and we are not ashamed that any one should know it. It is nothing to be ashamed of; and Gertrude is the last person to do anything wrong; and I believe you know that as well as I do!"

Poor Fan's heroics broke off suddenly, as she encountered the steel-grey eye of Mrs. Pratt fixed upon her in astonishment.

Opposition in any form always shocked her inexpressibly; she really felt it to be a sort of sacrilege; but Frances Lorimer was such a poor creature, that one could do nothing but pity her, trampled upon as she was by her younger sisters.

"Fanny is right," said Gertrude, trusting herself to speak, "we are very poor."

"Now do you know exactly how you stand?" went on Aunt Caroline, who allowed herself all the privileges of a near relation in the matter of questions.

"It is not known yet, exactly," answered Lucy, hastily, "but Mr. Devonshire and our father's lawyer, and, I thought, Uncle Septimus, are going into the matter after the sale."

"So your uncle tells me. He tells me also that there will be next to nothing for you girls. Have you made up your minds what you are going to do? Which of you goes out to the Sebastian Lorimers? I hear they have telegraphed for two. I should say Fanny and Phyllis had better go; the others are better able to look after themselves."

Silence; but not in the least disconcerted, Aunt Caroline went on.

"It is a pity that none of you has married; girls don't seem to marry in these days!" (with some complacency, the well-disciplined, well-dowered daughters of the house of Pratt being in the habit of "going off" in due order and season) "but India works wonders sometimes in that respect."

"Oh, let me go to India, Gerty!" cried Phyllis, in a very audible aside, while Gertrude bent her head and bit her lip, controlling the desire to laugh hysterically, which the naïve character of her aunt's last remark had excited.

"Now, Gertrude and Lucy," continued the speaker, "I am empowered by your uncle" (poor Septimus!) "to offer you a home for as long as you like. Either as a permanency, or until you have found suitable occupations."

"*We* are in India, Fan, that's why there is no mention of us," whispered naughty Phyllis.

"Aunt Caroline," broke in Gertrude, suddenly, lifting her head and speaking with great decision. "You are very kind, and we thank you. But we contemplate other arrangements."

"My dear Gertrude, other arrangements! And what 'arrangements,' pray, do you 'contemplate'?"

"Fanny, Lucy, Phyllis, shall I tell Aunt Caroline?"

They all consented; Fanny, whose willingness to join them had seemed before a doubtful matter, with the greatest promptness of them all.

"We think of going into business as photographers."

Gertrude dropped her bomb without delight. For a moment she saw herself and her sisters as they were reflected in the mind of Mrs. Septimus Pratt: naughty children, idle dreamers.

Aunt Caroline refused to be shocked, and Gertrude felt that her bomb had turned into a pea from a pea-shooter.

"Nonsense!" said Mrs. Pratt. "Gertrude, I wonder that you haven't more common sense. And before your younger sisters, too. But common sense," with unpleasant emphasis, "was never a family characteristic."

Lucy, who had remained silent and watchful throughout the last part of the discussion, if discussion it could be called, now rose to her feet.

"Aunt Caroline," she said in her clear young voice; "will you excuse us if we refuse to discuss this matter with you at present? We have decided nothing; indeed, how could we decide? Gertrude wrote yesterday to an old friend of our father's, who has the knowledge and experience we want; and we are waiting now for his advice."

"I think you are a set of wilful, foolish girls," cried Mrs. Pratt, losing her temper at last; "and heaven knows what will become of you! You are my dead sister's children, and I have my duties towards you, or I would wash my hands of you all from this hour. But your uncle shall talk to you; perhaps you will listen to *him*; though there's no saying."

She rose from her seat, with a purple flush on her habitually pale face, and without deigning to go through the formalities of farewell, swept from the room, followed by Lucy.

"A good riddance!" cried Fan. She too was flushed and excited, poor soul, with defiance.

Lucy, coming back from leading her aunt to the carriage, found Gertrude silent, pale, and trembling with rage. "How dare she!" she said below her breath.

"She is only very silly," answered Lucy; "I confess I began to wonder if I was an ill-conducted pauper, or a lunatic, or something of the sort, from the tone of her voice."

"She spoke so loud," said Gertrude, pressing her hand to her head.

"I never felt so labelled and docketed in my life," cried Phyllis; "*This is a poor person*, seemed to be written all over my clothes. Poor Fred's chuckles and 'By Joves' were much more comfortable."

Kettle came into the room with a letter addressed to Miss G. Lorimer.

"It is from Mr. Russel," she said, examining the postmark, and broke the seal with anxious fingers.

Mr. Russel was the friend of their father to whom she had applied for advice the day before. He carried on a large and world-famed business as a photographer in the north of England; to the disgust of a family that had starved respectably on scholarship for several generations.

Gertrude's mobile face brightened as she read the letter. "Mr. Russel is most encouraging," she said; "and very kind. He is actually coming to London to talk it over with us, and examine our work. And he even hints that one of us should go back with him to learn about things; but perhaps that will not be necessary."

Every one seized on the kind letter, and the air was filled with the praises of its writer, Fanny even going so far as to call him a darling.

Gertrude, walking up and down the room, stopped suddenly and said: "Let us make some good resolutions!"

"Yes," cried Phyllis, with her usual frankness; "let us pave the way to hell a little!"

"Firstly, we won't be cynical."

The motion was carried unanimously.

"Secondly, we will be happy."

This motion was carried, with even greater enthusiasm than the preceding one.

"Thirdly," put in Phyllis, coming up behind her sister, laying her nut-brown head on her shoulder, and speaking in tones of mock pathos: "Thirdly, we will never, never mention that we have seen better days!"

Thus, with laughing faces, they stood up and defied the Fates.

CHAPTER III

Ways and Means

O 'tis not joy and 'tis not bliss,
Only it is precisely this
   That keeps us all alive.
A.H. Clough[1]

"So you are really, really going to do it, Gerty?"

"Yes, really, Con."

It was the day before the sale, and the two girls, Gertrude Lorimer and Constance Devonshire, were walking round the garden together for the last time. It had been a day of farewells. Only an hour ago the unfortunate Fan had rolled off to Lancaster Gate[2] in a brougham belonging to the house of Pratt. Lucy was now steaming on her way to the north with Mr. Russel; and upstairs Phyllis was packing her boxes before setting out for Queen's Gate with Constance and her sister.

"If it hadn't been for Mr. Russel," went on Gertrude, with enthusiasm, "the whole thing would have fallen through. Of course, all the kind, common-sense people opposed the scheme tooth and nail; Mr. Russel told me in confidence that he had no

---

1   Arthur Hugh Clough (1819-61), "Life Is Struggle," lines 20-22.
    Clough's poetry conveys a loss of religious faith. His sister Ann Jemima Clough was a founding principal of Newnham College from 1879.

2   Area of central London adjacent to Paddington and Bayswater, on the northwest side of Kensington Gardens and Hyde Park, nearly opposite to Queen's Gate on the south side.

belief in common sense; that I was to remember that, before trusting myself to him in any respect."

"Well, I don't think that particularly reassuring myself."

Gertrude laughed.

"At least, he has justified it in his own case. Delightful person! he actually appeared here in the flesh, the very day after he wrote. Common sense would never have done such a thing as that."

"You are very intolerant, Gertrude."

"Oh, I hope not! Well, Mr. Russel insisted on going straight to the studio, and examining our apparatus and our work. He turned over everything, remained immersed, as it were, in photographs for such a long time, and was throughout so silent and so serious, that I grew frightened. At last, looking up, he said brusquely: 'This is good work.' He talked to us very seriously after that. Pointed out to us the inevitable risks, the chances of failure which would attend such an undertaking as ours; but wound up by saying that it was by no means a preposterous one, and that for his part, his motto through life had always been, 'nothing venture, nothing have.'"

"Evidently a person after your own heart, Gerty."

"He added, that our best plan would be, if possible, to buy the good-will of some small business; but, as we could not afford to wait, and as our apparatus was very good as far as it went, we must not be discouraged if no opportunity of doing so presented itself, but had better start in business on our own account. Moreover, he says, if the worst comes to the worst, we should always be able to get employment as assistant photographers."

"But, Gerty, why not do that at first? You would be so much more likely to succeed in business afterwards," said Conny, for her part no opponent of common sense; and who, despite much superficial frivolity, was at heart a shrewd, far-seeing daughter of the City.

"If I said that one was life and the other death," answered Gertrude, with her charming smile, "you would perhaps consider the remark unworthy a woman of business. And yet I am not sure that it does not state my case as well as any other. We want a home and an occupation, Conny; a real, living occupation. Think of little Phyllis, for instance, trudging by herself to some great shop in all weathers and seasons!"

"Little Phyllis! She is bigger than any of you, and quite able to take care of herself."

"I wish—it sounds unsisterly—that she were not so very good-looking."

"It's a good thing there's no person of the other sex to hear you, Gerty. You would be made a text for a sermon at once."

"'Felines and Feminines,' or something of the sort? But here is Phyllis herself."

Cool, careless, and debonair, the youngest Miss Lorimer advanced towards them; the April sunshine reflected in her eyes; the tints of the blossoms outrivalled in her cheeks.

"My dear Gertrude," she said, patronisingly, "do you know that it is twelve o'clock, that my boxes are packed and locked, and that not a rag of your own is put away?"

Gertrude explained that she did not intend leaving the house till the afternoon, but that the other two were to go on at once to Queen's Gate, and not keep Mrs. Devonshire waiting for lunch. This, after some protest, they consented to do; and in a few moments Gertrude Lorimer was standing alone in the familiar garden, from which she was soon to be shut out for ever.

Pacing slowly up and down the oft-trodden path, she strove to collect her thoughts; to review, at leisure, the events of the last few days. Her avowed contempt of the popular idol Common Sense notwithstanding, her mind teemed with practical details, with importunate questionings as to ways and means.

These matters seemed more perplexing without the calm and soothing influence of Lucy's presence; for Lucy had been borne off by the benevolent and eccentric Mr. Russel for a three-months' apprenticeship in his own flourishing establishment.

"I will see that your sister learns something of the management of a business, besides improving herself in those technical points which we have already discussed," had been his parting assurance. "While, as for you, Miss Lorimer, I depend on you to look round, and be on a fair way to settling down by the time the three months are up. Perhaps, one of these days, we shall prevail on you to pay us a visit yourself."

It had been decided that for the immediate present Gertrude and Phyllis should avail themselves of the Devonshires' invitation; while Fan, borne down by the force of a superior will, had been prevailed upon to seek a temporary refuge at the house of Mrs. Septimus Pratt.

Poor Aunt Caroline had been really shocked and pained by the firm, though polite, refusal of her nieces to accept her hospitality. Their differences of opinion notwithstanding, she could see no adequate cause for it. If her skin was thick, her heart was not of stone; and it chagrined her to think that her dead sister's children should, at such a time, prefer the house of strangers to her own.

But the young people were obdurate; and she had had at last to content herself with Fan, who was a poor creature, and only a spurious sort of relation after all.

Reviewing one by one all those facts which bore upon her present case; setting in order her thoughts; and gathering up her energies for the fight to come; Gertrude felt her pulses throb, and her bosom glow with resolve.

Of the darker possibilities of human nature and of life, this girl—who believed herself old, and experienced—had no knowledge, save such as had come to her in brief flashes of insight, in passing glimpses scarcely realised or remembered. Even had circumstances given her leisure, she was not a woman to have brooded over the one personal injury which had been dealt her; her pride was too deep and too delicate for this; rather she recoiled from the thought of it, as from an unclean contact.

If the arching forehead and mobile face bespoke imagination and keen sensibilities, the square jaw and resolute mouth gave token, no less, of strength and self-control.

"And all her sorrow shall be turned to labour,"[1]

said Gertrude to herself, half-unconsciously. Then something within her laughed in scornful protest. Sorrow? on this spring day, with the young life coursing in her veins, with all the world before her, an undiscovered country of purple mists and boundless possibilities.

There were hints of a vague delight in the sweet, keen air; whisperings, promises, that had nothing to do with pyrogallic acid and acetate of soda; with the processes of developing, fixing, or intensifying.

A great laburnum tree stood at one end of the lawn, half-flowered and faintly golden; a blossoming almond neighboured it, and beyond, rose a gnarled old apple tree, pink with buds. Birds were piping and calling to one another from all the branches; the leaves of the trees, the lawn, the shrubs, and bushes, wore the vivid and delicate verdure of early spring; life throbbed, and pulsed, and thrust itself forth in every available spot.

---

1 James Thomson (1834-82), *The City of Dreadful Night* (1880), book 21, line 54. This epic of modern London captures the mood of *fin-de-siècle* pessimism, a quality that resonates in Levy's work as well. Levy's essay "James Thomson: A Minor Poet" appeared in 1883. This line comes from a stanza considering Dürer's engraving "Melancolia."

Gertrude, as we know, was by way of being a poet. She had a rebellious heart that cried out, sometimes very inopportunely, for happiness.

And now, as she drank in the wonders of that April morning, she found herself suddenly assailed and overwhelmed by a nameless rapture, an extreme longing, half-hopeful, half-despairing. Sorrow, labour; what had she to do with these?

"I love all things that thou lovest
    Spirit of delight!"[1]

cried the voices within her, with one accord.

"Please, Miss," said Kettle, suddenly appearing, and scattering the thronging visions rather rudely; "the people have come from the Pantechnicon[2] about those cameras, and the other things you said was to go."

"Yes, yes," answered Gertrude, rubbing her eyes and wrinkling her brows—curious, characteristic brows they were; straight and thick, and converging slightly upwards—"everything that is to go is ready packed in the studio."

They had decided on retaining a little furniture, besides the photographic apparatus and studio fittings, for the establishment of the new home, wherever and whatever it should be.

"Very well, Miss Gertrude. And shall I bring you up a little luncheon?"

"No, thank you, Kettle. And I must say good-bye, and thank you for all your kindness to us."

"God bless you, Miss Gertrude, every one of you! I have made so bold as to give my address-card to Miss Phyllis; and if there's anything in which I can ever be of service, don't you think twice about it, but write off at once to Jonah Kettle."

Overcome by his own eloquence, and without waiting for a reply, the old man shuffled off down the path, leaving Gertrude strangely touched by this unexpected demonstration.

"We resolved not to be cynical," she thought. "Cynical! What is the meaning of the current commonplaces as to loss of friends with loss of fortune? How did they arise? What perverseness of vision could have led to the creation of such a person as Timon

---

1 Percy Bysshe Shelley (1792-1822), "Rarely, Rarely Comest Thou" (1820), stanza 5, lines 25-26.
2 Initial usage referred to a bazaar or craft shop that opened in Belgravia, London, but soon was modified to refer to a kind of storage warehouse.

of Athens,[1] for instance? If misery parts the flux of company,[2] surely it is the miserable people's own fault."

Balancing the mass of friends in need against one who was only a fair-weather friend, Gertrude refused to allow her faith in humanity to be shaken.

Ah, Gertrude, but it is early days!

CHAPTER IV

Number Twenty B

Bravant le monde et les sots et les sages,
Sans avenir, riche de mon printemps,
L'este et joyeux je montais six étages,
Dans un grenier qu'on est bien à vingt ans!
Béranger[3]

The Lorimers' tenacity of purpose, backed by Mr. Russel's support and countenance, at last succeeded in procuring them a respectful hearing from the few friends and relatives who had a right to be interested in their affairs.

Aunt Caroline, shifting her ground, ceased to talk of the scheme as beneath contempt, but denounced it as dangerous and unwomanly.

She spoke freely of loss of caste; damage to prospects—vague and delicate possession of the female sex—and of the complicated evils which must necessarily arise from an undertaking so completely devoid of chaperons.

Uncle Septimus said little, but managed to convey to his nieces quiet marks of support and sympathy; while the Devon-

---

1 Subject of Shakespeare's tragedy, *The Life of Timon of Athens*, a misanthrope.
2 Compare with Shakespeare's *As You Like It* II.i.51-52: "thus misery doth part / The flux of company."
3 Pierre-Jean de Béranger (1780-1857), "Le Grenier" ("The Garret"). W.M. Thackeray's modified translation as follows: "Making a mock of life and all its cares, / Rich in the glory of my rising sun, / Lightly I vaulted up four pair of stairs, / In the brave days when I was twenty-one" ("The Garret," *The Works of William Makepeace Thackeray* (London: Smith, Elder, 1910-1911), vol. 15, 1899, lines 5-8).

shires, after much preliminary opposition, had ended by throwing themselves, like the excellent people they were, heart and soul into the scheme.

To Constance, indeed, the change in her friends' affairs may be said to have come, like the Waverley pen,[1] as a boon and a blessing. She was the somebody to whom their ill wind, though she knew it not, was blowing good.

Like many girls of her class, she had good faculties, abundant vitality, and no interests but frivolous ones. And with the wealthy middle-classes, even the social business is apt to be less unintermittent, less absorbing, than with the better born seekers after pleasure.

Her friendship with the Lorimers, with Gertrude especially, may be said to have represented the one serious element in Constance Devonshire's life. And now she threw herself with immense zeal and devotion into the absorbing business of house-hunting, on which, for the time being, all Gertrude's thoughts were centred.

After the sale, and the winding up (mysterious process) of poor Mr. Lorimer's affairs, it was intimated to the girls that they were the joint possessors of £600; not a large sum, when regarded as almost the entire fortune of four people, but slightly in excess of that which they had been led to expect. I said almost, for it must not be forgotten that Fanny had a modest income of £50 coming to her from her mother, of which the principal was tied up from her reach.

There was nothing now to do but to choose their quarters, settle down in them, and begin the enterprise on which they were bent.

For many weary days, Gertrude and Conny, sometimes accompanied by Fred or Mr. Devonshire, paced the town from end to end, laden with sheaves of "orders to view" from innumerable house-agents.

Phyllis was too delicate for such expeditions, and sat at home with Mrs. Devonshire, or drove out shopping; amiable but ironical; buoyant but never exuberant; the charming child that everybody conspired to spoil, that everybody instinctively screened from all unpleasantness.

---

1 Made by Macniven and Cameron in Birmingham, the Waverly pen came in a box with a label bearing an image of Sir Walter Scott and the slogan: "They come as a boon and a blessing to men, / The Pickwick, the Owl, and the Waverly pen."

One day, the two girls came back to Queen's Gate in a state of considerable excitement.

"It certainly is the most likely place we have seen," said Gertrude, as she sipped her tea, and blinked at the fire with dazzled, short-sighted eyes.

"But such miles away from South Kensington," grumbled Conny, unfastening her rich cloak, and falling upon the cake with all the appetite born of honest labour.

"And the rent is a little high; but Mr. Russel says it would be bad economy to start in some cheap, obscure place."

"So we are to flaunt expensively," said Phyllis, lightly; "but all this is very vague, is it not Mrs. Devonshire? Please be more definite, Gerty dear."

"We have been looking at some rooms in Upper Baker Street,"[1] explained Gertrude, addressing her hostess; "there are two floors to be let unfurnished, above a chemist's shop."

"Two floors, and what else?" cried Conny; "you will never guess! Actually a photographer's studio built out from the house."

Mrs. Devonshire disapproved secretly of their scheme, and had only been won over to countenance it after days of persuasion.

"Some one has been failing in business there," she said, "or why should the studio stand empty?"

The girls felt this to be a little unreasonable, but Gertrude only laughed, and said: "No, but somebody has been dying. Our predecessor in business died last year."

"At least we should be provided with a ghost at once," said Phyllis; "I suppose if we go there we shall be 'Lorimer, late so-and-so?'"

"What ghouls you two are!" objected Conny, with a shudder; then resumed the more practical part of the conversation. "The studio is in rather a dilapidated condition; but if it were not it would only count for more in the rent; it has to be paid for one way or another."

---

1   In the 1880s, Upper Baker Street ran north of Marylebone Road to Regent's Park. From 1872 to 1885 Levy and her family lived at Sussex Place, just north of Upper Baker Street. In 1887, Arthur Conan Doyle published "A Study in Scarlet," the first Sherlock Holmes story, in which Holmes and Watson reside at 221B Baker Street, a fictitious address approximating Upper Baker Street.

"There are a great many photographers in Baker Street[1] already," demurred Mrs. Devonshire.

She liked the Lorimers, but feared them as companions for her daughter; there was no knowing on what wild freak they might lead Constance to embark.

"But, Mrs. Devonshire," protested Gertrude, with great eagerness, "I am told that it is the right thing for people of the same trade to congregate together; they combine, as it were, to make a centre, which comes to be regarded as the emporium of their particular wares."

Gertrude laughed at her own phrases, and Phyllis said:

"Don't look so poetical over it all, Gerty! Your hat has found its way to the back of your head, and there is a general look of inspiration about you."

She straightened the hat as she spoke, and put back the straggling wisps of hair.

"There is no bath-room!" went on Conny, sternly. She had a love of practical details and small opportunity for indulging it, except with regard to her own costume; and now she proceeded to plunge into elaborate statements on the subject of hot water, and the practicability of having it brought up in cans.

The end of it was that an expedition to Baker Street was organised for the next day; when the whole party drove across the park to that pleasant, if unfashionable, region, for the purpose of inspecting the hopeful premises.

It was a chill, bright afternoon, and notwithstanding that it was the end of May, the girls wore their winter cloaks, and Mrs. Devonshire her furs.

"What number did you say, Gertrude?" asked Phyllis, as the carriage turned into New Street, from Gloucester Place.[2]

"Twenty B."

As they came into Baker Street, a young man, slim, high-coloured, dark-haired, darted out, with some impetuosity, from the post-office at the corner, and raised his hat as his eye fell on the approaching carriage.

---

1 20 Upper Baker Street was the address of different photographic studios from 1877 to 1899, according to Michael Pritchard's *A Directory of London Photographers 1841-1908* (Bushey: ALLM Books, 1986), which confirms Mrs. Devonshire's observation here. According to Pritchard's data, there were several concurrent photography establishments on Upper Baker and Baker Streets in the 1880s.

2 Gloucester Place is southwest of Sussex Place, and New Street runs eastward into Upper Baker Street.

Constance bowed, colouring slightly.

"Who is your friend, Conny?" said her mother.

"Oh, a man I meet sometimes at dances. I believe his name is Jermyn. He dances rather well."

Conny spoke with somewhat exaggerated indifference, and the colour on her cheek deepened perceptibly.

"Here we are!" cried Phyllis.

The carriage had drawn up before a small, but flourishing-looking shop, above which was painted in gold letters; *Maryon; Pharmaceutical Chemist.*

"This is it."

Gertrude spoke with curious intensity, and her heart beat fast as they dismounted and rang the bell.

Mrs. Maryon, the chemist's wife, a thin, thoughtful-looking woman of middle-age, with a face at once melancholy and benevolent, opened the door to them herself, and conducted them over the apartments.

They went up a short flight of stairs, then stopped before the opening of a narrow passage, adorned with Virginia cork and coloured glass.

"We will look at the studio first, please," said Gertrude, and they all trooped down the little, sloping passage.

"Reminds one forcibly of a summer-house at a tea-garden, doesn't it?" said Phyllis, turning her pretty head from side to side. They laughed, and the melancholy woman was seen to smile.

Beyond the passage was a little room, designed, no doubt, for a waiting or dressing-room; and beyond this, divided by an aperture, evidently intended for curtains, came the studio itself, a fair-sized glass structure, in some need of repair.

"You will have to make this place as pretty as possible," said Conny; "you will be nothing if not aesthetic. And now for the rooms."

The floor immediately above the shop had been let to a dressmaker, and it was the two upper floors which stood vacant.

On the first of these was a fair-sized room with two windows, looking out on the street, divided by folding doors from a smaller room with a corner fire-place.

"This would make a capital sitting-room," said Conny, marching up and down the larger apartment.

"And this," cried Gertrude, from behind the folding-doors, which stood ajar, "could be fitted up beautifully as a kitchen."

"You will have to have a kitchen-range, my dears," remarked Mrs. Devonshire, who was becoming deeply interested, and whose spirits, moreover, were rising under the sense that here, at least, she could speak to the young people from the heights of knowledge and experience; "and water will have to be laid on; and you will certainly need a sink."

"This grey wall-paper," went on Conny, "is not pretty, but at least it is inoffensive."

"And the possibilities for evil of wallpapers being practically infinite, I suppose we must be thankful for small mercies in that respect," answered Gertrude, emerging from her projected kitchen, and beginning to examine the uninteresting decoration in her short-sighted fashion.

Upstairs were three rooms, capable of accommodating four people as bed-rooms, and which bounded the little domain.

Mr. and Mrs. Maryon and their servant inhabited the basement and the parlour behind the shop; and it was suggested by the chemist's wife that, for the present at least, the ladies might like to enter on some arrangement for sharing Matilda's services; the duties of that maiden, as matters now stood, not being nearly enough to fill up her time.

"That would suit us admirably," answered Gertrude; "for we intend to do a great deal of the work ourselves."

They drove away in hopeful mood; Mrs. Devonshire as much interested as any of them. It took, of course, some days before they were able to come to a final decision on the subject of the rooms. Various persons had to be consulted, and various matters inquired into. Mr. Russel came flying down from the north directly Gertrude's letter reached him. He surveyed the premises in his rapid, accurate fashion; entered into details with immense seriousness; pronounced in favour of taking the apartments; gave a glowing account of Lucy; and rushed off to catch his train.

A few days afterwards the Lorimers found themselves the holders of a lease, terminable at one, three, or seven years, for a studio and upper part of the house, known as 20B, Upper Baker Street.

Then followed a period of absorbing and unremitting toil. All through the sweet June month the girls laboured at setting things in order in the new home. Expense being a matter of vital consequence, they endeavoured to do everything, within the limits of possibility, themselves. Workmen were of course needed for repairing the studio and fitting the kitchen fireplace, but their services were dispensed with in almost every other case. The furniture stored at the Pantechnicon proved more than enough for their present needs; Gertrude and Conny between them laid down the carpets and hung up the curtains; and Fred, revealing an unsuspected talent for carpentering, occupied his leisure moments in providing the household with an unlimited quantity of shelves.

Indeed, the spectacle of that gorgeous youth hammering away in his shirt sleeves on a pair of steps, his immaculate hat and coat laid by, his gardenia languishing[1] in some forgotten nook, was one not easily to be overlooked or forgotten. It was necessary, of course, to buy some additional stock-in-trade, and this Mr. Russel undertook to procure for them at the lowest possible rates; adding, on his own behalf, a large burnishing machine. The girls had hitherto been accustomed to having their prints rolled for them by the Stereoscopic Company.[2]

In their own rooms everything was of the simplest, but a more ambitious style of decoration was attempted in the studio.

The objectionable Virginia cork and coloured glass of the little passage were disguised by various aesthetic devices; lanterns swung from the roof, and a framed photograph or two from Dürer and Botticelli, Watts and Burne-Jones,[3] was mingled artfully with the specimens of their own work which adorned it as a matter of course.

A little cheap Japanese china, and a few red-legged tables and chairs converted the waiting-room, as Phyllis said, into a perfect bower of art and culture; while Fred contributed so many rustic windows, stiles and canvas backgrounds to the studio, that his bankruptcy was declared on all sides to be imminent.

Over the street-door was fixed a large black board, on which was painted in gold letters:

---

1 An allusion to the Aesthetic Movement and the figure of the dandy soon after to be associated with Oscar Wilde's 1890 *The Picture of Dorian Gray*. The buttonhole flower was the chief accessory to the aesthete's wardrobe, while "languishing" became a quality that captured *fin-de-siècle* ennui.

2 The stereoscope is a device in which two objects photographed at slightly different angles are viewed together to give the impression of a three-dimensional object. There was a London Stereoscopic and Photographic Company at work as early as 1860 and as late as 1910.

3 Albrecht Dürer (1471-1528), German painter and engraver; Sandro Botticelli (1445-1510), Italian painter; George Frederic Watts (1817-1904), English painter; Sir Edward Burne-Jones (1833-98), English painter and designer associated with the Pre-Raphaelite Movement, a precursor to the Aesthetic Movement.

G. & L. Lorimer: The Photographic Studio[1]

and in the doorway was displayed a showcase, whose most conspicuous feature was a cabinet portrait[2] of Fred Devonshire, looking, with an air of mingled archness and shamefacedness, through one of his own elaborate lattices in Virginia cork.

The Mayrons surveyed these preparations from afar with a certain amused compassion, an incredulous kindliness, which were rather exasperating.

Like most people of their class, they had seen too much of the ups and downs of life to be astonished at anything; and the sight of these ladies playing at photographers and house decorators, was only one more scene in the varied and curious drama of life which it was their lot to witness.

"I wish," said Gertrude, one day, "that Mrs. Maryon were not such a pessimist."

"She *is* rather like Gilbert's patent hag[3] who comes out and prophesies disaster," answered Phyllis. "She always thinks it is going to rain, and nothing surprises her so much as when a parcel arrives in time."

"And she is so very kind with it all."

The sisters had been alone in Baker Street that morning; Constance being engaged in having a ball-dress tried on at Russell and Allen's;[4] and now Gertrude was about to set out for the British Museum, where she was going through a course of photographic reading, under the direction of Mr. Russel.

"Look," cried Phyllis, as they emerged from the house; "there goes Conny's impetuous friend. I have found out that he lodges just opposite us, over the auctioneer's."

"What busybodies you long-sighted people always are, Phyllis!"

---

1 Michael Pritchard's *A Directory of London Photographers 1841-1908* (Bushey: ALLM Books, 1986), lists a "New Photographic Studio" at 20 Upper Baker Street in 1882.

2 Similar to the *carte de visite*, a portrait photograph mounted on card stock that became very popular in the 1880s.

3 "Palsied hag" occurs in the vocal score (second song of the first act) of *Ruddigore; or the Witch's Curse* (1887) by W.S. Gilbert (1836-1911) and Arthur Sullivan (1842-1900). The lyrics convey a "writhing dame" who curses her assailant as she is being tortured by fire.

4 "Messrs. Russell and Allen, Old Bond Street, London, W." was an exclusive dress designer and supplier shop, according to photographs on the website of the Victoria and Albert Museum.

At Baker Street Station[1] they parted; Phyllis disappearing to the underground railway; Gertrude mounting boldly to the top of an Atlas omnibus.[2]

"Because one cannot afford a carriage or even a hansom cab," she argued to herself, "is one to be shut up away from the sunlight and the streets?"

Indeed, for Gertrude, the humours of the town had always possessed a curious fascination. She contemplated the familiar London pageant with an interest that had something of passion in it; and, for her part, was never inclined to quarrel with the fate which had transported her from the comparative tameness of Campden Hill to regions where the pulses of the great city could be felt distinctly as they beat and throbbed.

By the end of June the premises in Upper Baker Street were quite ready for occupation; but Gertrude and Phyllis decided to avail themselves of some of their numerous invitations, and strengthen themselves for the coming tussle with fortune with three or four weeks of country air.

At last there came a memorable evening, late in July, when the four sisters met for the first time under the roof which they hoped was to shelter them for many years to come.

Gertrude and Phyllis arrived early in the day from Scarborough, where they had been staying with the Devonshires, and at about six o'clock Fanny appeared in a four-wheel cab; she had been borne off to Tunbridge Wells by the Pratts, some six weeks before.

When she had given vent to her delight at rejoining her sisters, and had inspected the new home, Phyllis led her upstairs to the bedroom, Gertrude remaining below in the sitting-room, which she paced with a curious excitement, an irrepressible restlessness.

"Poor old Fan!" said Phyllis, re-appearing; "I don't think she was ever so pleased at seeing any one before."

---

1 The underground Metropolitan Railway station by this name opened in 1863 and was situated at the intersections of Upper Baker Street, York Place, and Marylebone Road.

2 The Atlas and the City Atlas omnibuses ran between St. John's Wood and London Bridge with a Baker Street stop approximately every 20 minutes from 8:15 in the morning to 11:25 at night, according to Edward Stanford's 1875 *London Guide*. Levy's "Ballade of an Omnibus," from *A London Place-Tree, and Other* Verse (1889), conveys the pleasures of viewing "the familiar London pageant" riding atop of an omnibus.

"Fancy, all these months with Aunt Caroline!"

"She says little," went on Phyllis; "but from the few remarks dropped, I should say that her sufferings had been pretty severe."

"Yes," answered Gertrude, absently. The last remark had fallen on unheeding ears; her attention was entirely absorbed by a cab which had stopped before the door. One moment, and she was on the stairs; the next, she and Lucy were in one another's arms.

"Oh, Gerty, is it a hundred years?"

"Thousands, Lucy. How well you look, and I believe you have grown."

Up and down, hand in hand, went the sisters, into every nook and corner of the small domain, exclaiming, explaining, asking and answering a hundred questions.

"Oh, Lucy," cried Gertrude, in a burst of enthusiasm, as they stood together in the studio, "this is work, this is life. I think we have never worked or lived before."

Fan and Phyllis came rustling between the curtains to join them.

"Here we all are," went on Gertrude. "I hope nobody is afraid, but that every one understands that this is no bed of roses we have prepared for ourselves."

"We shall have to work like niggers,[1] and not have very much to eat. I think we all realise that," said Lucy, with an encouraging smile.

"Plain living and high thinking," ventured Fanny; then grew overwhelmed with confusion at her own unwonted brilliancy.

"At least," said Phyllis, "we can all of us manage the plain living. And as a beginning, I vote we go upstairs to supper."

---

1 Most likely a colloquialism referring to African slaves; the word "nigger" was a commonplace in Victorian discourse. *The Jewish Chronicle* review of *The Romance of a Shop* (see Appendix A2) objects to this phrase as an instance of Levy's female characters speaking "vulgar slang."

CHAPTER V

This Working-Day World

O the pity of it.
Othello[1]

If a sudden reverse of fortune need not make us cynical, there is perhaps no other experience which brings us face to face so quickly and so closely with the realities of life.

The Lorimers, indeed, had no great cause for complaint; and perhaps, in condemning the Timons of this world, forgot that, as interesting young women, embarked moreover on an interesting enterprise, they were not themselves in a position to gauge the full depths of mundane perfidy.

Of course, after a time, they dropped off from the old set, from the people with whom their intercourse had been a mere matter of social commerce; but, as Phyllis justly observed, when you have no time to pay calls, no clothes to your back, no money for cabs, and very little for omnibuses, you can hardly expect your career to be an unbroken course of festivities.

On the other hand, many of their friends drew closer to them in the hour of need, and a great many good-natured acquaintances amused themselves by patronising the studio in Upper Baker Street, and recommending other people to go and do likewise.

Certainly these latter exacted a good deal for their money; were restive when posed, expected the utmost excellence of work and punctuality of delivery, and, like most of the Lorimers' customers, seemed to think the sex of the photographers a ground for greater cheapness in the photographs.

One evening, towards the middle of October, the girls had assembled for the evening meal—it could not, strictly speaking, be called dinner—in the little sitting-room above the shop.

They were all tired, for the moment discouraged, and had much ado to maintain that cheerfulness which they held it a point of honour never to abandon.

---

1 Shakespeare, *Othello* IV.i.196. Othello speaks of Desdemona's charms: "O Iago, the pity of it, Iago!"

"How the evenings do draw in!" observed Fan, who sat near the window, engaged in fancy-work.

Fanny's housekeeping, by the way, had been tried, and found wanting; and the poor lady had, with great delicacy, been relegated to the vague duty of creating an atmosphere of home for her more strong-minded sisters. Fortunately, she believed in the necessity of a thoroughly womanly presence among them, womanliness being apparently represented to her mind by any number of riband bows on the curtains, antimacassars[1] on the chairs, and strips of embroidered plush on every available article of furniture; and accepted the situation without misgiving.

"Yes," answered Lucy, rather dismally; "we shall soon have the winter in full swing, fogs and all."

She had been up to the studio of an artist at St. John's Wood[2] that morning, making photographs of various studies of drapery for a big picture, and the results, when examined in the darkroom later on, had not been satisfactory; hence her unusual depression of spirits.

"For goodness' sake, Lucy, don't speak in that tone!" cried Phyllis, who was standing idly by the window. "What does it matter about Mr. Lawrence's draperies? Nobody ever buys his pokey pictures. You've not been the same person ever since you developed those plates this afternoon."

"Don't you see, Phyllis, Mr. Russel introduced us to him; and besides, though he is obscure himself, he might recommend us to other artists if the work was well done."

"Oh, bother! Come over here, Lucy. Do you see that lighted window opposite? It is Conny's Mr. Jermyn's."

"What an interesting fact!"

"Conny said he danced well. I wish he would come and dance with us sometimes. It is ages and ages since I had a really good waltz."

"Phyllis! do you forget that you are in mourning?" cried Fanny, shocked, as she moved towards the table, where Lucy had lit the lamp.

---

1 A cloth used for putting over the back of a chair in order to keep it clean or to decorate it.

2 Suburban area of Victorian London northwest of Regent's Park associated with bohemian artists, referred to as the St. John's Wood Clique or School, and included Philip Hermogenes Calderon, John Evan Hodgson, William Frederick Yeames, and Val Prinsep, all living in this section of London in the 1870s-80s.

Gertrude came through the folding-doors bearing a covered dish. Her aspect also was undeniably dejected. Business had been slacker, if possible, than usual, during the past week; regarded from no point of view could their prospects be considered brilliant; and, to crown all, Aunt Caroline had paid them a visit in the course of the day, in which she had propounded some very direct questions as to the state of their finances; questions which it had been both difficult to answer and difficult to evade.

Phyllis ceased her chatter, which she saw at once to be out of harmony with the prevailing mood, and took her place in silence at the table.

At the same moment the studio-bell echoed with considerable violence throughout the house.

"What can any one want this time of night?" cried Fan, in some agitation.

"They must have pulled the wrong bell," said Lucy; "but one of us had better go down and see."

Gertrude lighted a candle, and went downstairs, and the rest proceeded rather silently with their meal.

In about five minutes Gertrude re-appeared with a grave face. "Well?"

They all questioned her, with lips and eyes.

"Some one has been here about work," she said, slowly; "but it's rather a dismal sort of job. It is to photograph a dead person."

"Gerty, what *do* you mean?"

"Oh, I believe it is quite usual. A lady—Lady Watergate—died to-day, and her husband wishes the body to be photographed to-morrow morning."

"It is very strange," said Fanny, "that he should select ladies, young girls, for such a piece of work!"

"Oh, it was a mere chance. It was the housekeeper who came, and we happened to be the first photographer's shop she passed. She seemed to think I might not like it, but we cannot afford to refuse work."

"But, Gertrude," cried Fan, "do you know what Lady Watergate died of? Perhaps scarlet fever, or smallpox, or something of the sort."

"She died of consumption," said Gertrude shortly, and put her arm round Phyllis, who was listening with a curious look in her great, dilated eyes.

"I wonder," put in Lucy, "if this poor lady can be the wife of *the* Lord Watergate?"

"I rather fancy so; I know he lives in Regent's Park, and the address for to-morrow is Sussex Place."[1]

A name so well known in the scientific and literary world was of course familiar to the Lorimers. They had, however, little personal acquaintance with distinguished people, and had never come across the learned and courteous peer in his social capacity, his frequent presence in certain middle-class circles notwithstanding.

Mrs. Maryon, coming up later on for a chat, under pretext of discussing the unsatisfactory Matilda, was informed of the new commission.

"Ah," she said, shaking her head, "it was a sad story that of the Watergates." So passionately fond of her as he had been, and then for her to treat him like that! But he took her back at the last and forgave her everything, like the great-hearted gentleman that he was. "And do you mean," she added, fixing her melancholy, humorous eyes on them, "that you young ladies are actually going by yourselves to the house to make a picture of the body?"

"I am going—no one else," answered Gertrude calmly, passing over Phyllis' avowed intention of accompanying her.

"She always has some dreadful tale about everybody you mention," cried Lucy, indignantly, when Mrs. Maryon had gone. "She will never rest content until there is something dreadful to tell of us."

"Yes, I'm sure she regards us as so many future additions to her Chamber of Horrors,"[2] said Phyllis, reflectively, with a smile.

"And oh," added Fan, "if she would only not compare us so constantly with that poor man who had the studio last year! It makes one positively creep."

"Nonsense," said Gertrude; "she is quite as fond of pleasant events as sad ones. Weddings, for instance, she describes with as much unction as funerals."

"We will certainly do our best to add to her stock of tales in that respect," cried Phyllis, with an odd burst of high spirits. "Who votes for getting married? I do. So do you, don't you, Fan?

---

1 Levy and her family lived at 11 Sussex Place from 1872 to 1885.
2 Madame Tussaud's Waxworks was established in this vicinity of London, Marylebone, Regent's Park, in 1835. It primarily exhibited death masks but also contained (as it does today) a "Chamber of Horrors" of waxwork figured murderers and their victims.

It must be such fun to have one's favourite man dropping in on one every evening."

★ ★ ★ ★ ★

At an early hour the next morning, Gertrude Lorimer started on her errand. She went alone; Lucy of course must remain in the studio; Phyllis was in bed with a headache, and Fan was ministering to her numerous wants. As she passed out, laden with her apparatus, Mdlle. Stéphanie, the big, sallow Frenchwoman who occupied the first floor, entered the house and grinned a vivacious "*Bon jour!*"

"A fine, bright morning for your work, miss!" cried the chemist from his doorstep; while his wife stood at his side, smiling curiously.

Gertrude went on her way with a considerable sinking of the heart. She had no difficulty in finding Sussex Place; indeed, she had often remarked it; the white curve of houses with the columns, the cupolas, and the railed-in space of garden which fronted the Park.

Lord Watergate's house was situated about midway in the terrace. Gertrude, on arriving, was shown into a large dining-room, darkened by blinds, and decorated in each gloomy corner by greenish figures of a pseudo-classical nature, which served the purpose of supports to the gas-globes.

At least a quarter of an hour elapsed before the appearance of the housekeeper, who ushered her up the darkened stairs to a large room on the second storey.

Here the blinds had been raised, and for a moment Gertrude was too dazzled to be aware with any clearness of her surroundings.

As her eyes grew accustomed to the light, she perceived herself to be standing in a daintily-furnished sleeping apartment, whose open windows afforded glimpses of an unbroken prospect of wood, and lawn, and water.

Drawn forward to the middle of the room, well within the light from the windows, was a small, open bedstead of wrought brass. A woman lay, to all appearance, sleeping there, the bright October sunlight falling full on the upturned face, on the spread and shining masses of matchless golden hair. A woman no longer in her first youth; haggard with sickness, pale with the last strange pallor, but beautiful withal, exquisitely, astonishingly beautiful.

Another figure, that of a man, was seated by the window, in a pose as fixed, as motionless, as that of the dead woman herself.

Gertrude, as she silently made preparations for her strange task, instinctively refrained from glancing in the direction of this second figure; and had only the vaguest impression of a dark, bowed head, and a bearded, averted face.

She delivered a few necessary directions to the housekeeper, in the lowest audible voice, then, her faculties stimulated to curious accuracy, set to work with camera and slides.

As she stood, her apparatus gathered up, on the point of departure, the man by the window rose suddenly, and for the first time seemed aware of her presence.

For one brief, but vivid moment, her eyes encountered the glance of two miserable grey eyes, looking out with a sort of dazed wonder from a pale and sunken face. The broad forehead, projecting over the eyes; the fine, but rough-hewn features; the brown hair and beard; the tall, stooping, sinewy figure: these together formed a picture which imprinted itself as by a flash on Gertrude's overwrought consciousness, and was destined not to fade for many days to come.

★ ★ ★ ★ ★

"They are some of the best work you have ever done, Gerty," cried Phyllis, peering over her sister's shoulder. The habits of this young person, as we know, resembled those of the lilies of the field;[1] but she chose to pervade the studio when nothing better offered itself, and in moments of boredom even to occupy herself with some of the more pleasant work.

Gertrude looked thoughtfully at the prints in her hand. They represented a woman lying dead or asleep, with her hair spread out on the pillow.[2]

"Yes," she said, slowly, "they have succeeded better than I expected. Of course the light was not all that could be wished."

---

1 Matthew 6.28: "Consider the lilies of the field; they toil not, neither do they spin."

2 Postmortem photography was widely practiced into the early twentieth century; in the nineteenth century advertisements for "likenesses of deceased persons" were common. Photographing the dead was and is practiced throughout Europe, North America, and other parts of the world. See Jay Ruby, *Secure the Shadow: Death and Photography in America* (Cambridge, MA: The MIT Press, 1995).

"Poor thing," said Phyllis; "what perfect features she has. Mrs. Maryon told us she was wicked, didn't she? But I don't know that it matters about being good when you are as beautiful as all that."

CHAPTER VI

To the Rescue

We studied hard in our styles,
      Chipped each at a crust like Hindoos,
For air, looked out on the tiles,
      For fun, watched each other's windows.
R. *Browning*[1]

"Mr. Frederick Devonshire, I positively refuse to minister any longer to such gross egotism! You've been cabinetted, vignetted, and carte de visited.[2] You've been taken in a snowstorm; you've been taken looking out of window, drinking afternoon tea, and doing I don't know what else. If your vanity still remains unsatisfied, you must get another firm to gorge it for you."

"You're a nice woman of business, you are! Turning money away from the doors like this," chuckled Fred. Lucy's simple badinage appealed to him as the raciest witticisms would probably have failed to do; it seemed to him almost on a par with the brilliant verbal coruscations of his cherished *Sporting Times*.[3]

"Our business," answered Lucy demurely, "is conducted on the strictest principles. We always let a gentleman know when he has had as much as is good for him."

"Oh, I say!" Fred appeared to be completely bowled over by what he would have denominated as this "side-splitter," and gave vent to an unearthly howl of merriment.

"Whatever is the matter?" cried his sister, entering the sitting-room. She and Gertrude had just come up together from the studio, where Conny had been pouring out her soul as to the hol-

---

1 Robert Browning (1812-89), "Youth and Art" (1864), lines 17-20. This poem is about two struggling artists, a singer and a sculptor, who "lodged in a street together" in their youth.

2 The cabinet portrait, the vignette, and the *carte de visite* were all different kinds of portrait photography used in the late nineteenth century.

3 As the title suggests, a newspaper on sports, first published in 1865.

lowness of the world, a fact she was in the habit periodically of discovering. "Fred, what a shocking noise!"

"Oh, shut up, Con, and let a fellow alone," grumbled Fred, subsiding into a chair. "Conny's been dancing every night this week—making me take her, too, by Jove!—and now, if you please, she's got hot coppers."[1]

Miss Devonshire deigned no reply to these remarks, and Phyllis, who, like all of them, was accustomed to occasional sparring between the brother and sister, threw herself into the breach.

"You're the very creature I want, Conny," she cried. "Come over here; perhaps you can enlighten me about the person who interests me more than any one in the world."

"Phyllis!" protested Fan, who understood the allusion.

"It's your man opposite," went on Phyllis, unabashed; "Lucy and I are longing to know all about him. There he is on the doorstep; why, he only went out half an hour ago!"

"That fellow," said Fred, with unutterable contempt; "that foreign-looking chap whom Conny dances half the night with?"

"Foreign-looking," said Phyllis, "I should just think he was! Why, he might have stepped straight out of a Venetian portrait; a Tintoretto, a Bordone,[2] any one of those *mellow* people."

"Only as regards colouring," put in Lucy, whose interest in the subject appeared to be comparatively mild. "I don't believe those old Venetian nobles dashed about in that headlong fashion. I often wonder what his business can be that keeps him running in and out all day."

Fortunately for Constance, the fading light of the December afternoon concealed the fact that she was blushing furiously, as she replied coolly enough, "Oh, Frank Jermyn? he's an artist; works chiefly in black and white for the illustrated papers, I think. He and another man have a studio in York Place together."

"Is he an Englishman?"

"Yes; his people are Cornish clergymen."

"All of them? 'What, all his pretty ones?'"[3] cried Phyllis; "but you are very interesting, Conny, to-day. Poor fellow, he looks a

---

1 According to the *Oxford English Dictionary*, slang for "a mouth and throat parched through excessive drinking," or the ill-effects the day after partying all night.

2 Jacopo Robusti Tintoretto (1518-94) and Paris Bordone (1500-71), both painters who studied under Titian.

3 See Shakespeare, *Macbeth* IV.iii.217: "All my pretty ones?" Macduff speaks these lines upon learning that his wife and children have been slaughtered.

little lonely sometimes; although he has a great many oddly-assorted pals."

"By the bye," went on Conny, still maintaining her severely neutral tone, "he mentioned the photographic studio, and wanted to know all about 'G. and L. Lorimer.'"

"Did you tell him," answered Phyllis, "that if you lived opposite four beautiful, fallen princesses, who kept a photographer's shop, you would at least call and be photographed."

"It is so much nicer of him that he does not," said Lucy, with decision.

Phyllis struck an attitude:

"It might have been, once only,
We lodged in a street together ..."[1]

she began, then stopped short suddenly.

"What a thundering row!" said Fred.

A curious, scuffling sound, coming from the room below, was distinctly audible.

"Mdlle. Stéphanie appears to be giving an afternoon dance," said Lucy.

"I will go and see if anything is the matter," remarked Gertrude, rising.

As a matter of fact she snatched eagerly at this opportunity for separating herself from this group of idle chatterers. She was tired, dispirited, beset with a hundred anxieties; weighed down by a cruel sense of responsibility.

How was it all to end? she asked herself, as, oblivious of Mdlle. Stéphanie's performance, she lingered on the little dusky landing. That first wave of business, born of the good-natured impulse of their friends and acquaintance, had spent itself, and matters were looking very serious indeed for the firm of G. and L. Lorimer.

"We couldn't go on taking Fred's guineas for ever," she thought, a strange laugh rising in her throat. "Perhaps, though, it was wrong of me to refuse to be interviewed by *The Waterloo Place Gazette*. But we are photographers, not mountebanks!" she added, in self-justification.

In a few minutes she had succeeded in suppressing all outward marks of her troubles, and had rejoined the people in the sitting-room.

---

1 Opening two lines of Robert Browning's "Youth and Art."

"Mrs. Maryon says there is nothing the matter," she cried, with her delightful smile, "and that there is no accounting for these foreigners."

Laughter greeted her words, then Conny, rising and shaking out her splendid skirts, declared that it was time to go.

"Aren't you ever coming to see us?" she said, giving Gertrude a great hug. "Mama is positively offended, and as for Papa— disconsolate is not the word."

"You must make them understand how really difficult it is for any of us to come," answered Gertrude, who had a natural dislike to entering on explanations in which such sordid matters as shabby clothes and the comparative dearness of railway tickets would have had to figure largely. "But we are coming one day, of course."

"I'll tell you what it is," cried Fred, as they emerged into the street, and stood looking round for a hansom; "Gertrude may be the cleverest, and Phyllis the prettiest, but Lucy is far and away the nicest of the Lorimer girls."

"Gerty is worth ten of her, *I* think," answered Conny, crossly. She was absorbed in furtive contemplation of a light that glimmered in a window above the auctioneer's shop opposite.

As the girls were sitting at supper, later on, they were startled by the renewal of those sounds below which had disturbed them in the afternoon.

They waited a few minutes, attentive; but this time, instead of dying away, the noise rapidly gathered volume, and in addition to the scuffling, their ears were assailed by the sound of shrill cries, and what appeared to be a perfect volley of objurgations. Evidently a contest was going on in which other weapons than vocal or verbal ones were employed, for the floor and windows of the little sitting-room shook and rattled in a most alarming manner.

Suddenly, to the general horror, Fanny burst into tears.

"Girls," she cried, rushing wildly to the window, "you may say what you like; but I am not going to stay and see us all murdered without lifting a hand. Help! Murder!" she shrieked, leaning half her body over the window-sill.

"For goodness' sake, Fanny, stop that!" cried Lucy, in dismay, trying to draw her back into the room. But her protest was drowned by a series of ear-piercing yells issuing from the room below.

"I will go and see what is the matter," said Gertrude, pale herself to the lips; for the whole thing was sufficiently blood-curdling.

"You'd better stay where you are," answered Lucy, in her most matter-of-fact tones, as she led the terrified Fan to an arm-chair.

Phyllis stood among them silent, gazing from one to the other, with that strange, bright look in her eyes, which with her betokened excitement; the unimpassioned, impersonal excitement of a spectator at a thrilling play.

"Certainly I shall go," said Gertrude, as a door banged violently below, to the accompaniment of a volley of polyglot curses.

"I will not stay in this awful house another hour," panted Fanny, from her arm-chair. "Gertrude, Gertrude, if you leave this room I shall die!"

With a sickening of the heart, for she knew not what horror she was about to encounter, Gertrude made her way downstairs, the cries and sounds of struggling growing louder at each step. At the bottom of the first flight she paused.

"Go back, Phyllis."

"It's no good, Gerty, I'm not going back."

"I am going to the shop; and if the Maryons are not there we must call a policeman."

Swiftly they went down the next flight, past the horrible doors, on the other side of which the battle was raging, still downwards, till they reached the little narrow hall. Here they drew up suddenly before a figure which barred the way.

Long afterwards Gertrude could recall the moment when she first saw Frank Jermyn under their roof; could remember distinctly—though all at the time seemed chaos—the sudden sensation of security that came over her at the sight of the kind, eager young face, the brilliant, steadfast eyes; at the sound of the manly, cheery voice.

There were no explanations; no apologies.

"There seems to be a shocking row going on," he said, lifting his hat; "I only hope that it does not concern any of you ladies."

In a few hurried words Gertrude told him what she knew of the state of affairs. Meanwhile the noise had in some degree subsided.

"Great heavens!" cried Frank; "there may be murder going on at this instant." And in less time than it takes to tell he had sprung past her, and was hammering with all his might at the closed door.

The girls followed timidly, and were in time to see the door fly open in response to the well-directed blows, and Mrs. Maryon herself come forward, pale but calm. Within the room all was now dark and silent.

Mrs. Maryon and the new comer exchanged a few hurried words, and the latter turned to the girls, who clung together a few paces off.

"There is no cause for alarm," he said. "Pray do not wait here. I will explain everything in a few minutes, if I may."

"Now please, Miss Lorimer, go back upstairs; there's nothing to be frightened at," chimed in Mrs. Maryon, with some asperity.

A few minutes afterwards Frank Jermyn knocked at the door of the Lorimers' sitting-room, and on being admitted, found himself well within the fire of four questioning pairs of feminine eyes.

"Pray sit down, sir," said Fan, who had been prepared for his arrival. "How are we ever to thank you?"

"There is nothing to thank me for, as your sisters can tell you," he said, bluntly. He looked a modest, pleasant little person enough as he sat there in his light overcoat and dress clothes, all the fierceness gone out of him. "I have merely come to tell you that nothing terrible has happened. It seems that the poor Frenchwoman below has been in money difficulties, and has been trying to put an end to herself. The Maryons discovered this in time, and it has been as much as they could do to prevent her from carrying out her plan. Hence these tears," he added, with a smile.

When once you had seen Frank Jermyn smile, you believed in him from that moment.

The girls were full of horror and pity at the tale.

"We have had a great shock," said Fan, wiping her eyes, with dignity. "Such a terrible noise. But you heard it for yourself."

A pause; the young fellow looked round rather wistfully, as though doubtful of what footing he stood on among them.

"We must not keep you," went on Fan, whose tongue was loosened by excitement; "no doubt (glancing at his clothes) you are going out to dinner."

She spoke in the manner of a fallen queen who alludes to the ceremony of coronation.

Frank rose.

"By the by," he said, looking down, "I have often wished—I have never ventured"—then looking up and smiling brightly, "I have often wondered if you included photographing at artists' studios in your work."

Lucy assured him that they did, and the young man asked permission to call on them the next day at the studio. Then he added—

"My name is Jermyn, and I live at Number 19, opposite."

"I think," said Lucy, in the candid, friendly fashion which always set people at their ease, "that we have an acquaintance in common, Miss Devonshire."

Jermyn acknowledged that such was the case; a few remarks on the subject were exchanged, then Frank went off to his dinner-party, having first shaken hands with each of the girls in all cordiality and frankness.

Mrs. Maryon came up in the course of the evening, to express her regret that the ladies had been frightened and disturbed; setting aside with cynical good-humour their anxious expressions of pity and sympathy for the heroine of the affair.

"It isn't for such as you to trouble yourselves about such as her," she said, "although I'm sorry enough for Steffany myself—and never a penny of last quarter's rent paid!"

"Poor woman," answered Lucy, "she must have been in a desperate condition."

"You see, miss," said Mrs. Maryon circumstantially, "she had been going on owing money for ever so long, though *we* knew nothing about it; and at last she was threatened with the bailiffs. Then what must she do but go down to the shop and make off with some of Maryon's bottles while we were at dinner. He found it out, and took one away from her this afternoon when you complained of the noise. Later he missed the second bottle, and went up to Steffany, who was uncorking it and sniffing it, and making believe she wanted to do away with herself."

"How unutterably horrible!" Gertrude shuddered.

"You heard how she went on when he tried to take it from her. Such strength as she has, too—it was as much as me and Maryon and the girl could do between us to hold her down."

"Where has she gone to now?" said Lucy.

"Oh, she don't sleep here, you know, miss. She's gone home with Maryon as meek as a lamb; took her bit of supper with us, quite cheerfully."

"What will she do, I wonder?"

"Ah," said Mrs. Maryon, thoughtfully; "there's no saying what she and many other poor creatures like her have to do. There'd be no rest for any of us if we was to think of that."

Gertrude lay awake that night for many hours; the events of the day had curiously shaken her. The story of the miserable Frenchwoman, with its element of grim humour, made her sick at heart.

Fenced in as she had hitherto been from the grosser realities of life, she was only beginning to realise the meaning of life. Only a plank—a plank between them and the pitiless, fathomless ocean[1] on which they had set out with such unknowing fearlessness; into whose boiling depths hundreds sank daily and disappeared, never to rise again.

★ ★ ★ ★ ★

Mademoiselle Stéphanie actually put in an appearance the next morning, and made quite a cheerful bustle over the business of setting her house in order, preparatory to the final flitting.

Gertrude passed her on the stairs on her way to the studio, but feigned not to notice the other's morning greeting, delivered with its usual crispness. The woman's mincing, sallow face, with its unabashed smiles, sickened her.

Phyllis, who was with her, laughed softly.

"She does not seem in the least put out by the little affair of yesterday," she said.

"Hush, Phyllis. Ah, there is the studio bell already. No doubt it is Mr. Jermyn," and she unconsciously assumed her most business-like air.

A day or two later Mademoiselle Stéphanie vanished for ever; and not long afterwards her place was occupied by a serious-looking umbrella-maker, who displayed no hankering for Mr. Maryon's bottles.

<h1 style="text-align:center">CHAPTER VII</h1>

A New Customer

Stately is service accepted, but lovelier service rendered,
Interchange of service the law and condition of Beauty.
A.H. Clough[2]

Frank Jermyn, whom we have left ringing at the bell, followed Gertrude down the Virginia-cork passage into the waiting-room.

---

1 "The Wreck of the Whaler 'Oscar'" (1890) by William Topaz McGonagall (1830?-1902) concludes with this line: "There's only a plank between them and a watery grave, which makes their lives unsure."

2 "The Bothie of Tober-Na-Vuolich" (1848) part 6, lines 70-71.

The curtains between this apartment and the studio were drawn aside, displaying a charming picture—Lucy, in her black gown and holland pinafore, her fair, smooth head bent over the re-touching frame; Phyllis, at an ornamental table, engaged in trimming prints, with great deftness and grace of manipulation.

Neither of the girls looked up from her work, and Frank took possession of one of the red-legged chairs, duly impressed with the business-like nature of the occasion; although, indeed, it must be confessed that his glance strayed furtively now and then in the direction of the studio and its pleasant prospect.

Gertrude explained that they were quite prepared to undertake studio work. Frank briefly stated the precise nature of the work he had ready for them, and then ensued a pause.

It was humiliating, it was ridiculous, but it was none the less true, that neither of these business-like young people liked first to make a definite suggestion for the inevitable visit to Frank's studio.

At last Gertrude said, "You would wish it done to-day?"

"Yes, please; if it be possible."

She reflected a moment. "It must be this morning. There is no relying on the afternoon light. I cannot arrange to go myself, but my sister can, I think. Lucy!"

Lucy came across to them, alert and serene.

"Lucy, would you take number three camera to Mr. Jermyn's studio in York Place?"

"Yes, certainly."

"I have some studies of drapery I should wish to be photographed," added Frank, with his air of steadfast modesty.

"I will come at once, if you like," answered Lucy, calmly.

"You will, of course, allow me to carry the apparatus, Miss Lorimer."

"Thank you," said Lucy, after the least possible hesitation.

Every one was immensely serious; and a few minutes afterwards Mrs. Maryon, looking out from the dressmaker's window, saw a solemn young man and a sober young woman emerge together from the house, laden with tripod-stand and camera, and a box of slides, respectively.

"I wish I could have gone myself," said Gertrude, in a worried tone; "but I promised Mrs. Staines to be in for her."

"Yes, he *is* a nice young man," answered Phyllis, unblushingly, looking up from her prints.

"Oh Phyllis, Phyllis, don't talk like a housemaid."

"I say, Gerty, all this is delightfully unchaperoned, isn't it?"

"Phyllis, how can you?" cried Gertrude, vexed.

The question of propriety was one which she always thought best left to itself, which she hated, above all things, to discuss. Yet even her own unconventional sense of fitness was a little shocked at seeing her sister walk out of the house with an unknown young man, both of them being bound for the studio of the latter.

She was quite relieved when, an hour later, Lucy appeared in the waiting-room, fresh and radiant from her little walk.

"Mrs. Staines has been and gone," said Gertrude. "She worried dreadfully. But what have you done with 'number three?'"

"Oh, I left the camera at York Place. I am going again to-morrow to do some work for Mr. Oakley, who shares Mr. Jermyn's studio."

"Grist for our mill with a vengeance. But come here and talk seriously, Lucy."

Phyllis, be it observed, who never remained long in the workshop, had gone out for a walk with Fan.

"Well?" said Lucy, balancing herself against a five-barred gate, Fred Devonshire's latest gift, aptly christened by Phyllis the White Elephant. "Well, Miss Lorimer?"

"I'm going to say something unpleasant. Do you realise that this latest development of our business is likely to excite remark?"

"'That people will talk,' as Fan says? Oh, yes, I realise that."

"Don't look so contemptuous, Lucy. It is unconventional, you know."

"Of course it is; and so are we. It is a little late in the day to quarrel with our bread-and-butter on that ground."

"It is a mere matter of convention, is it not?" cried Gertrude, more anxious to persuade herself than her sister. "Whether a man walks into your studio and introduces himself, or whether your hostess introduces him at a party, it comes to much the same thing. In both cases you must use your judgment about him."

"And whether he walks down the street with you, or puts his arm round your waist, and waltzes off with you to some distant conservatory, makes very little difference. In either case the chances are one knows nothing about him. I am sure half the men one met at dances might have been haberdashers or professional thieves for all their hostesses knew. And, as a matter of fact, we happen to know something about Mr. Jermyn."

"Oh, I have nothing to say against Mr. Jermyn, personally. I am sure he is nice. It was rather that my vivid imagination saw vistas of studio-work looming in the distance. It was quite different with Mr. Lawrence, you know," said Gertrude, whom her own arguments struck as plausible rather than sound. "One thing may lead to another."

"Yes, it is sure to," cried Lucy, who saw an opportunity for escaping from the detested propriety topic. "To-day, for instance, with Mr. Oakley. He is middle-aged, by the bye, Gerty, and married, for I saw his wife."

They both laughed; they could, indeed, afford to laugh, for, regarded from a financial point of view, the morning had been an unusually satisfactory one.

Gertrude's prophetic vision of vistas of studio work proved, for the next few days at least, to have been no baseless fabric of the fancy. The two artists at York Place kept them so busy over models, sketches, and arrangements of drapery, that the girls' hands were full from morning till night. Of course this did not last, but Frank was so full of suggestions for them, so genuinely struck with the quality of their work, so anxious to recommend them to his comrades in art, that their spirits rose high, and hope, which for a time had almost failed them, arose, like a giant refreshed,[1] in their breasts.

In all simplicity and respect, the young Cornishman took a deep and unconcealed interest in the photographic firm, and expected, on his part, a certain amount of interest to be taken in his own work.

Frank, as Conny had said, worked chiefly in black and white. He was engaged, at present, in illustrating a serial story for *The Woodcut*, but he had time on his hands for a great deal more work, time which he employed in painting pictures which the public refused to buy, although the committees were often willing to exhibit them.

"If they would only send me out to that wretched little war,"[2] he said. "There is nothing like having been a special artist for getting a man on with the pictorial editors."

---

1 Psalm 78.66: "So the Lord awaked as one out of sleep, and like a giant refreshed with wine."

2 Frank speaks of journalists covering wars overseas, a regular feature of British imperialism across the globe. In the 1870s and 1880s, the British were involved in military actions in the Balkans, Egypt, the Sudan, Southern Africa, and India. In early 1885, General Charles George Gordon, a British officer, was killed at Khartoum during a military conflict with the Mahdi (Mohammed Ahmed), a messianic Muslim. British interests in Egypt and the Sudan pertained to the strategic control of

There is nothing like the salt of healthy objective interests for keeping the moral nature sound. Before the sense of mutual honesty, the little barriers of prudishness which both sides had thought fit in the first instance to raise, fell silently between the young people, never again to be lifted up.

For good or evil, these waifs on the great stream of London life had drifted together; how long the current should continue thus to bear them side by side—how long, indeed, they should float on the surface of the stream at all, was a question with which, for the time being, they did not very much trouble themselves.

No one quite knew how it came about, but before a month had gone by, it became the most natural thing in the world for Frank to drop in upon them at unexpected hours, to share their simple meals, to ask and give advice about their respective work.

Fanny had accepted the situation with astonishing calmness. Prudish to the verge of insanity with regard to herself, she had grown to look upon her strong-minded sisters as creatures emancipated from the ordinary conventions of their sex, as far removed from the advantages and disadvantages of gallantry as the withered hag who swept the crossing near Baker Street Station.

Perhaps, too, she found life at this period a little dull, and welcomed, on her own account, a new and pleasant social element in the person of Frank Jermyn; however it may be, Fanny gave no trouble, and Gertrude's lurking scruples slept in peace.

One bright morning towards the end of January, Gertrude came careering up the street on the summit of a tall, green omnibus, her hair blowing gaily in the breeze, her ill-gloved hands clasped about a bulky note-book. Frank, passing by in painting-coat and sombrero, plucked the latter from his head and waved it in exaggerated salute, an action which evoked a responsive smile from the person for whom it was intended, but acted with quite a different effect on another person who chanced to witness it, and for whom it was certainly not intended. This was no other than Aunt Caroline Pratt, who, to Gertrude's dismay, came dashing past in an open carriage, a look of speechless horror on her handsome, horselike countenance.

Now it is impossible to be dignified on the top of an omnibus, and Gertrude received her aunt's frozen stare of nonrecognition

---

the Suez Canal, and Red Sea route to India. See "The Khartoum Expedition" in *The Illustrated London News*, 14 February 1885, for an account of these events. The article mentions the newspaper's "Special Artist" who sent "several interesting sketches," many included in the article.

with a humiliating consciousness of the disadvantages of her own position.

With a sinking heart she crept down from her elevation, when the omnibus stopped at the corner, and walked in a crestfallen manner to Number 20B, before the door of which the carriage, emptied of its freight, was standing.

Aunt Caroline did not trouble them much in these days, and rather wondering what had brought her, Gertrude made her way to the sitting-room, where the visitor was already established.

"How do you do, Aunt Caroline?"

"How do you do, Gertrude? And where have you been this morning?"

"To the British Museum."

Gertrude felt all the old opposition rising within her, in the jarring presence; an opposition which she assured herself was unreasonable. What did it matter what Aunt Caroline said, at this time of day? It had been different when they had been little girls; different, too, in that first moment of sorrow and anxiety, when she had laid her coarse touch on their quivering sensibilities.

Yet, when all was said, Mrs. Pratt's was not a presence to be in any way passed over.

"It is half-past one," said Aunt Caroline, consulting her watch; "are you not going to have your luncheon?"

"It is laid in the kitchen," explained Lucy; "but if you will stay we can have it in here."

"In the kitchen! Is it necessary to give up the habits of ladies because you are poor?"

"A kitchen without a cook," put in Phyllis, "is the most lady-like place in the world."

Mrs. Pratt vouchsafed no answer to this exclamation, but turned to Lucy.

"No luncheon, thank you. I may as well say at once that I have come here with a purpose; solely, in fact, from motives of duty. Gertrude, perhaps your conscience can tell you what brings me."

"Indeed, Aunt Caroline, I am at a loss—"

"I have come," continued Mrs. Pratt, "prepared to put up with anything you may say. Gertrude, it is to you I address myself, although, from Fanny's age, she is the one to have prevented this scandal."

"I do not in the least understand you," said Gertrude, with self-restraint.

Mrs. Pratt elevated her gloved forefinger, with the air of a well-seasoned counsel.

"Is it, or is it not true, that you have scraped acquaintance with a young man who lodges opposite you; that he is in and out of your rooms at all hours; that you follow him about to his studio?"

"Yes," said Gertrude, slowly, flushing deeply, "if you choose to put it that way; it is true."

"That you go about to public places with him," continued Aunt Caroline; "that you have been seen, two of you and this person, in the upper boxes of a theatre?"

"Yes, it is true," answered Gertrude; and Lucy, mindful of a coming storm, would have taken up the word, but Gertrude interrupted her.

"Let me speak, Lucy; perhaps, after all, we do owe Aunt Caroline some explanation. Aunt, how shall I say it for you to understand? We have taken life up from a different standpoint, begun it on different bases. We are poor people, and we are learning to find out the pleasures of the poor, to approach happiness from another side. We have none of the conventional social opportunities for instance, but are we therefore to sacrifice all social enjoyment? You say we 'follow Mr. Jermyn to his studio;' we have our living to earn, no less than our lives to live, and in neither case can we afford to be the slaves of custom. Our friends must trust us or leave us; must rely on our self-respect and our judgment. Convention apart, are not judgment and self-respect what we most of us do rely on in our relations with people, under any circumstances whatever?"

It was only the fact that Aunt Caroline was speechless with rage that prevented her from breaking in at an earlier stage on poor Gertrude's heroics; but at this point she found her voice. Sitting very still, and looking hard at her niece with a remarkably unpleasant expression in her cold eye, she said in tones of concentrated fury:

"Fanny is a fool, and the others are children; but don't *you*, Gertrude, know what is meant by a lost reputation?"

This was too much for Gertrude; she sprang to her feet.

"Aunt Caroline," she cried, "you are right; Lucy and Phyllis are very young. It is not fit that they should hear such conversation. If you wish to continue it, I will ask them to go away."

A pause; the two combatants standing pale and breathless, facing one another. Then Lucy went over to her sister and took her hand; Fanny sobbed; Phyllis glanced from one to the other with her bright eyes.

Now, Gertrude's conduct had been distinctly injudicious; open defiance, no less than servile acquiescence, was understood and appreciated by Mrs. Pratt; but Gertrude, as Lucy, who secretly admired her sister's eloquence, at once perceived, had spoken a tongue not understanded of Aunt Caroline.

As soon, in these non-miraculous days, strike the rock for water, as appeal to Aunt Caroline's finer feelings or imaginative perceptions.

"If you will not listen to me," she said, suddenly assuming an air of weariness and physical delicacy, "it must be seen whether your uncle can influence you. I am not equal to prolonging the discussion."

Pointedly ignoring Gertrude, she shook hands with the other girls; angry as she was, their shabby clothes and shabby furniture smote her for the moment with compassion. Poverty seemed to her the greatest of human calamities; she pitied even more than she despised it.

To Lucy, indeed, who escorted her downstairs, she assumed quite a gay and benevolent manner; only pausing to ask on the threshold, with a good deal of fine, healthy curiosity underlying the elaborate archness of her tones:

"Now, how much money have you naughty girls been making lately?"

Lucy stoutly and laughingly evaded the question, and Aunt Caroline drove off smiling, refusing, like the stalwart warrior that she was, to acknowledge herself defeated. But it was many a long day before she attempted again to interfere in the affairs of the Lorimers.

Perhaps she would have been more ready to renew the attack, had she known how really distressed and disturbed Gertrude had been by her words.

CHAPTER VIII

A Distinguished Person

... I can give no reason, nor I will not;
More than have a lodged hate and a certain loathing
I bear Antonio.
Merchant of Venice[1]

One morning, towards the middle of March, the sisters were much excited at receiving a letter containing an order to photograph a picture in a studio at St. John's Wood.

It was written in a small legible handwriting, was dated from The Sycamores, and signed, Sidney Darrell.

"I wonder how he came to hear of us?" said Lucy, who cherished a particular admiration for the works of this artist.

"Perhaps Mr. Jermyn knows him," answered Gertrude.

"He would probably have spoken of him to us, if he did."

"Here," said Gertrude, "is Mr. Jermyn to answer for himself."

Frank, who had been admitted by Matilda, came into the waiting-room, where the sisters stood, a look as of the dawning spring-time in his vivid face and shining eyes.

"I have brought the proofs from *The Woodcut*," he said, drawing a damp bundle from his painting-coat. The Lorimers always read the slips of the story he was illustrating, and then a general council was held to decide on the best incident for illustration.

Lucy took the bundle and handed him the letter.

"Aren't you tremendously pleased?" he said.

"Do you know anything about this?" asked Lucy.

"How?"

"I mean, did you recommend us to him?"

"Not I. This letter is simply the reward of well-earned fame."

"Thank you, Mr. Jermyn; I really think you must be right. Do you know Sidney Darrell?"

"I have met him. But he is a great swell, you know, Miss Lucy, and he is almost always abroad."

"Yes," put in Gertrude; "his exquisite Venetian pictures!"

---

1 Shakespeare, *Merchant of Venice* IV.i.59-61.

"Oh, Darrell is a clever fellow. Too fond of the French school, perhaps, for my taste. And the curious thing is, that, though his work is every bit as solid as it is brilliant, there is something rather sensational about his reputation."

"All this," cried Gertrude, "sounds exciting."

"I think that must be owing to the man himself," went on Frank. "Oakley knows him fairly well; says you may meet him one night at dinner, and he will ask you up to his studio. The first thing next morning you get a note putting you off; he is very sorry, but he is starting that day for India."

"Does he paint Indian pictures?"

"No, but is bitten at times with the 'big game' craze; shoots tigers and sticks pigs, and so on. I believe his studio is quite a museum of trophies of the chase."

"By the by, Lucy, which of us is to go to The Sycamores tomorrow morning?"

"You must go, Gerty; I can't trust any one else to finish off those prints of little Jack Oakley, and they have been promised so long."

Gertrude consulted the letter.

"I shall have to take the big camera, which involves a cab."

"I wish I could have walked up with you," said Frank; "but, strange to say, I am very busy this week."

"I wish we were busy," answered Gertrude; "things are a little better, but it is slow work."

"I consider this letter of Darrell's a distinct move forward," cried hopeful Frank; "*he* will be able to recommend you to artists who are not a lot of out-at-elbow fellows," he added, holding out his hand in farewell, with a bright smile that belied the rueful words. "Now, please don't forget you are all coming to tea with Oakley and me on Sunday afternoon. And Miss Devonshire— you gave her my invitation?"

"Yes," said Lucy, promptly; then added after a pause: "May her brother come too; he says he would like to?"

Frank scanned her quickly with his bright eyes.

"Certainly, if you like; he is not a bad sort of cub."

And then he departed abruptly.

"That was quite rude, for Mr. Jermyn," said Gertrude.

Lucy turned away with a slight flush on her fair face.

"It would be quite rude for anybody," she said, and went over to the studio. Phyllis was spending the day at the Devonshires, but came back for the evening meal, by which time her sisters' excitement on the subject of Darrell's letter had subsided; and no mention was made of it while they were at table.

After the meal, Phyllis went over to the window, drew up the blind, and amused herself, as was her frequent custom, by looking into the street.

"I wish you wouldn't do that," said Lucy; "any one can see right into the room."

"Why do you waste your breath, Lucy? You know it is never any good telling me not to do things, when I want to."

Gertrude, who had herself a secret, childish love for the gas-lit street, for the sight of the hurrying people, the lamps, the hansom cabs, flickering in and out the yellow haze, like so many fire-flies, took no part in the dispute, but set to work at repairing an old skirt of Phyllis', which was sadly torn.

Meanwhile the spoilt child at the window continued her observations, which seemed to afford her considerable amusement.

"There is a light in Frank Jermyn's window—the top one," she cried; "I suppose he is dressing. He told me he had an early dance in Harley Street.[1] I wish *I* were going to a dance."

There was a look of mischief in Phyllis' eyes as she looked round at Lucy, who was buried in the proof-sheets from *The Woodcut*.

"Phyllis, you are coughing terribly. Do come away from that draughty place," cried Gertrude, with real anxiety.

"Oh, I'm all right, Gerty. Ah, there goes Master Frank. It is wet underfoot, and he has turned up his trousers, and his pumps are bulging from his coat-pocket. I wonder how many miles a week he walks on his way to dances?"

"It is quite delightful to see a person with such an enjoyment of every phase of existence," said Gertrude, half to herself.

"You poor, dear *blasée* thing. It *is* a pretty sight to see the young people enjoying themselves, as the little boy said in *Punch*,[2] is it not? I wonder if Mr. Jermyn is going to walk all the way? Perhaps he will take the omnibus at the corner. He never 'soars higher than a 'bus,' as he expresses it."

---

1 Fashionable street south of Regent's Park.

2 *Punch Magazine*, published weekly, from its first issue in 1841, was a popular vehicle for British humor, and noted primarily for its abundant cartoons. See Appendix B2, Figure 1.

Wearying suddenly of the sport, Phyllis dropped the blind, and, coming over to Gertrude, knelt on the floor at her feet.

"It is a little dull, ain't it, Gerty, to look at life from a top-floor window?"

A curious pang went through Gertrude, as she tenderly stroked the nut-brown head.

"You haven't heard our news," she said, irrelevantly. "There, read that." And taking Mr. Darrell's note from her pocket, she handed it to Phyllis.

The latter read it through rather languidly.

"Yes, I suppose it is a good thing to be employed by such a person," she remarked. "Sidney Darrell?—Didn't I tell you I met him last week at the Oakleys, the day I went to tea?"

★ ★ ★ ★ ★

The Sycamores was divided from the road by a high grey wall, beyond which stretched a neglected-looking garden of some size, and, on the March morning of which I write, this latter presented a singularly melancholy appearance.

The house itself looked melancholy also, as houses will which are very little lived in, and appeared to consist almost entirely of a large studio, built out like a disproportionate wing from the main structure.

Gertrude was led at once to the studio by a serious-looking manservant, who announced that his master would join her in a few minutes.

The apartment in which Gertrude found herself was of vast size, and bore none of the signs of neglect and disuse which marked the house and garden.

It was fitted up with all the chaotic splendour which distinguishes the studio of the modern fashionable artist; the spoils of many climes, fruits of many wanderings, being heaped, with more regard to picturesqueness than fitness, in every available nook.

Going up to the carved fire-place, Gertrude proceeded to warm her hands at the comfortable wood-fire, a position badly adapted for taking stock of the great man's possessions, of which, as she afterwards confessed, she only carried away a prevailing impression of tiger-skins and Venetian lanterns.

The fire-light played about her slim figure and about the faded richness of a big screen of old Spanish leather, which fenced in the little bit of territory in the immediate neighbourhood of the fire-place; a spot in which had been gathered the most luxurious lounges and the choicest ornaments of the whole collection; and where, at the present moment, the air was heavy with the scent of tuberose,[1] several sprays of which stood on a small table in a costly jar of Venetian glass.

In a few minutes the sound of footsteps outside, and of the rich, deep notes of a man's voice were audible.

"Et non, non, non,
Vous n'êtes plus Lisette,
Ne portez plus ce nom."[2]

As the footsteps drew nearer the words of the song could be clearly distinguished.

Gertrude turned towards the door, which fronted the fire-place, and as she did so the song ceased, the curtain was pushed aside, and a person, presumably the singer, came into the room.

He was a man of middle height, and middle age, with light brown hair, parted in the centre, and a moustache and Vandyke beard of the same colour. He was not, strictly speaking, hand-some, but he wore that air of distinction which power and the assurance of power alone can confer. His whole appearance was a masterly combination of the correct and the picturesque.

He advanced deliberately towards Gertrude.

"Allow me, Miss Lorimer, to introduce myself."

He spoke carelessly, yet with a note of disappointment in his voice, and a shade of moodiness in his heavy-lidded eyes.

Gertrude, looking up and meeting the cold, grey glance, became suddenly conscious that her hat was shabby, that her boots were patched and clumsy, that the wind had blown the wisps of hair about her face. What was there in this man's gaze that made her, all at once, feel old and awkward, ridiculous and dowdy; that made her long to snatch up her heavy camera and flee from his presence, never to return?

What, indeed? Gertrude, we know, had a vivid imagination, and that perhaps was responsible for the sense of oppression, defiance, and self-distrust with which she followed Mr. Darrell

---

1 According to *The Language of Flowers* (1885), the tuberose symbolizes dangerous pleasures.

2 "And no, no, no, / You are no longer Lisette / Don't use that name any more." Refrain of "Ce n'est plus Lisette" (1816) by Pierre-Jean de Béranger. In this popular song, Lisette's newly acquired accessories of wealth appear to be at the expense of her respectability.

across the room to one of the easels, on which was displayed a remarkable study in oils of a winter aspect of the Grand Canal at Venice.

There was certainly, superficially speaking, no ground for her feeling in the artist's conduct. With his own hands he set up and fixed the heavy camera on the tripod stand, questioned her, in his low, listless tones, as to her convenience, and observed, by way of polite conversation, that he had had the pleasure of meeting her sister the week before at the Oakleys.

To her own unutterable vexation, Gertrude found herself rather cowed by the man and his indifferent politeness, through which she seemed to detect the lurking contempt; and as his glance of cold irony fell upon her from time to time, from beneath the heavy lids, she found herself beginning to take part not only against herself but also against the type of woman to which she belonged.

Having made the necessary adjustments, and given the necessary directions, Darrell went over to the fire-place, and cast himself into a lounge, where the leather screen shut out his well-appointed person from Gertrude's sight. She, on her part, set about her task without enjoyment, and was glad when it was over and she could pack up the dark-slides. As she was unscrewing the camera from the stand, the curtain before the doorway was pushed aside for the second time, and a man entered unannounced. At the same moment Darrell advanced from behind his screen, and the two men met in the middle of the room.

"Delighted to see you back, my dear fellow."

It seemed to Gertrude that a shade of deference had infused itself into the artist's manner, as he cordially clasped hands with the new comer.

This person was a tall, sinewy man of from thirty-five to forty years of age, with stooping shoulders and a brown beard. From her corner by the easel Miss Lorimer could see his face, and her casual glance falling upon it was arrested by a sudden sense of recognition.

Where had she seen them before; the ample forehead, the clear, grey eyes, the rough yet generous lines of the features?

This man's face was sunburnt, cheery, smiling; the face which it recalled had been pale, haggard, worn with watching and sorrow. Then, as by a flash, she saw it all again before her eyes; the dainty room flooded with October sunlight; the dead woman lying there with her golden hair spread on the pillow; the bearded, averted face, and stooping form of the figure that crouched by the window.

"I only hope," she reflected, "that he will not recognise me. The recollections that the sight of me would summon up could scarcely be pleasant. I have no wish to enact the part of skeleton at the feast." [1]

With a desponding sense that she had no right to her existence, Gertrude gathered up her possessions and made her way across the room.

Darrell came forward slowly, "Oh, put down those heavy things," he said.

Lord Watergate, for it was he, went over to the fire-place and stood there warming his hands.

"May I trouble you to have a cab called?"

Gertrude spoke in her most dignified manner.

"Certainly. But won't you come to the fire?"

Darrell rang a bell which stood on the mantelshelf, and indicated to Gertrude a chair by the screen.

Gertrude, however, preferred to stand, and for some moments the three people on the tiger-skin hearthrug stared into the fire in silence.

Then Darrell said in an offhand manner:

"Miss Lorimer has been kind enough to photograph my 'Grand Canal' for me."

Lord Watergate, looking up suddenly, met Gertrude's glance. For a moment a puzzled expression came into his eyes, then changed to one of recognition and recollection. After some hesitation, he said:

"It must be difficult to do justice in a photograph to such a picture."

She threw him back his commonplace:

"Oh, the gradations of tone often come out surprisingly well."

Inwardly she was saying, "How he must hate the sight of me."

Darrell looked from one to the other, dimly suspicious of their mutual consciousness, then rejected the suspicion as an absurd one.

"I will write to you about those sketches," he said, as the cab was announced.

Lucy and Phyllis were frisking about the studio, as young creatures will do in the spring, when Gertrude entered, weary and dispirited, from her expedition to The Sycamores.

The girls fell upon her at once for news.

---

1   Title of poem "The Skeleton at the Feast" (1886) by Irish poet James Jeffrey Roche (1847-1908).

She flung herself into the sitter's chair, which half revolved with the violence of the action.

"Say something nice to me," she cried. "Compliment me on my beauty, my talents, my virtues. There is no flattery so gross that I could not swallow it."

Phyllis looked from her to Lucy and tapped her forehead in significant pantomime.

"You are everything that is most delightful," said Lucy; "only do tell us about the great man."

"He was odious," cried Gertrude.

"She has never been quarrelling, I will not say with her own, but with *our* bread-and-butter," said Phyllis, in affected dismay.

"I will never go there again, if that's what you mean."

"But what is the matter, Gerty? I found him quite polite."

"Polite? It is worse than rudeness, a politeness which says so plainly: 'This is for my own sake, not for yours.'"

"You are really cross, Gerty; what has the illustrious Sidney been doing to you?" said Lucy, who did not suffer from violent likes and dislikes.

"Oh," cried Gertrude, laughing ruefully; "how shall I explain? He is this sort of man;—if a woman were talking to him of—of the motions of the heavenly bodies, he would be thinking all the time of the shape of her ankles."

"Great heavens, Gerty, did you make the experiment?"

Phyllis opened her pretty eyes their widest as she spoke.

"We all know," remarked Lucy, with a twinkle in her eye, "that it is best to begin with a little aversion."

Phyllis struck an attitude:

"'Friends meet to part, but foes once joined—'" [1]

"Girls, what has come over you?" exclaimed Gertrude, dismayed.

"Gerty is shocked," said Lucy; "one is always stumbling unawares on her sense of propriety."

"She is like the Bishop of Rumtyfoo," [2] added Phyllis; "she does draw the line at such unexpected places."

---

1 George Gordon, Lord Byron (1788-1824), "The Giaour" (1813), lines 653-54: "Friends meet to part; Love laughs at faith; / True foes, once met, are joined till death!"

2 "The Bishop of Rum-Ti-Foo," in W.S. Gilbert's *The Bab Ballads* (1869).

CHAPTER IX

Show Sunday

La science l'avait gardé naïf.

Alphonse Daudet[1]

The last Sunday in March was Show Sunday; and Frank, who was of a festive disposition, had invited all the people he knew in London to inspect his pictures and Mr. Oakley's before they were sent in to the Royal Academy.

Mr. Oakley was a middle-aged Bohemian, who had made a small success in his youth and never got beyond it. It had been enough, however, to launch him into the artistic world, and it was probably only owing to the countenance of his brothers of the brush[2] that he was able to sell his pictures at all. Oakley was an accepted fact, if nothing more; the critics treated him with respect if without enthusiasm; the exhibition committees hung him, though not indeed on the line, and the public bought his pictures, which had the advantage of being moderate in price and signed with a name that everybody knew.

Of course this indifferent child of the earth had a wife and family; and he had been only too glad to share his studio expenses with young Jermyn, whose father, the Cornish clergyman, had been a friend of his own youth.

"I wonder," said Gertrude, as the Lorimers dressed for Frank's party, "if there will be a lot of gorgeous people this afternoon?" And she looked ruefully at the patch on her boot, with a humiliating reminiscence of Darrell's watchful eye.

"I don't expect so," answered Phyllis, whose pretty feet were appropriately shod. "You know what dowdy people one meets at the Oakleys. Oh, of course they know others, but they don't turn up, somehow."

"Then there will be Mr. Jermyn's people," said Lucy, inspecting her gloves with a frown.

---

1 "Science has protected his youthfulness," from the novel *Jack* (1876).

2 Allusion to the Pre-Raphaelite Brotherhood, a group of Victorian male artists and writers including Dante Gabriel Rossetti, John Everett Millais, and William Holman Hunt; the phrase suggests male professional networking, in contrast to the Lorimer sisters, who lack female colleagues.

"A lot of pretty, well-dressed girls, no doubt," answered Phyllis; "I expect that well-beloved youth has a wife in every port, or at least a young woman in every suburb."

"*Apropos*," said Gertrude, "I wonder if the Devonshires will be there. We never seem to see Conny in these days."

"Isn't it rather a strain on friendship," answered Phyllis, shrewdly, "when two sets of our friends become acquainted, and seem to prefer one another to *us*, the old and tried and trusty friend of each?"

"What horrid things you say sometimes, Phyllis," objected Lucy, as the three sisters trooped downstairs.

Fanny was not with them; she was spending the day with some relations of her mother's.

A curious, dreamlike sensation stole over Gertrude at finding herself once again in a roomful of people; and as an old war-horse is said to become excited at the sound of battle, so she felt the social instincts rise strongly within her as the familiar, forgotten pageant of nods and becks and wreathed smiles burst anew upon her.

Frank shot across the room, like an arrow from the bow, as the Lorimers entered.

"How late you are," he said; "I was beginning to have a horrible fear that you were not coming at all."

"How pretty it all is," said Lucy, sweetly. "Those great brass jars with the daffodils are charming; and what an overwhelming number of people."

Conny came up to them, splendid as ever, but with a restless light in her eyes, an unnatural flush on her cheek.

"How do you do, girls?" she said, abruptly. "You look seedy, Gerty." Then, as Frank moved off to fetch them some tea: "I do so hate afternoon affairs, don't you?"

"How pretty Frank looks," whispered Phyllis to Lucy; "I like to see him flying in and out among the people, as though his life depended on it, don't you? And the daffodil in his coat just suits his complexion."

"Phyllis, don't be so silly!"

Lucy refrained from smiling, but her eyes followed, with some amusement, the picturesque and active figure of her host, as he went about his duties with his usual air of earnestness and candour.

"Come and look at the pictures, Lucy. That's what you're here for, you know," remarked Fred, who had joined their group, and was looking the very embodiment of Philistine comeliness. "I haven't seen you for an age," he added, as they made their way to one of the easels.

"That is your own fault, isn't it?" said Lucy, lightly.

"Conny has got it into her head that you don't care to see us."

"How can Conny be so silly?"

"Don't tell her I told you. She would be in no end of a wax," he added, as Phyllis and Constance pressed by them in the crush.

Gertrude was still standing near the doorway, sipping her tea, and looking about her with a rather wistful interest. She had caught here and there glimpses of familiar faces, faces from her own old world—that world which, taken *en masse*, she had so fervently disliked; but no one had taken any notice of the young woman by the doorway, with her pale face and suit of rusty black.

"I feel like a ghost," she said to Frank, as she handed him her empty cup.

"You do look horribly white," he answered, with genuine concern; "I wish you were looking as well as your sisters—Miss Phyllis for instance."

He glanced across as he spoke with undisguised admiration at the slim young figure, and blooming face of the girl, who stood smiling down with amiable indifference at one of his own canvasses.

Phyllis Lorimer belonged to that rare order of women who are absolutely independent of their clothes.

By the side of her old black gown and well-worn hat, Constance Devonshire's elaborate spring costume looked vulgar and obtrusive; and Constance herself, in the light of her friend's more delicate beauty, seemed *bourgeoise* and overblown.

The effect of this contrast was not lost on two men who, at this point of the proceedings, strolled into the room, and whom the Oakleys came forward with some *empressement*[1] to receive.

"I have brought you Lord Watergate," Gertrude heard one of them say, in a voice which she recognised at once, the sound of which filled her with a vague sense of discomfort.

"Darrell, by all that's wonderful!" said Frank, *sotto voce*, his eyes shining with enthusiasm; "there, with the light Vandyke beard—but you know him already."

"Hasn't he a Show Sunday of his own?" replied Gertrude, in a voice that implied that the wish was father to the thought.

---

1   Haste, eagerness (French).

"He has a gallery all to himself in Bond Street[1] this season. I wonder if he will sing this afternoon."

"Mr. Darrell is a person of many accomplishments it seems."

"Oh, rather!" and Frank went off to offer a pleased and modest welcome to the illustrious guest.

Sidney Darrell, having succeeded in escaping from the Oakleys and their tea-table, made his way across the room, stopping here and there to exchange greetings with the people that he knew, and moving with that ostentatious air of lack of purpose which is so often assumed in society to mask a set and deliberate plan.

"How do you do, Miss Lorimer?" He stopped in front of Phyllis and held out his hand.

Phyllis' flower-face brightened at this recognition from the great man.

"Now, don't you think this is the most ridiculous institution on the face of the earth?" said Darrell, as he took his place beside her, for Conny had moved off discreetly at his approach.

"Which institution? Tea, pictures, people?"

"Their incongruous combination under the name of Show Sunday."

"Oh, I think it's fun. But then I have never seen the sort of thing before."

"You are greatly to be envied, Miss Lorimer."

"How lovely Phyllis is looking," cried Conny, who had joined Gertrude near the doorway; "she grows prettier every day."

"Do you think so?" answered Gertrude. "She looks to me more delicate than ever, with that flush on her cheek, and that shining in her eyes."

"Nonsense, Gerty; you are quite ridiculous about Phyllis. She appears to be amusing Mr. Darrell, at any rate. She says just the sort of things Mr. Lorimer used to. She is more like him than any of you."

"Yes." Gertrude winced; then, looking up, saw Mr. Oakley and a tall man standing before her.

"Lord Watergate, Miss Lorimer."

The grey eyes looked straight into hers, and a deep voice said—

"We have met before. But I scarcely ventured to regard myself as introduced to you."

---

1 Area of fashionable shops and galleries.

Lord Watergate smiled as he spoke, and, with a sense of relief, Gertrude felt that here, at least, was a friendly presence.

"I met you at The Sycamores on Wednesday."

"If it could be called a meeting. That's a wonderful picture of Darrell's."

"Yes."

"Oakley has been telling me about the great success in photography of you and your sisters."

"I don't know about success!" Gertrude laughed.

"You look so tired, Miss Lorimer; let me find you a seat."

"No, thank you; I prefer to stand. One sees the world so much better."

"Ah, you like to see the world?"

"Yes; it is always interesting."

"It is to be assumed that you are fond of society?"

"Does one follow from the other?"

"No; I merely hazarded the question."

"One demands so much more of a game in which one is taking part," said Gertrude; "and with social intercourse, one is always thinking how much better managed it might be."

They both laughed.

"Now what is your ideal society, Miss Lorimer?"

"A society not of class, caste, or family—but of picked individuals."

"I think we tend more and more towards such a society, at least in London," said Lord Watergate; then added, "You are a democrat, Miss Lorimer."

"And you are an optimist, Lord Watergate."

"Oh, I'm quite unformulated. But let us leave off this mutual recrimination for the present; and perhaps you can tell me who is the lady talking to Sidney Darrell."

Lord Watergate's attention had been suddenly caught by Phyllis; Gertrude noted that he was looking at her with all his eyes.

"That is one of my sisters," she said.

He turned towards her with a start; there was a note of constraint in his tones as he said—

"She is very beautiful."

What was there in his voice, in his face, that suddenly brought before Gertrude's vision the image of the dead woman, her golden hair, and haggard beauty?

Phyllis, on her part, had been aware of the brief but intense gaze which the grey eyes had cast upon her from the other side of the room.

"Who is that person talking to my sister?" she said.

Darrell looked across coldly, and answered: "Oh, that's Lord Watergate, the great physiologist."[1]

"I have never met a lord before."

"And, after all, this isn't much of a lord, because the peer is quite swallowed up in the man of science."

Oakley came up, entreating Darrell to sing.

"But isn't it quite irregular, to-day?"

"Oh, we don't pretend to be fashionable. This isn't 'Show Sunday,' pure and simple, but just a pretext for seeing one's friends."

"By the by," said the artist, as Oakley went off to open the little piano, "is it any good my sending the sketches this week? though it's horribly bad form to talk shop."

"You must ask my sister about those things."

"Oh, your sister is far and away too clever for me."

"Gertrude is clever, but not in the way you mean."

"Nevertheless, I am horribly afraid of her."

Darrell went over to the piano and sang a little French song, with perfect art, in his rich baritone. Gertrude watched him, as he sat there playing his own accompaniment, and a vague terror stole over her of this irreproachable-looking person, who did everything so well; whose quiet presence was redolent of an immeasurable, because an unknown strength; and who, she felt (indignantly remembering the cold irony of his glance) could never, under any circumstances, be made to appear ridiculous.

At the end of the song, Phyllis came over to Gertrude.

"Aren't we going, Gerty?" she said; "It is quite unfashionable to 'make a night of it' like this. One is just supposed to look round and sail off to half-a-dozen other studios."

Lord Watergate, who stood near, caught the half-whispered words, and smiled, as one smiles at the nonsense of a pretty child. Gertrude saw the expression of his face as she answered—

"Yes, it is time we went. Tell Lucy; there she is with Mr. Jermyn."

Darrell came over to them as they were going, and shook hands, first with Gertrude, and then with Phyllis.

---

1 Physiology in the Victorian period referred to the study of processes in animals, including neuromuscular, brain, and cardiac function, as well as the recognition of chemical control mechanisms in the body. Physiologists also helped to establish the place of scientific method and experimental analysis in British education.

"Thank you," he said to the latter, "for a very pleasant afternoon."

Both he and Lord Watergate lingered in York Place till the other guests had departed, when they fell upon Frank for further information respecting the photographic studio.

"It doesn't look as if it paid them," remarked Darrell, by way of administering a damper to loyal Frank's enthusiasm.

"I wonder," said Lord Watergate, "if they would think it worth while to prepare some slides for me?"

"For the Royal Institution lectures?"[1] Darrell sat down to the piano as he spoke, and ran his hands over the keys. "She is a charming creature—Phyllis."

"Charming!" cried Frank; "and so is Miss Lucy. And Gertrude is charming, too; she is the clever one."

"Oh, yes, Gertrude is the clever one; you can see that by her boots."

Meanwhile the Lorimers and the Devonshires were walking up Baker Street together, engaged, on their part also, in discussing the people from whom they had just parted.

"You are quite wrong, Gerty, about Mr. Darrell," cried Phyllis; "he is very nice, and great fun."

"What, the fellow with the goatee?" said Fred.

"Oh, Fred, his beautiful Vandyke beard!"

"I don't care, I don't like him."

"Nor do I, Fred," said Gertrude, with decision, as the whole party turned into Number 20B, and went up to the sitting-room.

"I think really you are a little unreasonable," said Lucy, putting her arm round her sister's waist; "he seemed quite a nice person."

"He looks," put in Conny, speaking for the first time, "as though he meant to have the best of everything. But so do a great many of us mean that."

"But not," cried Gertrude, "by trampling over the bodies of other people. Ah, you are all laughing at me. But can one be expected to think well of a person who makes one feel like a strong-minded clown?"

They laughed more than ever at the curious image summoned up by her words; then Phyllis remarked, critically—

---

1   The Royal Institution in Albemarle Street offered different series of public lectures on science attended by women, men, and children. These lectures contributed to the popularization of science in the nineteenth century; some of the celebrated lecturers included Humphry Davy, Michael Faraday, and John Tyndall.

"There is one thing I don't like about him, and that is his eye. I particularly detest that sort of eye; prominent, with heavy lids, and those little puffy bags underneath."

"Phyllis, spare us these realistic descriptions," protested Lucy, "and let us dismiss Mr. Darrell, for the present at least. Perhaps our revered chaperon will tell us something of her experiences with a certain noble lord," she added, placing in her dress, with a smile of thanks, the gardenia of which Fred had divested himself in her favour.

"It was very nice of him," said Gertrude, gravely, "to get Mr. Oakley to introduce him to me, if only to show me that the sight of me did not make him sick."

"I like his face," added Lucy; "there is something almost boyish about it. Do you remember what Daudet says of the old doctor in *Jack*, 'La science l'avait gardé naïf.'" [1]

"What a set of gossips we are," cried Conny, who had taken little part in the conversation. "Come along, Fred; you know we are dining at the Greys to-night."

"Botheration! They are certain to give me Nelly to take in," grumbled Fred, who, like many of his sex, was extremely modest where his feelings were concerned, but cherished a belief that the mass of womankind had designs upon him; "and we never know what on earth to say to one another."

"There goes Mr. Jermyn," observed Phyllis, as the door closed on the brother and sister; "he said something about coming in here to-night."

Lucy, who was seated at some distance from the window, allowed herself to look up, and smiled as she remarked—

"What ages ago it seems since we used to wonder about him and call him 'Conny's man.'"

"'Conny's man,'" added Phyllis, with a curl of her pretty lips, "who does not care two straws for Conny."

---

1 The chapter epigraph from Daudet's novel is repeated here in the context of Lord Watergate as a "man of science."

CHAPTER X

Summing Up

J'ai peur d'Avril, peur de l'émoi
Qu'éveille sa douceur touchante.
Sully Prudhomme [1]

April had come round again; and, like M. Sully Prudhomme, Gertrude was afraid of April.

As Fanny had remarked to Frank, the month had very painful associations for them all; but Gertrude's terror was older than their troubles, and was founded, not on the recollection of past sorrow, so much as on the cruel hunger for a present joy. And now again, after all her struggles, her passionate care for others, her resolute putting away of all thoughts of personal happiness, now again the Spring was stirring in her veins, and voices which she had believed silenced for ever arose once more in her heart and clamoured for a hearing.

Often, before business hours, Gertrude might be seen walking round Regent's Park at a swinging pace, exorcising her demons; she was obliged, as she said, to ride her soul on the curb, and be very careful that it did not take the bit between its teeth—this poor, weak Gertrude, who seemed such a fountain-head of wisdom, such a tower of strength to the people among whom she dwelt.

At this period, also, she had had recourse, in the pauses of professional work, to her old consolation of literary effort, and had even sent some of her productions to Paternoster Row with the same unsatisfactory results as of yore, she and Frank uniting their voices in that bitter cry of the rejected contributor, which in these days is heard through the breadth and length of the land.

One morning she came into the studio after her walk, to find Lucy engaged in focussing Frank, who was seated, wearing an air of immense solemnity, in the sitter's chair. Phyllis, meanwhile,

---

1 René François Armand Sully Prudhomme (1839-1907), "Douceur d'Avril" (1875), lines 1-2. "I am afraid of April, afraid of feelings / Aroused by its touching sweetness."

hovered about, bestowing hints and suggestions on them both, secretly enjoying the quiet humour of the scene.

"It is Mr. Jermyn's birthday present," she announced, as Gertrude entered. "He is going to send it to Cornwall, which will be a nice advertisement for us."

Frank blushed slightly; and Lucy cried from beneath her black cloth, "Don't get up, Mr. Jermyn; Gertrude will excuse you, I am sure."

Gertrude, laughing, retreated to the waiting-room; where, throwing herself into a chair, and leaning both her elbows on a rickety scarlet table, she stared vaguely at the little picture of youth and grace which the parted curtains revealed to her.

How could they be so cheerful, so heedless? cried her heart, with a sudden impatience. Was this life, this ceaseless messing about in a pokey glass out-house, this eating and drinking and sleeping in the shabby London rooms?

Was any human creature to be blamed who rebelled against it? Did not flesh and blood cry out against such sordidness, with all the revel of the spring-time going on in the world beyond?

It is base and ignoble perhaps to scorn the common round, the trivial task, but is it not also ignoble and base to become so immersed in them as to desire nothing beyond?

"What mean thoughts I am thinking," cried Gertrude to herself, shocked at her own mood; then, gazing mechanically in front of her, saw Lucy disappear into the dark-room, and Frank come forward with outstretched hand.

"At last I can say 'good-morning,' Miss Lorimer."

Gertrude gave him her hand with a smile; Jermyn's was a presence that somehow always cleared the moral atmosphere.

"You will never guess," said Frank, "what I have brought you."

As he spoke, he drew from his pocket a number of *The Woodcut*, damp from the press, and opening it at a particular page, spread it on the table before her.

Phyllis, becoming aware of these proceedings, came across to the waiting-room and leaned over her sister's shoulder.

"Oh, Gerty, what fun."

On one side of the page was a large wood engraving representing four people on a lawn-tennis court. Three of them were girls, in whom could be traced distinct resemblance to the three Lorimers; while the fourth, a man, had about him an unmistakable suggestion of Jermyn himself. The initials "F.J." were writ large in a corner of the picture, and on the opposite page were the following verses:—

What wonder that I should be dreaming*
    Out here in the garden to-day?
The light through the leaves is streaming;
        Paulina cries, "Play!"

The birds to each other are calling;
The freshly-cut grasses smell sweet—
To Teddy's dismay comes falling
        The ball at my feet!

"Your stroke should be over, not under."
"But that's such a difficult way!"
The place is a spring-tide wonder
        Of lilac and may.

Of lilac and may and laburnam;
Of blossom—*"we're losing the set!*
Those volleys of Jenny's, return them,
        Stand close to the net!"

ENVOI.
You are so fond of the may-time,
    My friend far away,
Small wonder that I should be dreaming
    Of you in the garden to-day.[1]

The verses were signed "G. Lorimer"; and Gertrude's eyes rested on them with the peculiar tenderness with which we all of us regard our efforts the first time that we see ourselves in print.

"How nice they look, Gerty," cried Phyllis. "And Mr. Jermyn's picture. But I think they have spoilt it a little in the engraving."

"It is rather a come down after *Charlotte Corday*, isn't it?" said Gertrude, pleased yet rueful.

Frank, who had been told the history of that unfortunate tragedy, answered rather wistfully—

"We have all to get off our high horse, Miss Lorimer, if we want to live. I had ten guineas this morning for that thing; and

---

* From *Lawn Tennis*.

---

1 Under the title "A Game of Lawn Tennis," this poem appeared in Levy's last collection of poems, *A London Plane-Tree, and Other Verse* (1889).

there is the *Death of Œdipus* with its face to the wall in the studio—and likely to remain there, unless we run short of firewood one of these days."

"Do you remember," said Gertrude, "how Warrington threw cold water on Pendennis by telling him to stick to poems like the *Church Porch* and abandon his beloved *Ariadne in Naxos*?"[1]

"Yes," answered Frank, "and I never could share Warrington's—and presumably Thackeray's—admiration for those verses."

"Nor I," said Gertrude, as Lucy emerged triumphantly from the dark-room and announced the startling success of her negatives.

She was shown the wonderful poem, and the no less wonderful picture, and then Phyllis said—

"Don't gloat so over it, Gerty." For Gertrude was still sitting at the table absorbed in contemplation of the printed sheet spread out before her.

Gertrude laughed and pushed the paper away; and Lucy quoted gravely—

"'We all, the foolish and the wise,
Regard our verse with fascination,
Through asinine-paternal eyes,
And hues of fancy's own creation!'"[2]

A vociferous little clock on the mantelpiece struck ten.

"I must be off," said Frank; "there will be my model waiting for me. I am afraid I have wasted a great deal of your time this morning."

"No, indeed," said Lucy, as Gertrude rose and folded the seductive *Woodcut*, with a get-thee-behind-me-Satan[3] air; "though I am glad to say we are quite busy."

"There are Lord Watergate's slides," added Phyllis; "and Mr.

---

1   In W.M. Thackeray (1811-63), *The History of Pendennis* (1850), the title character writes poetry, including "The Church Porch," and a play, *Ariadne in Naxos*, which his friend Warrington, a journalist, ridicules. In Greek mythology, Ariadne is left on the island of Naxos after she helps Theseus escape from the Minotaur.

2   Frederick Locker-Lampson (1821-95), "Advice to a Poet" (1868), stanza 8, lines 1-4.

3   These words are spoken by Jesus in the Gospels of Matthew, Mark, and Luke.

Darrell's sketches to finish off; not to speak of possible chance-comers."

"How do you get on with Darrell?" said Frank, who seemed to have forgotten his model, and made no movement to go.

"He has only been here once," answered Lucy, promptly; "but I like what I have seen of him."

"So do I," cried Phyllis.

"And I," added Frank.

In the face of this unanimity Gertrude wisely held her peace.

"Well then, good-bye," said Frank, reluctantly holding out his hand to each in turn—to Lucy, last. "I am dining out to-night and to-morrow, so shall not see you for an age, I suppose."

"Gay person," said Lucy, whose hand lingered in his; held there firmly, and without resistance on her part.

"It's a bore," cried Frank, making wistful eyebrows, and looking at her very hard.

Gertrude started, struck for the first time by something in the tone and attitude of them both. With a shock that bewildered her, she realised the secret of their mutual content; and, stirred up by this unconscious revelation, a conflicting throng of thoughts, images, and emotions arose within her.

Gertrude worked like a nigger that day, which, fortunately for her state of mind, turned out an unusually busy one. Lucy was industrious too, but went about her work humming little tunes, with a serenity that contrasted with her sister's rather feverish laboriousness. Even Phyllis condescended to lend a hand to the finishing off of the prints of Sidney Darrell's sketches.

All three were rather tired by the time they joined Fanny round the supper-table, who, herself, presented a pathetic picture of ladylike boredom.

The meal proceeded for some time in silence, broken occasionally by a professional remark from one or other of them; then Lucy said—

"You're not eating, Fanny."

"I'm not hungry," answered Fan, with an injured air.

She looked more like a superannuated baby than ever, with her pale eyebrows arched to her hair, and the corners of her small thin mouth drooped peevishly.

"This pudding isn't half bad, really, Fan," said Phyllis, good-naturedly, as she helped herself to a second portion. "I should advise you to try it."

Fanny's under-lip quivered in a touchingly infantile manner, and, in another moment, splash! fell a great tear on the table-cloth.

"It's all very well to talk about pudding," she cried, struggling helplessly with the gurgling sobs. "To leave one alone all the blessed day, and not a word to throw at one when you do come upstairs, unless, if you please, it's 'pudding!' Pudding!" went on Fan, with contemptuous emphasis, and abandoning herself completely to her rising emotions. "You seem to take me for an idiot, all of you, who think yourselves so clever. What do you care how dull it is for me up here all day, alone from morning till night, while you are amusing yourselves below, or gadding about at gentlemen's studios."

"That sounds just like Aunt Caroline," said Phyllis, in a stage-whisper; but Lucy, rising, went round to her weeping sister, and, gathering the big, silly head, and wide moist face to her bosom, proceeded to administer comfort after the usual inarticulate, feminine fashion.

"Fanny is right," cried Gertrude, smitten with sudden remorse. "It is horribly dull for her, and we are very thoughtless."

"I am sorry I said anything about it," sobbed Fanny; "but flesh and blood couldn't stand it any longer."

"You were quite right to tell us, Fan. We have been horrid," cried Lucy, as she gently led her from the room. "Come upstairs with me, and lie down. You have not been looking well all the week."

In about ten minutes Lucy re-appeared alone, to find the table cleared, and her sisters sewing by the lamplight.

"Fan has gone to bed," she announced; "she was a little hysterical, and I persuaded her to undress."

"It *is* dull for her, I know," said Gertrude, really distressed; "but what is to be done?"

"And she has been so good all these months," answered Lucy. "She has had none of the fun, and all the anxiety and pinching, and this is the first complaint we have heard from her."

"Yes, she has come out surprisingly well through it all."

Gertrude sighed as she spoke, secretly reproaching herself that there was not more love in her heart for poor Fanny.

Mrs. Maryon appeared at this point to offer the young ladies her own copy of the *Waterloo Place Gazette*, a little bit of neighbourly courtesy in which she often indulged, and which to-night was especially appreciated, as creating a diversion from an unpleasant topic.

"'A woman shot at Turnham Green,'" cried Phyllis, glancing down a column of miscellaneous items, while the lamplight fell on her bent brown head. "'More fighting in Africa.' Ah, here's something interesting at last.—'We understand that the exhibition of Mr. Sidney Darrell, A.R.A's[1] pictures, to be held in the Berkeley Galleries, New Bond Street, will be opened to the public on the first of next month. The event is looked forward to with great interest in artistic circles, as the collection is said to include many works never before exhibited in London.' *I* shall go like a shot; sha'n't you, Gerty?"

"Yes, and slip little dynamite machines[2] behind the pictures. Let me look at that paper, Phyllis."

Phyllis pushed it towards her, and, as she took it up, her eye fell on the date of the month printed at the top of the page.

"Do you know," she said, "that it is a year to-day that we finally decided on starting our business?"

"Is it?" said Lucy. "Do you mean from that day when Aunt Caroline came and pitched into us all?"

"Yes; and when Mr. Russel's letter appeared on the scene, just as we were thinking of rushing in a body to the nearest chemist's for laudanum."

"And when we made a lot of good resolutions; do you remember?" cried Phyllis.

"What were they?" said Gertrude. "One was, that we would be happy."

"Well, I think we have kept that one at least," observed Lucy, with decision.

Gertrude looked across at her sister rather wistfully, as she answered, "Yes, on the whole. What was the other resolution? That we would not be cynical, was it not?"

"There hasn't been the slightest ground for cynicism; quite the other way," said Lucy. "It is not much credit to us to have kept that resolution."

"Oh, I don't know," observed Phyllis, lightly; "some people have been rather horrid; have forgotten all about us, or not been nice. Don't you remember, Gerty, how Gerald St. Aubyn dodged round the corner at Baker Street the other day because he didn't

---

1 Associate of the Royal Academy.
2 Dynamite terrorism escalated in London in the 1880s, including attacks on several government buildings and one in the London Underground Railway in 1883 and Victoria Station in 1884. *The Pall Mall Gazette* describes the dynamite used as "infernal machines," small and heavy boxes that were also found in other London railway stations in 1884 (*Pall Mall Gazette*, 26 February 1884). See Barbara Arnett Melchiori, *Terrorism in the Late Victorian Novel* (Dover, NH: Croom Helm, 1985).

care to be seen bowing to two shabby young women with heavy parcels? And, Lucy, have you forgotten what you told us about Jack Sinclair, when you met him, travelling from the north? How he never took any notice of you, because you happened to be riding third class, and had your old gown on? Jack, who used to make such a fuss about picking up one's pocket-handkerchief and opening the door for one."

"It seems to me," said Gertrude, "that to think about those sort of things makes one almost as mean as the people who do them."

"And directly a person shows himself capable of doing them, why, it ceases to matter about him in the least," added Lucy, with youthful magnificence.

Gertrude was silent a moment, then said, with something of an effort: "Let us direct our attention to the charming new people we have got to know. One gets to know them in such a much more pleasant way, somehow."

Lucy bent her head over her work, hiding her flushed face as she answered, "That is the best of being poor; one's chances of artificial acquaintanceships are so much lessened. One gains in quality what one loses in quantity."

"How moral we are growing," cried Phyllis. "We shall be quoting Scripture next, and saying it is harder for the camel to get through the needle's eye, &c., &c." [1]

Gertrude laughed.

"There is another point to consider," she said. "I suppose you both know that we are not making our fortunes?"

"Yes," answered Lucy; "but, at the same time, the business has almost doubled itself in the course of the last three months."

"That sounds more prosperous than it really is, Lucy. If it hadn't done so, we should have had to think seriously of giving it up. And, as it is, we cannot be sure, till the end of the year, that we shall be able to hold on."

"You mean the end of the business year; next June?"

"Yes; Mr. Russel is coming, and there is to be a great overhauling of accounts."

Gertrude lay awake that night long after her sisters were asleep. Her brief rebellious mood of the morning had passed away, and, looking back on the year behind her, she experienced a measure of the content which we all feel after something

---

1 "It is easier for a camel to pass through the eye of a needle than for a rich man to enter the kingdom of God," from Matthew 19.24.

attempted, something done. That she had been brought face to face with the sterner side of life, had lost some illusions, suffered some pain, she did not regret. It seemed to her that she had not paid too great a price for the increased reality of her present existence.

She fell asleep, then woke at dawn with a low cry. She had been dreaming of Lucy and Frank; had seen their faces, as she had seen them the day before, bright with the glow of the light which never was on sea and land. Oh, she had always known, nay, hoped, that this, or rather something akin to this, would come; yet sharp was the pang that ran through her at the recollection.

It had always seemed to her highly improbable that her sisters, portionless as they were, should remain unmarried. One day, she had always told herself, they would go away, and she and Fanny would be left alone. She did not wish it otherwise. She had a feminine belief in love as the crown and flower of life; yet, as the shadow of the coming separation fell upon her, her spirit grew desolate and afraid; and, lying there in the chill grey morning, she wept very bitterly.

CHAPTER XI

A Confidence

> It may be one will dance to-day,
>   And dance no more to-morrow;
> It may be one will steal away,
>   And nurse a lifelong sorrow;
> What then? The rest advance, evade,
>   Unite, disport, and dally,
> Re-set, coquet, and gallopade,
>   Not less—in "Cupid's Alley."
> *Austin Dobson*[1]

"Mr. Darrell has sent us a card for his Private View," announced Gertrude, as they sat at tea one Saturday afternoon in the sitting-room.

---

1 Henry Austin Dobson (1840-1921), "Cupid's Alley," *Proverbs in Precelain* (1877), stanza 9.

"Oh, let me look, Gerty," cried Phyllis, taking possession of the bit of pasteboard. "'The Misses Lorimer and friends.' Why Conny might go with us."

Constance Devonshire had dropped in upon them unexpectedly that afternoon, after an absence of several weeks. She was looking wretchedly ill. Her usually blooming complexion had changed to a curious waxen colour; her round face had fallen away; there were dark hollows under the unnaturally brilliant eyes.

"I should rather like to go, if you think you may take me," she said; then added, with an air of not very spontaneous gaiety; "I suppose it will be what the society papers call a 'smart function.'"

Stoicism, it has been observed, is a savage virtue. There was something of savagery in Conny's fierce reserve; in the way in which she resolutely refused to acknowledge, what was evident to the most casual observer, that there was something seriously amiss with her health and spirits.

"Is it not fortunate," said Lucy, "that Uncle Sebastian should have sent us that cheque? Now we shall be able to get ourselves some decent clothes."

"I mean to have a grey cachemire walking-dress, and my evening dress shall be grey too," announced Phyllis, who was one of the rare people who can wear that colour to advantage. Fanny, who had rigid ideas about mourning, declared with an air of severity that her own new outfit should be black, then sighed, as though to call attention to the fact of her constancy to the memory of the dead, in the face of the general heedlessness.

"Gerty is thinking of rose-colour, is she not?" asked Phyllis, innocently, as she marked Gertrude's rapidly-suppressed movement of irritation.

"As regards a gown for this precious Private View—I am not going to it."

"The head of the firm ought to show up on such an occasion, as a mere matter of business," observed Lucy, smiling amiably at every one in general.

"Yes, really, Gerty," added Phyllis, "you are the person to inspire confidence as to the quality of our work. No one would suspect *us*"—indicating herself and her two other sisters—"of being clever. It would be considered unlikely that nature should heap up *all* her benefits on the same individuals."

"Am I such a fright?" asked Gertrude, a little wistfully.

"No, darling; but there could be no doubt about your brains with that face."

"Wait a few years," said Conny; "she will be the best looking of you all."

"We will 'wait till she is eighty in the shade,'"[1] quoted Phyllis; "but when one comes to think of it, what a well-endowed family we are. Not only is our genius good-looking; that is a comparatively common case; but our beauties are so exceedingly intelligent; aren't they, Lucy?"

Constance Devonshire was right. Sidney Darrell's Private View at the Berkeley Galleries, held on the last day of April, was a very smart function indeed. There were duchesses, beauties, statesmen, and clever people of every description galore. In the midst of them all Darrell himself shone resplendent; gracious, urbane, polished; infusing just the right amount of cordiality into his many greetings, according to the deserts of the person greeted.

"I never saw any one who possessed to greater perfection the art of impressing his importance on other people," whispered Conny to Gertrude, as the two girls strolled off together into one of the smaller rooms. Lucy had been led off by Frank and one of his friends. That young woman was never long in any mixed assembly without attracting persons of the male sex to her side.

As for Phyllis, radiant in the new grey costume, its soft tints set off by a knot of Parma violets at the throat, she was making the round of the pictures under the escort of no less a person than Lord Watergate, who had come up to the Lorimers at the moment of their entrance; and Fanny, in a jetted mantle and bonnet, clanked about with Mr. Oakley, happy in the consciousness of being for once in the best society.

"What a dreary thing a London crowd is," grumbled Conny, who was not accustomed, in her own set, to being left squireless.

"Oh, but this is fun. So different from the parties one used to go to," said Gertrude, smiling, as Lord Watergate and her sister came up to them, to direct their attention to a particular canvas in the other room.

As they sauntered, in a body, to the entrance, Darrell came up with a young man of the masher type[2] in his wake, whom he introduced to Phyllis as Lord Malplaquet.

"Lord Malplaquet is dying to hear your theories of life," he

---

1 Gilbert and Sullivan, *The Mikado* (1885), act 2. The expression suggests someone older than eighty since "in the shade" implies less revelatory lighting.

2 A man who makes passes at women.

said playfully, bestowing a beaming and confidential smile upon her.

"Mr. Darrell, you shall not amuse yourself at my expense," she responded gaily, as she plunged into the crowd under the wing of her new escort, who was staring at her with the languid yet undisguised admiration of his class.

"Now this is the real thing," said Lord Watergate to Gertrude, as they stopped before the canvas they had come to seek.

"Yes," said Gertrude, in mechanical acquiescence.

She was thinking: "What a mean soul I must have. Every one seems to like and admire this Sidney Darrell: and I suspect everything about him—even his art. For the sake of a prejudice; of a little hurt vanity, perhaps, as well."

"That, 'yes,' hasn't the ring of the true coin, Miss Lorimer."

"This is scarcely the time and place for criticism, Lord Watergate," laughed Gertrude.

"For hostile criticism, you mean. You are a terrible person to please, are you not?"

As the room began to clear Darrell took Frank aside, and glancing in the direction of the sisters, who had re-united their forces, said: "You know those girls, intimately, I believe."

"Yes." (Very promptly.)

"I wonder if that beautiful Phyllis would sit to me?"

"She would probably be immensely honoured."

"Well, you see, it's this: I want her for Cressida." [1]

"Rather a disagreeable sort of subject, isn't it?" said Frank, doubtfully; then added, with professional interest: "I didn't know you had such a picture on hand, Mr. Darrell."

"The idea occurred to me this very afternoon. It was the sight of the fair Phyllis, in fact, which suggested it."

"Were you thinking of the scene in the orchard, or in the Greek camp?"

"Neither; one could hardly ask a lady to sit for such a picture. No, it is Cressida, before her fall, I want; as she stands at the street corner with Pandarus, waiting for the Trojan heroes to pass, don't you know? Half ironical, half wistful; with the light of that little *tendre* for Troilus just beginning to dawn in her eyes. She would be the very thing for it."

"Are you going to propose it to her?" said Frank, who looked as if he did not much relish the idea.

---

1 Shakespeare, *Troilus and Cressida*.

"I shall ask her to sit for me, at any rate. There's the dragon-sister to be got round first."

"Indeed you are mistaken about Miss Lorimer."

Darrell gave a short laugh. "I beg your pardon, my dear fellow!"

Frank frowned, and Darrell, going forward to the Lorimers, preferred his request.

Phyllis looked pleased; and Gertrude, suppressing the signs of her secret dislike to the scheme, said, quietly:

"Phyllis must refer you to her sister Fanny. It depends on whether she can spare the time to bring her to your studio."

She glanced up as she spoke, and met, almost with open defiance, the heavy grey eyes of the man opposite. From these she perceived the irony to have faded; she read nothing there but a cold dislike.

It was an old, old story the fierce yet silent opposition between these two people; an inevitable antipathy; a strife of type and type, of class and class, rather than of individuals: the strife of the woman who demands respect, with the man who refuses to grant it.

★ ★ ★ ★ ★

Phyllis was in high feather at her successful afternoon, at the compliment paid her by the great Sidney in particular; and Fanny rather brightened at the prospect of what bore even so distant a resemblance to an occupation, as chaperoning her sister to a studio.

Only Conny was silent and depressed, and when they reached Baker-street, followed Gertrude to her room. Here she flung herself on the bed, regardless of her new transparent black hat, and its daffodil trimmings.

"Gerty, 'the world's a beast, and I hate it!'" [1]

"You are not well, Conny. If you would only acknowledge the fact, and see a doctor."

"Gerty, come here."

Gertrude went over to the bed, secretly alarmed; something in her friend's tones frightened her.

Conny crushed her face against the pillows, then said in smothered tones:

"I can't bear it any longer. I must tell some one or it will kill me."

1 W.S. Gilbert, *Tom Cobb; or Fortune's Toy* (1875), act 1.

Gertrude grew pale; instinctively she felt what was coming; instinctively she desired to ward it off.

"Can't you guess? Oh, you may say it is humiliating, unworthy; I know that." She raised her face suddenly: "Oh, Gerty, how can I help it? He is so different from them all; from the sneaks who want one's money; from the bad imitations of fashionable young men, who snub, and patronise, and sneer at us all. Who could help it? Frank—"

"Conny, Conny, you musn't tell me this."

Gertrude caught her friend in her arms, so as to shield her face. She disapproved, generally speaking, of confidences of this kind, considering them bad for both giver and receiver; but this particular confidence she felt to be simply intolerable.

"Gerty, what have I done, what have I said?"

"Nothing, really nothing, Con, dear old girl. You have told me nothing."

A pause; then Conny said, between the sobs which at last had broken forth: "How can I bear my life? How can I bear it?"

Gertrude was very pale.

"We all have to bear things, Conny; often this kind of thing, we women."

"I don't think I *can*."

"Yes, you will. You have no end of pluck. One day you are going to be very happy."

"Never, Gerty. We rich girls always end up with sneaks—no decent person comes near us."

"There are other things which make happiness besides— pleasant things happening to one."

"What sort of things?"

Gertrude paused a minute, then said bravely: "Our own self-respect, and the integrity of the people we care for."

"That sounds very nice," replied Conny, without enthusiasm, "but I should like a little of the more obvious sorts of happiness as well."

Gertrude gave a laugh, which was also a sob.

"So should I, Conny, so should I."

CHAPTER XII

Gertrude Is Anxious

Lady, do you know the tune?
Ah, we all of us have hummed it!
I've an old guitar has thrummed it
Under many a changing moon.
Thackeray[1]

When Frank next saw Sidney Darrell, the latter told him that he had abandoned the idea of the "Cressida," and was painting Phyllis Lorimer in her own character.

"Grey gown; Parma violets; grey and purplish background. Shall let Sir Coutts have it, I think," he added; "it will show up better at his place than amid the *profanum vulgus* of Burlington House."[2]

"Mr. Darrell doesn't often paint portraits, does he?" Lucy said, when Jermyn was discussing the matter one evening in Baker Street.

"Not often; but those that he has done are among his finest work. That one of poor Lady Watergate for instance—it is Carolus Duran[3] at his very best."

"By the bye, what an incongruous friendship it always seems to me—Lord Watergate and Mr. Darrell," said Lucy.

"Oh, I don't know that it's much of a friendship," answered Frank.

"Lord Watergate often drops in at The Sycamores," put in Phyllis, helping herself from a smart *bonbonnière* from Charbonnel and Walker's;[4] for Sidney found many indirect means of paying his pretty model; "I think he is such a nice old person."

"Old," cried Fanny; "he is not old at all. I looked him out in

---

1 "Mrs. Katherine's Lantern" (1867), stanza 6, lines 1-4.
2 *Profanum vulgus*, i.e., the vulgar rabble. The Royal Academy moved to Burlington House in Piccadilly from the east wing of the National Gallery in 1868.
3 Charles Auguste Emile Carolus-Duran (1838-1917); French academic painter chiefly known for his portrait paintings.
4 Charbonnel et Walker, London chocolatier established in 1875.

Mr. Darrell's Peerage. He is thirty-seven, and his name is Ralph."

"'I love my love with an R..' You said it just in that way, Fan," laughed Phyllis. "Yes, it is an odd friendship, if one comes to think of it—that big, kind, simple, Lord Watergate, and my elaborate friend, Sidney."

"Mr. Darrell is a perfect gentleman," interposed Fan, with dignity.

The occasional mornings at The Sycamores, afforded a pleasant break in the monotony of her existence. Darrell treated her with a careful, if ironical politeness, which she accepted in all good faith.

"Fan, as they call her, is a fool, but none the worse for that," had been his brief summing up of the poor lady, whom, indeed, he rather liked than otherwise.

It was the end of May, and the sittings had been going on in a spasmodic, irregular fashion, throughout the month. Both the girls enjoyed them. Darrell, like the rest of the world, treated Phyllis as a spoilt child; gave her sweets and flowers galore; and what was better, tickets for concerts, galleries, and theatres, of which her sisters also reaped the benefit.

Gertrude secretly disliked the whole proceeding, but, aware that she had no reasonable objection to offer, wisely held her peace; telling herself that if one person did not turn her little sister's head, another was sure to do so; and perhaps the sooner she was accustomed to the process the better.

"Why won't you come up and see my portrait?" Phyllis had pleaded; "I am going next Sunday, so you can have no excuse."

"I shall see it when it is finished," Gertrude had answered.

"Oh, but you can get a good idea of what it will look like, already. It is a great thing, life-size, and ends at about the knees. I am standing up and looking over my shoulder, so. I suppose Mr. Darrell has found out how nicely my head turns round on my neck."

Gertrude had laughed, and even attempted a pun in her reply, but she did not accompany her sister to The Sycamores. Indeed, more subtle reasons apart, she had little time to spare for unnecessary outings.

The business, as businesses will, had taken a turn for the better, and the two members of the partnership had their hands full. Rumours of the Photographic Studio had somehow got abroad, and various branches of the public were waking up to an interest in it.

People who had theories about woman's work; people whose friends had theories; people who were curious and fond of novelty; individuals from each of these sections began to find their way to Upper Baker Street. Gertrude, as we know, had refused at an early stage of their career to be interviewed by *The Waterloo Place Gazette*; but, later on, some unauthorised person wrote a little account of the Lorimers' studio in one of the society papers, of which, if the taste was questionable, the results were not to be questioned at all.

Moreover, it had got about in certain sets that all the sisters were extremely beautiful, and that Sidney Darrell was painting them in a group for next year's Academy, a *canard* certainly not to be deprecated from a business point of view.

Such things as these, do not, of course, make the solid basis of success, but in a very overcrowded world, they are apt to be the most frequent openings to it. In these days, the aspirant to fame is inclined to over-value them, forgetting that there is after all something to be said for making one's performance such as will stand the test of so much publicity.

The Lorimers knew little of the world, and of the workings of the complicated machinery necessary for getting on in it; and while chance favoured them in the matter of gratuitous advertisement, devoted their energies to keeping up their work to as high a standard as possible.

Life, indeed, was opening up for them in more ways than one. The calling which they pursued brought them into contact with all sorts and conditions of men, among them, people in many ways more congenial to them than the mass of their former acquaintance; intercourse with the latter having come about in most cases through "juxtaposition" rather than "affinity."

They began to get glimpses of a world more varied and interesting than their own, of that world of cultivated, middle-class London, which approached more nearly, perhaps, than any other to Gertrude's ideal society of picked individuals.

And it was Gertrude, more than any of them, who appreciated the new state of things. She was beginning, for the first time, to find her own level; to taste the sweets of genuine work and genuine social intercourse. Fastidious and sensitive as she was, she had yet a great fund of enjoyment of life within her; of that impersonal, objective enjoyment which is so often denied to her sex. Relieved of the pressing anxieties which had attended the beginning of their enterprise, the natural elasticity of her spirits asserted itself. A common atmosphere of hope and cheerfulness pervaded the little household at Upper Baker Street.

The evening of which I write was one of the last of May, and Frank had come in to bid them farewell, before setting out the next morning for a short holiday in Cornwall; "the old folks," as he called his parents, growing impatient of their only son's prolonged absence.

"The country will be looking its very best," cried Frank, who loved his beautiful home; "the sea a mass of sapphire with the great downs rolling towards it. I mean to have a big swim the very first thing. No one knows what the sea is like, till they have been to Cornwall. And St. Colomb—I wish you could see St. Colomb! Why, the whole place is smaller than Baker Street. The little bleak, grey street, with the sou'wester blowing through it at all times and seasons—there are scarcely two houses on the same level. And then—

"The little grey church on the windy hill,"[1]

and beyond, the great green vicarage garden, and the vicarage, and the dear old folks looking out at the gate."

He rose reluctantly to go. "One day I hope you will see it for yourselves—all of you."

With which impersonal statement, delivered in a voice which rather belied its impersonal nature, Frank dropped Lucy's hand, which he had been holding with unnecessary firmness, and departed abruptly from the room.

Gertrude looked rather anxiously towards her sister, who sat quietly sewing, with a little smile on her lips. How far, she wondered, had matters gone between Lucy and Frank? Was the happiness of either or both irrevocably engaged in the pretty game which they were playing? Heaven forbid that her sisterly solicitude should lead her to question the "intentions" of every man who came near them; a hideous feminine practice abhorrent to her very soul. Yet, their own position, Gertrude felt, was a peculiar one, and she could not but be aware of the dangers inseparable from the freedom which they enjoyed; dangers which are the price to be paid for all close intimacy between young men and women.

After all, what do women know about a man, even when they live opposite him? And do not men, the very best of them, allow

---

1 Matthew Arnold (1822-88), "The Forsaken Merman" (1849), line 71:
   "To the little gray church on the windy hill."

themselves immense license in the matter of loving and riding away?

As for Frank, he never made the slightest pretence that the Lorimers enjoyed a monopoly of his regard. He talked freely of the charms of Nellie and Carry and Emily; there was a certain Ethel, of South Kensington, whose praises he was never weary of sounding. Moreover, there could be no doubt that at one time or other he had displayed a good deal of interest in Constance Devonshire; dancing with her half the night, as Fred had expressed it; a mutual fitness in waltz-steps scarcely being enough to account for his attentions. And even supposing a more serious element to have entered into his regard for Lucy, was he not as poor as themselves, and was it not the last contingency for a prudent sister to desire?

"What a calculating crone I am growing," thought Gertrude; then observing the tranquil and busy object of her fears, laughed at herself, half ashamed.

The next day Mr. Russel came to see them, and entered on a careful examination of their accounts: compared the business of the last three months with that of the first; praised the improved quality of their work, and strongly advised them, if it were possible, to hold on for another year. This they were able to do. Although, of course, the money invested in the business had returned anything but a high rate of interest, their economy had been so strict that there would be enough of their original funds to enable them to carry on the struggle for the next twelve months, by which time, if matters progressed at their present rate, they might consider themselves permanently established in business.

Before he went Mr. Russel said something to Lucy which disturbed her considerably, though it made her smile. He had been for many years a widower, living with his mother, but the old lady had died in the course of the year, and now he suggested, modestly enough, that Lucy should return as mistress to the home where she had once been a welcome guest.

The girl found it difficult to put her refusal into words; this kind friend had hitherto given everything and asked nothing; but there was a delicate soul under the brusque exterior, and directly he divined how matters stood, he did his best to save her compunction.

"It really doesn't matter, you know. Please don't give it another thought." He had observed in an off-hand manner, which had amused while it touched her.

Lucy was magnanimous enough to keep this little episode to herself, though Gertrude had her suspicions as to what had occurred.

CHAPTER XIII

A Romance

When strawberry pottles are common and cheap
    Ere elms be black or limes be sere,
When midnight dances are murdering sleep,
    Then comes in the sweet o' the year!
Andrew Lang[1]

The second week in June saw Frank back in his old quarters above the auctioneer's. He had arrived late in the evening, and put off going to see the Lorimers till the first thing the next day. It was some time before business hours when he rang at Number 20B, and was ushered by Matilda into the studio, where he found Phyllis engaged in a rather perfunctory wielding of a feather-duster.

She was looking distractingly pretty, as he perceived when she turned to greet him. Her close-fitting black dress, with the spray of tuberose at the throat, and the great holland apron with its braided bib suited her to perfection; the sober tints setting off to advantage the delicate tones of her complexion, which in these days was more wonderfully pink and white than ever.

"And how are your sisters? I needn't ask how you are?" cried Frank, who in the earlier stages of their acquaintance had been rather surprised at himself for not falling desperately in love with Phyllis Lorimer.

"Everybody is flourishing," she answered, leaning against the little mantelshelf in the waiting-room, and looking down upon Frank's sunburnt, uplifted face.

A look of mischief flashed into her eyes as she added, "There is a great piece of news."

Frank grasped the back of the frail red chair on which he sat

---

1 Andrew Lang (1844-1912), "Ballade of Summer," *Rhymes à la Mode* (1885), lines 1-4; author of novels, poetry, criticism, and children's fairy tales.

astride in a manner rather dangerous to its well-being, and said abruptly, "Well, what is it?"

"One of us is going to be married."

"Oh!" said Frank, with a sort of gasp, which was not lost on his interlocutor.

"I am not going to tell you which it is. You must guess," went on Phyllis, looking down upon him demurely from under her drooped lids, while a fine smile played about her lips.

"Oh, I'll begin at the beginning," said poor Frank, with rather strained cheerfulness. "Is it Miss Gertrude?"

Phyllis played a moment with the feather-duster, then answered slowly, "You must guess again."

"Is it Miss Lucy?" (with a jerk).

A pause. "No," said Phyllis, at last.

Frank sprang to his feet with a beaming countenance and caught both her hands with unfeigned cordiality. "Then it is you, Miss Phyllis, that I have to congratulate."

Her eyes twinkled with suppressed mirth as she answered ruefully, "No, indeed, Mr. Jermyn!"

Frank dropped her hands, wrinkling his brows in perplexity, then a light dawned on him suddenly, and was reflected in his expressive countenance.

"It must be Fan!" He forgot the prefix in his astonishment.

Phyllis nodded. "But you musn't look so surprised," she said, taking a chair beside him. "Why shouldn't poor old Fan be married as well as other people?"

"Of course; how stupid of me not to think of it before," said Frank, vaguely.

"It is quite a romance," went on Phyllis; "she and Mr. Marsh wanted to be married ages and ages ago. But he was too poor, and went to Australia. Now he is well off, and has come back to marry Fan, like a person in a book. A touching tale of young love, is it not?"

"Yes; I think it a very touching and pretty story," said Frank, severely ignoring the note of irony in her voice.

He had all a man's dislike to hearing a woman talk cynically of sentiment; that should be exclusively a masculine privilege.

"Perhaps," said Phyllis, "it takes the bloom off it a little, that Edward Marsh married on the way out. But his wife died last year, so it is all right."

Frank burst out laughing, Phyllis joining him. A minute later Gertrude and Lucy came in and confirmed the wonderful news; and the four young people stood gossiping, till the sound of the studio bell reminded them that the day's work had begun.

Jermyn came in, by invitation, to supper that night, and was introduced to the new arrival, a big, burly man of middle age, whose forest of black beard afforded only very occasional glimpses of his face.

As for Fanny, it was touching to see how this faded flower had revived in the sunshine. The little superannuated airs and graces had come boldly into play; and Edward Marsh, who was a simple soul, accepted them as the proper expression of feminine sweetness.

So she curled her little finger and put her head on one side with all the vigour that assurance of success will give to any performance; gave vent to her most illogical statements in her most mincing tones, uncontradicted and undisturbed; in short, took advantage to the full of her sojourn (to quote George Eliot) in "the woman's paradise where all her nonsense is adorable." [1]

"I don't know what those girls will do without me," Fanny said to her lover, who took the remark in such good faith as to make her believe in it herself; "we must see that we do not settle too far away from them."

And she delicately set a stitch in the bead-work slipper which she was engaged in "grounding" for the simple-hearted Edward.

Fanny patronised her sisters a good deal in these days; and it must be owned—such is the nature of woman—that her importance had gone up considerably in their estimation.

As for Mr. Marsh, he regarded his future relatives with a mixture of alarm and perplexity that secretly delighted them. Never for a moment did his allegiance to Fanny falter before their superior charms; never for a moment did the fear of such a contingency disturb poor Fanny's peace of mind.

Only the girls themselves, in the depths of their hearts, wondered a little at finding themselves regarded with about the same amount of personal interest as was accorded to Matilda, by no means a specimen of the sparkling *soubrette*. Gertrude, who had rather feared the effect of the contrast of Fanny's faded charms with the youthful prettiness of the two younger girls, was relieved, and at the same time a little indignant, to perceive that, as far as Edward Marsh was concerned, Phyllis' hair might be red and Lucy's eyes a brilliant green.

---

1 George Eliot (1819-80), *Daniel Deronda* (1876), book 3, chapter 27. The lines refer to Gwendolen Harleth on the brink of what turns into a wretched marriage.

For once, indeed, Fan's tactlessness had succeeded where the finest tact might have failed. In dropping at once into position as the Fanny of ten years ago; as the incarnation of all that is sweetest and most essentially feminine in woman; in making of herself an accepted and indisputable fact, she had unconsciously done the very best to secure her own happiness.

"There really is something about Fanny that pleases men. I have always said so," Phyllis remarked, as she watched the lovers sailing blissfully down Baker Street, on one of their many house-hunting expeditions.

"You know," added Lucy, "she always dislikes walking about alone, because people speak to her. No one ever speaks to us, do they, Gerty?"

"Nor to me—at least, not often," said Phyllis, ruefully.

"Phyllis, will you never learn where to draw the line?" cried Gertrude; "but it is quite true about Fan. She must be that mysterious creature, a man's woman."

"Mr. Darrell likes her," broke forth Phyllis, after a pause; "he laughs at her in that quiet way of his, but I am quite sure that he likes her. I hope," she added, "that she won't get married before my portrait is finished. But it wouldn't matter, I could go without a chaperon."

"No, you couldn't," said Gertrude, shortly.

"Why are you seized with such notions of propriety all of a sudden?"

"I have no wish to put us to a disadvantage by ignoring the ordinary practices of life."

"Then put up the shutters and get rid of the lease. But, Gerty, we needn't discuss this unpleasant matter yet awhile. By the by, Mr. Darrell is going to ask me to sit for him in a picture, after the portrait. He has made sketches for it already—something out of one of Shakespeare's plays."

"Oh, I am tired of Mr. Darrell's name. Go and see that your dress is in order for the Devonshires' dance to-night."

"*Apropos*," said Lucy, as Phyllis flitted off on the congenial errand, "why is it that we never see anything of Conny in these days?"

"She is going out immensely this season," answered Gertrude, dropping her eyelids; "but, at any rate, we get a double allowance of Fred to compensate."

"Silly boy," cried Lucy, flushing slightly, "he has actually made me promise to sit out two dances with him. Such waste, when one is dying for a waltz."

"Oh, there will be plenty of waltzing. I wish you could have my share," sighed Gertrude, who had been won over by Conny's entreaties to promise attendance at the dance that night.

"It is time you left off these patriarchal airs, Gerty. You are as fond of dancing as any of us; and I mean you to spin round all night like a teetotum."

"What a charming picture you conjure up, Lucy."

"You people with imaginations are always finding fault. Fortunately for me, I have no imagination, and very little humour," said Lucy, with an air of genuine thankfulness that delighted her sister.

Thus, with work and play, and very much gossip, the summer days went by. The three girls found life full and pleasant, and Fanny had her little hour.

CHAPTER XIV

Lucy

Who is Silvia? What is she,
That all our swains commend her?
Two Gentlemen of Verona [1]

There was no mistaking the situation. At one of the red-legged tables sat Fred, his arms spread out before him, his face hidden in his arms; while Lucy, with a troubled face, stood near, struggling between her genuine compunction and an irrepressible desire to laugh.

It was Sunday morning; the rest of the household were at church, and the two young people had had the studio to themselves without fear of disturbance; a circumstance of which the unfortunate Fred had hastened to avail himself, thereby rushing on his fate.

They had now reached that stage of the proceedings when the rejected suitor, finding entreaty of no avail, has recourse to manifestations of despair and reproach.

"You shouldn't have encouraged a fellow all these years," came hoarsely from between the arms and face of the prostrate swain.

---

1 Shakespeare, *Two Gentlemen of Verona* IV.ii.38-39.

"'All these years!' how can you be so silly, Fred?" cried Lucy, with some asperity. "Why, I shall be accused next of encouraging little Jack Oakley, because I bowled his hoop round Regent's Park for him last week."

Lucy did not mean to be unkind; but the really unexpected avowal from her old playmate had made her nervous; a refusal to treat it seriously seemed to her the best course to pursue. But her last words, as might have been supposed, were too much for poor Fred. Up he sprang, "a wounded thing with a rancorous cry"—[1]

"There is another fellow!"

Back started Lucy, as if she had been shot. The hot blood surged up into her face, the tears rose to her eyes.

"What has that to do with it?" she cried, stung suddenly to cruelty; "what has that to do with it, when, if you were the only man in the world, I would not marry you?"

Fred, hurt and shocked by this unexpected attack from gentle Lucy, gathered himself up with something more like dignity than he had displayed in the course of the interview.

"Oh, very well," he said, taking up his hat; "perhaps one of these days you will be sorry for what you have done. I'm not much, I know, but you won't find many people to care for you as I would have cared." His voice broke suddenly, and he made his way rather blindly to the door.

Lucy was trembling all over, and as pale as, a moment ago, she had been red. She wanted to say something, as she watched him fumbling unsteadily with the door-handle; but her lips refused to frame the words.

Without lifting his head he passed into the little passage. Lucy heard his retreating footsteps, then her eye fell on a roll of newspapers at her feet. She picked them up hastily.

"Fred," she cried, "you have forgotten these."

But he vouchsafed no answer, and in another moment she heard the outer door shut.

She stood a moment with the ridiculous bundle in her hand— *Tit-Bits*[2] and a pink, crushed copy of *The Sporting Times*—then something between a laugh and a sob rose in her throat, the

---

1 Tennyson, "Maud" (1855), part I, line 363.

2 George Newnes launched the popular weekly penny newspaper *Tit-Bits* in 1881, which contained snippets of information and advice, short stories and jokes, advertisements and contests, aimed at upper working-class and lower middle-class readers.

papers fell to the ground, and sinking on her knees by the table, she buried her face in her hands and burst into bitter weeping.

Gertrude, coming in from church some ten minutes later, found her sister thus prostrate.

The sight unnerved her from its very unusualness; bending over Lucy she whispered, "Am I to go away?"

"No, stop here."

Gertrude locked the door, then came and knelt by her sister.

"Oh, poor Fred, and I was so horrid to him," wept the penitent.

"Ah, I was afraid it would come."

Gertrude stroked the prone, smooth head; she feared that the thought of some one else besides Fred lay at the bottom of all this disturbance. She was very anxious for Lucy in these days; very anxious and very helpless. There was only one person, she knew too well, who could restore to Lucy her old sweet serenity, and he, alas, made no sign.

What was she to think? One thing was clear enough; the old pleasant relationship between themselves and Frank was at an end; if renewed at all, it must be renewed on a different basis. A disturbing element, an element of self-consciousness had crept into it; the delicate charm, the first bloom of simplicity, had departed for ever.

It was now the middle of July, and for the last week or two they had seen scarcely anything of Jermyn, beyond the glimpses of him as he lounged up the street, with his sombrero crushed over his eyes, all the impetuosity gone from his gait.

That he distinctly avoided them, there could be little doubt. Though he was to be seen looking across at the house wistfully enough, he made no attempt to see them, and his greetings when they chanced to meet were of the most formal nature.

The change in his conduct had been so marked and sudden, that it was impossible that it should escape observation. Fanny, with an air of superior knowledge, gave it out as her belief that Mr. Jermyn was in love; Phyllis held to the opinion that he had been fired with the idea of a big picture, and was undergoing the throes of artistic conception; Gertrude said lightly, that she supposed he was out of sorts and disinclined for society; while Lucy held her peace, and indulged in many inward sophistries to convince herself that her own unusual restlessness and languor had nothing to do with their neighbour's disaffection.

It was these carefully woven self-deceptions that had been so rudely scattered by Fred's words; and Lucy, kneeling by the scarlet table, had for the first time looked her fate in the face, and diagnosed her own complaint.

"Lucy," said Gertrude, after a pause, "bathe your eyes and come for a walk in the Park; there is time before lunch."

Lucy rose, drying her wet face with her handkerchief.

"Let me look at you," cried Gertrude. "What is the charm? Where does it lie? Why are these sort of things always happening to you?"

"Oh," answered Lucy, with an attempt at a smile, "I am a convenient, middling sort of person, that is all. Not uncomfortably clever like you, or uncomfortably pretty like Phyllis."

The two girls set off up the hot dusty street, with its Sunday odour of bad tobacco. Regent's Park wore its most unattractive garb; a dead monotony of July verdure assailed the eye; a verdure, moreover, impregnated and coated with the dust and soot of the city. The girls felt listless and dispirited, and conscious that their walk was turning out a failure.

As they passed through Clarence Gate, on their way back, Frank darted past them with something of his normal activity, lifting his hat with something like the old smile.

"He might have stopped," said Lucy, pale to the lips, and suddenly abandoning all pretence of concealment of her feelings.

"No doubt he is in a hurry;" answered Gertrude, lamely. "I daresay he is going to lunch in Sussex Place. Lord Watergate's Sunday luncheon parties are quite celebrated."

The day dragged on. The weather was sultry and every one felt depressed. Fanny was spending the day with relations of her future husband's; but the three girls had no engagements and lounged away the afternoon rather dismally at home.

All were relieved when Fanny and Mr. Marsh came in at supper-time, and they seated themselves at the table with alacrity. They had not proceeded far with the meal, when footsteps, unexpected but familiar, were heard ascending the staircase; then some one knocked, and before there was time to reply, the door was thrown open to admit Frank Jermyn.

He looked curiously unlike himself as he advanced and shook hands amid an uncomfortable silence that everybody desired to break. His face was pale, and no longer moody, but tense and eager, with shining eyes and dilated nostrils.

"You will stay to supper, Mr. Jermyn?" said Gertrude, at last, in her most neutral tones.

"Yes, please." Frank drew a chair to the table like a person in a dream.

"You are quite a stranger," cried arch, unconscious Fan, indicating with head and spoon the dish from which she proposed to serve him.

Frank nodded acceptance of the proffered fare, but ignored her remark.

Silence fell again upon the party, broken by murmurs from the enamoured Edward, and the ostentatious clatter of knives and forks on the part of people who were not eating. Every one, except the plighted lovers, felt that there was electricity in the air.

At last Frank dropped his fork, abandoning, once for all, the pretence of supper.

"Miss Lucy," he cried across the table to her, "I have a piece of news."

She looked up, pale, with steady eyes, questioning him.

"I am going abroad to-morrow."

"Oh, where are you going?" cried Fanny, vaguely mystified.

"I am going to Africa."

He did not move his eyes from Lucy as he spoke; her head had drooped over her plate. "They are sending me out as special from *The Woodcut*, in the place of poor Leadpoint, who has died of fever. I heard the first of it last night, and this morning it was finally settled. It makes," cried Frank, "an immense difference in my prospects."

Edward Marsh, who objected to Frank as a spoilt puppy, always expecting other people to be interested in his affairs, asked the young man bluntly the value of his appointment. But he met with no reply; for Frank, his face alight, had sprung to his feet, pushing back his chair.

"Lucy, Lucy," he cried in a low voice, "won't you come and speak to me?"

Lucy rose like one mesmerised; took, with a presence of mind at which she afterwards laughed, the key of the studio from its nail, and followed Frank from the room, amidst the stupefaction of the rest of the party.

It was a sufficiently simple explanation which took place, some minutes later, in the very room where, a few hours before, poor Fred had received his dismissal.

"But why," said Lucy, presently, "have you been so unkind for the last fortnight?"

"Ah, Lucy," answered Frank; "you women so often misjudge us, and think that it is you alone who suffer, when the pain is on both sides. When it dawned upon me how things stood with you and me—dear girl, you told me more than you knew yourself—I reflected what a poor devil I was, with not the ghost of a prospect. (I have been down on my luck lately, Lucy.) And I saw, at the same time, how it was with Devonshire; I thought, he is a good fellow, let him have his chance, it may be best in the end—"

"Oh, Frank, Frank, what did you think of me? If these are men's arguments I am glad that I am a woman," cried Lucy, clinging to the strong young hand.

"Well, so am I, for that matter," answered Frank; and then, of course, though I do not uphold her conduct in this respect, Lucy told him briefly of Fred Devonshire's offer and her own refusal.

It was late before these two happy people returned to the sitting-room, to receive congratulations on the event, which, by this time, it was unnecessary to impart.

Fanny wondered aloud why she had not thought of such a thing before; and felt, perhaps, that her own *rechauffé* love affair was quite thrown into the shade. Phyllis smiled and made airy jests, submitting her soft cheek gracefully to a brotherly kiss.

Edward Marsh looked on mystified and rather shocked, and Gertrude remained in the background, with a heart too full for speech, till the lovers made their way to her, demanding her congratulations.

"Don't think me too unworthy," said Frank, in all humility.

"I am glad," she said.

Glancing up and seeing the two young faces, aglow with the light of their happiness, she looked back with a wistful amusement on her own doubts and fears of the past weeks.

As she did so, the beautiful, familiar words flashed across her consciousness—

"Blessed are the pure in heart, for they shall see God."[1]

★　★　★　★　★

Late that night, when the guests had departed and the rest of the household was asleep, Gertrude heard Lucy moving about in the room below, and, throwing on her dressing-gown, went down stairs. She found her sister risen from the table, where she had been writing a letter by the lamp-light.

"Aren't you coming to bed, Lucy? Remember, you have to be up very early."

The shadow of the coming separation, which at first had only seemed to give a more exquisite quality to her happiness, lay on

---

1 Matthew 5.8.

Lucy. She was pale, and her steadfast eyes looked out with the old calm, but with a new intensity, from her face.

"Read this," she said, "it seemed only fair."

Stooping over the table, Gertrude read—

"Dear Fred,—I am engaged to Frank Jermyn, who goes abroad to-morrow. I am sorry if I seemed unkind, but I was grieved and shocked by what you said to me. Very soon, when you have quite forgiven me, you will come and see us all, will you not? Acknowledge that you made a mistake, and never cease to regard me as your friend.—L.L."

Gertrude thought: "Then I shall not have to tell Conny, after all."

CHAPTER XV

Cressida

Beauty like hers is genius.
D. G. Rossetti[1]

Lucy slept little that night. At the first flush of the magnificent summer dawn she was astir, making her preparations for the traveller's breakfast.

She had changed suddenly, from a demure and rather frigid maiden to a loving and anxious woman. Perhaps the signet-ring on her middle finger was a magic ring, and had wrought the charm.

Frank's notice to quit had been so short, that he had been obliged to apply for various necessaries to Darrell, who, with Lord Watergate, had supplied him with the main features of a tropical outfit. His ship sailed that day, at noon, so there was little time to be lost. He came over at an unconscionably early hour to Number 20B, for there was much to be said and little opportunity for saying it.

Lucy, displaying a truly feminine mixture of the tender and the practical, packed his bag, strapped his rugs, and put searching

---

1 Dante Gabriel Rossetti (1828–82), "Genius in Beauty," *The House of Life* (1881), sonnet 18, line 1.

questions as to his preparations for travel. Already, womanlike, she had taken him under her wing, and henceforward the minutest detail of his existence would be more precious to her than anything on earth.

Gertrude, when she had kissed the vivid young face in sisterly farewell, saw the lovers drive off to the station and wondered inwardly at their calmness.

Later in the day, coming into the studio, she found Lucy quietly engaged in putting a negative into the printing-frame.

"It is his," she said, looking up with a smile; "I never felt that I had a right to do it before."

At luncheon, Phyllis reminded her that to-night was the night of Mr. Darrell's *conversazione* [1] at the Berkeley Galleries for which he had sent them two tickets.

"It's no good expecting Lucy to go; you will have to take me, Gerty," she announced.

Gertrude had a great dislike to going, and she said—

"Can't Fanny take you?"

"Edward and I are dining at the Septimus Pratts'," replied Fanny.

After much hesitation, she and her betrothed had had to resign themselves to the inevitable, and dispense with the services of a chaperon; a breach of decorum which Mr. Marsh, in particular, deplored.

"Are you very anxious about this party?" pleaded Gertrude.

"Oh Gerty, of course. And if you won't take me, I'll go alone," cried Phyllis, with unusual vehemence.

Gertrude was indignant at her sister's tone; then reflected that it was, perhaps, hard on Phyllis, to cut off one of her few festivities.

Phyllis, indeed, had not been very well of late, and demanded more spoiling than ever. She coughed constantly, and her eyes were unnaturally bright.

Gertrude ended by submitting to the sacrifice, and at ten o'clock she and Phyllis found themselves in Bond Street, where the rooms were already thronged with people.

Phyllis had blazed into a degree of beauty that startled even her sister, and made her the frequent mark for observation in that brilliant gathering.

---

1 A fashionable social event for invited guests to have an intellectual discussion, in this case about an art exhibition, along with refreshments and sometimes chamber music.

Her grey dress was cut low, displaying the white and rounded slenderness of her shoulders and arms; the soft brown hair was coiled about the perfect head in a manner that afforded a view of the neck and its graceful action; her eyes shone like stars; her cheeks glowed exquisitely pink. Wherever she went, went forth a sweet strong fragrance, the breath of a great spray of tuberose which was fastened in her bodice, and which had arrived for her that day from an unnamed donor.

Darrell's greeting to both the sisters had been of the briefest. He had shaken hands unsmilingly with Phyllis; he and Gertrude had brought their finger-tips into chill and momentary contact, without so much as lifting their eyes, and Gertrude had felt humiliated at her presence there.

She had not seen Darrell since his Private View, more than six weeks ago; and now, as she stood talking to Lord Watergate, her eye, guided by a nameless curiosity, an unaccountable fascination, sought him out. He was looking ill, she thought, as she watched him standing in his host's place, near the doorway, chatting to an ugly old woman, whom she knew to be the Duchess of Kilburne; ill, and very unhappy. Happiness indeed, as she instinctively felt, is not for such as he—for the egotist and the sensualist.

Her acute feminine sense, sharpened perhaps by personal soreness, had pierced to the second-rateness of the man and his art. Beneath his arrogance and air of assured success, she read the signs of an almost craven hunger for pre-eminence; of a morbid self-consciousness; an insatiable vanity. And for all the stupendous cleverness of his workmanship, she failed to detect in his work the traces of those qualities which, combined with far less skill than his, can make greatness.

As for her own relations to Darrell, the positions of the two had shifted a little since the first. In the brief flashes of intercourse which they had known, a drama had silently enacted itself; a war without words or weapons, in which, so far, she had come off victor. For Sidney had ceased to regard her as merely ridiculous; and she, on her part, was no longer cowed by his aggressive personality, by the all-seeing, languid glance, the arrogant, indifferent manner. They stood on a level platform of unspoken, yet open distaste; which, should occasion arise, might blaze into actual defiance.

Lord Watergate, as I have said, was talking to Gertrude; but his glance, as she was quick to observe, strayed constantly toward Phyllis. She had wondered before this, as to the measure of his admiration for her sister; it seemed to her that he paid her the tribute of a deeper interest than that which her beauty and her brightness would, in the natural course of things, exact.

As for Phyllis, she was enjoying a triumph which many a professional beauty might have envied. People flocked round her, scheming for introductions, staring at her in open admiration, laughing at her whimsical sallies.

"That young person has a career before her."

"Who is she?"

"Oh, one of Darrell's discoveries. Works at a photographer's, they say."

"Darrell is painting her portrait."

"No, not her portrait; but a study of 'Cressida.'"

"Cressida!"

"'There's language in her eye, her cheek, her lip;
Nay, her foot speaks—'" [1]

"Hush, hush!"

Such floating spars of talk had drifted past Gertrude's corner, and had been caught, not by her, but by her companion.

Lord Watergate frowned, as he mentally finished the quotation, which struck him as being in shocking taste. He had adopted, unconsciously, a protective attitude towards the Lorimers; their courage, their fearlessness, their immense ignorance, appealed to his generous and chivalrous nature. He made up his mind to speak to Darrell about that baseless rumour of the Cressida.

Gertrude, on her part, was not too absorbed in conversation to notice what her sister was doing. She saw at once that, in spite of some thrills of satisfied vanity, Phyllis was not enjoying herself. There was a restless, discontented light in her eyes, a half-weary recklessness in her pose, as she leant against the edge of a tall screen, which filled Gertrude with wonder and anxiety. She felt, as she had felt so often lately, that Phyllis, her little Phyllis, whom she had scolded and petted and yearned over for eighteen years, was passing beyond her ken, into regions where she could never follow.

---

1 Shakespeare, *The History of Troilus and Cressida* IV.v.56-57. Following these lines are: "Her wanton spirits look out / At every joint and motive of her body."

The evening wore itself away as such evenings do, in aimless drifting to and fro, half-hearted attempts at conversation, much mutual staring, and a determined raid on the refreshment buffet, on the part of people who have dined sumptuously an hour ago.

"Our English social institutions," Darrell said aside to Lord Watergate; "the private view, where every one goes; the *conversazione*, where no one talks."

Lord Watergate laughed, and went back to Gertrude, to propose an attack on the buffet, by way of diversion; and Sidney, with his inscrutable air of utter purposelessness, made his way through the crowd to where Phyllis stood in conversation with two young men.

Some paces off from her he paused, and stood in silence, looking at her.

Phyllis shot her glance to his, half-petulant, half-supplicating, like that of a child.

It was late in the evening, and this was the first attempt he had made to approach her. Darrell advanced a step or two, and Phyllis lowered her eyes, with a sudden and vivid blush.

"At last," said Darrell, in a low voice, as the two young men instinctively moved off before him.

"You are just in time to say 'goodnight' to me, Mr. Darrell."

Darrell smiled, with his face close to hers. His smile was considered attractive—

"Seeming more generous for the coldness gone."[1]

"It is not 'good-night,' but 'good-bye,' that I have come to say."

The brilliant and rapid smile had passed across his face, leaving no trace.

"What do you mean, Mr. Darrell?"

"I mean that I am going away tomorrow."

"For ever and ever?" Phyllis laughed, as she spoke, turning pale.

"For several months. I have important business in Paris."

"But you haven't finished my portrait, Mr. Darrell."

Sidney looked down, biting his lip.

"Shall you be able to finish it in time for the Grosvenor?"[2]

---

1 George Eliot, *The Spanish Gypsy* (1868), book 1, line 468.

2 The Grosvenor Gallery, New Bond Street, opened in London in 1877 and gained a reputation for experimental and unconventional art, in contrast to exhibits at the Royal Academy. The Grosvenor was associ-

"Possibly not."

"Now you are disagreeable," cried Phyllis, in a high voice; "and ungrateful, too, after all those long sittings."

"Not ungrateful. Thank you, thank you, thank you!" Under cover of the crowd he had taken both her hands, and was pressing them fiercely at each repetition, while his miserable eyes looked imploringly into hers.

"You are hurting me." Her voice was low and broken. She shrank back afraid.

"Good-bye—Phyllis."

Gertrude, coming back from the refreshment-room a minute later, found Phyllis standing by herself, in an angle formed by one of the screens, pale to the lips, with brilliant, meaningless eyes.

"We are going home," said Gertrude, walking up to her.

"Oh, very well," she answered, rousing herself; "the sooner the better. I am not well." She put her hand to her side. "I had that pain again that I used to have."

Lord Watergate, who stood a little apart, watching her, came forward and gave her his arm, and they all three went from the room.

In the cab Phyllis recovered something of her wonted vivacity.

"Isn't it a nuisance," she said, "Mr. Darrell is going away for a long time, and doesn't know when he will be able to finish my portrait."

Gertrude started.

"Well, I suppose you always knew that he was an erratic person."

"You speak as if you were pleased, Gerty. I am very disappointed."

"Put not your trust in princes, Phyllis, nor in fashionable artists, who are rather more important than princes, in these days," answered Gertrude, secretly hoping that their relations with Darrell would never be renewed. "He has tired of his whim," she thought, indignant, yet relieved.

Mrs. Maryon opened the door to them herself.

Phyllis shuddered as they went upstairs. "That bird of ill-omen!" she cried, beneath her breath.

---

ated with the Aesthetic Movement, and Oscar Wilde described this gallery as a revival of the love of beauty. Founded by Blanche and Sir Coutts Lindsay, the Grosvenor exhibited paintings by George Frederic Watts and Edward Burne-Jones; it is mentioned in the first chapter of Wilde's *The Picture of Dorian Gray* (1890).

"Poor Mrs. Maryon. How can you be so silly?" said Gertrude, who herself had noted the long and earnest glance which the woman had cast on her sister.

In the sitting-room they found Lucy sewing peacefully by the lamplight.

"You hardly went to bed at all last night; you shouldn't be sitting up," said Gertrude, throwing off her cloak; while Phyllis carefully detached the knot of tuberose from her bodice, as she delivered herself for the second time of her grievance.

Afterwards, going up to the mantelpiece, she placed the flowers in a slender Venetian vase, its crystal flecked with flakes of gold, which Darrell had given her; took the vase in her hand, and swept upstairs without a word.

"I do not know what to think about Phyllis," said Gertrude.

"You are afraid that she is too much interested in Mr. Darrell?"

"Yes."

"She does not care two straws for him," said Lucy, with the conviction of one who knows; "her vanity is hurt, but I am not sure that that will be bad for her."

"He is the sort of person to attract—" began Gertrude; but Lucy struck in—

"Why, Gerty, what are you thinking of? he must be forty at least; and Phyllis is a child."

Something in her tones recalled to Gertrude that clarion-blast of triumph, in the wonderful lyric—

"Oh, my love, my love is young!" [1]

"At any rate," she said, as they prepared to retire, "I am thankful that the sittings are at an end. Phyllis was getting her head turned. She is looking shockingly unwell, moreover, and I shall persuade her to accept the Devonshires' invitation for next month."

---

1 *The Passionate Pilgrim*, poem 12, line 10. This miscellany of poems by known and unknown authors was first published in the late sixteenth century; many later editions erroneously attributed all the poems to Shakespeare.

CHAPTER XVI

A Wedding

A human heart should beat for two,
    Whate'er may say your single scorners;
And all the hearths I ever knew
    Had got a pair of chimney-corners.
    F. Locker: London Lyrics [1]

The next day, at about six o'clock, just as they had gone upstairs from the studio, Constance Devonshire was announced, and came sailing in, in her smartest attire, and with her most gracious smile on her face.

"I have come to offer my congratulations," she cried, going up to Lucy; "you know, I have always thought little Mr. Jermyn a nice person."

Lucy laughed quietly.

"I am glad you have brought your congratulations in person, Conny. I rather expected you would tell your coachman to leave cards at the door."

Conny turned away her face abruptly.

"What is the good of coming to see such busy people as you have been lately? ... And with so much love-making going on at the same time! What does Mrs. Maryon think of it all?"

"Oh, she finds it very tame and hackneyed, I am afraid."

"You see," added Phyllis, who lounged idly in an arm-chair by the window, pale but sprightly, "the course of true love runs so monotonously smooth in this household. And Mrs. Maryon has a taste for the dramatic."

Conny laughed; and at this point the door was thrown open to admit Aunt Caroline, whose fixed and rigid smile was intended to show that she was in a gracious mood, and was accepted by the girls as a signal of truce.

"What is this a little bird tells me, Lucy?" she cried archly, for Mrs. Pratt shared the liking of her sex for matters matrimonial.

Fanny, who was, in fact, none other than the little bird who

---

1   Frederick Locker-Lampson, "Old Letters," *London Lyrics* (1857), stanza 10.

had broken the news, put her head on one side in unconsciously avine fashion, and smiled benevolently at her sister.

"I am engaged to Mr. Jermyn," said Lucy, her clear voice lingering proudly over the words.

Conny winced suddenly; then turned to gaze through the window at the blank casements above the auctioneer's shop.

"Then you have found out who Mr. Jermyn *is*?" went on Aunt Caroline, still in her most conciliatory tones.

"We never wanted to know," said Lucy, unexpectedly showing fight.

Aunt Caroline flushed, but she had come resolved against hostile encounter, in which, hitherto, she had found herself overpowered by force of numbers; so she contented herself with saying—

"And have you any prospect of getting married?"

"Frank has gone to Africa for the present," said Lucy.

Aunt Caroline looked significant.

"I only hope," she said afterwards to Fanny, who let her out at the street-door, "that your sister has not fallen into the hands of an unscrupulous adventurer. It will be time when the young man comes home, if he ever does, for Mr. Pratt to make the proper inquiries."

Fanny had risen into favour since her engagement; Mr. Marsh, also, had won golden opinions at Lancaster Gate.

"I believe," Fanny replied, speaking for once to the point, "that Frank Jermyn is going to write, himself, to Mr. Pratt, at the first opportunity."

Meanwhile, upstairs in the sitting-room, Conny was delivering herself of her opinion that they had all behaved shamefully to Aunt Caroline.

"She had a right to know. And it is very good of her to trouble about such a set of ungrateful girls at all," she cried. "You can't expect every one besides yourselves to look upon Frank Jermyn as dropped from heaven."

"Aunt Caroline is cumulative—not to be judged at a sitting," pleaded Gertrude.

Very soon Constance herself rose to go.

"I shall not see you again unless you come down to us; which, I suppose, you won't," she said. "We go to Eastbourne on Friday; and afterwards to Homburg. Mama is going to write and invite you in due form."

"It is very kind of Mrs. Devonshire. Lucy and I cannot possibly leave home, but Phyllis would like to go," answered Gertrude; a remark of which Phyllis herself took no notice.

"Well then, good-bye. Lucy, Fred sends his congratulations. Phyllis, my dear, we shall meet ere long. Fanny, I shall look out for your wedding in the paper. Come on, Gerty, and let a fellow out!"

On the other side of the door her manner changed suddenly.

"Do come home and dine, Gerty."

"I can't, Con, possibly."

"Gerty, of course I can guess about Fred. I knew it was no good, but I can't help being sorry."

"It was out of the question, poor boy."

"Oh, don't pity him too much. He'll get over it soon enough. His is not a complaint that lasts."

There was a significant emphasis on the last words, that did not escape Gertrude.

"You look better, Conny, than when I last saw you."

"Oh, I'm all right. There's nothing the matter with me but too many parties."

"I think dancing has agreed with you."

"I don't know about dancing. I have taken to sitting in conservatories under pink lamps. That is better sport, and far more becoming to the complexion."

"I shouldn't play that game, Conny. It never ends well."

"Indeed it does. Often in St. George's, Hanover Square.[1] You are shocked, but I do not contemplate matrimony just at present. But I see you agree with *Chastelard*—

"'I do not like this manner of a dance;
This game of two and two; it were much better
To mix between the dances, than to sit,
Each lady out of earshot with her friend.'"[2]

"Have you been taking to literature?"

"Yes; to the modern poets and the French novelists particularly. When next you hear of me, I shall have taken probably to slumming; shall have found peace in bearing jellies to aged paupers. Then you might write a moral tale about me."

Gertrude sighed, as the door closed on Constance. It was the

---

1 St. George's Church is south of Hanover Square, located south of Oxford Street and east of New Bond Street.

2 Algernon Charles Swinburne (1837-1909), *Chastelard* (1866), act 1, scene 2.

Devonshires who, throughout their troubles, had shown them the most unwavering kindness; and on the Devonshires, it seemed, they were doomed to bring misfortune.

At the end of August, Fanny was quietly married at Marylebone Church. She would have dearly liked a "white wedding;" and secretly hoped that her sisters would suggest what she dared not—a white satin bride and white muslin bridesmaids. Truth to tell, such an idea never entered the heads of those practical young women; and poor Fanny went soberly to the altar in a dark green travelling dress, which was becoming if not festive.

Aunt Caroline and Uncle Septimus came up from Tunbridge Wells for the wedding, and the Devonshires, who were away, lent their carriage. It was a sober, middle-aged little function enough, and every one was glad when it was over.

Aunt Caroline said little, but contented herself with sending her hard, keen eyes into every nook and corner, every fold and plait, every dish and bowl; while she mentally appraised the value of the feast.

One result of the encounters with her nieces was this, that she was more outwardly gracious and less inwardly benevolent than before; a change not wholly to be deprecated.

Lucy, with bright eyes, listened, with the air of one who has a right to be interested, to the words of the marriage service, taking afterwards her usual share in practical details. She was upheld, no doubt, by the consciousness of the letter in her pocket; a letter which had come that very morning; was written on thin paper in a bold hand; and in common with others from the same source, was bright and kind; tender and hopeful; and very full of confidential statements as to all that concerned the writer.

Phyllis, pale but beautiful, alternated between langour and a fitful sprightliness; her three weeks at Eastbourne seemed to have done her little good; while Gertrude went through her part mechanically, and remembered remorsefully that she had never been very nice to Fanny.

As for the bride, she was subdued and tearful, as an orthodox bride should be; and invited all her sisters in turn to come and stay with her at Notting Hill[1] directly the honeymoon in Switzerland should be over. Edward Marsh suffered the usual insignifi-

---

1   An area west of Kensington Gardens, north of Campden Hill, and east of Holland Park; it was a relatively inexpensive neighborhood of London in the Victorian period.

cance of bridegrooms; but did all that was demanded of him with exactness.

In the evening, when that blankness which invariably follows a wedding had fallen upon the sisters, Mrs. Maryon came up into the sitting-room, and beguiled them with tales of the various brides she had known; who, if they had not married in haste, must certainly, to judge by the sequel, have repented at leisure.

CHAPTER XVII

A Special Edition

We bear to think
You're gone,—to feel you may not come,—
To hear the door-latch stir and clink,
Yet no more you!....
E.B. Browning[1]

It was true enough, no doubt, that Phyllis did not care for Darrell in Lucy's sense of the word; but at the same time it was sufficiently clear that he had been the means of injecting a subtle poison into her veins.

Since the night of the *conversazione* at the Berkeley Galleries, when he had bidden her farewell, a change, in every respect for the worse, had crept over her.

The buoyancy, which had been one of her chief charms, had deserted her. She was languid, restless, bored, and more utterly idle than ever. The flippancy of her lighter moods shocked even her sisters, who had been accustomed to allow her great license in the matter of jokes; the moodiness of her moments of depression distressed them beyond measure.

At Eastbourne she had amused herself with getting up a tremendous flirtation with Fred, to the Devonshires' annoyance and the satisfaction of the victim himself, whose present mood it suited and who hoped that Lucy would hear of it.

After Phyllis' visit to Eastbourne, which had been closely followed by Fanny's wedding, the household at Upper Baker Street

---

1 "Parting Lovers" (1860), lines 57-60, from the posthumous collection *Last Poems*.

underwent a period of dulness, which was felt all the more keenly from the cheerful fulness of the previous summer. Every one was out of town. In early September even the country cousins have departed, and people have not yet begun to return to London, where it is perhaps the most desolate period of the whole year.

Work, of course, was slack, and they had no longer the preparations for Fanny's wedding to fall back upon.

The air was hot, sunless, misty; like a vapour bath, Phyllis said. Even Gertrude, inveterate cockney as she was, began to long for the country. Nothing but a strong sense of loyalty to her sister prevented Lucy from accepting a cordial invitation from the "old folks." Phyllis openly proclaimed that she was only awaiting *der erste beste*[1] to make her escape for ever from Baker Street.

Phyllis, indeed, was in the worst case of them all; for while Lucy had the precious letters from Africa to console her, Gertrude had again taken up her pen, which seemed to move more freely in her hand than it had ever done before.

So the days went on till it was the middle of September, and life was beginning to quicken in the great city.

One sultry afternoon, the Lorimers were gathered in the sitting-room; both windows stood open, admitting the hot, still, autumnal air; every sound in the street could be distinctly heard.

Lucy sat apart, deep in a voluminous letter on foreign paper which had come for her that morning, and which she had been too busy to read before. Phyllis was at the table, yawning over a copy of *The Woodcut*; which was opened at a page of engravings headed: "The War in Africa; from sketches by our special artist."[2] Gertrude sewed by the window, too tired to think or talk. Now and then she glanced across mechanically to the opposite house, whence in these days of dreariness, no picturesque, impetuous young man was wont to issue; from whose upper windows no friendly eyes gazed wistfully across.

The rooms above the auctioneer's had, in fact, a fresh occupant; an ex-Girtonian without a waist, who taught at the High School for girls hard-by.[3]

---

1 The first (person, job, etc.) that comes along (German).

2 See p. 98, note 2, on British imperial interests and military actions in "the scramble for Africa" of the late nineteenth century.

3 See p. 55, note 2. The "Girton Girl" became a popular figure of the new woman: college-educated, independent, and—as the following paragraph suggests—not fashionably dressed. See Andrew Lang's "Ballade of the Girton Girl" published in *Rhymes à la Mode* (1885).

The Lorimers chose to regard her as a usurper; and with the justice usually attributed to their sex, indulged in much sarcastic comment on her appearance; on her round shoulders and swinging gait; on the green gown with balloon sleeves, and the sulphur-coloured handkerchief which she habitually wore.

Presently Lucy looked up from her letter, folded it, sighed, and smiled.

"What has your special artist to say for himself?" asked Phyllis, pushing away *The Woodcut*.

"He writes in good spirits, but holds out no prospect of the war coming to an end. He was just about to go further into the interior, with General Somerset's division. Mr. Steele of *The Photogravure*, with whom he seems to have chummed, goes too," answered Lucy, putting the letter into her pocket.[1]

"Perhaps his sketches will be a little livelier in consequence. They are very dull this week."

Phyllis rose as she spoke, stretching her arms above her head. "I think I will go and dine with Fan. She is such fun."

Fanny had returned from Switzerland a day or two before, and was now in the full tide of bridal complacency. As mistress of a snug and hideous little house at Notting Hill, and wedded wife of a large and affectionate man, she was beginning to feel that she had a place in the world at last.

"I will come up with you," said Lucy to Phyllis, "and brush your hair before you go."

The two girls went from the room, leaving Gertrude alone. Letting fall her work into her lap, she leaned in dreamy idleness from the window, looking out into the street, where the afternoon was deepening apace into evening. A dun-coloured haze, thin and transparent, hung in the air, softening the long perspective of the street. School hours were over, and the Girtonian, her arm swinging like a bell-rope, could be discerned on her way home, a devoted *cortège* of school-girls straggling in her wake. From the corner of the street floated up the cries of the newspaper boys, mingling with the clatter of omnibus wheels.[2]

An empty hansom cab crawled slowly by. Gertrude noticed that it had violet lamps instead of red ones.

---

1   The photogravure process was developed in the 1850s and is described as having the subtlety of a photograph and the artistic quality of a litho-graph.

2   Two of Levy's poems from *A London Plane-Tree, and Other Verse* (1889)—"Ballade of an Omnibus" and "Ballade of a Special Edition"— offer related London images.

A lamplighter was going his rounds, leaving a lengthening line of orange-coloured lights to mark his track. The recollection of summer, the presage of winter, were met in the dusky atmosphere.

"How the place echoes," thought Gertrude. It seemed to her that the boys crying the evening papers were more vociferous than usual; and as the thought passed through her mind, she was aware of a hateful, familiar sound—the hoarse shriek of a man proclaiming a "special edition" up the street.

No amount of familiarity could conquer the instinctive shudder with which she always listened to these birds of ill-omen, these carrion, whose hideous task it is to gloat over human calamity. Now, as the sound grew louder and more distinct, the usual vague and sickening horror crept over her. She put her hands to her ears. "It is some ridiculous race, no doubt."

She let in the sound again.

Her fears were unformulated, but she hoped that Lucy upstairs in the bed-room had not heard.

The cry ceased abruptly; some one was buying a paper; then was taken up again with increased vociferousness. Gertrude strained her ears to listen.

"Terrible slaughter, terrible slaughter of British troops!" floated up in the hideous tones.

She listened, fascinated with a nameless horror.

"A regiment cut to pieces! Death of a general! Special edition!" The fiend stood under the window, vociferating upwards.

In an instant Gertrude had slipped down the dusky staircase, and was giving the man sixpence for a halfpenny paper. Standing beneath the gas-jet in the passage, she opened the sheet and read; then, still clutching it, sank down white and trembling on the lowest stair.

Noiseless, rapid footfalls came down behind her, some one touched her on the shoulder, and a strange voice said in her ear, "Give it to me."

She started up, putting the hateful thing behind her.

"No, no, no, Lucy! It is not true."

"Yes, yes, yes! don't be ridiculous, Gerty."

Lucy took the paper in her hands, bore it to the light, and read, Gertrude hiding her face against the wall.

The paper stated, briefly, that news had arrived at head-quarters of the almost total destruction of the troops which, under General Somerset, had set out for the interior of Africa some weeks before. A few stragglers, chiefly native allies, had reached the coast in safety, and had reported that the General himself had been among the first to perish.[1]

Messrs. Steele and Jermyn, special artists of *The Photogravure* and *The Woodcut*, respectively, had been among those to join the expedition. No news of their fate had been ascertained, and there was reason to fear that they had shared the doom of the others.

"It is not true." Lucy's voice rang hollow and strange. She stood there, white and rigid, under the gas-jet.

Mrs. Maryon, who had bought a paper on her own account, issued from the shop-parlour in time to see the poor young lady sway forward into her sister's arms.

★ ★ ★ ★ ★

Those were dark days that followed. At first there had been hope; but as time went on, and further details of the catastrophe came to light, there was nothing for the most sanguine to do but to accept the worst.

Gertrude herself felt that the one pale gleam of uncertainty which yet remained was, perhaps, the most cruel feature of the case. If only Lucy's hollow eyes could drop their natural tears above Frank's grave she might again find peace.

Frank's grave! Gertrude found herself starting back incredulous at the thought.

Death, as a general statement, is so easy of utterance, of belief; it is only when we come face to face with it that we find the great mystery so cruelly hard to realise; for death, like love, is ever old and ever new.

"People always come back in books," Fanny had said, endeavouring, in all good faith, to administer consolation; and Lucy had actually laughed.

"Your sister ought to be able to do better for herself," Edward Marsh said, later on, to his wife.

But Fanny, who had had a genuine liking for kind Frank, disagreed for once with the marital opinion.

"He was good, and he loved her. She has always that to remember," Gertrude thought, as she watched Lucy going about her business with a calmness that alarmed her more than the most violent expressions of sorrow would have done.

---

1 The 7 February 1885 edition of *The Illustrated London News* reported the death of the special correspondent of *The Standard* during the Khartoum Relief Expedition.

"Dear little Frank! I wonder if he is really dead," Phyllis reflected, staring with wide eyes at the house opposite, rather as if she expected to see a ghost issue from the door.

Fortunately for the Lorimers they had little time for brooding over their troubles. Their success had proved itself no ephemeral one. As people returned to town, work began to flow in upon them from all sides, and their hands were full. Labour and sorrow, the common human portion, were theirs, and they accepted them with courage, if not, indeed, with resignation. September and October glided by, and now the winter was upon them.

CHAPTER XVIII

Phyllis

Die æltre Tochter gæhnet
"Ich will nicht verhungern bei euch,
Ich gehe morgen zum Grafen,
Und der ist verliebt und reich."
Heine [1]

"Lucy, dear, you must go."

"But, Gerty, you can never manage to get through the work alone."

"I will make Phyllis help me. It will be the best thing for her, and she works better than any of us when she chooses."

The sisters were standing together in the studio, discussing a letter which Lucy held in her hand—an appeal from the heart-broken "old folks" that she, who was to have been their daughter, should visit them in their sorrow.

---

1 Heinrich Heine (1797-1856), *Buch der Lieder* [*Book of Songs*] (1827): "Then yawns the eldest daughter, / 'I will starve no longer here; / I will go to the Count to-morrow, / He is rich, and he loves me dear.'" From "Homeward Bound," *Poems and Ballads of Heinrich Heine*(1881), translated by Emma Lazarus. Heine was a German poet, Jewish by birth and a converted Christian, who wrote with intense ambivalence about his identity. Levy's interest in Heine appears in many of her essays on Jewish subjects, and Lady Katie Magnus included Levy's translation of one of Heine's poems in her book *Jewish Portraits* (1888).

"It is simply your duty to go," went on Gertrude, who was consumed with anxiety concerning her sister; then added, involuntarily, "if you think you can bear it."

A light came into Lucy's eyes.

"Is there anything that one cannot bear?"

She turned away, and began mechanically fixing a negative into one of the printing frames. She remembered how, on that last day, Frank had planned the visit to Cornwall. Was he not going to show her every nook and corner of the old home, which many a time before he had so minutely described to her? The place had for long been familiar to her imagination, and now she was in fact to make acquaintance with it; that was all. What availed it to dwell on contrasts?

The sisters spoke little of Lucy's approaching journey, which was fixed for some days after the receipt of the letter; and one cold and foggy November afternoon found her helping Mrs. Maryon with her little box down the stairs, while Matilda went for a cab.

At the same moment Gertrude issued from the studio with her outdoor clothes on.

"No one is likely to come in this Egyptian darkness," she said; "it is four o'clock already, and I am going to take you to Paddington."[1]

"That will be delightful, if you think you may risk it," answered Lucy, who looked very pale in her black clothes.

"I have left a message with Mrs. Maryon to be delivered in the improbable event of 'three customers coming in,' as they did in *John Gilpin*,"[2] said Gertrude, with a feeble attempt at sprightliness.

Matilda appeared at this point to announce that the cab was at the door.

"Where is Phyllis?" cried Lucy. "I have not said good-bye to her."

"She went out two hours ago, miss," put in Mrs. Maryon, in her sad voice.

"No doubt," said Gertrude, "she has gone to Conny's. I think she goes there a great deal in these days."

---

1 Paddington Station was the London terminal for the Great Western Railway. As in Levy's time, Paddington is located in Bayswater, a short distance west of the Lorimers' shop.

2 William Cowper (1731-1800), *The Diverting History of John Gilpin* (1782).

Mrs. Maryon looked up quickly, then set about helping Matilda hoist the box on to the cab.

"How bitterly cold it is," cried Gertrude, with a shudder, as they crossed the threshold.

An orange-coloured fog hung in the air, congealed by the sudden change of temperature into a thick and palpable mass.

"I shouldn't be surprised if we had snow," observed Mrs. Maryon, shaking her head.

"Oh, how could Phyllis be so wicked as to go out?" cried Gertrude, as the cab drove off: "and her cough has been so troublesome lately."

"I think she has been looking more like her old self the last week or two," said Lucy; then added, "Do you know that Mr. Darrell is back? I forgot to tell you that I met him in Regent's Park the other day."

"I hope he will not wish to renew the sittings; but no doubt he has found some fresh whim by this time. I wish he had let Phyllis alone; he did her no good."

"Poor little soul, I am afraid she finds it dismal," said Lucy.

"I mean to plan a little dissipation for us both when you are away—the theatre, probably," said Gertrude, who felt remorsefully that in her anxiety concerning Lucy she had rather neglected Phyllis.

"Yes, do, and take care of yourself, dear old Gerty," said Lucy, as the cab drew up at Paddington station.

The sisters embraced long and silently, and in a few minutes Lucy was steaming westward in a third-class carriage, and Gertrude was making her way through the fog to Praed Street station.[1] At Baker Street she perceived that Mrs. Maryon's prophecy was undergoing fulfilment; the fog had lifted a little, and flakes of snow were falling at slow intervals.

Before the door of Number 20B a small brougham was standing—a brougham, as she observed by the light of the street lamp, with a coronet emblazoned on the panels.

"Lord Watergate is in the studio, miss," announced Mrs. Maryon, who opened the door; "he only came a minute ago, and preferred to wait. I have lit the lamp." As Gertrude was going

---

1   Praed Street Station was the underground railway station, on the Metro-
    politan line (now the Circle and District lines) adjacent to Paddington
    Station and the Great Western Hotel. The narration implies that
    Gertrude returns home from Paddington Station by way of the under-
    ground railway to Baker Street Station.

towards the studio the woman ran up to her, and put a note in her hand. "I forgot to give you this," she said. "I found it in the letter-box a minute after you left."

Gertrude, glancing hastily at the envelope, recognised, with some surprise, the childish handwriting of her sister Phyllis, and concluded that she had decided to remain overnight at the Devonshires.

"She might have remembered that I was alone," she thought, a little wistfully as she opened the door of the waiting-room.

Lord Watergate advanced to meet her, and they shook hands gravely. She had not seen him since the night of the *conversazione* at the Berkeley Galleries. His ample presence seemed to fill the little room.

"It is a shame," he said, "to come down upon you at this time of night."

She laid Phyllis' note on the table, and turned to him with a smile of deprecation.

"Won't you read your letter before we embark on the question of slides?"

"Thank you. I will just open it."

She broke the seal, advanced to the lamp, and cast her eye hastily over the letter. But something in the contents seemed to rivet her attention, to merit more than a casual glance. For some moments she stood absorbed in the carelessly-written sheet; then, suddenly, an exclamation of sorrow and astonishment burst from her lips.

Lord Watergate advanced towards her.

"Miss Lorimer, you are in some trouble. Can I help you, or shall I go away?"

She looked up, half-bewildered, into the strong and gentle face. Then realising nothing, save that here was a friendly human presence, put the letter into his hand.

This is what he read.

"My Dear Gerty,—This is to tell you that I am not coming home to-night—am not coming home again at all, in fact. I am going to marry Mr. Darrell, who will take me to Italy, where the weather is decent, and where I shall get well. For you know, I am horribly seedy, Gerty, and very dull.

"Of course you will be angry with me; you never liked Sidney, and you will think it ungrateful of me, perhaps, to go off like this. But oh, Gerty, it has been so dismal, especially since we heard about poor little Frank. Sidney hates a fuss,

and so do I. We both of us prefer to go off on the Q.T., as Fred says. With love from
    "Phyllis."

As Lord Watergate finished this characteristic epistle, an exclamation more fraught with horror than Gertrude's own burst from his lips. He strode across the room, crushing the paper in his hands.

"Lord Watergate!" Gertrude faced him, pale, questioning: a nameless dread clutched at her.

Something in her face struck him. Stopping short in front of her, in tones half paralysed with horror, he said—

"Don't you know?"

"Do I know?" she echoed his words, bewildered.

"Darrell is married. He does not live with his wife; but it is no secret."

The red tables and chairs, the lamp, Lord Watergate himself, whose voice sounded fierce and angry, were whirling round Gertrude in hopeless confusion; and then suddenly she remembered that this was an old story; that she had known it always, from the first moment when she had looked upon Darrell's face.

Gertrude closed her eyes, but she did not faint. She remained standing, while one hand rested on the table for support. Yes, she had known it; had stood by powerless, paralysed, while this thing approached; had seen it even as Cassandra[1] saw from afar the horror which she had been unable to avert.

Opening her eyes, she met the gaze, grieved, pitiful, indignant, of her companion.

"What is to be done?"

Her lips framed the words with difficulty.

A pause; then he said—

"I cannot hold out much hope. But will you come with me to—to—his house and make inquiries?"

She bowed her head, and gathering herself together, led the way from the room.

The snow was falling thick and fast as they emerged from the house, and Lord Watergate handed her into his brougham. It had grown very dark, and the wind had risen.

---

1 A daughter of Priam, the king of Troy during the Trojan War, who possessed the gift of prophecy; more generally "Cassandra" refers to one who predicts misfortunes.

"The Sycamores," said Lord Watergate to his coachman, as he took his seat by Gertrude, and drew the fur about her knees.

Mrs. Maryon, watching from the shop window, shrugged her shoulders.

"Who would have thought it? But you never can tell. And that Phyllis! It's twice I've seen her with the fair-haired gentleman, with his beard cut like a foreigner's. It's what you'd expect from her, poor creature—but Gertrude!"

"They have got the rooms on lease," grumbled Mr. Maryon, from among his pestles and mortars.

CHAPTER XIX

The Sycamores

How the world is made for each of us!
    How all we perceive and know in it
Tends to some moment's product thus,
    When a soul declares itself—to wit,
By its fruit the thing it does!
Robert Browning[1]

The carriage rolled on its way through the snow to St. John's Wood, while its two occupants sat side by side in silence. Now that they had set out, each felt the hopelessness of the errand on which they were bound, to which only that first stifling moment of horror, that absolute need of action, had prompted them.

The brougham stopped in the road before the gate of The Sycamores.

"We had better walk up the drive," said Lord Watergate, and opened the carriage door.

By this time the snow lay deep on the road and the roofs of the houses; the trees looked mere blotches of greyish-white, seen through the rapid whirl of falling flakes, which it made one giddy to contemplate.

"A terrible night for a journey," thought Lord Watergate, as he opened the big gate; but he said nothing, fearing to arouse false hopes in the breast of his companion.

---

1 "By the Fire-Side" (1855), stanza 49.

They wound together up the drive, the dark mass of the house partly hidden by the curving, laurel-lined path, and further obscured by the veil of falling snow.

Then, suddenly, something pierced through Gertrude's numbness; she stopped short.

"Look!" she cried, beneath her breath.

They were now in full sight of the house. The upper windows were dark; the huge windows of the studio were shuttered close, but through the chinks were visible lines and points of mellow light.

Lord Watergate laid his hand on her arm. He thought: "That is just like Darrell, to have doubled back. But even then we may be too late."

He said: "Miss Lorimer, if they are there, what are you going to do?"

"I am going to tell my sister that she has been deceived, and to bring her home with me."

Gertrude spoke very low, but without hesitation. Somewhere, in the background of her being, sorrow, and shame, and anger were lurking; at present she was keenly conscious of nothing but an irresistible impulse to action.

"That she has been deceived!" Lord Watergate turned away his face. Had Phyllis, indeed, been deceived, and was it not a fool's errand on which they were bent?

They mounted the steps, and he rang the bell; then, by the light of the hanging lamp, while the snow swirled round and fell upon them both, he looked into her white, tense face.

"Do not hope for anything. It is most probable that they are not there."

A long, breathless moment, then the door was thrown open, revealing the solemn manservant standing out against the lighted vestibule.

"I wish to see Mr. Darrell," said Lord Watergate, shortly.

"He's not at home, your lordship."

Gertrude pressed her hand to her heart.

"He is at home to me, as you perfectly well know."

"He has gone abroad, your lordship."

Gertrude swayed forward a little, steadying herself against the lintel, where she stood in darkness behind Lord Watergate.

"There are lights in the studio, and you must let me in," said Lord Watergate, sternly.

The man's face betrayed him.

"I shall lose my place, my lord."

"I am sorry for you, Shaw. You had better make off, and leave the responsibility with me."

The man wavered, took the coin from Lord Watergate's hand, then, turning, went slowly back to his own quarters.

Gertrude came forward into the light.

"You must not come in, Lord Watergate."

Her mind worked with curious rapidity; she saw that a meeting between the two men must be avoided.

"I cannot let you go alone. You do not know—"

"I am prepared for anything. Lord Watergate, spare my sister's shame."

She had passed him, with set, tragic face. He saw the slim, rapid figure, in the black, snow-covered dress, make its way down the passage, then disappear behind the curtain which guarded the entrance to the studio.

Gertrude had entered noiselessly, and, pausing on the threshold, hidden in shadow, remained there motionless a moment's space.

Every detail of the great room, seen but once before, smote on her sense with a curious familiarity. It had been wintry daylight on the occasion of her former presence there; now a mellow radiance of shaded, artificial light was diffused throughout the apartment, a radiance concentrated to subdued brilliance in the immediate neighbourhood of the fireplace.

A wood fire, with leaping blue flames, was piled on the hearth, its light flickering fitfully on the surrounding objects; on the tiger-skin rug, the tall, rich screen of faded Spanish leather; on Darrell himself, who lounged on a low couch, his blonde head outlined against the screen, a cloud of cigarette smoke issuing from his lips, as he looked from under his eye-lids at the figure before him.

It was Phyllis who stood there by the little table, on which lay some fruit and some coffee, in rose-coloured cups. Phyllis, yet somebody new and strange; not the pretty child that her sisters had loved, but a beautiful wanton in a loose, trailing garment, shimmering, wonderful, white and lustrous as a pearl; Phyllis, with her brown hair turned to gold in the light of the lamp swung above her; Phyllis, with diamonds on the slender fingers, that played with a cluster of bloom-covered grapes.

For a moment, the warmth, the overpowering fragrance of hot-house flowers, most of all, the sight of that figure by the table, had robbed Gertrude of power to move or speak. But in her heart the storm, which had been silently gathering, was growing ready to burst. For the time, the varied emotions which devoured her had concentrated themselves into a white heat of fury, which kindled all her being.

The flames leapt, the logs crackled pleasantly. Darrell blew a whiff of smoke to the ceiling; Phyllis smiled, then suddenly into that bright scene glided a black and rigid figure, with glowing eyes and tragic face; with the snow sprinkled on the old cloak, and clinging in the wisps of wind-blown hair.

"Phyllis," it said in level tones; "come home with me at once. Mr. Darrell cannot marry you; he is married already."

Phyllis shrank back, with a cry.

"Oh, Gerty, how you frightened me! What do you mean by coming down on one like this?"

Her voice shook, through its petulance; she whisked round so suddenly that her long dress caught in the little table, which fell to the ground with a crash.

Darrell had sprung to his feet with an exclamation. "By God, what brings that woman here!"

Gertrude turned and faced him.

His face was livid with passion; his prominent eyes, for once wide open, glared at her in rage and hatred.

Gertrude met his glance with eyes that glowed with a passion yet fiercer than his own.

Elements, long smouldering, had blazed forth at last. Face to face they stood; face to face, while the silent battle raged between them.

Then with a curious elation, a mighty throb of what was almost joy, Gertrude knew that she, not he, the man of whom she had once been afraid, was the stronger of the two. For one brief moment some fierce instinct in her heart rejoiced.

Phyllis, cowering in the background, Phyllis, pale as her splendid dress, shrank back, mystified, afraid. Her light soul shivered before the blast of passions in which, though she had helped to raise them, she felt herself to have no part nor lot.

Reckoned by time, the encounter of those two hostile spirits was but brief; a moment, and Darrell had dropped his eyes, and was saying in something like his own languid voice—

"To what may I ascribe this—honour?"

Gertrude turned in silence to her sister—

"Take off that—" (she indicated the shimmering garment with a pause), "and come with me."

Darrell sneered from the background; "Your sister has decided on remaining here."

"Phyllis!" said Gertrude, looking at her.

Phyllis began to sob.

"Oh, Gerty, what shall I do? Don't look at me like that. My dress is there behind the screen; and my hat. Oh, Gerty, I shall never get it on; I am so much taller."

With rapid fingers Gertrude had unfastened her own long, black cloak, and was wrapping it about her sister.

"Great heavens," cried Darrell, coming forward and seizing her hands; "You shall not take her away! You have no earthly right to take her against her will."

With a cold fury of disgust she shook off his touch.

"Oh, Sidney, I think I'd better go. I oughtn't to have come." Phyllis' voice sounded touchingly childish.

Something in the pleading tones stirred his blood curiously.

"Do you know," he cried, addressing himself to Gertrude, who was deliberately drawing the rings from her sister's passive hands, "Do you know what a night it is? That if you take her away you will kill her? Great God, you paragon of virtue, don't you see how ill she is?"

She swept her glance over him in icy disdain; then going up to the mantelpiece, laid the rings on the shelf.

"I swear to you," he cried, "that I will leave the house this hour, this minute. That I will never return to it; that I will never see her again—Phyllis!"

At the last word, his voice had dropped to a low and passionate key; he stretched out his arms, but Gertrude coming between them put her strong desperate grasp about Phyllis, who swayed forward with closed eyes. Darrell retreated with a muffled exclamation of grief and rage and baffled purpose, and Gertrude half led, half carried her sister from the room, the hateful satin garment trailing noisily behind them from beneath the black cloak.

A tall figure came forward from the doorway; the door was standing open; and the white whirlpool was visible against the darkness outside.

"She has fainted," said Gertrude, in a low voice.

Lord Watergate lifted her gently in his arms. At the same moment Darrell emerged from the studio, then remained rooted to the spot, dismayed and sullen, at the sight of his friend.

"You are a scoundrel, Darrell," said Lord Watergate, in very clear, deliberate tones; then, his burden in his arms, he stepped out into the darkness, Gertrude closing the door behind them.

Half an hour later the brougham stopped before the house in Upper Baker Street.

Lord Watergate, when he had carried the fainting girl upstairs, went himself for a doctor.

"I think I have killed her," said Gertrude, before he went, looking up at him from over the prostrate figure of her sister; "and if it were all to be done again—I would do it."

Mrs. Maryon asked no questions; her genuine kindness and helpfulness were called forth by this crisis; and her suspicions of Gertrude had vanished for ever.

CHAPTER XX

In the Sick-Room

A riddle that one shrinks
To challenge from the scornful sphinx.
D. G. Rossetti[1]

The doctor's verdict was unhesitating enough. Phyllis' doom, as more than one who knew her foresaw, was sealed. The shock and the exposure had only hastened an end which for long had been inevitable. Consumption, complicated with heart disease, both in advanced stages, held her in their grasp; added to these, a severe bronchial attack had set in since the night of the snowstorm, and her life might be said to hang by a thread. It might be a matter of days, said the cautious physician, of weeks, or even months.

"Would a journey to the south, at an earlier stage of her illness, have availed to save her?" Gertrude asked, with white, mechanical lips.

It was possible, was the answer, that it would have prolonged her life. But almost from the first, it seemed, the shadow of the grave must have rested on this beautiful human blossom.

"Death in her face," muttered Mrs. Maryon, grimly; "I saw it there, I have always seen it."

Meanwhile, people came and went in Upper Baker Street; sympathetic, inquisitive, bustling.

---

1   "Jenny" (1870), lines 280-81. These lines conclude the stanza that
     begins: "Yet, Jenny, looking long at you, / The woman almost fades from
     view. / A cipher of a man's changeless sum / Of lust, past, present, and
     to come, / Is left."

Fanny, dismayed and tearful, appeared daily at the invalid's bedside, laden with grapes and other delicacies.

"Poor old Fan," said Phyllis; "how shocked she would be if she knew everything. Don't you think it is your duty, Gerty, to Mr. Marsh, to let him know?"

Aunt Caroline drove across from Lancaster Gate, rebuke implied in every fold of her handsome dress.

"I cannot think," she remarked to her friends, "how Gertrude could have reconciled such culpable neglect of that poor child's health to her conscience."

Gertrude avoided her aunt, saying to herself, in the bitterness of her humiliation: "It is the Aunt Carolines of this world who are right. I ought to have listened to her. She understood human nature better than I."

The Devonshires, who had not long returned from Germany, were unremitting in their kindness, the slackened bonds between the two families growing tight once more in this hour of need.

Lord Watergate made regular inquiries in Baker Street. Gertrude found his presence more endurable than that of the people with whom she had to dissemble; he knew her secret; it was safe with him and she was almost glad that he knew it.

Gertrude had written a brief note to Lucy, telling her that Phyllis was very ill, but urging her to remain a week, at least, in Cornwall.

"She will need all the strength she can get up," thought Gertrude. She herself was performing prodigies of work without any conscious effort.

Frozen, tense, silent, she vibrated between the studio and the sick-room, moving as if in obedience to some hidden mechanism, a creature apparently without wants, emotions, or thoughts.

She had gathered from Phyllis' cynically frank remarks, that it was by the merest chance she had not been too late and that Darrell had returned to The Sycamores.

"We were going to cross on our way to Italy that very night," Phyllis said. "We drove to Charing Cross,[1] and then the snow began to fall, and I had such a fit of coughing that Sidney was frightened, and took me home to St. John's Wood."

Gertrude, who had received these confidences in silence, turned her head away with an involuntary, instinctive movement of repugnance at the mention of Darrell's Christian name.

---

1   Charing Cross Station opened in 1864 as the terminal for the South Eastern Railway.

"Gerty," said Phyllis, who lay back among the pillows, a white ghost with two burning red spots on her cheeks, "Gerty, it is only fair that I should tell you: Sidney isn't as bad as you think. He went away in the summer, because he was beginning to care about me too much; he only came back because he simply couldn't help himself. And—and, you will go out of the room and never speak to me again—I knew he had a wife, Gerty; I heard them talking about her at the Oakleys, the very first day I saw him. She was his model; she drinks like a fish, and is ten years older than he is—I put that in the letter about getting married, because I didn't quite know how to say it. I thought that very likely you knew."

Gertrude had walked to the window, and was pulling down the blind with stiff, blundering fingers. It was growing dusk and in less than half an hour Lucy would be home. It was just a week since she had set out for Cornwall.

"Shall you tell Lucy?" came the childish voice from among the pillows.

"I don't know. Lie still, Phyllis, and I will see if Mrs. Maryon has prepared the jelly for you."

"Kind old thing, Mrs. Maryon."

"Yes, indeed. She quite ignores the fact that we have no possible claim on her."

Gertrude met Mrs. Maryon on the dusky stairs, dish in hand.

"Do go and lie down, Miss Lorimer; or we shall have you knocked up too, and where should we be then? You mustn't let Miss Lucy see you like that."

Gertrude obeyed mechanically. Going into the sitting-room, she threw herself on the little hard sofa, her face pressed to the pillow.

She must have fallen into a doze, for the next thing of which she was aware was Lucy's voice in her ear, and opening her eyes she saw Lucy bending over her, candle in hand.

"Have you seen her?" she asked, sitting up with a dazed air.

"I am back this very minute. Gertrude, what have you been doing to yourself?"

"Oh, I am all right." She rose with a little smile. "Let me look at you, Lucy. Actually roses on your cheek."

"Gertrude, Gertrude, what has happened to you? Have I come—Oh, Gerty, have I come too late?"

"No," said Gertrude, "but she is very ill."

Lucy put her arms round her sister.

"And I have left you alone through these days. Oh, my poor Gerty."

They went upstairs together, and Lucy passed into the invalid's room, Gertrude remaining in the outer apartment, which was her own.

In about ten minutes Lucy came out sobbing. "Oh, Phyllis, Phyllis," she wept below her breath.

Gertrude, paler than ever, rose without a word, and went into the sick-room.

"Poor old Lucy, she looked as if she were going to cry. I asked her if she had any message for Frank," said Phyllis, as her sister sat down beside her, and adjusted the lamp.

"You are over-exciting yourself. Lie still, Phyllis."

"But, Gerty, I feel ever so much better to-night."

Silence. Gertrude sewed, and the invalid lay with closed eyes, but the flutter of the long lashes told that she was not asleep.

"Gerty!" In about half an hour the grey eyes had unclosed, and were fixed widely on her sister's face.

"What is it?"

"Gerty, am I really going to die?"

"You are very ill," said Gertrude, in a low voice.

"But to die—it seems so impossible, so difficult, somehow. Frank died; that was wonderful enough; but oneself!"

"Oh, my child," broke from Gertrude's lips.

"Don't be sorry. I have never been a nice person, but I don't funk somehow. I ought to, after being such a bad lot, but I don't. Gerty!"

"What is it?"

"Gerty, you have always been good to me; this last week as well. But that is the worst of you good people; you are hard as stones. You bring me jelly; you sit up all night with me—but you have never forgiven me. You know that is the truth."

Gertrude knelt by the bedside, a great compunction in her heart; she put her hand on that of Phyllis, who went on—

"And there is something I should wish to tell you. I am glad you came and fetched me away. The very moment I saw your angry, white face, and your old clothes with the snow on, I was glad. It is funny, if one comes to think of it. I was frightened, but I was glad."

Gertrude's head drooped lower and lower over the coverlet; her heart, which had been frozen within her, melted. In an agony of love, of remorse, she stretched out her arms, while her sobs came thick and fast, and gathered the wasted figure to her breast.

"Oh, Phyllis, oh, my child; who am I to forgive you? Is it a question of forgiveness between us? Oh, Phyllis, my little Phyllis, have you forgotten how I love you?"

Chapter XXI

The Last Act

Just as another woman sleeps.
D. G. Rossetti[1]

It was not till a week or two later that Gertrude brought herself to tell Lucy what had happened during her absence. It was a bleak afternoon in the beginning of December; in the next room lay Phyllis, cold and stiff and silent for ever; and Lucy was drearily searching in a cupboard for certain mourning garments which hung there. But suddenly, from the darkness of the lowest shelf, something shone up at her, a white, shimmering object, lying coiled there like a snake.

It was Phyllis' splendid satin gown, which Gertrude had flung there on the fateful night, and, from sheer repugnance, had never disturbed.

"But you must send it back," Lucy said, when in a few broken words her sister had explained its presence in the cupboard.

Lucy was very pale and very serious. She gathered up the satin gown, which nothing could have induced Gertrude to touch, folded it neatly, and began looking about for brown paper in which to enclose it.

The ghastly humour of the little incident struck Gertrude. "There is some string in the studio," she said, half-ironically, and went back to her post in the chamber of death.

In her long narrow coffin lay Phyllis; beautiful and still, with flowers between her hands. She had drifted out of life quietly enough a few days before; to-morrow she would be lying under the newly-turned cemetery sods.

Gertrude stood a moment, looking down at the exquisite face. On the breast of the dead girl lay a mass of pale violets which Lord Watergate had sent the day before, and as Gertrude looked,

---

1   "Jenny" (1870), line 177. The speaker describes Jenny as sleeping, although it is unclear whether she is dead or asleep.

there flashed through her mind, what had long since vanished from it, the recollection of Lord Watergate's peculiar interest in Phyllis.

It was explained now, she thought, as the image of another dead face floated before her vision. That also was the face of a woman, beautiful and frail; of a woman who had sinned. She had never seen the resemblance before; it was clear enough now.

Then she took up once again her watcher's seat at the bed-side, and strove to banish thought.

To do and do and do; that is all that remains to one in a world where thinking, for all save a few chosen beings, must surely mean madness.

She had fallen into a half stupor, when she was aware of a subtle sense of discomfort creeping over her; of an odour, strong and sweet and indescribably hateful, floating around her like a winged nightmare. Opening her eyes with an effort, she saw Mrs. Maryon standing gravely at the foot of the bed, an enormous wreath of tuberose in her hand.

Gertrude rose from her seat.

"Who sent those flowers?" she said, sternly.

"A servant brought them; he mentioned no name, and there is no card attached."

The woman laid the wreath on the coverlet and discreetly withdrew.

Gertrude stood staring at the flowers, fascinated. In the first moment of the cold yet stifling fury which stole over her, she could have taken them in her hands and torn them petal from petal.

One instant, she had stretched out her hand towards them; the next, she had turned away, sick with the sense of impotence, of loathing, of immeasurable disdain.

What weapons could avail against the impenetrable hide of such a man?

"She never cared for him," a vindictive voice whispered to her from the depths of her heart.

Then she shrank back afraid before the hatred which held pos-session of her soul. The passion which had animated her on the fateful evening of Phyllis' flight, the very strength which had caused her to prevail, seemed to her fearful and hideous things. She would fain have put the thought of them away; have banished them and all recollection of Darrell from her mind for ever.

It was a bleak December morning, with a touch of east wind in the air, when Phyllis was laid in her last resting-place.

To Gertrude all the sickening details of the little pageant were as the shadows of a nightmare. Standing rigid as a statue by the open grave, she was aware of nothing but the sweet, stifling fragrance of tuberose, which seemed to have detached itself from, and prevailed over, the softer scents of rose and violet, and to float up unmixed from the flower-covered coffin.

Lucy stood on one side of her, silent and pale with down-dropt eyes; Fanny sobbed vociferously on the other. Lord Watergate faced them with bent head. The tears rolled down Fred Devonshire's face as the burial service proceeded. Aunt Caroline looked like a vindictive ghost. Uncle Septimus wept silently.

It seemed a hideous act of cruelty to turn away at last and leave the poor child lying there alone, while the sexton shovelled the loose earth on to her coffin; hideous, but inevitable; and at midday Gertrude and Lucy drove back in the dismal coach to Baker Street, where Mr. Maryon had put up alternate shutters in the shop-window,[1] and the umbrella-maker had drawn down his blinds.

Gertrude, as she lay awake that night, heard the rain beating against the window-panes, and shuddered.

CHAPTER XXII

Hope and a Friend

Alas, I have grieved so I am hard to love.
Sonnets from the Portuguese[2]

Gertrude was sitting by the window with Constance Devonshire one bleak January afternoon.

Conny's face wore a softened look. The fierce, rebellious misery of her heart had given place to a gentler grief, the natural human sorrow for the dead.

This was a farewell visit. The next day she and her family were setting out for the South of France.

---

1 As a sign of mourning, shopkeepers would close their shutters and private residents would draw their blinds.
2 Elizabeth Barrett Browning, *Sonnets From the Portuguese* (1850), sonnet 35, line 12.

"I tried to make Fred come with me to-day," Constance was saying; "but he is dining with some kindred spirits at the Café Royal, and then going on to the Gaiety.[1] He said there would be no time."

Fred had been once to Baker Street since the unfortunate interview with Lucy; had paid a brief visit of condolence, when he had been very much on his dignity and very afraid of meeting Lucy's eye. The re-establishment of the old relations was not more possible than it usually is in such cases.

"How long do you expect to be at Cannes?" Gertrude said, after one of the pauses which kept on stretching themselves baldly across the conversation.

"Till the end of March, probably. Isn't Lucy coming up to say 'good-bye' to a fellow?"

"She will be up soon. She is much distressed about the over-exposure of some plates, and is trying to remedy the misfortune. Do you know, by the by, that we are thinking of taking an apprentice? Mr. Russel has found a girl—a lady—who will pay us a premium, and probably live with us."

"I think that is a good plan," said Conny, staring wistfully out of the window.

How strange it seemed, after all that had happened, to be sitting here quietly, talking about over-exposed negatives, premiums, and apprentices.

Looking out into the familiar street, with its teeming memories of a vivid life now quenched for ever, she said to herself, as Gertrude had often said: "It is not possible."

One day, surely, the door would open to give egress to the well-known figure; one day they would hear his footstep on the stairs, his voice in the little room. Even as the thought struck her, Constance was aware of a sound as of some one ascending, and started with a sudden beating of the heart.

The next moment Matilda flung open the door, and Lord Watergate came, unannounced, into the room.

Gertrude rose gravely to meet him.

Since the accident, which had brought him into such intimate connection with the Lorimers' affairs, his kindness had been as unremitting as it had been unobtrusive.

Gertrude had several times reproached herself for taking it as a matter of course; for being roused to no keener fervour of grat-

---

1 The Gaiety Theatre, located in the Strand, opened in 1868 and ran operettas, dramas, and burlesques.

itude; yet something in his attitude seemed to preclude all expression of commonplaces.

It was no personal favour that he offered. To stretch out one's hand to a drowning creature is no act of gallantry; it is but recognition of a natural human obligation.

Lord Watergate took a seat between the two girls, and, after a few remarks, Constance declared her intention of seeking Lucy in the studio.

"Tell Lucy to come up when she has soaked her plates to her satisfaction," said Gertrude, a little vexed at this desertion.

To have passed through such experiences together as she and Lord Watergate, makes the casual relations of life more difficult. These two people, to all intents and purposes strangers, had been together in those rare moments of life when the elaborate paraphernalia of everyday intercourse is thrown aside; when soul looks straight to soul through no intervening veil; when human voice answers human voice through no medium of an actor's mask.

We lose with our youth the blushes, the hesitations, the distressing outward marks of embarrassment; but, perhaps, with most of us, the shyness, as it recedes from the surface, only sinks deeper into the soul.

As the door closed on Constance, Lord Watergate turned to Gertrude.

"Miss Lorimer," he said, "I am afraid your powers of endurance have to be further tried."

"What is it?" she said, while a listless incredulity that anything could matter to her now stole over her, dispersing the momentary cloud of self-consciousness.

Lord Watergate leaned forward, regarding her earnestly.

"There has been news," he said, slowly, "of poor young Jermyn."

Gertrude started.

"You mean," she said, "that they have found him—that there is no doubt."

"On the contrary; there is every doubt."

She looked at him bewildered.

"Miss Lorimer, there is, I am afraid, much cruel suspense in store for you, and possibly to no purpose. I came here to-day to prepare you for what you will hear soon enough. I chanced to learn from official quarters what will be in every paper in England to-morrow. There is a rumour that Jermyn has been seen alive."

"Lord Watergate!" Gertrude sprang to her feet, trembling in every limb.

He rose also, and continued, his eyes resting on her face meanwhile:—

"Native messengers have arrived at head-quarters from the interior, giving an account of two Englishmen, who, they say, are living as prisoners in one of the hostile towns. The descriptions of these prisoners correspond to those of Steele and Jermyn."

"Lucy!" came faintly from Gertrude's lips.

"It is chiefly for your sister's sake that I have come here. The rumour will be all over the town to-morrow. Had you not better prepare her for this, at the same time impressing on her the extreme probability of its baselessness?"

"I wish it could be kept from her altogether."

"Perhaps even that might be managed until further confirmation arrives. I cannot conceal from you that at present I attach little value to it. It was in the nature of things that such a rumour should arise; neither of the poor fellows having actually been seen dead."

"What steps will be taken?" asked Gertrude, after a pause. She had not the slightest belief that Frank would ever be among them again; she and Lucy had gone over for ever to the great majority of the unfortunate.

"A rescue-party is to be organised at once. The war being practically at an end, it would probably resolve itself into a case of ransom, if there were any truth in the whole thing. I may be in possession of further news a little before the newspapers. Needless to say that I shall bring it here at once."

He took up his hat and stood a moment looking down at her.

"Lord Watergate, we do not even attempt to thank you for your kindness."

"I have been able, unfortunately, to do so little for you. I wish to-day that I had come to you as the bringer of good tidings; I am destined, it seems, to be your bird of ill-omen."

He dropped his eyes suddenly, and Gertrude turned away her face. A pause fell between them; then she said—

"Will it be long before news of any reliability can reach us?"

"I cannot tell; it may be a matter of days, of weeks, or even months."

"I fear it will be impossible to keep the rumour from my poor Lucy."

"I am afraid so. I trust to you to save her from false hopes."

"So I am to be Cassandra," thought Gertrude, a little wistfully. She was always having some hideous *rôle* or other thrust upon her.

Lord Watergate moved towards the door.

A sudden revulsion of feeling came over her.

"Perhaps," she said, "it is true."

He caught her mood. "Perhaps it is."

They stood smiling at one another like two children.

Constance Devonshire coming upstairs a few minutes later found Gertrude standing alone in the middle of the room, a vague smile playing about her face. A suspicion that was not new gathered force in Conny's mind. Going up to her friend she said, with meaning—

"Gerty, what has Lord Watergate been saying to you?"

"Conny, Conny, can you keep a secret?"

And then Gertrude told her of the new hope, vague and sweet and perilous, which Lord Watergate had brought with him.

"But it is true, Gerty; it really is," Conny said, while the tears poured down her cheeks; "I have always known that the other thing was not possible. Oh, Gerty, just to see him, just to know he is alive—will not that be enough to last one all the days of one's life?"

But this mood of impersonal exaltation faded a little when Constance went back to Queen's Gate, where everything was in a state of readiness for the projected flitting. She lay awake sobbing with mingled feelings half through the night.

"Even Gerty," she thought; "I am going to lose her too." For she remembered the smile in Gertrude's eyes that afternoon when she had found her standing alone after Lord Watergate's visit; a smile to which she chose to attach meanings which concerned the happiness of neither Frank nor Lucy.

CHAPTER XXIII

A Dismissal

O thou of little faith, what hast thou done?[1]

Lucy has always since maintained that the days which followed Lord Watergate's communication were the very worst that she ever went through. The fluctuations of hope and fear, the delays, the prolonged strain of uncertainty coming upon her afresh, after all that had already been endured, could be nothing less than torture even to a person of her well-balanced and well-regulated temperament.

"To have to bear it all for the second time," thought poor Gertrude, whose efforts to spare her sister could not, in the nature of things, be very successful.

A terrible fear that Lucy would break down altogether and slip from her grasp, haunted her night and day. The world seemed to her peopled with shadows, which she could do nothing more than clutch at as they passed by, she herself the only creature of any permanence of them all. But gradually the tremulous, flickering flame of hope grew brighter and steadier; then changed into a glad certainty. And one wonderful day, towards the end of March, Frank was with them once more: Frank, thinner and browner perhaps, but in no respect the worse for his experiences; Frank, as they had always known him—kind and cheery and sympathetic; with the old charming confidence in being cared for.

"And I was not there," he cried, regretful, self-reproachful, when Lucy had told him the details of their sad story.

"I thought always, 'If Frank were here!'"

"I think I should have killed him," said Frank, in all sincerity; and Lucy drew closer to him, grateful for the non-fulfilment of her wish.

They were standing together in the studio. It was the day after Jermyn's return, and Gertrude was sitting listlessly upstairs, her busy hands for once idle in her lap. In a few days April would have come round again for the second time since their father's death.

---

1 Matthew 14.31 reads: "And immediately Jesus stretched forward his hand, and caught him [Peter], and said unto him, O thou of little faith, wherefore didst thou doubt?"

What a lifetime of experience had been compressed into those two years, she thought, her apathetic eyes mechanically following the green garment of the High School mistress, as she whisked past down the street.

She knew that it is often so in human life—a rapid succession of events; a vivid concentration of every sort of experience in a brief space; then long, grey stretches of eventless calm. She knew also how it is when events, for good or evil, rain down thus on any group of persons.—The majority are borne to new spheres, for them the face of things has changed completely. But nearly always there is one, at least, who, after the storm is over, finds himself stranded and desolate, no further advanced on his journey than before.

The lightning has not smitten him, nor the waters drowned him, nor has any stranger vessel borne him to other shores. He is only battered, and shattered, and weary with the struggle; has lost, perhaps, all he cared for, and is permanently disabled for further travelling. Gertrude smiled to herself as she pursued the little metaphor, then, rising, walked across the room to the mirror which hung above the mantelpiece. As her eye fell on her own reflection she remembered Lucy Snowe's words—

"I saw myself in the glass, in my mourning dress, a faded, hollow-eyed vision. Yet I thought little of the wan spectacle…. I still felt life at life's sources."[1]

That was the worst of it; one was so terribly vital. Inconceivable as it seemed, she knew that one day she would be up again, fighting the old fight, not only for existence, but for happiness itself. She was only twenty-five when all was said; much lay, indeed, behind her, but there was still the greater part of her life to be lived.

She started a little as the handle of the door turned, and Mrs. Maryon announced Lord Watergate. She gave him her hand with a little smile: "Have you been in the studio?" she said, as they both seated themselves.

"Yes; Jermyn opened the door himself, and insisted on my coming in, though, to tell you the truth, I should have hesitated about entering had I had any choice in the matter—which I hadn't."

---

1 Charlotte Brontë (1816-55), *Villette* (1853), chapter four. Lucy Snowe, the narrator of this novel, an orphan cast out in the world on her own resources, has just been described as "a worn-out creature." The full passage Levy quotes is: "The blight, I believed, was chiefly external: I still felt life at life's sources."

"Lucy has picked up wonderfully, hasn't she?"

"She looks her old self already. Jermyn tells me they are to be married almost immediately."

"Yes. I suppose they told you also that Lucy is going to carry on the business afterwards."

"In the old place?"

"No. We have got rid of the rest of the lease, and they propose moving into some place where studios for both of them can be arranged."

"And you?"

"It is uncertain. I think Lucy will want me for the photography."

"Miss Lorimer, first of all you must do something to get well. You will break down altogether if you don't."

Something in the tone of the blunt words startled her; she turned away, a nameless terror taking possession of her.

"Oh, I shall be all right after a little holiday."

"You have been looking after everybody else; doing everybody's work, bearing everybody's troubles." He stopped short suddenly, and added, with less earnestness, "*Quis custodet custodiem?*[1] Do you know any Latin, Miss Lorimer?"

She rose involuntarily; then stood rather helplessly before him. It was ridiculous that these two clever people should be so shy and awkward; those others down below in the studio had never undergone any such uncomfortable experience; but then neither had had to graft the new happiness on an old sorrow; for neither had the shadow of memory darkened hope.

Gertrude went over to the mantelshelf, and began mechanically arranging some flowers in a vase. For once, she found Lord Watergate's presence disturbing and distressing; she was confused, unhappy, distrustful of herself; she wished when she turned her head that she would find him gone. But he was standing near her, a look of perplexity, of trouble, in his face.

"Miss Lorimer," he said, and there was no mistaking the note in his voice, "have I come too soon? Is it too soon for me to speak?"

She was overwhelmed, astonished, infinitely agitated. Her soul shrank back afraid. What had the closer human relations ever brought her but sorrow unutterable, unending? Some blind instinct within her prompted her words, as she said, lifting her

---

1 "Who will keep the keeper?" Levy (or Lord Watergate) singularizes the conventional adage: *quis custodiet ipsos custodes?*

head, with the attitude of one who would avert an impending blow—

"Oh, it is too soon, too soon."

He stood a moment looking at her with his deep eyes.

"I shall come back," he said.

"No, oh, no!"

She hid her face in her hands, and bent her head to the marble. What he offered was not for her; for other women, for happier women, for better women, perhaps, but not for her.

When she raised her head he was gone.

The momentary, unreasonable agitation passed away from her, leaving her cold as a stone, and she knew what she had done. By a lightning flash her own heart stood revealed to her. How incredible it seemed, but she knew that it was true: all this dreary time, when the personal thought had seemed so far away from her, her greatest personal experience had been silently growing up—no gourd of a night, but a tree to last through the ages. She, who had been so strong for others, had failed miserably for herself.

Love and happiness had come to her open-handed, and she had sent them away. Love and happiness? Oh, those will o' the wisps had danced ere this before her cheated sight. Love and happiness? Say rather, pity and a mild peace. It is not love that lets himself be so easily denied.

Happiness? That was not for such as she; but peace, it would have come in time; now it was possible that it would never come at all.

All the springs of her being had seemed for so long to be frozen at their source; now, in this one brief moment of exaltation, half-rapture, half-despair, the ice melted, and her heart was flooded with the stream.

Covering her face with her hands, she knelt by his empty chair, and a great cry rose up from her soul:—the human cry for happiness—the woman's cry for love.

CHAPTER XXIV

At Last

We sat when shadows darken,
　　And let the shadows be;
Each was a soul to hearken,
　　Devoid of eyes to see.

You came at dusk to find me;
　　I knew you well enough....
Oh, Lights that dazzle and blind me—
　　It is no friend, but Love!
A. Mary F. Robinson[1]

Hotel Prince de Galles, Cannes,
April 27th.

My dearest Gerty,—You shall have a letter to-day, though it is more than you deserve. Why do you never write to me? Now that you have safely married your young people, you have positively no excuse. By the by, the poor innocent mater read the announcement of the wedding out loud at breakfast to-day.— Fred got crimson and choked in his coffee, and I had a silent fit of laughter. However, he is all right by now, playing tennis with a mature lady with yellow hair, whom he much affects, and whom papa scornfully denominates a "hotel hack."

All this, let me tell you, is preliminary. I have a piece of news for you, but somehow it won't come out. Not that it is anything to be ashamed of. The fact is, Gerty, I am going the way of all flesh, and am about to be married. Believe me, it is the most sensible course for a woman to take. I hope you will follow my good example.

Do you remember Sapho's words: "J'ai tant aimé; j'ai besoin d'être aimée"?[2] Do not let the quotation shock you; neither take

---

1　A. Mary F. Robinson (1857-1944), "Love Without Wings," *An Italian Garden: A Book of Songs* (1886), stanza 2, lines 1-8. See Appendix C3.

2　"I have loved so much; I have need to be loved," *An Italian Garden: A Book of Songs* (1886), a few phrases from the end of Alphonse Daudet's novel *Sappho* (1884).

it too seriously. I think Mr. Graham—you know Lawrence Graham?—does care as caring goes and as men go. He came out here, on purpose, a fortnight ago, and yesterday we settled it between us...."

Gertrude read no further; the thin, closely-written sheet fell from her hand; she sat staring vaguely before her.

Conny's letter, with its cheerfulness, partly real, partly affected, hurt her taste, and depressed her rather unreasonably.

This was the hardest feature of her lot: for the people she loved, the people who had looked up to her, she had been able to do nothing at all.

She was sitting alone in the dismantled studio on this last day of April. To-morrow Lucy and Frank would have returned from Cornwall, and have taken possession of the new home.

Her own plans for the present were vague.

One of her stories, after various journeys to editorial offices, had at last come back to her in the form of proof, supplemented, moreover, by what seemed to her a handsome cheque.

She had arranged, on the strength of this, to visit a friend in Florence, for some months; after that period she would in all probability take part with Lucy in the photography business.

There was no fire lighted, and the sun, which in the earlier part of the day had warmed the room, had set. Most of the furniture and properties had already gone to the new studio, but some yet remained, massed and piled in the gloom.

The black sign-board, with its gold lettering, stood upright and forlorn in a corner, as though conscious that its day was over for ever. Gertrude had been busying herself with turning out a cupboard, but the light had failed, and she had ceased from her work.

A very dark hour came to Gertrude, crouching there in the dusk and cold, amid the dismantled workshop which seemed to symbolize her own life.

She who held unhappiness ignoble and cynicism a poor thing, had lost for the moment all joy of living and all belief. The little erection of philosophy, of hope, of self-reliance, which she had been at such pains to build, seemed to be crumbling about her ears; all the struggles and sacrifices of life looked vain things. What had life brought her, but disillusion, bitterness, an added sense of weakness?

She rose at last and paced the room.

"This will pass," she said to herself; "I am out of sorts; and it is not to be wondered at."

She sat down in the one empty chair the room contained, and leaning her head on her hand, let her thoughts wander at will.

Her eyes roved about the little dusky room which was so full of memories for her. Shadows peopled it; dream-voices filled it with sound.

Lucy and Phyllis and Frank moved hither and thither with jest and laughter. Fanny was there too, tampering amiably with the apparatus; and Darrell looked at her once with cold eyes, although, indeed, he had been a rare visitor at the studio.

Then all these phantoms faded, and she seemed to see another in their stead; a man, tall and strong, his face full of anger and sorrow—Lord Watergate, as he had been on that never-forgotten night. Then the anger and sorrow faded from his face, and she read there nothing but love—love for herself shining from his eyes.

Then she hid her face, ashamed.

What must he think of her? Perhaps that she scorned his gift, did not understand its value; had therefore withdrawn it in disdain.

Oh, if only she could tell him this:—that it was her very sense of the greatness of what he offered that had made her tremble, turn away, and reject it. One does not stretch out the hand eagerly for so great a gift.

She had told him not to return and he had taken her at her word. She was paying the penalty, which her sex always pays one way or another, for her struggles for strength and independence. She was denied, she told herself with a touch of rueful humour, the gracious feminine privilege of changing her mind.

Lord Watergate might have loved her more if he had respected her less, or at least allowed for a little feminine waywardness. Like the rest of the world, he had failed to understand her, to see how weak she was, for all her struggles to be strong.

She pushed back the hair from her forehead with the old resolute gesture. Well, she must learn to be strong in earnest now; the thews and sinews of the soul, the moral muscles, grow with practice, no less than those of the body. She must not sit here brooding, but must rise and fight the Fates.

Hitherto, perhaps, life had been nothing but failures, but mistakes. It was quite possible that the future held nothing better in store for her. That was not the question; all that concerned her was to fight the fight.

She lit a solitary candle, and began sorting some papers and prints on the table near.

"If he had cared," her thoughts ran on, "he would have come back in spite of everything."

Doubtless it had been a mere passing impulse of compassion which had prompted his words, and he had caught eagerly at her dismissal of him. Or was it all a delusion on her part? That brief, rapid moment, when he had spoken, had it ever existed save in her own imagination? Worst thought of all, a thought which made her cheek burn scarlet in the solitude, had she misinterpreted some simple expression of kindness, some frank avowal of sympathy; had she indeed refused what had never been offered?

She felt very lonely as she lingered there in the gloom, trying to accustom herself in thought to the long years of solitude, of dreariness, which she saw stretching out before her.

The world, even when represented by her best friends, had labelled her a strong-minded woman. By universal consent she had been cast for the part, and perforce must go through with it.

She heard steps coming up the Virginia cork passage and concluded that Mrs. Maryon was bringing her an expected postcard from Lucy.

"Come in," she said, not raising her head from the table.

The person who had come in was not, however, Mrs. Maryon.

He came up to the table with its solitary candle and faced her.

When she saw who it was her heart stood still; then in one brief moment the face of the universe had changed for her for ever.

"Lord Watergate!"

"I said I would come again. I have come in spite of you. You will not tell me that I come too soon, or in vain?"

"You must not think that I did not value what you offered me," she said simply, though her voice shook; "that I did not think myself deeply honoured. But I was afraid—I have suffered very much."

"And I.... Oh, Gertrude, my poor child, and I have left you all this time."

For the light, flickering upwards, had shown him her weary, haggard face; had shown him also the pathetic look of her eyes as they yearned towards him in entreaty, in reliance,—in love.

He had taken her in his arms, without explanation or apology, holding her to his breast as one holds a tired child.

And she, looking up into his face, into the lucid depths of his eyes, felt all that was mean and petty and bitter in life fade away into nothingness; while all that was good and great and beautiful gathered new meaning and became the sole realities.

EPILOGUE

There is little more to tell of the people who have figured in this story.

Fanny continues to flourish at Notting Hill, the absence of children being the one drop in her cup and that of her husband.

"But, perhaps," as Lucy privately remarks, "it is as well; for I don't think the Marshes would have understood how to bring up a child."

For Lucy, in common with all young matrons of the day, has decided views on matters concerned with the mental, moral, and physical culture of the young. Unlike many thinkers, she does not hesitate to put her theories into practice, and the two small occupants of her nursery bear witness to excellent training.

The photography, however, has not been crowded out by domestic duties; and no infant with pretensions to fashion omits to present itself before Mrs. Jermyn's lens. Lucy has succumbed to the modern practice of specialising, and only the other day carried off a medal for photographs of young children from an industrial exhibition. Her husband is no less successful in his own line. Having permanently abandoned the paint-brush for the needle, he bids fair to take a high place among the black and white artists of the day.[1]

The Watergates have also an addition to their household, in the shape of a stout person with rosy cheeks and stiff white petticoats, who receives a great deal of attention from his parents. Gertrude wonders if he will prove to have inherited his father's scientific tastes, or the literary tendencies of his mother. She devoutly hopes that it is the former.

Conny flourishes as a married woman no less than as a girl. She and the Jermyns dine out now and then at one another's houses; her old affection for Gertrude continues, in spite of the fact that their respective husbands are quite unable (as she says) to hit it off.

Fred has not yet married; but there is no reason to believe him inconsolable. It is rather the embarrassment of choice than any other motive which keeps him single.

Aunt Caroline, having married all her daughters to her satisfaction, continues to reign supreme in certain circles at Lancaster Gate. She speaks with the greatest respect of her niece, Lady

---

1   A steel etching needle is used in lithography.

Watergate, though she has been heard to comment unfavourably on the shabbiness of the furniture in Sussex Place.

As for Darrell, shortly after Phyllis's death, he went to India at the invitation of the Viceroy and remained there nearly two years.

It was only the other day that the Watergates came face to face with him. It was at a big dinner, where the most distinguished representatives of art and science and literature were met. Gertrude turned pale when she saw him, losing the thread of her discourse, and her appetite, despite her husband's reassuring glances down the table.

But Darrell went on eating his dinner and looking into his neighbour's eyes, in apparent unconsciousness of, or unconcern at, the Watergates' proximity.

The Maryons continue in the old premises, increasing their balance at the banker's, and enlarging their experience of life.

The Photographic Studio is let to an enterprising young photographer, who has enlarged and beautified it beyond recognition.

As for the rooms above the umbrella maker's: the sitting-room facing the street; the three-cornered kitchen behind; the three little bed-rooms beyond;–when last I passed the house they were to let unfurnished, with great fly-blown bills in the blank casements.

THE END.

Appendix A: Contemporary Reviews of The Romance of a Shop

1. From "The Newest Books," *British Weekly* 4 (26 October 1888): 420-21

We do not remember to have previously seen the name Amy Levy on a title-page, and it was with some fears we took up *The Romance of a Shop* (Fisher Unwin). The first pages, however, dispelled these fears, and we shall watch with eagerness to see that name again, for a more charming story we have not read for a long time. It reminds one of Mr. W.D. Howells,[1] and would add to his reputation. It is a simple narrative of the adventures of four sisters who are suddenly thrown out of comparative opulence and take to photography as a means of gaining a living. This seems a sufficiently tame theme, but touched by a true artist's hand it gives out flashes of wit on every page. Miss Levy is familiar with the best literature, and has travelled out of the common paths in her reading; but she uses her knowledge without pretentiousness, and aims at nothing that is too high for her. Her characters are very cleverly managed, each eliciting what is characteristic in the others; the sentiment of the story is healthy and bracing, and it is told in perfect English. We most heartily welcome a new writer who can produce work like *The Romance of a Shop*.

2. "The Romance of a Shop," *The Jewish Chronicle* (2 November 1888): 13

Miss Amy Levy has written a bright and animated novel about some sisters who conducted a high-art photographic studio in a second-floor in Baker Street. By poetical license the studio is referred to in the title of the work as a shop. However, it is only with the title, and with one highly unpleasant and unnatural incident that we have to quarrel. The three girls, nay four—for the

---

1   William Dean Howells (1837-1920), American novelist and literary critic. Levy replied to his essay extolling the novels of Henry James in her essay "The New School of American Fiction" (1884). She compares Howells's novels to photographs "where no artistic hand has grouped the figures, only posed them very stiffly before the lens."

delightful superannuated Baby is not more than thirty—are a very interesting group, with their courage, their ignorance, and their unconventionality. In these days when a novel is so often only the Newgate Calendar[1] in a thin disguise, it is refreshing to read about women who do not commit a murder, nor even contemplate one, and with whom no detective has any business. When hard times come upon the Lorimers they bravely take up the burden of work and make a vow to abjure cynicism and to seek for happiness. How they succeed will be best learnt by a perusal of the book. Each of the four girls has a distinct individuality, especially charming, childish Phyllis, to whom the author is singularly unjust. Phyllis has very original and amusing views on most matters. Unfortunately she has a tendency to rather vulgar slang, a foible which is shared by her sister's friend, Constance Devonshire, a young lady whose attire is as splendid as her name, but who invariably speaks of herself as a "fellow." Even the author writes that her young ladies "work like niggers."

For the Lorimer girls work meant a very novel and interesting life, the finding of new friends, and for each the unfolding of a love-story. That anxiety, trials and sorrows should come to them was but natural, or their story would not have been, as it is, distinctly worth the telling.

3. "The Romance of a Shop," supplement to *The Spectator* 61 (3 November 1888): 1536-37

Miss Levy has already earned a place in the world of letters by the freshness and charm of her verses, and she has written, we believe, short tales for the magazines; but as a writer of fiction this is her most ambitious effort. On the whole, *The Romance of a Shop* is, we think, decidedly a success. The experienced reviewer will no doubt readily discover weak points in the characters and in the plot; but the writer understands in no slight measure the novelist's art, and the *dramatis personae* have a certain vitality which prevents us from regarding them as mere puppets. Three girls, hitherto accustomed to affluence, are suddenly left orphans, and nearly penniless; and the two elder, Gertrude and Lucy Lorimer, with the independence which is characteristic of the times, resolve to trust to their own exertions for a maintenance.

---

1 Publications recording crimes of the eighteenth century that became a popular source for plots. Many nineteenth-century British novels borrowed crime stories from these volumes, such as Dickens's *Oliver Twist*.

The youngest, Phyllis by name, who has considerable vivacity and much beauty, follows her sisters' lead. She is a spoilt pet, and blurts out whatever comes into her mind with somewhat startling frankness. There is also a half-sister, Fanny, weak, kind, and help-less, who, as far as the reviewer is concerned, may be left out of the reckoning. In the days of their wealth, Gertrude and Lucy had studied photography, and with a capital of £600, all that is left out of the wreck of their father's fortune, they now lease a shop and try to earn their own living. The battle they fight and the difficulties in which they are placed in this novel position, their gradual success as artists, and their struggles as women—for if love did not find its way into the studio, the novelist's vocation would be gone—all this is described with much ability. Perhaps the narrative is too much broken into scenes which injure its con-tinuity, and one or two striking positions are scarcely made the best of. The dialogue is bright and sometimes witty, and the reader's attention, hardened novel-reader though he may be, is fully sustained. Lucy Lorimer's character will charm him, though he may find it difficult to say why; but he will protest probably, and certainly we do, against the author's treatment of Phyllis. The easy and flippant way in which she falls from virtue, not from passionate love, but because she was dull, is, it may be hoped, untrue to Nature. Surely there must be a series of downward steps before a girl sinks into a gulf like that. Novel-writers have a good deal in their power, and one is glad to find that Gertrude, on whom the heat and burden of the day have fallen, has a joyous prospect before her when the curtain falls. There are plenty of epigrammatic sayings in the book, and pleasant sallies of mirth. In appearance as well as in substance, for the publishers have done their part well, this tale may be commended.

4. From George Saintsbury, "New Novels," *The Academy* (10 November 1888): 301-03

It appears to us that with a little more experience Miss Amy Levy may write a very good novel. The notion of young ladies, who are suddenly turned out of affluence into poverty, supporting them-selves by trade or something like it, is, of course, not new, but it is not yet exhausted. The last time we met it, it was dressmaking, now it is photography. One is as good as the other; indeed, fingers stained with chemicals are, perhaps, better from many points of view than pins in the mouth. There are youthfulnesses in this *Romance of a Shop*, no doubt. The episode of Phyllis, the youngest sister, and her unscrupulous artist-lover, is a little out of place, and wants stronger handling. Moreover, Miss Levy really must not fold her heroine to her lover's breast at the end "like a tired child." She might as well make the lover himself "pass his hand over his fevered brow." But these things may be mended; and there is a quality of "liveness" in the book, a faculty of dialogue, and some scraps and bits of character drawing here and there, which carry the reader pleasantly through for the present, and give good promise for the future.

5. From H.C. Brewer, "New Novels," *The Graphic* (24 November 1888): 558

"The Romance of a Shop," by Amy Levy (1 vol.: T. Fisher Unwin), is presumably its author's first work of fiction; and, on that presumption, is of considerable promise. She has the power, by no means an ordinary one even with novelists of mark, of giving distinctness to her characters, so that one could tell at once who was speaking without any further key than a word or two, when his or her acquaintance has once been made. This is notably the case with the three sisters whose sisterhood is none the less unmistakeable, and who live and work together under the same conditions. Their individual unlikeness in their family likeness is exceedingly well rendered. No doubt there are symptoms of portraiture throughout the story: but this only makes whatever success it has the more conspicuous, seeing that nothing is so difficult, in the whole art of fiction, as actual portraiture: nothing—paradoxical as the assertion may seem—is so almost certain to give an air of unreality. Possibly that is one reason why, despite the excellence of its character-drawing, one rises from "The Romance of a Shop" with a certain impression of general improbability, even although no single situation or incident can be called improbable. In itself, the story is not very agreeable; but it is treated sympathetically and with a promising degree of vigour and trenchancy, so that the result is interesting. Moreover, there is at least one genuinely dramatic scene—that in which poor foolish Phyllis is parted from her despicable lover, who has magnetised her by the force of his selfishness and vanity. We are glad that Amy Levy has not mistaken feeble-minded self-indulgence for manly strength, after the manner of lady novelists in general. Her novel gives not only promise for the future, but much present interest and pleasure.

6. Oscar Wilde, "Amy Levy," *The Woman's World* 3 (1890): 51-52

The gifted subject of these paragraphs, whose distressing death has brought sorrow to many who knew her only from her writings, was born at Clapham, and spent the greater part of her short and outwardly uneventful life in London. Her family was Jewish, but she herself, as she grew up, gradually ceased to hold the orthodox doctrines of her nation, retaining, however, a strong race feeling. At a very early age she showed a marked turn for writing, and some of her childish verses, still preserved, are both correct and original. During the years 1880 and 1881 she was a student at Newnham College, Cambridge, and while still in residence published her first volume of verse, "Xantippe." The modest little paper-covered book, which contains only thirty pages, was published in Cambridge, and was, we believe, never advertised. Its merit, however, attracted a good deal of attention, and the whole edition was sold out. "Xantippe,"[1] the longest and most important poem, had been written three years earlier, and had already appeared (in May, 1880) in the *University Magazine*. Xantippe on her death-bed relates the disappointment of her life, beginning with her love for her husband, and her longing to share his thoughts:—

> "I guided by his wisdom and his love,
> Led by his words, and counselled by his care,
> Should lift the shrouding veil from things which be.
> And at the flowing fountain of his soul
> Refresh my thirsting spirit."

But Socrates wanted no such companion or disciple in his wife, and gradually her love turned to bitterness:—

> "Then faded that vain fury: hope died out;
> A huge despair was stealing on my soul:
> A sort of fierce acceptance of my fate—
> He wished a household vessel—well! 'twas good

---

1   See Introduction for discussion of Levy's dramatic monologue, "Xantippe," the wife of Socrates.

For he should have it......
......till at last I grew
As ye have known me—eye exact to mark
The texture of the spinning; ear all keen
For aimless talking when the moon is up
And ye should be a sleeping; tongue to cut,
With quick incision, thwart the merry words
Of idle maidens."

This poem—surely a most remarkable one to be produced by a girl still at school—is distinguished, as nearly all Miss Levy's work is, by the qualities of sincerity, directness, and melancholy. In expression it is less simple and lucid than some of her later verse, far less so, for instance, than the two short poems which we publish in this issue; but its spirit is the same, and no intelligent critic could fail to see the promise of greater things.

"A Minor Poet, and other Verse," published in 1884, showed a distinct advance. This, too, is but a thin volume, with no single superfluous line in it. The two epitaphs with which it closes, and the dedication "to a dead poet"[1] with which it opens, are perhaps the most perfect and complete things in it; these, if they stood alone, would be enough to mark their writer as a poet of no mean excellence.

A third volume of poems was nearly ready for publication at the time of her death, and is to appear immediately.[2] Some of the pieces to be included in it have appeared already in various papers and magazines, and two or three of these are among her very best work.

Her prose work consists almost entirely of fiction. The few magazine articles which she wrote are good of their kind, but they lack that special individuality which makes the value of her other writing. Of her short stories, two or three are slight and careless, written from a very superficial stratum of thought or feeling, and produced with the utmost facility. Of these stories she herself was the first to speak slightingly, and she would never have sanctioned their republication. But even these are marked by a strong vital-

---

1 Levy published an essay on James Thomson (1834-82) entitled "James Thomson: A Minor Poet" in 1883; the dedication suggests that Thomson's *City of Dreadful Night* inspired the title poem as well as her own poetic career as a female bard of London.

2 *A London Plane-Tree, and Other Verse* was published in late 1889.

ity. They are careless, but not dull; they show how much the touch of the real artist tells, even in second-rate work. But besides these there are a few other short stories which are by no means second-rate. Among these may be named "Cohen of Trinity," "Eldorado at Islington," "Addenbrooke," "Wise in Her Generation"—one of her latest, which we give in our present number—and "The Recent Telepathic Occurrence at the British Museum."[1] This last is a good example of Miss Levy's extraordinary power of condensation. The story occupied only about a page of this magazine, and it gives the whole history of a wasted and misunderstood love. There is not so much as a name in it, but the relation of the man and woman stands out vivid as if we had known and watched its growth.

Miss Levy's two novels, "The Romance of a Shop" and "Reuben Sachs," were both published last year. The first is a bright and clever story, full of sparkling touches; the second is a novel that probably no other writer could have produced. Its directness, its uncompromising truth, its depth of feeling, and, above all, its absence of any single superfluous word, make it, in some sort, a classic. Like all her best work it is sad, but the sadness is by no means morbid. The strong undertone of moral earnestness, never preached, gives a stability and force to the vivid portraiture, and prevents the satiric touches from degenerating into mere malice. Truly the book is an achievement.

To write thus at six-and-twenty is given to very few; and from the few thus endowed their readers may safely hope for yet greater things later on. But "later on" has not come for the writer of "Reuben Sachs," and the world must forego the full fruition of her power. The loss is the world's, but perhaps not hers. She was never robust; not often actually ill, but seldom well enough to feel life a joy instead of a burden; and her work was not poured out lightly, but drawn drop by drop from the very depth of her own feeling. We may say of it that it was in truth her life's blood.

---

1 See Appendix B4 for "Eldorado at Islington." "Addenbrooke" was published in *Belgravia* in March 1889; "Cohen of Trinity" is in *Reuben Sachs*, ed. Susan David Bernstein (Peterborough, ON: Broadview Press, 2006); the other stories are in Melvyn New, ed., *The Complete Novels and Selected Writings of Amy Levy, 1861-1889* (Gainesville: UP of Florida, 1993).

Appendix B: Other Writing by Levy

[Levy published short fiction, essays, and poetry in a range of magazines, most frequently in *London Society, The Jewish Chronicle,* and *The Woman's World*, each representing a different facet—as the titles suggest—of her diverse audience. During the last three years of her life, Levy contributed several stories, essays, and poems to *The Woman's World*, edited by Oscar Wilde, and three of these ("The Poetry of Christina Rossetti," "Women and Club Life," and "Eldorado at Islington") appear in this appendix. In another periodical aimed at a female audience, *Atalanta*, a magazine founded by the prolific and popular woman writer L.T. Meade expressly for modern girls, Levy published "Readers at the British Museum." Here she describes the history of this national library whose reading room was open without fee to both women and men. Levy researched in this library her essay on Christina Rossetti's poetic career. This essay also suggests how Levy viewed the field of Victorian poetry by women, and as such, offers a context for understanding her treatment of female creativity in *The Romance of a Shop*, as well as a literary context for her own poetry. "Women and Club Life" investigates the array of London clubs available to women by the late 1880s; Levy herself belonged to the University Club for Ladies, which continues today as the University Club for Women. Taken together, these four documents give a detailed portrait of late-Victorian London life for women, and thus offer a context for Levy's novel.

Of the six selected poems, the first five come from Levy's final collection, *A London Plane-Tree, and Other Verse* (1889). Besides the contrast between pastoral and urban settings in "The Village Garden," a poem that anticipates William Butler Yeats's "The Lake Isle of Innisfree," these lyrics intimate same-sex desires, and the welter of contradictory emotions with which modern women like Levy struggled. "A Ballad of Religion and Marriage," circulated privately over twenty-five years after Levy's death, articulates the dilemmas of the female speaker caught between tradition and modernity, between the circumscribed domestic life of conventional marriage and certified by institutional religion, and modern visions of transformation, including evolutionary theory.]

1. "The Poetry of Christina Rossetti," *The Woman's World* 1 (February 1888): 178-80

A woman-poet of the first rank is among those things which the world has yet to produce. Even the broken, beautiful strains which float up to us from Lesbos, tell of a singer whose lyre had few strings; whose voice, exquisite as it must have been, but few notes.

Only twice, I think, has Mrs. Browning achieved excellence— in "Sonnets from the Portuguese" and the "Great God Pan;"[1] and when we have named Sappho[2] and Mrs. Browning, who remains to be added to the list of poetesses with any claim to a place in the first class?

But if no woman has grown to the stature of a Dante, a Homer, or a Shakespeare, it cannot be denied that, within the narrow limits imposed by her hitherto narrow range of vision, of emotion, of experience and opportunity, woman has produced work which will bear the severest test. The creator of "Come unto these Yellow Sands" need not have been ashamed to acknowledge,

Γέσπερε, πάντα φέρεις, ὅσα ψαίυολις ἐοκέδας ἀύως;[3]

---

1 Elizabeth Barrett Browning (1806-61) published "Sonnets from the Portuguese" (1846) and "The Dead Pan," as well as her epic verse-novel *Aurora Leigh* (1856) about a woman poet living and working independently in London.

2 A Greek lyric poet born in Lesbos in the seventh century BCE. In 1885 Henry Wharton published a translation of Sappho that restored for the first time in English the feminine pronoun as the object of address. Women poets who were Levy's contemporaries, such as Vernon Lee and Michael Field (Katherine Bradley and Edith Cooper), wrote in the Sapphic tradition, which became linked to lesbian desire.

3 "Hesperus, you bring all things that lightgiving dawn has scattered" (Greek). Compare with Shakespeare, *All's Well That Ends Well* II.i.164: "Moist Hesperus hath quench'd her sleepy lamp." The line "Come unto these yellow sands" refers to Ariel's song in *The Tempest* I.ii.375.

nor he who sang "Ye banks and braes of bonnie Doon,"[1] to claim as his own the tragedy-lyric of "Auld Robin Gray." If I may be allowed the paradox, there has been no excellent woman-poet, but much woman's poetry of excellence.

The name of Christina Rossetti stands high among the producers of such poetry. With unusual opportunities of culture, breathing from the first an atmosphere almost uniquely favourable to artistic production, she had never to contend with those obstacles which are apt to confront her sex at the outset of a literary career. On the other hand, steeped as she must have been in strong and peculiar influences, she ran the risk of losing her artistic individuality. These influences, indeed, have left their mark on her work; but it is always her own voice—no echo—her woman's voice, curiously sweet, fantastically sad, which floats up to us as we listen to her singing.

Miss Rossetti was born in London, in 1830, of Italian parents. As in the case of Dante Gabriel Rossetti,[2] her talent was a precocious one, and as early as 1847 she appears as the author of a book of poems, "Verses," dedicated to her mother, privately printed at the press of her grandfather, Mr. Pollidori, at 15, Park Villas East, Regent's Park.

This modest little volume, which may be seen by the curious in the Large Room of the British Museum, is introduced by a preface from the printer, who explains that the poems are printed by his own desire. As the work of so young a poet, they are, indeed, remarkable. Those qualities which stamp the work of her maturity—the quaint yet exquisite choice of words; the felicitous *naïveté*, more Italian than English; the delicate, unusual melody of the verse; the richness, almost to excess, of imagery—are all apparent in these first-fruits of her muse. And not less apparent are the mysticism and the almost unrelieved

---

1 Robert Burns (1759-96), "Ye Banks and Braes o' Bonnie Doon," a popular Scottish song. Lady Anne Lindsay (1750-1825) wrote "Auld Robin Gray."

2 Dante Gabriel Rossetti (1828-82), poet and artist who co-founded the Pre-Raphaelite Brotherhood in 1848. Christina Rossetti was the model for some of her brother's paintings, including "The Girlhood of Mary Virgin" (1849).

melancholy which we associate with Christina Rossetti's better-known poetry. Indeed, there is here to be found that youthful exaggeration of sadness, that perverse assumption of the cypress, to which a half-complacent, half-mournful poet of our own time has alluded—

"Our youth began with tears and sighs,
With seeking what we could not find;
Our verses were all threnodies..." [1]

Miss Rossetti's verses, at this period, were all threnodies, more or less.

"The City of the Dead," the most important poem in the "Verses," contains many passages of great beauty, and testifies throughout to the strong imagination of the writer, no less than to her power over her instrument. A little poem, dated as far back as 1842, is interesting; it will, perhaps, be remembered by some that another woman-poet, a sweet singer, as undervalued in our day as she was overvalued in her own—Mrs. Hemans[2]—chose the same subject for her first poetic effort. Here are Miss Rossetti's lines:—

"TO MY MOTHER.
"To-day's your natal day;
    Sweet flowers I bring;
Mother, accept, I pray,
    My offering.

"And may you happy live,
    And long us bless;
Receiving, as you give,
    Great happiness."

In 1850, our poet, under the name of Ellen Alleyn, contributed several poems to the *Germ*,[3] that wonderful little peri-

---

1 Andrew Lang (1844-1912), "Ballade of Middle Age," *Rhymes à la Mode* (1885), lines 1-3.
2 Felicia Hemans (1793-1835).
3 *The Germ* (subtitled "Thoughts toward Nature in Poetry, Literature, and Art") ran for four issues, from January to April 1850. In this magazine, the Pre-Raphaelite Brotherhood, including Rossetti's brothers Dante Gabriel and William, asserted their aesthetic principles.

odical whose career, as short-lived as it was glorious, is now a matter of history. Ellen Alleyn's verses have, with one exception, been found worthy a place in the latest edition of Christina Rossetti's poetry. "Repining," the longest, in some ways the most important, though distinctly the least *réussi*[1] of them all, has never, I believe, been reprinted.[2] Vague, mystic, melancholy, it contains passages stamped with the right stamp. I quote a few lines, which seem to me unmistakable, coming as they do from a poet of twenty:—

"What is this thing? Thus hurriedly
To pass into eternity;
To leave the earth so full of mirth;
To lose the profit of our birth;
To die and be no more; to cease,
Having numbness which is not peace."

The italics are my own.

It was not till fifteen years after the printing of the "Verses" that Miss Rossetti came before the public with a volume of poems. "Goblin Market, and other Poems," appeared in 1862, a dainty little book enriched by two beautiful designs from the pencil of her brother, Dante Gabriel Rossetti. This was followed, in 1866, by "The Prince's Progress, and other Poems," also with two designs from the same hand, and, in 1872, by "Sing Song," a charming book of rhymes for children; and, in 1881, by "A Pageant, and other Poems." Besides the little masque of the months, which gives its name to the book, this last volume contains many poems of considerable interest, including a series of Petrarchian sonnets, written from the point of view of an imaginary Laura.

"Had the great poetess of our own day," says Miss Rossetti, "been unhappy instead of happy, her circumstances would have invited her to bequeath us, in lieu of the Portuguese Sonnets, an inimitable *monna innominata*, drawn, not from fancy, but from feeling, and worthy to occupy a niche beside Beatrice and

---

1 Successful (French).
2 "Repining" was reprinted in *New Poems by Christina Rossetti* (1896), edited by William Michael Rossetti. Levy quotes lines 197-202.

Laura."[1] Few of us, I think, would wish to have reversed the decree of Fate in this respect.

The list of Christina Rossetti's works includes, besides those mentioned, two volumes of prose tales, and several volumes of devotional pieces in both prose and verse. But it is with her poetry alone, and moreover with her best poetry, that I have to deal. This latter is undoubtedly contained in the two volumes of her maturity—"Goblin Market" and "The Prince's Progress." These, with but few additions or alterations, have been reprinted in one volume; and with this volume the general reader who wishes to make acquaintance with Christina Rossetti's poetry may content himself.

"Goblin Market," which occupies the first twenty pages of the book, is a whimsical fairy fancy, full of beauties, yet curiously unequal. Here and there, as in other productions of the poet, we are reminded of the magic notes which rang out for us in "Christabel" and "Kubla Khan;"[2] though, indeed, the sweet music of our minstrel, weird, exotic, vaguely fascinating as it is, tinkles faintly within sound of those mighty strains.

For "The Prince's Progress," a vaguely allegorical poem of some length, there is not much to be said as a work of sustained imagination; it contains, however, occasional felicities, and concludes with a passage of such rare beauty that I cannot do better than quote some of it here. The Prince, who has been variously tempted to linger unconscionably long on his journey to his betrothed, arrives at last at the palace to find the Princess dead—worn out by waiting. Her maidens reproach him—

"Too late for love, too late for joy,
        Too late, too late!
You loitered on the road too long,
        You trifled at the gate:
The enchanted dove upon her branch
        Died without a mate...
The enchanted princess in her tower
        Slept, died, behind the grate;

---

1 Christina Rossetti (1830-94), preface to her sonnet sequence, "Monna Innominata," in *A Pageant and Other Poems* (1881). "Monna innominata" (Italian) means "unnamed lady." The "great poetess" refers to Elizabeth Barrett Browning.

2 Samuel Taylor Coleridge (1772-1834), both poems published in *Christabel; Kubla Khan, a Vision; The Pains of Sleep* (1816).

Her heart was starving all this while
    You made it wait.

★★★

"Is she fair now as she lies?
    Once she was fair;
Meet queen for any kingly king,
    With gold-dust in her hair.
Now these are poppies in her locks,
    White poppies she must wear;
Must wear a veil to shroud her face,
    And the want graven there;
Or is the hunger fed at length,
    Cast off the care?

"We never saw her with a smile,
    Or with a frown;
Her bed seemed never soft to her,
    Though tossed of down;
She little heeded what she wore,
    Kirtle, or wreath, or gown;
We think her white brows often ached
    Beneath her crown....

"Her heart sat silent through the noise
    And concourse of the street;
There was no hurry in her hands,
    No hurry in her feet;
There was no bliss drew nigh to her
    That she might run to meet.

"You should have wept her yesterday,
    Wasting upon her bed:
But wherefore should you weep to-day
    That she is dead?" [1]

But it is, perhaps, when she is least mystic, least involved—when she is simplest, most direct, most human, that Christina Rossetti is at her best.

---

[1] "The Prince's Progress" (1866), lines 479-88, lines 501-18, lines 525-34.

"A Royal Princess," while retaining all the writer's indescribable charm of manner, glows throughout with genuine passion;

"Shows a heart within, blood-tinctured of a veined humanity."[1]

It is terribly appropriate reading for these days, the tale of the luxuriously-reared Princess whose castle is attacked by the starving mob. I quote, with reluctance—for no quotation can give an idea of the beauty of this poem—the last stanzas:—

> "'Sit and roast there with your meat, sit and bake there with
>   your bread,
> You who sat to see us starve,' one shrieking woman said;
> 'Sit on your throne and roast with your crown upon your
>   head.'
>
> "Nay, this thing will I do, while my mother tarrieth,
> I will take my fine spun gold, but not to sew therewith,
> I will take my gold and gems and rainbow fan and wreath;
>
> "With a ransom in my lap, a king's ransom in my hand,
> I will go down to this people, will stand face to face, will
>   stand
> Where they curse king, queen, and princess of this cursèd
>   land.
>
> "They shall take all to buy them bread, take all I have to
>   give;
> I, if I perish, perish; they to-day shall eat and live;
> I, if I perish, perish; that's the goal I half conceive."[2]

In "Maude Clare" is again apparent the dramatic power which gives life to "A Royal Princess." This little poem is worthy to take a place in our ballad-literature, the traces of whose influence it so deeply shows. In a few vivid verses we are told how the stately

---

1   Elizabeth Barrett Browning, "Lady Geraldine's Courtship" (1844), line 166.
2   "A Royal Princess" (1866), lines 94-105. "I, if I perish" also echoes a line spoken by Queen Esther in the Hebrew Book of Esther when she decides to appear unbidden before her husband King Ahasueras and reveal her Jewish identity. Rossetti's eighth sonnet in "Monna Innominata" explores the story of Esther and opens with this line: "'I, if I perish, perish'—Esther spake."

Maude Clare followed her faithless lover and his bride to the church, overwhelming the one with reproaches, the other with taunts:—

> "'Take my share of a fickle heart,
> 　　Mine of a paltry love:
> Take it or leave it as you will,
> 　　I wash my hands thereof.'
>
> "'And what you leave,' said Nell, 'I'll take;
> 　　And what you spurn, I'll wear;
> For he's my lord for better and worse,
> 　　And him I love, Maude Clare.
>
> "'Yea, though you're taller by the head,
> 　　More wise, and much more fair,
> I'll love him till he loves me best,
> 　　Me best of all, Maude Clare.'" [1]

Only a woman could have written this poem.

Almost perfect, in their way, are "The Hour and the Ghost," "The Ghost's Petition," and "Wife to Husband." Who that has read them can forget these lines (from the last), with their plaintive refrain?—

> "Blank sea to sail upon,
> 　　Cold bed to sleep in:
> 　　　　Good-bye.
> While you clasp, I must be gone
> 　　For all your weeping:
> 　　　　I must die.
>
> "A kiss for one friend,
> 　　And a word for two:
> 　　　　Good-bye.
> A lock that you must send,
> 　　A kindness you must do:
> 　　　　I must die.

1　"Maude Clare" (1862), lines 37-48.

"Not a word for you,
   Not a lock or kiss:
      Good-bye.
We, one, must part in two;
   Verily death is this:
      I must die." [1]

I should be disposed to place this group of poems—"A Royal
Princess," "Maude Clare," "The Hour and the Ghost," "The
Ghost's Petition," and "Wife to Husband"—very high in our literature. And of great excellence are Miss Rossetti's more purely
lyric poems—for instance, the lines beginning, "When I am dead,
my dearest," and those headed "A Birthday," both of which have
been made familiar to us by their musical setting. Nor must it be
forgotten that Miss Rossetti has been among the numerous
writers of our day who have ventured frequently within the
sonnet's scanty plot of ground. Many of her sonnets are good, but
none, I think, of that supreme excellence which gives to such productions their *raison-d'être*.

There is a fatal fascination about sonnet-writing, to which too
many of our poets have succumbed. The critic who objected to
sonnets on the ground that they looked like bricks, was undoubtedly a crude person, but not altogether without his perceptions.
Certain dramatic and descriptive qualities notwithstanding, it is
as a lyric poet that Miss Rossetti must be classified; that is to say,
if we are to occupy ourselves with terms and labels in the matter.
Hers is, at best, a poetic personality difficult to grasp, difficult to
classify. As with Shelley and Coleridge, she is at one moment
intensely human, intensely personal; at another, she paddles away
in her rainbow shell, and is lost to sight as she dips over the
horizon-line of her halcyon sea.

A fervid human spirit; a passionate woman's heart; an imagination deep and tender; a fancy vivid and curious; is it to be wondered at that the poet in whom such qualities are met should
elude the hard and fast measurements of the critic? Her muse
personifies itself for us, an elfin sprite with iridescent wings, and
eyes that startle us with their mournful human gaze.

I hesitate to pronounce what should seem to be meant for a
verdict on Christina Rossetti's poetry, still less to indulge in
prophecy as to its power of resisting the action of the waves of

---

1   "Wife to Husband" (1862), lines 13-30.

Time. If, indeed, the art be not always worthy of the artist; if the vessel, at times, obscure the flame within; if manner grow here and there to mannerism, *naïveté* to bathos, subtlety to thinness; it must be remembered how delicate, how fine, how unique is that art at its best. Christina Rossetti stands alone, as Dante Gabriel Rossetti stood alone. From the branches of a wondrous tree, transplanted by chance to our clime, we pluck the rare, exotic fruit, and the unfamiliar flavour is very sweet. It is not here the place for criticism of the author of "The House of Life." But of Christina Rossetti let it be said that if she is not great, at least, artistically speaking, she is good.

2. "Women and Club Life," *The Woman's World* 1 (June 1888): 364-67

"Send your horse home and stop and dine here with me, Julia; I've asked Trixy Rattlecash and Emily Sheppard," says Mr. du Maurier's Miss Firebrace, as she reclines at ease in the luxurious club-chair.

"Can't, my dear girl; my sainted old father-in-law's just gone back to Yorkshire, and poor Bolly's all alone," replies Mrs. Bolingbroke Tompkins with a sigh of regret for the freedom of spinsterhood and the charms of club life.

It is not ten years since the appearance of this little bit of dialogue and its accompanying sketch in the pages of *Punch*,[1] and already the world has drifted into a stolid acceptance of the fact of feminine club life; has come to look on, without surprise or amusement, at the rapid growth of women's clubs, adapted to the various requirements of various classes.

Demand, say the makers of that mischievous pseudoscience, political economy, creates supply. What has hitherto been felt as a vague longing—the desire among women for a corporate life, for a wider human fellowship, a richer social opportunity—has assumed the definite shape of a practical demand, now that so many women of all ranks are controllers of their own resources.

From the high and dry region of the residential neighbourhood the women come pouring down to those pleasant shores where the great stream of human life is dashing and flowing.

In class-room and lecture-theatre, office and art-school, college and club-house alike, woman is waking up to a sense of the hundred and one possibilities of social intercourse; possibili-

---

1 "Female Clubs v. Matrimony," *Punch's Almanack for 1878* (December 14, 1877). See Figure 1. The cartoonist is George Du Maurier (1834-96).

Figure 1.

PUNCH'S ALMANACK FOR 1878. [December 14, 1877.

FEMALE CLUBS v. MATRIMONY

Miss Firebrace. "Send your Horse Home, and stop and Dine here with me, Julia! I've asked Trixy Rattlecash and Emily Sheppard."

Mrs. Bolingbroke Tompkins, *née Julia Wildrake* (with a sigh of regret for the freedom of Spinsterhood and the charms of Club life). "Can't, my dear Girl! My sainted old Father-in-Law's just gone back to Yorkshire, and poor Bolly's all alone!"

ties which, save in exceptional instances, have hitherto for her been restricted to the narrowest of grooves.

The female club must be regarded as no isolated and ludicrous phenomenon, but as the natural outcome of the spirit of an age which demands excellence in work from women no less than from men, and as one of the many steps towards the attainment of that excellence.

As Miss Simcox points out, in a recent number of the *Nineteenth Century*,[1] no great performance in art or science can justly be expected from a class which is debarred from the inestimable advantages of a corporate social life.

To turn from the general to the particular: it is now my intention to enumerate and consider the most important of those

1 Edith Simcox (1844-1901), "The Capacity of Women," *The Nineteenth Century* (Sept. 1887): 391-402. Simcox challenges George Romanes's essay, "Mental Differences between Men and Women," *The Nineteenth Century* (May 1887): 654-72.

ladies' clubs in London, which have followed so closely on the heels of Mr. du Maurier's little skit.

Of these, the Albemarle Club (founded in 1881) is, perhaps, the best known. Its members consist of ladies and men in about equal numbers, from whom an annual subscription of five guineas is exacted, the original entrance-fee of eight guineas having been suspended by the committee in 1884. In the large, conveniently-situated house in Albemarle Street, ladies can entertain their friends of both sexes, make appointments, or merely pass the time pleasantly in the perusal of periodical literature.

How many a valuable acquaintance has been improved, how many an important introduction obtained in that convenient neutral territory of club-land!

Here, at last, is a chance of seeing something of A or B or C apart from her sisters, her cousins, and her aunts—all excellent people, no doubt, but with whom we personally have nothing in common, and whose acquaintance we have no desire to cultivate. And here is a haven of refuge, where we can write our letters and read the news, undisturbed by the importunities of a family circle, which can never bring itself to regard feminine leisure and feminine solitude as things to be respected.

Of more recent date is the Alexandra Club for ladies only, situated in Grosvenor Street, whose list of members, no less than that of the Albemarle, includes many names well known in society, and in artistic and political circles. For this club no lady is eligible "who has been, or would probably be, precluded from attending Her Majesty's Drawing-Rooms;" a nice phrase, full of the sound and fury of exclusiveness, and signifying not so much after all.

There is an entrance-fee of three guineas, and an annual subscription of three and two guineas for town and country members respectively; and sleeping accommodation is available at moderate charges, including beds for ladies'-maids.

Men may not be introduced to the club as visitors—a restriction which, in my opinion, places it at a disadvantage with the Albemarle.

It is a significant fact that, established as recently as 1884, the Alexandra already numbers about 600 members.

Not the least interesting of female clubs is the University Club for Ladies, which came into existence at the beginning of last year. For this are eligible as members the graduates of any University; registered medical practitioners of the United Kingdom;

students or lecturers who have been in residence for at least three terms either at Newnham or Girton College, Cambridge, or at Somerville or Lady Margaret Hall, Oxford; undergraduates of any University who have passed the examination next after matriculation; and students who have passed the first professional examination of any medical corporation. It will be seen, therefore, that this is a club of workers; and the working woman not being apt to have much spare cash at her disposal, it has been organised on a more modest basis than either of those before alluded to. A guinea entrance-fee and a guinea annual subscription represent the expenses of membership; nor have the University ladies aspired, so far, to the dignity of a club-house, but have contented themselves with a small but daintily-furnished set of rooms on the upper floors of a house in New Bond Street. Simple meals at moderate charges can be obtained of the housekeeper; but if Cornelia Blimber[1] or the Princess Ida[2] objects to the austerity of this scholar's fare, an arrangement has been entered into with the Grosvenor Restaurant opposite, by which more luxurious cates can be supplied to her on the shortest notice.

Here, amid Morris papers[3] and Chippendale chairs, old acquaintances are renewed, old gossip resuscitated, and any amount of "shop" of various descriptions discussed.

"And where have all my playmates sped,
    Whose ranks were once so serried?
Why, some are wed, and some are dead,
    And some are only buried.
Frank Petre, then so full of fun,
    Is now St. Blaise's prior;
And Travers, the attorney's son,
    Is member for the shire."[4]

---

1   An intellectual woman in *Dombey and Son* (1846-48) whom Charles Dickens satirizes as "dry and sandy with working in the graves of deceased languages" (chap. 11).

2   The title of a Gilbert and Sullivan opera performed at the Savoy Theatre in 1884 and based on Alfred Tennyson's *The Princess* (1847), a poem about Princess Ida who renounces men and marriage and opens a university for women.

3   The wallpapers designed by William Morris's firm. Morris was a Victorian writer, socialist, and artist. Levy mentions his wallpapers in *The Romance of a Shop* (chap. I).

4   Frederick Locker-Lampson (1821-95), "The Jester's Moral" (1868), lines 49-56.

The suburban high-school mistress, in town for a day's shopping or picture-seeing, exchanges here the discomfort of the pastrycook's or the costliness of the restaurant for the comforts of a quiet meal and a quiet read or chat in the cosy club precincts; the busy journalist rests here from her labours of "private viewing," strengthening herself with tea and newspapers before setting out for fresh lands to conquer. The mingled sense of independence and *esprit de corps* which made college life at once so pleasant and so wholesome are not wanting here in the colder, more crowded regions of London club-land.

Differing somewhat in scope from the clubs described above is the Somerville Club,★ in Oxford Street, which aims at combining the usual advantages of the club proper with those of the class or college; organising debates, lectures, and social evenings for the benefit of its members. These latter are drawn from all classes of society; the annual subscription is ten shillings. The original idea of its founders was to create a social centre for women to whom the ordinary social advantages are not easily accessible. Only women are eligible as members, but men may be introduced as visitors. Reading-room, library, &c., are provided, as at other clubs, and refreshments can be obtained at very moderate charges.

The ice, then, may be considered to have been fairly broken, and the woman's club to have take its place among our social institutions. There is, so far, no good reason to suppose that, intoxicated by the sweets of club liberty, ladies have been led away into any of those extravagances prophesied by Mr. du Maurier and other humorists.

The female club-lounger, the *flâneuse* of St. James's Street, latch-key in pocket and eye-glasses on nose, remains a creature of the imagination. The clubs mentioned are sober, business-like haunts enough, to which no dutiful wife or serious-minded maiden need feel ashamed of belonging. If the Alexandra, with its talk of Drawing-Rooms, aims rather more at smartness than the rest, it is none the worse for that; nor are we to blame the "frivolous" woman for following in the wake of her professional sister.

But it is to the professional woman, when all is said, that the club offers the most substantial advantages. What woman engaged in art, in literature, in science, has not felt the drawbacks

---

★ The original subscription to the Somerville Club (founded in 1878) was five shillings. This club dissolved itself at the end of last year, and has recently re-established itself on a slightly different basis. After June, 1888, an entrance-fee of ten shillings will be charged.

of her isolated position? Apart from that intellectual solitude to which Miss Simcox alludes in the article before quoted, she has had to contend with every practical disadvantage.

She has had to fight her way unknown and single-handed; to compete with a guild of craftsmen all more or less known to one another, having easy access to one another, bound together by innumerable links of acquaintance and intercourse. It is all uphill work with her, unless she be somebody's sister, or somebody's wife, or unless she have the power and the means of setting in motion an elaborate social machinery to obtain what every average follower of his calling has come to regard as a right.

The number of professional women of all kinds has increased so greatly, and is still so greatly increasing, that, with a little more *esprit de corps*, women might do a great deal for themselves and for one another. A level platform of intercourse for members of the same craft, regardless of distinction of sex, may assuredly be looked forward to in no distant future; but at present I believe the fact of sex to have too great social insistence to render such an arrangement practicable, though such institutions as the Albemarle Club are steps in the right direction.

Not long ago, indeed, a motion was brought forward for the admission of women into the Savile Club. Its rejection must be a matter of regret to all women engaged in literature and education; but the fact that such a motion was brought forward and considered is of itself significant.

At this point we seem to hear the voice of some excellent Conservative upraised in protest. "You have dismissed Trixy Rattlecash and Julia Wildrake," it says, "but do you hold up anything so admirable after all? Is Cornelia Blimber elbowing her way into a man's club-room such an edifying spectacle, when all is said? Is it such a beautiful thing that Mrs. Jellaby[1] should absent herself from home at all hours of the day, or the Princess Ida take to haunting the neighbourhood of Bond Street? Are we expected to rejoice over the fact that Blanche and Psyche can entertain Cyril and Florian[2] at a club dinner, or to sympathise with the selfishness of Penthesilea[3] in disregarding the social claims of her family?"

---

1 Dickens's caricature of a lady philanthropist in *Bleak House* (1852-53).

2 In *The Princess*, Cyril and Florian crossdress as women to gain admission to Princess Ida's university; eventually their identities are detected by two tutors, Lady Blanche, Professor of Abstract Science, and Lady Psyche, Professor of Humanities.

3 Queen of the Amazons and a revered warrior in the Trojan War.

In reply, I can only say that I am considering things as they are, not as they might be. We are in England, not in Utopia; it is the nineteenth century, and not the Golden Age; the land is not flowing with milk and honey; those commodities can only be obtained by strenuous and competitive effort.

It is not for me to rejoice over, or to deplore, the complete and rapid change of the female position which has taken place in this country during the last few years. It is a phenomenon for our observation rather than an accident for our intervention; the result of complex and manifold circumstance over which none of us can be thought to have much control. The tide has set in and there is no stemming it.

It is not without regret that one sees the old order changing and giving place to new in this respect. The woman who owns no interests beyond the circle of home, who takes no thought for herself, who is content to follow where love and superior wisdom are leading—this ideal of feminine excellence is not, indeed, to be relinquished without a sigh.

But she is, alas! too expensive a luxury for our civilisation; we cannot afford her.

To ignore blindly this fact, to refuse obstinately to face it, only means the bringing down of sorrow and distress on the heads of everyone concerned.

A day has come when the most conservative among us must realise the necessity for women of leaving off weeping and taking to working, no less than man.

Now an unmixed diet of work is no more suited for Jill than it is for Jack; she must be left, moreover, to choose her own games, and play after her own fashion. A course of worsted-work and morning class to a woman desirous of the peaceful amenities of club-land would be about as enlivening as the celebrated game of chevy-chase, in *Vice Versâ*,[1] to the young gentlemen of Dr. Grinstone's Academy.

There is no reason to suppose that because she is a member of a club a woman will develop the selfishness of her husband and brother; that, for instance, she will seek to emulate the young man in *Punch* who wondered why his family went to the expense of taking in the papers, considering he saw them all at his club!

---

1 Thomas Anstey Guthrie (1856-1934), *Vice Versâ, or a Lesson to Fathers* (1882), a humorous novel about a schoolboy who magically changes bodies with his father for a week.

Do we hear of unladylike excesses among the students of Girton or of Somerville Hall? Of the undue extravagance and evil habits of those hard-working and self-respecting bodies? And who does not remember the prophetic chorus of many Cassandras and Isaiahs which greeted the establishment of lectures for women at Cambridge?

Let it be remembered that, while the old state of affairs was in many respects beautiful and satisfactory, it was the source of much and of increasing evil; adapted rather for the happiness of the chosen few than of the unchosen many. To its upholders in these days can only be attributed an unphilosophic disregard of the greatest happiness of the greatest number.

And yet, in the words of Clough's undergraduate:—

"Often I find myself saying—old faith and doctrine abjuring,
Into the crucible casting philosophies, facts, convictions—
Were it not well that the stem should be naked of leaf and of
    tendril,
Poverty-stricken, the barest, the dismallest stick of the
    garden,
Flowerless, leafless, unlovely for ninety and nine long
    summers,
So at the hundredth, at last, were bloom for one day at the
    summit,
So but that fleeting flower were lovely as Lady Maria?"[1]

Often I find myself saying it, perhaps; but always to return, as the hero of the poem did, to the recollection that interchange of service is, after all, the law and condition of beauty. Let us, then, remember that, while we lose much, we gain perhaps more, by the new state of affairs.

3. "Readers at the British Museum," *Atalanta: Every Girl's Magazine* (April 1889): 449-54

Those readers of *Atalanta*[2] who have been to the British Museum will probably have obtained a momentary glimpse of the great Reading Room, with its book-lined walls, its radiating

---

1   Arthur Hugh Clough (1819-61), *The Bothie of Tober-na-Vuolich: A Long Vacation Pastoral* (1848) part 5, lines 43-49, a poem about a student reading party in Scotland.

2   *Atalanta* (1887-98) was a magazine for British middle-class girls.

Figure 2.

"For out of old fieldes, as men saithe,
    Cometh al this new corne fro yere to yere,
And out of old bookes, in good faithe,
    Cometh al this new science that men lere."
    The Assembly of Foules.

rows of seats, and its characteristic, suggestive scent of leather bindings.

Under the great dome—almost the largest in the world—they will have noticed a motley crowd of readers, in various stages of industry and idleness, absorbed in their books, bustling hither and thither with important faces, gossiping, lounging, wrapped in thought, or even, in some rare instances, fast asleep like the man in the picture.[1]

The great library of the Museum, which has recently been described as incomparably the best, and is, with the exception of the National Library at Paris, the largest in the world, attracts to itself in ever-increasing numbers all sorts and conditions of men and women. Students as sharply contrasted as the dry-as-dust, paper-laden old scholar of our illustrations and the trim young person in the *pince-nez*, jostle one another from the opening of

---

1 The original essay included several sketches of readers, both women and men. Here Levy describes the drawing that appears at the head of the article. See Figure 2.

the doors at 9 A.M., to those hours of the afternoon or evening when the lavender-white light of the electric lamps shines somewhat fitfully through the thick atmosphere.

The "Room" has indeed become a centre, a general workshop, where in these days of much reading, much writing, and competitive examinations, the great business of book-making, article-making, cramming, may be said to have their headquarters, while it has not ceased to be the resort of the genuine student who loves knowledge for its own sake.

The library and the Reading Room, or rather a reading-room, are as old as the Museum itself.

In the middle of the eighteenth century the trustees of Sir Hans Sloane, an eminent Chelsea physician, offered, in accordance with his will, his valuable collection of curiosities, manuscripts, and books to the nation, at a price greatly below its actual value. This bequest suggested the notion of a National Museum. In 1753 the foundation charter of the British Museum was granted, and in 1759 the nucleus of our present world-famed collection was stowed away in Montague House, a mansion originally belonging to the Duke of Montague, situated where the Museum buildings now stand.

The library was from the first an important feature of the collection.

In the years which elapsed between the act of incorporation and the purchase of Montague House several valuable additions had been made to Sir Hans Sloane's treasure of books, MSS., including the Harleian and Cottonian MSS[1] and the library of another private collector, Major Edwards.[2]

But the most important addition of all was that of the Royal Library, presented in 1757 by George II. to the nation.

This collection, brought together by the kings of England from Henry VIII. to William III., included the libraries of Archbishop Cranmer and of Isaac Casaubon,[3] the great scholar, and the

---

1 Some of the manuscripts include the Lindisfarne Gospels, Beowulf, and the Magna Carta.
2 Major Arthur Edwards (1680-1743) bequeathed 2,000 volumes to the Cottonian Library, one of the British Museum's foundational collections.
3 Isaac Casaubon (1559-1614), English classical scholar who served as royal librarian under Henry IV.

Alexandrian Codex of the Bible.[1] With the Royal Library passed also the privilege of being supplied with a copy of every publication entered at Stationers' Hall;[2] a privilege which, retained to this day, gives to our National Library one of its most important and characteristic features.

Since this first sowing of the seed the library has been enriched by gifts and purchases too numerous to mention; though a word must be said of the King's Library, presented (or sold) by George IV. to the Museum.

This collection, brought together by the agents of George III., includes many books printed by Caxton,[3] and early editions of the classics. Its choiceness is partly owing to the fact that it was collected during the period of the suppression of the Jesuit houses, whose valuable libraries were, consequently, for sale.

Of rare value also is the Grenville Library, bequeathed in 1845 by Mr. Grenville, one of the trustees of the Museum.

Among other treasures it contains a unique copy of a hitherto undiscovered edition of *The Canterbury Tales*, printed in 1498 by Wynkyn de Worde;[4] a second edition (Caxton) of the same work; a first edition of Shakespeare's collected dramatic works; and the only known fragment of the New Testament in English, translated by Tyndale and Roy,[5] printed in 1525 at Cologne, when the translators had to interrupt the printing and flee for their lives. Besides its vast stores of MSS. and printed books of many periods and in many tongues, the Museum boasts a collection of

---

1 This ancient manuscript in book or "codex" form of the New Testament, written in Greek, dates from the fourth century CE. Originally found in Alexandria, Egypt, the Alexandrian Codex was acquired by the Royal Library of the kings and queens of England in 1627, and later became part of the library archives of the British Museum.

2 In order to establish copyright, all publications from 1554 to 1924 had to be registered at Stationers' Hall in London. Publishers were obligated to supply complimentary copies for copyright libraries in the United Kingdom: the British Library, the Bodleian Library of Oxford University, the Cambridge University Library, National Library of Scotland, and the library of Trinity College Dublin.

3 William Caxton (1422-91), the first printer of books in English, including *The Canterbury Tales*.

4 Another early modern printer who came to London as Caxton's assistant and established printing in Fleet Street around 1500.

5 William Tyndale (1494?-1536) translated the New Testament and the Pentateuch; William Roy worked as an amanuensis for Tyndale.

newspapers dating from 1588 downwards; and one of books on vellum surpassing that of every other library with the exception of the Bibliothèque Nationale, including a first edition of the Bible known as the Mazarin Bible, printed in 1454.

A room was set apart for readers from the opening of the British Museum at Montague House in 1759.

It was a basement apartment, opening by glass doors on to a pleasant garden, and contained an oak table with chairs for twenty readers. A superintendent was appointed to answer questions and help the readers generally with their work, but these were few in number, and three years after the opening of the library to the public there is an entry to the effect that "no company coming to the Reading Room, Dr. Templeman [the superintendent] ventured to go away about two o'clock."

We hear later on however of this same Dr. Templeman, that, strolling in the garden of Montague House in office hours, he was met by a trustee of the Museum, who, indignant at this neglect of duty, called out to him, "Go back, sir!" Not long afterwards his resignation was sent in. In July, 1759, Gray,[1] the poet, writes from London to a friend:—"I am just settled in my new habitation in Southampton Row, and though a solitary and dispirited creature, not unquiet nor wholly unpleasant to myself. The Museum will be my chief amusement. I this day passed through the jaws of a Great Leviathan that lay in my way, into the presence of Dr. Templeman, Superintendent of the Reading Room, who congratulated himself on so much good company." Gray, himself, as he goes on to explain, made the fifth reader present.

But if the company was small, it was certainly select. Besides that of Gray, we find the names of Hume[2] among the earliest readers: Johnson[3] was admitted in 1761, and one cannot help regretting that the Reading Room of the present day was unknown to him.

In that large and crowded building, with its opportunities for gossip and lounging, the Doctor would have been in his element. Fleet Street, I firmly believe, would have been abandoned in favour of Bloomsbury, and those thundering sledge-hammers of

---

1   Thomas Gray (1716-71), most often noted for his poem, "Elegy Written in a Country Churchyard" (1751).
2   David Hume (1711-76), Scottish philosopher, historian, and economist.
3   Samuel Johnson (1709-84), English man of letters who wrote *The Lives of the Poets* (1779-81), *Rasselas* (1759), and *The Dictionary of the English Language* (1755).

common-sense would have echoed in the tall stone galleries, or sounded more faintly under the dome of the Reading Room itself.

Isaac Disraeli, father of Lord Beaconsfield,[1] was among the habitual readers at the end of the last century, and he records that there were never more than a dozen of them present.

The French Revolution brought about an increase in the number of readers, many of the refugees, some people of distinction among them, seeking consolation from books in the land of exile.

The names of Scott, Sydney Smith, Lamb (recommended by Godwin), and Hallam,[2] figure among the list of readers in the first years of the present century.

As time went on applications for admission to the library became more and more numerous; and the original arrangements for the accommodation of readers at Montague House were found quite inadequate.

One apartment after another was made use of as Reading Room, but it was not till 1857 that the present structure was completed.

This we owe to the genius of Anthony Panizzi,[3] an Italian political exile, but a naturalized Englishman, and formerly superintendent of the Reading Room.

He planned and closely overlooked the carrying out of his scheme which has given us a library and Reading Room unparalleled for arrangement in the world.

The vast, circular apartment, whose aspect is no doubt famil-

---

1 Isaac D'Israeli (1766-1848) remained Jewish all his life despite his having his children baptized in 1817 and their surname changed to "Disraeli." His son Benjamin Disraeli (1804-81) twice served as Prime Minister (1868, 1874-80). He was made the Earl of Beaconsfield by Queen Victoria in 1876.

2 Sir Walter Scott (1771-1832), Scottish author known for his historical novels, including *Ivanhoe* (1819); Sydney Smith (1771-1845), English essayist; Charles Lamb (1775-1834), English essayist; William Godwin (1756-1836), philosopher and novelist, father of Mary Shelley, author of *Frankenstein* (1818); Arthur Henry Hallam (1811-33), Cambridge University friend of Alfred, Lord Tennyson and subject of Tennyson's poem *In Memoriam* (1850).

3 Sir Anthony Panizzi (1797-1879) was instrumental in the expansion of the library, and the establishment of the Reading Room. He was Keeper of Printed Books (1837-56) and Principal Librarian (1856-66).

iar to many of my readers, can accommodate at the present day no less than 460 readers. The desks and tables are models of comfort and convenience; the lighting is by electric light; and so carefully is the temperature regulated by means of an elaborate ventilating apparatus, that an enthusiastic American lady once compared the atmosphere of the place in summer to that of a cool and shady dell.

Let the people who grumble at the closeness of the densely crowded apartment take this to heart, and bear in mind that the unwholesome condition of a former reading room was such as to give rise to a peculiar complaint, known at the time as museum megrims. But perhaps, as a writer in *Blackwood* [1] points out, the fact which most strikes us in connection with the Museum library is its wonderful accessibility. Any person above the age of twenty-one, who can induce one householder to vouch for his good behaviour, has the whole collection of books within his easy reach.

It is a mere matter of transcribing the name and press-mark of any volume from the catalogue, of taking your seat and waiting for the attendant to bring what you have ordered.

There is rarely, if ever, a long delay, and no limit is fixed to the number of books which a reader may demand.

Not only the Reading Room, but the surrounding libraries, are models of arrangement, where millions of books are stowed in such a manner that any one of them may be obtained on the shortest notice.

A French professor told me that he found it on the whole a greater saving of time to come over and read in the Museum during his vacations than to remain in Paris, where the National Library, though larger than our own, and very valuable, and furnished moreover with a reading room, is not so easily accessible.

Perhaps, alas! it is this very accessibility which has brought about such frequent abuse of the privilege of reading at the library, where many people have no scruple in taking up the time of the officials, or crowding out genuine workers from the desks in pursuit of such futilities as answers to word-competitions, chess-problems, or mere novel-reading.

The lower shelves of the Reading Room are filled with books of reference, and these may be taken out by the reader at will, a chart of their positions being furnished. There is an extra room

---

1 [Unsigned], "The British Museum and the People Who Go There," *Blackwood's Magazine* (August 1888): 196-217.

devoted to the consultation of newspapers, and an apartment known as the large room, where may be seen works too valuable to be carried into the Reading Room, or where, sometimes, by the kindness of the officials, readers under the age of twenty-one anticipate the privilege of their majority.

As for the readers who come and go in these various apartments, they include, as I have said, all sorts and conditions of men and women. To begin with, they might be roughly classified into *habitués* and occasional visitors. It is naturally the former class that comes most under observation, and the people composing it, various as they are, develop after a time certain qualities in common.

What are his marks? A premature baldness, a roundness in the shoulders, a slouching gait, an increasing tendency to short-sight, a growing disinclination for the use of the clothes-brush. These are the marks of the Reading Room *habitué*.

Rich and poor, old and young, competent and incompetent, the successes and failures of life and of literature may be met beneath the dome in indistinguishable fellowship.

To each and all, no doubt, the "Room" presents its attractions, for each and all has its uses. For some it is a workshop, for others a lounge; there are those who put it to the highest uses, while in many cases it serves as a shelter,—a refuge, in more senses than one, for the destitute.

4. "Eldorado at Islington," *The Woman's World* 2 (1889): 488-89

The houses in the terrace were of grey stucco, with bow-windows and flights of steps out of all proportion to their size.

The main road ran along the bottom, and the remaining two sides were bounded by stretches of blank wall, above which a few sickly plane-trees were fluttering their leaves in the August air.

Eleanor Lloyd, from her window in the roof, could see not only the wall and the plane-trees, but, by dint of craning her neck, the High Street itself, with its ceaseless stream of trams and omnibuses. There was a public-house at the corner, and, as the door swung backwards and forwards, Eleanor caught glimpses of the lively barmaid behind her tall white tap-handles. A group of flower-girls, with uncurled feathers and straight fringes, stood outside on the pavement, jesting with the 'busmen and passers-by. Eleanor, who was a "lady," (Heaven help her!) used sometimes to envy the barmaid and the flower-girls their social opportunity.

This evening, over everything, over the sordid street, the dusty trees, the clustering roofs—over the girl at the window with her pale face, strong young shoulders, and shabby gown—brooded the spirit of the tired summer.

The summer, which, by stream and sea, is lusty from June to September, drags on weary and dispirited through its later weeks in the City.

The hot, gusty, grit-laden air blew from the east; it moved querulously among the plane-trees, and lifted at intervals the hair on Eleanor's forehead.

She had been sitting there all the afternoon, and now the sun was setting. There was nothing for her to do. Her little pupils in the neighbouring square had gone to the sea; her brothers and sisters played noisily in the basement parlour; even poor Eddy had fallen asleep on the sofa, with the crutch, that was of so little use to him, at his side.

And now, as a great red flame lit up the west, there came over Eleanor one of those half-rapturous fits of longing, those fierce yearnings for happiness, which most of us know in youth; which are not noble, not beautiful, perhaps; certainly in no way to be encouraged; which are only infinitely cruel and infinitely sad.

So the cry went up from her, the human, passionate cry from this helpless, fluttering creature caught—oh, the irony of it!—in a pitiless network of suburban streets.

A man with bent, shabby shoulders and lagging gait, turned up the terrace from the High Street.

At the parlour window of the Lloyds' house a worn-out-looking woman, with a patient face, watched him and sighed.

In their youth, no doubt, the husband and wife had dreamed of other things than those long years of ceaseless labour with their scant reward.

Hard-working, unassuming, delicately just, he was not, perhaps, of the stuff of which rich men are made.

The children clamoured up into the parlour to greet their father. Eddy held out a little thin hand from the sofa; Eleanor, with the dreams still in her dazzled eyes, slid into the darkened room—darkened on behalf of carpet and curtains—and took her place at the tea-table.

"Did you see your letter, father?" said the wife, as she lifted the teapot of Britannia metal.

Mr. Lloyd, who had taken the long blue envelope from the mantelpiece, laid it unopened beside his plate.

The room was very hot, and the blind flapped drearily in the wind. There was a household loaf on the table, some thick, thin-spread bread-and-butter, and a dish of watercress—a tough and sinewy August growth.

Even the children tackled the meal languidly, and after a few minutes their father set down his cup, took up his letter, and broke the seal.

A long, closely-written sheet of paper unrolled itself beneath his hand. He straightened the glasses on his tired eyes and began to read. He read it once, he read it twice, then lifting a perplexed face, said faintly—

"Mother, what does this mean?"

She was at his side, leaning over him, in a moment. She, too, read the letter, then stood strangely silent.

"Children," said their father, "a wonderful thing has happened. It seems that I am a rich man. My brother, from whom I parted in anger many years ago, is dead. He died as he had lived—alone; but at the last remembered me and forgave me...."

His voice died away; and the wife, looking from her children's faces, on which a radiant comprehension was slowly dawning, to her husband's prematurely grizzled head, burst suddenly into weeping.

"My wife," he said—taking her into his arms—"there is no more cause to weep."

II.

Mrs. Lloyd brushed her husband's coat and hat the next morning even more carefully than usual, with a view to his visit to the lawyer.

"If it had come sooner!" she thought, as she watched the bent, beloved figure down the street.

Then she went back to her household duties.

The burden of those long years was not to be shaken off in an hour. She had stiffened, perhaps, into a habit of sorrow and of poverty; it is certain that she laboured faithfully throughout the day at her sordid cares—scarcely able to realise the strange fortune which had befallen them.

But not so the children. For them the good news was a reality. They drew together, building their castles in the air, which, unlike such erections generally, had foundations of solid gold, and even in their unsubstantial upper storeys were fitted up with a sagacity characteristic of the early-wise children of the poor.

Eddy, from his sofa, spoke wistfully of marvellous cures, of health-giving breezes, of great doctors whose services he could now command. Eleanor moved about the house with new life, speaking little, but dreaming, dreaming, dreaming through the summer hours.

The wonderful day sped to its close. Once more the family gathered round the tea-table, the tired father taking his seat at the head.

"Did you go to that lawyer, father? A nice fellow he must be, I should say!" cried Eddy, who was a privileged person.

"And, father, did you tell them at the office that you are not going there any more?" added Eleanor, with a new gladness in her voice, a new light in her eyes, which to-day, at least, were the eyes of a pretty girl.

"Your father is tired," said the mother seeing that her husband neither moved nor spoke, but sat with his elbow on the table, shading his face with his hand.

"No, no," he said quickly, "I am not tired ..."

Then, lifting his head suddenly, he spoke out with curious harshness—

"Wife, children, you must put to-day and yesterday out of your heads. It has all been a mistake."

Half-imploring, half-defiant, he swept the dismayed circle of faces with his glance; then, dropping his eyes, went on—

"The money was never ours, never could be ours. It was the fruit of cruelty and extortion; it was wrung from the starving poor. It is money that no honest man can touch."

He covered his face with his hand, and there was silence in the room.

Then, all at once, the youngest of the children broke into loud crying, and Eleanor, with flaming cheeks and blazing eyes, sprang to her feet.

"I knew it!" she cried, and the anger and sorrow of her voice were sad to hear. "I knew it could not be true that we were going to be happy. It is a shame, a shame, but I knew it!" And she went from the room.

Her father followed her into the narrow passage, shutting the door behind them.

She stood silent, motionless, with her forehead pressed to the wall.

He stretched out a tired, trembling hand and laid it on her shoulder.

"My dear"—the harsh note of pain had faded from his voice; it was only very wistful and weary—"My dear, I am very sorry. But you would not wish it otherwise, I know."

He was a man of few words—simple, timid, little given to demonstrations of affection.

"You do not wish it otherwise?" he said again.

No answer; but he felt the shoulder shaking with sobs beneath his touch.

In the poor girl's simple heart she held her father's decision as absolutely without alternative, as he had done himself. Her anger was impersonal, directed against Fate, and at the pathetic sound of her father's voice she had melted into tears.

Meantime, in the parlour, the mother comforted her children. It was Eleanor who had believed in Eldorado, and yet who had cried, "I knew it!" The mother, whose heart had throughout refused to accept the glad tidings, made no such proclamation. She quieted the crying child, handed Eddy his tea, and taking up the loaf, began to cut it.

This evening the sun had been allowed to stream in through the window, regardless of the poor carpet and curtains. Perceiving this, Mrs. Lloyd laid down her knife and, stirred by the familiar thrifty instinct, walked firmly across the room and quietly drew down the blind.

5. Poetry

[The first five poems appeared in Levy's third and last collection of poetry, *A London-Plane Tree, and Other Verse* (London: T. Fisher Unwin, 1889). With the exception of "In the Mile End Road," none of these five poems is currently in print. "The Village Garden" conveys a yearning for the city despite the attractions of the countryside, and anticipates the poetry of William Butler Yeats, who was familiar with Levy's verse. The other poems suggest the complexities of desire, sexuality, and gender that resonate with Levy's own history as a Jewish and possibly lesbian "new woman" of London. "The Ballad of Religion and Marriage," privately circulated over twenty-five years after Levy's death, contemplates the cultural status of the traditions of marriage and religion, both under question. See the Introduction (pp. 20-21) for additional commentary relevant to these poems.]

"The Village Garden," *A London Plane-Tree, and Other Verse*
(London: T. Fisher Unwin, 1889): 30-31

To E.M.S.[1]

Here, where your garden fenced about and still is,
 Here, where the unmoved summer air is sweet
With mixed delight of lavender and lilies,
 Dreaming I linger in the noontide heat.

Of many summers are the trees recorders,
 The turf a carpet many summers wove;
Old-fashioned blossoms cluster in the borders,
 Love-in-a-mist and crimson-hearted clove.

All breathes of peace and sunshine in the present,
 All tells of bygone peace and bygone sun,
Of fruitful years accomplished, budding, crescent,
 Of gentle seasons passing one by one.

Fain would I bide, but ever in the distance
 A ceaseless voice is sounding clear and low;—
The city calls me with her old persistence,
 The city calls me—I arise and go.

Of gentler souls this fragrant peace is guerdon;
 For me, the roar and hurry of the town,
Wherein more lightly seems to press the burden
 Of individual life that weighs me down.

I leave your garden to the happier comers
 For whom its silent sweets are anodyne.
Shall I return? Who knows, in other summers
 The peace my spirit longs for may be mine?

---

1 Euphemia Malder Stevens and Levy met as classmates at Brighton High
 School. Levy appointed Stevens her executrix.

Believe me, this was true last night,
Tho' it is false to-day.
A.M.F. Robinson[1]

A fair dream to my chamber flew:
Such a crowd of folk that stirred,
Jested, fluttered; only you,
You alone of all that band,
Calm and silent, spake no word.
Only once you neared my place,
And your hand one moment's space
Sought the fingers of my hand;
Your eyes flashed to mine; I knew
All was well between us two.

★★★★★

On from dream to dream I past,
But the first sweet vision cast
Mystic radiance o'er the last.

★★★★★

When I woke the pale night lay
Still, expectant of the day;
All about the chamber hung
Tender shade of twilight gloom;
The fair dream hovered round me, clung
To my thought like faint perfume:—
Like sweet odours, such as cling
To the void flask, which erst encloses
Attar of rose; or the pale string
Of amber which has lain with roses.

"In the Mile End Road," *A London Plane-Tree, and Other Verse* 50

How like her! But 'tis she herself,
    Comes up the crowded street,

---

1 A. Mary F. Robinson (1857-1944).

How little did I think, the morn,
    My only love to meet!

Whose else that motion and that mien?
    Whose else that airy tread?
For one strange moment I forgot
    My only love was dead.

"Contradictions," *A London Plane-Tree, and Other Verse* 51

Now, even, I cannot think it true,
My friend, that there is no more you.
Almost as soon were no more I,
Which were, of course, absurdity!
Your place is bare, you are not seen,
Your grave, I'm told, is growing green;
And both for you and me, you know,
There's no Above and no Below.
That you are dead must be inferred,
And yet my thought rejects the word.

"The Two Terrors," *A London Plane-Tree, and Other Verse* 64

Two terrors fright my soul by night and day:
The first is Life, and with her come the years;
A weary, winding train of maidens they,
With forward-fronting eyes, too sad for tears;
Upon whose kindred faces, blank and grey,
The shadow of a kindred woe appears.
Death is the second terror; who shall say
What form beneath the shrouding mantle nears?

Which way she turn, my soul finds no relief,
My smitten soul may not be comforted;
Alternately she swings from grief to grief,
And, poised between them, sways from dread to dread.
For there she dreads because she knows; and here,
Because she knows not, inly faints with fear.

"A Ballad of Religion and Marriage" [1]

Swept into limbo is the host
    Of heavenly angels, row on row;
The Father, Son, and Holy Ghost,
    Pale and defeated, rise and go.
The great Jehovah is laid low,
    Vanished his burning bush and rod—
Say, are we doomed to deeper woe?
    Shall marriage go the way of God?

Monogamous, still at our post,
    Reluctantly we undergo
Domestic round of boiled and roast,
    Yet deem the whole proceeding slow.
Daily the secret murmurs grow;
    We are no more content to plod
Along the beaten paths—and so
    Marriage must go the way of God.

Soon, before all men, each shall toast
    The seven strings unto his bow,
Like beacon fires along the coast,
    The flames of love shall glance and glow.
Nor let nor hindrance man shall know,
    From natal bath to funeral sod;
Perennial shall his pleasures flow
    When marriage goes the way of God.

Grant, in a million years at most,
    Folk shall be neither pairs nor odd—
Alas! we sha'n't be there to boast
    "Marriage has gone the way of God!"

---

1 Twelve copies of the poem were privately printed by Clement Shorter
and circulated in 1915.

Appendix C: Literary Contexts

1. From John Ruskin, "The Two Servants" from "Fiction—Fair and Foul," *The Nineteenth Century* 10 (October 1881): 516-31

[John Ruskin (1819-1900) was an eminent man of letters and social reformer in the Victorian period who wrote extensively about the arts and whose five-volume *Modern Painters* (1846-60) prompted the first published use of the word "realism" in relation to forms of artistic representation. This excerpt comes from the last of five essays on contemporary fiction that Ruskin published in the magazine *The Nineteenth Century* in 1880-81. Here he criticizes "foul" modern fiction that portrays what he viewed as the ugliness of "low" subject matter, including characters of lower classes and urban life. To explain his aesthetics of "fair" fiction, Ruskin modifies the Romantic symbol of the Grecian vase, from John Keats's "Ode to a Grecian Urn," by emphasizing its usefulness. In his concern about the moral and cultural excesses of his age, Ruskin anticipates both the Decadence Movement in the arts and the social theory of degeneracy of *fin-de-siècle* Western culture.]

I have assumed throughout these papers, that everybody knew what Fiction meant; as Mr. Mill[1] assumed in his Political Economy, that everybody knew what wealth meant. The assumption was convenient to Mr. Mill, and persisted in: but, for my own part, I am not in the habit of talking, even so long as I have done in this instance, without making sure that the reader knows what I am talking about; and it is high time that we should be agreed upon the primary notion of what a Fiction is.

A feigned, fictitious, artificial, super-natural, put-together-out-of-one's-head, thing. All this it must be, to begin with. The best type of it being the most practically fictile—a Greek vase. A thing which has two sides to be seen, two handles to be carried by, and a bottom to stand on, and a top to be poured out of, this, every right fiction *is*, whatever else it may be. Planned rigorously, rounded smoothly, balanced symmetrically, handled handily, lipped softly for pouring out oil and wine. Painted daintily at last with images of eternal things—

---

1 John Stuart Mill (1806-73), *Principles of Political Economy* (1848).

For ever shalt thou love, and she be fair.[1]

Quite a different thing from a 'cast',—this work of clay in the hands of the potter, as it seemed good to the potter to make it. Very interesting, a cast from life may perhaps be; more interesting, to some people perhaps, a cast from death;—most modern novels are like specimens from Lyme Regis,[2] impressions of skeletons in mud.

'Planned rigorously'—I press the conditions again one by one—it must be, as ever Memphian labyrinth or Norman fortress. Intricacy full of delicate surprise; covered way in secrecy of accurate purposes, not a stone useless, nor a word nor an incident thrown away.

'Rounded smoothly'—the wheel of Fortune revolving with it in unfelt swiftness; like the world its story rising like the dawn, closing like the sunset, with its own sweet light for every hour.

'Balanced symmetrically'—having its two sides clearly separate, its war of good and evil rightly divided. Its figures moving in majestic law of light and shade.

'Handled handily'—so that, being careful and gentle, you can take easy grasp of it and all that it contains; a thing given into your hand thenceforth to have and to hold. Comprehensible, not a mass that both your arms cannot get round; tenable, not a confused pebble heap of which you can only lift one pebble at a time.

'Lipped softly'—full of kindness and comfort: the Keats line indeed the perpetual message of it—'For ever shalt thou love, and she be fair.' All beautiful fiction is of the Madonna, whether the Virgin of Athens or of Judah—Pan-Athenaic always.[3]

And all foul fiction is *leze majesté*[4] to the Madonna and to womanhood. For indeed the great fiction of every human life is the shaping of its Love, with due prudence, due imagination, due persistence and perfection from the beginning of its story to the end; for every human soul, its Palladium. And it follows that all right imaginative work is beautiful, which is a practical and brief

---

1 John Keats (1795-1821), "Ode to a Grecian Urn" (1820), line 20.
2 Seaside village on the coast of Dorset in southern England, the site of many discoveries of fossils in the early nineteenth century.
3 Matthew Arnold (1822-88) extolled Greek culture or "Hellenism" as a standard for an aesthetic ideal of "sweetness and light" in *Culture and Anarchy* (1869).
4 Offensive conduct (French).

law concerning it. All frightful things are either foolish, or sick, visits of frenzy, or pollutions of plague.

Taking thus the Greek vase at its best time, for the symbol of fair fiction: of foul, you may find in the great entrance-room of the Louvre, filled with the luxurious *orfèvrerie*[1] of the sixteenth century, types perfect and innumerable: Satyrs carved in serpentine, Gorgons platted in gold, Furies with eyes of ruby, Scyllas with scales of pearl; infinitely worthless toil, infinitely witless wickedness; pleasure satiated into idiocy, passion provoked into madness, no object of thought, or sight, or fancy, but horror, mutilation, distortion, corruption, agony of war, insolence of disgrace, and misery of Death.

It is true that the ease with which a serpent, or something that will be understood for one, can be chased or wrought in metal; and the small workmanly skill required to image a satyr's hoof and horns, as compared to that needed for a human foot or forehead, have greatly influenced the choice of subject by incompetent smiths; and in like manner, the prevalence of such vicious or ugly story in the mass of modern literature is not so much a sign of the lasciviousness of the age, as of its stupidity, though each react on the other, and the vapour of the sulphurous pool becomes at last so diffused in the atmosphere of our cities, that whom it cannot corrupt, it will at least stultify.

★★★

All healthy and helpful literature sets simple bars between right and wrong; assumes the possibility, in men and women, of having healthy minds in healthy bodies, and loses no time in the diagnosis of fever or dyspepsia in either; least of all in the particular kind of fever which signifies the ungoverned excess of any appetite or passion. The 'dulness' which many modern readers inevitably feel, and some modern blockheads think it creditable to allege, in Scott,[2] consists not a little in his absolute purity from every loathsome element or excitement of the lower passions; so that people who live habitually in Satyric or hircine conditions of thought find him as insipid as they would a picture of Angelico's.[3] The accurate and trenchant separation between him and the common railroad-station novelist is that, in his total method of

---

1 Goldsmith's trade or gold plate (French).
2 Sir Walter Scott (1771-1832), Scottish poet and author of historical novels such as *Waverley* (1814) and *Ivanhoe* (1819).
3 Fra Angelico (1400-55), Dominican friar and Florentine painter of religious frescoes.

conception, only lofty character is worth describing at all; and it becomes interesting, not by its faults, but by the difficulties and accidents of the fortune through which it passes, while in the railway novel, interest is obtained with the vulgar reader for the vilest character, because the author describes carefully to his recognition the blotches, burrs and pimples in which the paltry nature resembles his own. The 'Mill on the Floss'[1] is perhaps the most striking instance extant of this study of cutaneous disease. There is not a single person in the book of the smallest importance to anybody in the world but themselves, or whose qualities deserved so much as a line of printer's type in their description. There is no girl alive, fairly clever, half educated, and unluckily related, whose life has not at least as much in it as Maggie's, to be described and to be pitied. Tom is a clumsy and cruel lout, with the making of better things in him (and the same may be said of nearly every Englishman at present smoking and elbowing his way through the ugly world his blunders have contributed to the making of); while the rest of the characters are simply the sweepings-out of a Pentonville[2] omnibus.*

And it is very necessary that we should distinguish this essentially Cockney literature developed only in the London suburbs, and feeding the demand of the rows of similar brick houses, which branch in devouring cancer round every manufacturing town,— from the really romantic literature of France. George Sand[3] is often immoral; but she is always beautiful, and in the characteristic novel I have named, 'Le Péché de Mons. Antoine,' the five principal characters, the old Cavalier Marquis,—the Carpenter,— M. De Chateaubrun,—Gilberte,—and the really passionate and generous lover, are all as heroic and radiantly ideal as Scott's Colonel Mannering, Catherine Seyton, and Roland Graeme;[4]

---

* I am sorry to find that my former allusion to the boating expedition in this novel has been misconstrued by a young authoress of promise into disparagement of her own work; not supposing it possible that I could only have been forced to look at George Eliot's by a friend's imperfect account of it. [Ruskin's note.]

---

1 George Eliot (1819-80), *The Mill on the Floss* (1860), a novel about the difficulties of a sister and brother growing up in rural England.
2 Pentonville is an area of London on the borders of East and West Ends near St. Pancras and Bloomsbury, as well as Clerkenwell and Finsbury.
3 George Sand (1804-76), French novelist who portrayed the struggles of independent women.
4 The first a character from *Guy Mannering* (1815), the other two from *The Abbot* (1820).

while the landscape is rich and true with the emotion of years of life passed in glens of Norman granite and beside bays of Italian sea. But in the English Cockney school,[1] which consummates itself in George Eliot, the personages are picked up from behind the counter and out of the gutter; and the landscape, by excursion train to Gravesend,[2] with return ticket for the City-road.

2. From Oscar Wilde, "The Decay of Lying: A Dialogue," *The Nineteenth Century* 25 (January 1889): 35-56

["The Decay of Lying" is often cited as Oscar Wilde's manifesto for Aestheticism and Decadence. Like Ruskin, Wilde assails the mundane sordidness of realism in modern literature. Unlike Ruskin, Wilde endeavors to divorce art and the life of the mind from nature; he celebrates urban culture over rural landscapes, and questions the unambiguous ethical codes that Ruskin values. In Wilde's aesthetic scheme, the novelist should not assemble "dull facts" of everyday life, but instead should privilege imaginative exaggeration or "lying," an artistic practice he links to poetry. Wilde structures his critique in the form of a conversation between Cyril and Vivian, who espouses the "doctrine of the new aesthetics." Toward the end of the essay, Vivian summarizes this theory: "As a method Realism is a complete failure, and the two things that every artist should avoid are modernity of form and modernity of subject-matter." Aphorisms such as "Life imitates Art far more than Art imitates Life" form the Preface to Wilde's novel, *The Picture of Dorian Gray* (1890). Amy Levy knew Wilde both from the London literary salon scene and as the editor of *The Woman's World* where Levy published several essays, short fiction, and poems.]

Scene.—The Library of a Country House in England.
Persons.—Cyril and Vivian.

Cyril (coming in through the open window from the terrace). My dear Vivian, don't coop yourself up all day in the library. It is a

---

1   A term first published in *Blackwood's Magazine* in 1817 to describe London poets of humble origins, including Leigh Hunt (1784-1859), William Hazlitt (1778-1830), and Keats.

2   Gravesend in Kent had a reputation as a second-rate excursion spot.

perfectly lovely afternoon. Let us go and lie on the grass and smoke cigarettes and enjoy nature.

Vivian. Enjoy nature! I am glad to say that I have entirely lost that faculty. People tell us that art makes us love nature more than we loved her before; that it reveals her secrets to us; and that after a careful study of Corot[1] and Constable[2] we see things in her that had escaped us. My own experience is that the more we study art, the less we care for nature. What art really reveals to us is nature's lack of design, her curious crudities, her extraordinary monotony, her absolutely unfinished condition. When I look at a landscape I cannot help seeing all its defects. It is fortunate for us, however, that nature is so imperfect, as otherwise we should have had no art at all. Art is our spirited protest, our gallant attempt to teach Nature her proper place. As for the infinite variety of Nature, that is a pure myth. It is not to be found in Nature herself, but in the imagination, or fancy, or cultivated blindness, of the man who looks at her.

C. Well, you need not look at the landscape. You can lie on the grass and smoke and talk.

V. But nature is so uncomfortable. Grass is hard and lumpy and damp, and full of horrid little black insects. Why, even Maple can make you a more comfortable seat than nature can. Nature pales before the Tottenham Court Road.[3] I don't complain. If nature had been comfortable, mankind would never have invented architecture, and I prefer houses to the open air. In a house we all feel of the proper proportions. Everything is subordinated to us, fashioned for our use and our pleasure. Egotism itself, which is so necessary to a proper sense of human dignity, is absolutely the result of indoor life. Out of doors one becomes abstract and impersonal. One's individuality absolutely leaves one. And then nature is so indifferent, so unappreciative. Whenever I am walking in the park here, I always feel that I am no more to nature than the cattle that browse on the slope, or the burdock that blooms in the ditch. Nothing is clearer than that Nature hates Mind. Thinking is the most unhealthy thing in the world, and people die of it just as of any other disease. Fortunately, in England at least, it is not catching. Our splendid physique as a people is entirely due to our national stupidity. I only hope we

---

1 Jean-Baptiste-Camille Corot (1796-1875), French realist painter.
2 John Constable (1776-1837), English landscape painter.
3 A major London street that runs through Bloomsbury and intersects with Oxford Street where it turns south into Charing Cross Road.

shall be able to keep this great historic bulwark of our happiness for many years to come; but I am afraid that we are beginning to be over-educated; at least everybody who is incapable of learning has taken to teaching—that is really what our enthusiasm for education has come to. In the meantime you had better go back to your wearisome uncomfortable Nature, and leave me to correct my proofs....

C. What is the subject?

V. I intend to call it 'The Decay of Lying: A Protest.'

C. Lying! I should have thought our politicians kept up that habit.

V. I assure you they do not. They never rise beyond the level of misrepresentation, and actually condescend to prove, to discuss, to argue. How different from the temper of the true liar, with his frank, fearless statements, his superb irresponsibility, his healthy, natural disdain of proof of any kind! After all, what is a fine lie? Simply that which is its own evidence. If a man is sufficiently unimaginative to produce evidence in support of a lie, he might just as well speak the truth at once. No, the politicians won't do, and besides, what I am pleading for is lying in art. Shall I read you what I have written? It might do you a great deal of good.

C. Certainly, if you give me a cigarette. Thanks....

V. (reading in a very clear, musical voice). 'The Decay of Lying: A Protest.—One of the chief causes of the curiously commonplace character of most of the literature of our age is undoubtedly the decay of lying as an art, a science, and a social pleasure. The ancient historians gave us delightful fiction in the form of fact; the modern novelist presents us with dull facts under the guise of fiction. The blue-book is rapidly becoming his ideal both for method and manner. He has his tedious "*document humain*," his miserable little "*coin de la création*," [1] into which he peers with his microscope. He is to be found at the Librairie Nationale, or at the British Museum, shamelessly reading up his subject. He has not even the courage of other people's ideas, but insists on going directly to life for everything, and ultimately, between encyclopædias and personal experience, he comes to the ground, having drawn his types from the family circle or from the weekly washerwoman, and having acquired an amount of useful information from which he never, even in his most thoughtful moments, can thoroughly free himself.

---

1 Corner of creation or invention (French).

'The loss that results to literature in general from this false ideal of our time can hardly be overestimated. People have a careless way of talking about a "born liar," just as they talk about a "born poet." But in both cases they are wrong. Lying and poetry are arts—arts, as Plato saw, not unconnected with each other—and they require the most careful study, the most disinterested devotion. Indeed, they have their technique, just as the more material arts of painting and sculpture have, their subtle secrets of form and colour, their craft-mysteries, their deliberate artistic methods. As one knows the poet by his fine music, so one can recognise the liar by his rich rhythmic utterance, and in neither case will the casual inspiration of the moment suffice. Here, as elsewhere, practice must precede perfection. But in modern days while the fashion of writing poetry has become far too common, and should, if possible, be discouraged, the fashion of lying has almost fallen into disrepute. Many a young man starts in life with a natural gift for exaggeration which, if nurtured in congenial and sympathetic surroundings, or by the imitation of the best models, might grow into something really great and wonderful. But, as a rule, he comes to nothing. He either falls into careless habits of accuracy—'

C. My dear Vivian!

V. Please don't interrupt in the middle of a sentence. 'He either falls into careless habits of accuracy, or takes to frequenting the society of the aged and the well-informed. Both things are equally fatal to his imagination, as indeed they would be fatal to the imagination of anybody, and in a short time he develops a morbid and unhealthy faculty of truth-telling, begins to verify all statements made in his presence, has no hesitation in contradicting people who are younger than himself, and often ends by writing novels which are so like life that no one can possibly believe them....

'Even Mr. Robert Louis Stevenson,[1] that delightful master of delicate and fanciful prose, is tainted with this modern vice, for we positively know no other name for it. There is such a thing as robbing a story of its reality by trying to make it too true, and *The Black Arrow* is so inartistic that it does not contain a single anachronism to boast of, while the transformation of Dr. Jekyll reads dangerously like an experiment out of the *Lancet*.[2] As for

---

1 Robert Louis Stevenson (1850-94), Scottish author of *The Strange Case of Dr. Jekyll and Mr. Hyde* (1886) and *The Black Arrow* (1888).
2 British medical journal first published in 1823.

Mr. Rider Haggard,[1] who really has, or had once, the makings of a perfectly magnificent liar, he is now so afraid of being suspected of genius that when he does tell us anything marvellous, he feels bound to invent a personal reminiscence, and to put it into a footnote as a kind of cowardly corroboration. Nor are our other novelists much better. Mr. Henry James[2] writes fiction as if it was a painful duty, and wastes upon mean motives and imperceptible "points of view" his neat literary style, his felicitous phrases, his swift and caustic satire. Mrs. Oliphant[3] prattles pleasantly about curates, lawn-tennis parties, domesticity, and other wearisome things.... *Robert Elsmere*[4] is of course a masterpiece—a masterpiece of the "genre ennuyeux," the one form of literature that the English people seem to thoroughly enjoy. Indeed it is only in England that such a novel could be possible. As for that great and daily increasing school of novelists for whom the sun always rises in the East-End,[5] the only thing that can be said about them is that they find life crude, and leave it raw.

'In France, though nothing so deliberately tedious as *Robert Elsmere* has been produced, things are not much better. M. Guy de Maupassant,[6] with his keen mordant irony and his hard vivid style, strips life of the few poor rags that still cover her, and shows us foul sore and festering wound. He writes lurid little tragedies in which everybody is ridiculous; bitter comedies at which one cannot laugh for very tears. M. Zola,[7] true to the lofty principle

---

1 Henry Rider Haggard (1856-1925), English novelist of imperial romances, including *King Solomon's Mines* (1886) and *She* (1887).

2 Henry James (1843-1916), American novelist who spend most of his professional life in England, and author of *The Portrait of a Lady* (1881).

3 Margaret Oliphant (1828-97), Scottish author of literary criticism and fiction, including the "Chronicles of Carlingford," a series of novels set in a town near London.

4 Mary Augusta (Mrs. Humphry) Ward (1851-1920), *Robert Elsmere* (1888), on the mid-Victorian crisis of religious faith and doubt.

5 Allusion to the social realism of contemporary novels set in impoverished and working-class sections of London such as Walter Besant's *All Sorts and Conditions of Men* (1882) and Margaret Harkness's *A City Girl* (1888). Wilde employs cartographic metaphors of London similar to Ruskin's complaint about the ugliness of "foul fiction" associated with Pentonville.

6 Guy de Maupassant (1850-93), of the French naturalist school of realism, as was Émile Zola, who defined naturalism as "nature seen through a temperment."

7 Émile Zola (1840-1902) was the leading novelist in the French school of naturalism, which maintained that social and economic environment as well as laws of nature such as inheritance were crucial in representing everyday life.

that he lays down in one of his pronunciamientos on literature, "L'homme de génie n'a jamais de l'esprit,"[1] is determined to show that, if he has not got genius, he can at least be dull.... From any ethical standpoint his work is just what it should be. He is perfectly truthful, and describes things exactly as they happen. What more can any moralist desire? I have no sympathy at all with the moral indignation of our time against M. Zola. It is simply the rage of Caliban[2] on seeing his own face in a glass.... M. Ruskin once described the characters in George Eliot's novels as being like the sweepings of a Pentonville omnibus,[3] but M. Zola's characters are much worse. They have their dreary vices, and their drearier virtues. The record of their lives is absolutely without interest. Who cares what happens to them? In literature we require distinction, charm, beauty, and imaginative power. We don't want to be harrowed and disgusted with an account of the doings of the lower orders.

3. A. Mary F. Robinson, "Will," *Women's Voices: an Anthology of the Most Characteristic Poems by English, Scotch, and Irish Women*, ed. Elizabeth A. Sharp (London: Walter Scott, 1887) 330

[Two poems by Levy, including "The Two Terrors" in Appendix B5, appeared in Sharp's anthology.]

The world is a garment for me to wear,
The days are my glance and the dark my hair.

Alone in the kingdom of space I stand
With Hell and Heaven in either hand.

Life is the smile, Death the sigh of me,
Who was, who am, who ever shall be.

Men and their gods pass away, but still
I am maker and end, I am God, I am Will.

---

1 The man of genius never has need of wit (French).

2 Character from Shakespeare's *The Tempest* described as "a savage and deformed slave."

3 See Appendix C1.

4. Michael Field, "The Moon Rose Full: The Women Stood," *Long Ago* (London: George Bell and Sons, 1889) 26-27

[This poem, written by two women, Katherine Bradley and Edith Cooper, who used the pen name "Michael Field," is an example of the Sapphic poetics of same-sex desire evident in late Victorian poetry. Many of Levy's later poems, including "The Dream" and "In the Mile End Road" in Appendix B5, might be read alongside Field's poetry.]

The moon was shining in its fulness
When they stood around the altar

A. Maidenhood, maidenhood, where have you gone in leaving me?
B. No longer will I come to you, no longer will I come.[1]

The moon rose full: the women stood
As though within a sacred wood
Around an altar—thus with awe
The perfect, virgin orb they saw
Supreme above them; and its light
Fell on their limbs and garments white.
Then with pale, lifted brows they stirred
Their fearful steps at Sappho's word,
And in a circle moved around,
Responsive to her music's sound,
That through the silent air stole on,
Until their breathless dread was gone,
And they could dance with lightsome feet,
And lift the song with voices sweet.
Then once again the silence came:
Their lips were blanched as if with shame
That they in maidenhood were bold
Its sacred worship to unfold;
And Sappho touched the lyre alone,
Until she made the bright strings moan.
She called to Artemis aloud—
Alas, the moon was wrapt in cloud!—

---

1 This epigraph, from Sappho, appears in Greek in the original version in *Long Ago*.

"Oh, whither art thou gone from me?
Come back again, virginity!
For maidenhood still do I long,
The freedom and the joyance strong
Of that most blessèd, secret state
That makes the tenderest maiden great.
O moon, be fair to me as these,
And my regretful passion ease,
Restore to me my only good,
My maidenhood, my maidenhood!"
She sang: and through the clouded night
An answer came of cruel might—
"To thee I never come again."
O Sappho, bitter was thy pain!
Then did thy heavy steps retire,
And leave, moon-bathed, the virgin quire.

5. Dollie Radford, "From Our Emancipated Aunt in Town," *Songs and Other Verses* (London: John Lane, 1895) 87-93

[Radford's poem offers a comical view of the "new woman" figure of late-Victorian literature. The poem might be compared with Levy's "A Ballad of Religion and Marriage."]

All has befallen as I say,
The old régime has passed away,
        And quite a new one

Is being fashioned in a fire,
The fervours of whose burning tire
        And quite undo one.

The fairy prince has passed from sight,
Away into the ewigkeit,[1]
        With best intention

I served him, as you know my dear,
Unfalteringly through more years
        Than ladies mention.

---

1 Eternity (German).

And though the fairy prince has gone,
With all the props I leaned upon,
         And I am stranded,

With old ideals blown away,
And all opinion, in the fray,
         Long since disbanded.

And though he's only left to me,
Of course quite inadvertently,
         The faintest glimmer

Of humour, to illume my way,
I'm thankful he has had his day,
         His shine and shimmer.

Le roi est mort—but what's to come?—
Surcharged the air is with the hum
         Of startling changes,

And our great "question" is per force
The vital one, o'er what a course
         It boldly ranges!

Strange gentlemen to me express
A quiet "at homes" their willingness,
         To ease our fetters

And ladies, in a fleeting car,
Will tell me that the moderns are
         My moral betters.

My knees I know are much too weak
To mount the high and shaky peak
         Of latest ethics,

I'm tabulated, and I stand
By evolution, in a band
         Of poor pathetics

Who cannot go alone, who cling
To many a worn out tottering thing
         Of a convention;

To many a prejudice and hope,
And to the old proverbial rope
      Of long dimension.

It is to you to whom I look
To beautify our history book,
      For coming readers,

To you my nieces, who must face
Our right and wrong, and take your place
      As future leaders.

And I, meanwhile, shall still pursue
All that is weird and wild and new
      In song and ballet,

In lecture, drama, verse and prose,
With every cult that comes and goes
      Your aunt will dally.

A microscopic analyst
Of female hearts, she will subsist
      On queerest notions,

And subtlest views of maid and wife
Ever engaged in deadly strife
      With the emotions.

But while you walk, and smile at her,
In quiet lanes, which you prefer
      To public meetings,

Remember she prepares your way,
With many another Aunt to-day,
      And send her greetings.

Appendix D: The Woman Question

1. From Grant Allen, "The Girl of the Future," *The Universal Review* 7 (1890): 49-64

[In her 1889 calendar Levy mentions several visits with Grant Allen when they discussed the woman question. Allen's writing, both fiction and essays, reflects his belief in eugenics. His essay "Plain Words on the Woman Question" appeared in the *Fortnightly Review* in October 1889, a month after Levy's death, but it is in this essay that he alludes to Levy's suicide. He also wrote a poem on the same topic, "For Amy Levy's Urn."]

High up in the front rank of social problems which engage the minds of thinking people in this age of transition, I suppose we may place the fundamental problem of how the Community may best be provided in future with constant relays of sound and efficient citizens. The Marriage Problem, most people call it, with illogical glibness; for that phrase begs the question from the very outset by tacitly taking for granted the continued existence in time to come of the institution of marriage. The Sex Problem, I dare say Miss Schreiner[1] and Mrs.Caird[2] would call it—thumbscrews will not drive me to violate the genius of our mother tongue by describing this last lady as "Mrs. Mona Caird:" but to speak of it as a problem of Sex rather than as a problem of Paternity and Maternity is to fall into the besetting sin of women who lightly meddle with these high matters—the error of treating marriage or its substitute mainly from the point of view of the personal convenience of the two adults involved, and very little indeed from the vastly more important and essential point of view of the soundness and efficiency of the children to be begotten. Were I to choose a name for it myself, I would call it rather the Child Problem, or if we want to be very Greek, out of respect to Girton,[3] the Problem of Paedopoietics.

---

1 Olive Schreiner (1855-1920), author of *The Story of an African Farm* (1883), an early "New Woman" novel.
2 Mona Caird (1854-1922), novelist and essayist whose 1888 essay "Marriage" in the *Westminster Review* spurred a controversy over the marriage question.
3 Girton was the first college established for women at Cambridge University. See p. 55, note 2.

★★★

.... it must be clear at once to every sensible mind that if any good thing is ever to come out of the present ferment, the opinions of men who have thought much upon these subjects, and the opinions of women (if any) who have thought a little, should be openly collated, compared, and debated upon. It is only by such frank sifting of the very best and fullest thought—the product of long and earnest study—that advance has ever been made in any direction. And if it be objected that no advance is here needed, the answer is obvious. You can't stand still. Change is in the air: change is close upon us: revolutionary ideas as to marriage permeate our society, and what is specially important, our women in particular. The wife is beginning to clamour for easier divorce: the spinster is beginning to kick against lottery wedlock.

★★★

It isn't the Quantity but the Quality of our fresh material that is now at stake. The East End and the scrofulous pensioners will pullulate in a thousand garrets as of yore: the nervous woman will still bring forth abundantly her rickety offspring with great regularity at measured intervals of twenty-four months: even the broken-down product of the Oxford Local Examination[1] system will continue to produce on an average two congenitally hysterical and anaemic infants before she finally fades away into thin air at her third childbed. But the question is, will our existing system provide us with mothers capable of producing sound and healthy children, in mind and body, or will it not? If it doesn't, then inevitably and infallibly it will go to the wall. Not all the Mona Cairds and Olive Schreiners that ever lisped Greek can fight against the force of natural selection. Survival of the fittest is stronger than Miss Buss,[2] and Miss Pipe,[3] and Miss Helen Glad-

---

1 Introduced in 1858, these rigorous examinations, taken at the end of a course of study, were intended to elevate middle-class secondary education for persons not entering academic professions. Levy passed the Cambridge local examinations in 1878.

2 Frances Mary Buss (1827-94), advocate for women's rights who fought for the admission of women to Cambridge University.

3 Hannah Pipe (1831-1906) founded Laleham Lodge, a boarding school for girls in Clapham from 1856 to 1908.

stone,[1] and the staff of the Girls' Public Day School Company, Limited,[2] all put together. The race that lets its women fail in their maternal functions will sink to the nethermost abyss of limbo, though all its girls rejoice in logarithms, smoke Russian cigarettes, and act Aeschylean tragedies in most aesthetic and archaic chitons. The race that keeps up the efficiency of its nursing mothers will win in the long run, though none of its girls can read a line of Lucian or boast anything better than equally-developed and well-balanced minds and bodies.

$$\star\star\star$$

One of the most striking among the innumberable inconveniences of our exisiting marriage system is the fact that it makes practically no provision for what Mr. Galton[3] aptly terms 'eugenics'—that is to say, a systematic endeavour towards the betterment of the race by the deliberate selection of the best possible sires, and their union for reproductive purposes with the best possible mothers. On the contrary, it leaves the breeding of the human race entirely to chance, and it results too often in the perpetuation of disease, insanity, hysteria, folly, and every other conceivable form of weakness or vice in mind and body. Indeed, to see how foolish is our practice in the reproduction of the human race, we have only to contrast it with the method we pursue in the reproduction of those other animals whose purity of blood, strength, and excellence has become of importance to us.

$$\star\star\star$$

We have only to ask, Is it probable that in the time to come men and women will voluntarily begin here and there, sporadically, so to readjust their natural relations in a manner pleasing to themselves, and satisfactory to their natural instincts, that something like the end here proposed may finally be achieved by slow devel-

---

1 Helen Gladstone (1814-80), the younger sister of the statesman William Ewart Gladstone, rebelled against her father and brothers who tried to control and restrain her "aberrant" behavior.
2 The Girls' Public Day School Company was established in 1872 for the purpose of providing girls with a rigorous and nondenominational academic education similar to public school programs for boys. Levy attended the Brighton High School for Girls, one of the first schools established by this organization.
3 Francis Galton (1822-1911) developed the theory of eugenics, influenced by his cousin Charles Darwin's theory of evolution by natural selection.

opment? In short, will Free Temporary Unions, or Free Relations with no definite union at all, tend to grow up side by side with marriage, or even ultimately with certain classes, to supersede marriage; and if so, will they have in part the effect here suggested, of encouraging the production of the greatest number of sane and sound children by the best parents, all round, and discouraging the production of undesirable children by the mentally, morally, or physically deficient?

It cannot be denied that this question is now fairly confronting us. The Free Union is an actuality. It is a growing actuality. It is beginning to be recognized. It is almost becoming respectable....

There has been of late years a great movement in England and America for the Higher Instruction of Women. Colleges have been opened; High Schools have been started; Senior Classics have been led like lambs to the slaughter; our girls have been crammed with Mathematics like Strasbourg geese with Indian meal, till they are bursting with vast stocks of unassimilated knowledge. The raw material has been pushed in at one end of the mill with indiscriminate zeal, and has come out at the other, turned and shaped to pattern, with wooden regularity. All life and spontaneity, to be sure, has been crushed out in the process; but no matter for that: our girls are now 'highly cultivated.' A few hundred pallid little Amy Levys sacrificed on the way are as nothing before the face of our fashionable Juggernaut. Newnham[1] has slain its thousands, and Girton its tens of thousands; the dark places of the earth are full of cruelty. But still, in spite of all its hideous and inhuman errors, 'the movement' has this at least of good augury in it—that now for the first time in the history of the world, mankind has begun to think about the upbringing of its women.

.... Is it not conceivable—nay, even probable—that before many years are out some educational reformer may propose, instead of stuffing girls with Sophocles and examining them in the Rudiments of Faith and Religion till they are as flat as pancakes and as dry as broomsticks, a new and daring scheme—to develop their bodies in muscle, nerve, and organ; to exercise their minds in logical reasoning; and to instruct them in the main truths of the universe around them, and their own relations to it? May not our women yet be taught to understand their own body, and the light cast upon it by the analogy of other bodies; their

---

1 See Introduction (pp. 14-16) for background on Levy as a student at Newnham College. See Appendix E2, a photograph of Levy and her classmates.

own mind, and the light cast upon it by the history and evolution of other minds; the cosmos in which they live, and the phenomena, organic or inorganic, stellar or terrestrial, it presents to their view; the society of which they are members, and the origin and development of its structure and functions? Such an Education of Women I firmly believe we may yet see; though I know Mrs. Grundy[1] will fight tooth and nail in her very last ditch to prevent its ultimate realization.

But you cannot have Education without having in the long run Emancipation as well. When you have given your women a training in gymnastic, music, hygiene, propaedeutic; in logic, mathematics, chemistry, physics; in astronomy, geology, biology, psychology; in history, sociology, politics, economics; in asthetics, ethics, and the application of all those to their own functions; and when you have at the same time taught them how to play at games for pure love of them, while simultaneously encouraging their sense of fun and humour; in short, when you have developed all sides of their nature equally, instead of stuffing them with a few dry linguistic facts, and getting them to walk two and two abreast, in weary, dreary file along the Marine Parade—then, I venture to predict, you will inevitably find their education has emancipated them.

Being myself one of those (if, indeed, the plural be admissible) who believe in the emancipation of woman, I am not afraid of this result; on the contrary, I hail the prospect with effusion. At present to be sure, very few men, and no women, believe in emancipation. Nevertheless, progress is steadily though unconsciously being made in that direction. The Instruction of Women, which aims, not at equable development of mind and body, but at one-sided overloading of the memory with dry details of language, and which succeeds, not in practising the intellect, but in cramping and thwarting it, so as to produce in the end an unwholesome mind in a stunted body—the Instruction of Women must nevertheless in the end give place, assuredly, to the Education of Women: and when Education comes, why Emancipation cannot be far distant. Women will then be as gods, having eaten of the tree of knowledge of good and evil. The keys of ethics, of history, of sociology, of economics, will be in their hands to unlock the problem of their sex's destiny. It will no longer be possible for man to persuade them in their blindness

---

1   A symbol of exaggerated moral propriety; the term is based on a character from Thomas Morton's play *Speed the Plough* (1798).

that their absolute subjection to, and appropriation by, one single lord and master is a necessary corner-store of all social order. It will no longer be possible for men to persuade them that marriage, which sprang from capture and slavery, and which crystallizes in its very form the brutal selfishness and jealousy of the stronger sex, is an element of eternal and immutable morality. They will see that our existing system, instead of being, as its apologists always hypocritically pretend, a pure system of marriage alone, is really a joint system of marriage and prostitution, in which the second element is a necessary corollary and safeguard of the first. And they will begin to inquire how far it is right of them to sacrifice so many of their own sex to man's unhappy collective need, merely in order that they may hand over the remainder, bound hand and foot, to man's unreasonable individual despotism.

★★★

For the self-supporting woman is free and independent. Owing nothing to any man, it is not likely she will go on accepting without a murmur for an indefinite period, the unproved dogma of man's natural right to monopolize individually whatever member of her sex he can buy or acquire for himself, without appeal or chance of revision. Already, indeed, the self-supporting woman is beginning to assert her individual freedom. She tramps about the world alone, all unmarried as she is, with neither protector nor chaperon. She sets at naught the stringent laws of matron-made etiquette. She goes on walking tours. She lives where she likes, and dines where she chooses. As often as not, she has rooms in Gower Street,[1] and spends her holiday by herself in a hotel at Florence. She is even beginning to demand a latch-key. There are London chambers, erected for her special benefit, in which she has actually claimed and already obtained that masculine privilege. And when once you begin to give your women a latch-key, trust me, you may feel sure that the moral order, based on marriage by capture and the slavery of the wife, is tottering, all unbeknown, to its rotten foundations.

★★★

---

1 Located adjacent to the University of London in Bloomsbury, Gower Street runs south from Euston Road. Levy's friends, Vernon Lee and Mary Robinson, lived there.

And when women are more soundly brought up and more physically educated; when their natural instincts are developed by healthy sports, and allowed free play in fuller social intercourse; when the scales have fallen from their eyes in ethical matters, and they have begun to think and reason instead of blindly swallowing whatever Authority tells them—do you believe the self-supporting woman or the endowed girl will go on for ever contentedly selling herself to empty-headed fools, or contentedly acquiescing in the disuse of her own highest feminine functions through enforced spinsterhood? No, indeed. All experience shows us she will do nothing of the sort. She will make her own choice and guide her own life in the way that seems good to her. She will follow her own highest ideal, and refuse to be misled by any specious argument-mongering. She will form her own code of public opinion. She will take the noblest and purest man she can get, and become by him the parent of sound and beautiful offspring. Then our best fathers and our best mothers will no longer run the risk of being thrown away in vain, and a practical system of eugenics, or nature's own plan of distinctive selection, will have automatically established itself.

Of course it will be long in coming; for men have so moulded women to their own will that a woman of independent mind is a great rarity. How could it be otherwise? Men have only married and made mothers of the 'nice girls' who had no craving for freedom; while the best and freest women have died unwed or gone to the bad hopelessly. But it may come in the end for all that—when our women are educated.

★★★

Remember, what I have to say comes in the end merely to this— that in the future we shall perhaps have a few more George Eliots and a few less Dorotheas[1] than formerly; that an increasing number of women, as they become educated and emancipated, will follow in the path that educated and emancipated women have trod already before them—and will possibly even be a little less tabooed for it.

---

1 Dorothea Brooke is the heroine in George Eliot's novel *Middlemarch* (1871-72).

2. From Clementina Black, "The Organization of Working Women," *The Fortnightly Review* 52 (November 1889): 695-704

[The issue of women working outside the home was a crucial component of "the woman question" debates of the late Victorian period. This essay describes the complex economic and social conditions of urban working women and stresses the importance of women's trade unions, the focus of Black's efforts during the last years of Levy's life, when the two women were close friends.]

The effects of economic competition upon the position of women have been twofold and contradictory. To the comparatively educated and prosperous it has brought greater independence and freedom; to the poor it has brought increased poverty, and, in some instances, a slavery which I believe to be worse than any of which record exists in the world.

Let me examine a little the way in which it seems to me that these two contradictory effects have been produced. Let me also own, beforehand, that there have been other causes which have contributed to produce them. Very few effects in our complicated modern life arise from the pressure of one clear and separate cause; most of them are resultants of many causes working in different directions, and with differing degrees of force. It is not so easy to calculate the relative force of each of these causes, and that is why one man's solution of a social problem is apt to differ so widely from another's. To me it appears that in this problem of women's work the strongest acting force has been that of economic competition, and for the moment I shall treat of it only.

Economic competition pressing more and more severely upon men has rendered it necessary for women to enter the labour market. A certain number of women became wage-earners instead of living on the wages of others and doing work which, though often in the highest degree useful and valuable, was not measured by a market price. Now, there is a vast difference between the position of a person who earns a livelihood or who owns property and that of one who depends for support upon the earnings or the property of another. The old proverb expresses the fact crudely enough, but truly: "He who pays the piper calls the tune." Speaking roughly, economic dependence means personal subservience; and economic independence means personal freedom. And this difference is even more marked in the case of whole classes than of individuals. The standing of a member of a wage-earning or property-owing class, even if this particular member neither earns nor owns, is more independent than that of a member of a supported class. A son who lives on an allowance from his father has more individual freedom than a daughter who does the same; on the other hand a daughter living thus has more freedom to-day, when numbers of women live by their own work, than was enjoyed fifty years ago by one who did live by her own work, when such a position was exceptional and the general rules of womanly life were those of a supported class. "Of course I do not propose to live in lodgings by myself. It would not be respectable." It was Harriet Martineau, a woman of independent temper if ever there was one, who wrote thus, when she was over thirty years old, to her mother.[1] Hundreds of women are living in precisely that manner at the present day and enjoying the respect of their neighbours. The need of earning money has compelled them to become free, and has compelled the world to recognise their freedom.[2]

This same need has also greatly raised the standard of their work. Work that is done to be paid for must be done regularly; it must be set in the first place, whatever else goes to the wall. Roughly speaking, when the work of women did not represent money—when it was not a commodity for the market—it was not treated with the same respect and consideration as that of men. Nay, the lingering tradition that women do not, or should not, work for money, still causes their work to be treated with less regard, and by this very circumstance helps to prevent it, in too many cases, from rising to an equal standard of efficiency with that of men. Precisely the same lingering tradition still indirectly hampers their liberty of action in those points where the need of earning money does not come in.

★★★

---

1 Harriet Martineau (1802-76) was a prominent woman of letters who wrote on a variety of subjects across different genres. She is best known for her writing on political economy, *Illustrations of Political Economy*, serialized from 1832-35, several novels, including *Deerbrook* (1839), her autobiography (1877), and her translation of Auguste Comte, the founder of sociology. She was also a staunch abolitionist and published on this topic as well.

2 Black and her sisters lived in lodgings in London (see Introduction).

Nor is it only the women who actually work who have secured more liberty. It would be difficult to maintain two different standards for persons of the same rank and education; and the fact that some women, because they have to work, have to live alone and to go about alone at all hours, has made it possible for all women to do so. This same necessity of working for money has made it necessary that women should be better trained, and the more thorough training has made them both better fitted to control their own lives and more anxious to do so. Thus economic competition has driven some of them into the labour market, and has in doing so caused not them only, but most women of their class, to receive better education and greater freedom—to the immense advantage, as I believe, not only of themselves, but also of those men and children of whom they may become wives and mothers.

That is one side of the picture. On the other hand, where wages were already low and conditions hard, the entrance of women into the labour market has served to intensify competition and increase these evils. When the husband's wage is very low, the wife goes to work that she may supplement his earnings. She can afford to work for something less than her single neighbour, because her husband partly supports her. He in his turn can afford to work for a little less than a man who has no wife at work. Thus one undersells another, and the weakest and the most enduring are in the long run the worst paid. And not only are they the worse paid, but also the most heavily worked. A woman who only earns a penny an hour has got to work a good many hours a day if she is to live by her work, and the woman who is in this case, is in a condition of worse slavery than any likely to be enforced by a slave-holder to whose interest it is that his slave should not die. I think the comparatively well-to-do have very little notion of the lives led by hundreds of working women in English towns.

★★★

Charity cannot avail to help. Charitable donations can only be, in effect, a rate in aid of wages and therefore in the end a force towards the reduction of wages. It is only by standing together that the workers in a trade can resist reductions of wage, and it is they and they only who can. All that the outsider can do is to show them how to do this for themselves, to supply the initial expenses of meetings, &c., to give perhaps temporary assistance in secretarial work, and to be ready to indemnify those who are made scapegoats in the early days before the union has accumulated funds enough to do this business for itself, and finally to secure for the combined workers, the invaluable protection of public opinion.

The first attempt to do these things for women was made about fifteen years ago by Mrs. Emma Paterson,[1] who was the daughter of a national schoolmaster and the wife of a cabinet-maker. She founded the Women's Protective and Provident League (since named the Women's Trades Union Provident League), of which she remained honorary secretary until her death three years ago. The fight was an uphill one. Trade Union was in those days a name of terror to the untrained and the unthinking, exactly as Socialism is now.[2] But a little band of earnest workers—Mrs. Paterson the most earnest of all—pursued their purpose quietly. The first union which they established was that of the women employed in bookbinding, which still exists and has a good balance at the bank. This society is the oldest trade society of women in England. It has at present about two hundred and fifty members, a sadly inadequate percentage of the number of women employed in the trade in London, but I am sorry to say a large number if compared with the membership of most women's unions. Several other societies in London followed, most of which still continue, but none of which is sufficiently large to fulfil the main function of a union, which is to secure good conditions of pay, hours, treatment, and surroundings....

***

---

1   Emma Anne Smith Paterson (1848-86) founded the Women's Protective and Provident League in 1876.

2   Socialism in 1880s London represented to some a radical and even anarchistic ideology, but there were several kinds of socialist groups in London during this period. Robert Owen introduced the concept of socialism in 1827 through his design of communal living along economic principles. The 1880s saw the revival of socialism with much debate on what form it should take in Great Britain. The Social Democratic Foundation (SDF) was founded in 1881, followed by William Morris's Socialist League in 1884, the same year that the Fabian Society started as a group of middle-class intellectuals. Like several of her friends, including Eleanor Marx, Olive Schreiner, Vernon Lee, and Clementina Black, Levy attended the Socialist League and the Fabian Society occasionally; Black was a more regular participant.

A vast impetus to the cause of unionism among women was given by the success of the match-girls' strike, and by the formation, under Mrs. Besant's able guidance, of their numerous union.[1]

★★★

The committee hope very shortly to secure an office in the heart of the East End. But meetings and offices and the printing and circulation of tracts and handbills all cost money. Money help and personal help are needed. The first and great essential— sadly wanting hitherto—seems now to be present; the women themselves are awake and ready. With those of us who see, who understand, and who care, it rests to take up the work of helping them, so that they may now at last deliver themselves from the bondage in which many of them have been born and lived.

---

1 Annie Besant (1847-1933) published an article, "White Slavery in London," about the poor wages and the dangers of phosphorous fumes to the health of women workers in the matchstick factory of Bryant and May. Besant helped these workers form a union, which led to a strike of 1,400 matchworkers in July 1888. The matchworkers' grievances echoed those of many women in other industries. Besant was a member of the Socialist Democratic League and also campaigned for birth control, and toward the end of her life, for Indian Home Rule, or governance by Indian nationalists rather than British colonists.

Appendix E: Victorian Photography

1. From [Lady Elizabeth Eastlake], "Photography," *Quarterly Review* 101 (April 1857): 442-68

[Lady Elizabeth Rigby Eastlake (1809-1893) was an art historian and literary critic, the first woman to contribute regularly to the *Quarterly Review*. Her 1848 review of Charlotte Brontë's *Jane Eyre* excoriated the novel for its "pervading tone of ungodly discontent." In 1856 she also published a harsh review of John Ruskin's *Modern Painters* where she characterized his art criticism as "morbid and diseased." A photographer herself, Eastlake terms photography in this 1857 essay "a new form of communication." After providing a brief history of this new medium, Eastlake addresses the question of whether photography should be regarded as an artistic form or as a mechanical device to register nature.]

It is now more than fifteen years ago that specimens of a new and mysterious art were first exhibited to our wondering gaze. They consisted of a few heads of elderly gentlemen executed in a bistre-like colour upon paper. The heads were not above an inch long, they were little more than patches of broad light and shade, they showed no attempt to idealise or soften the harshnesses and accidents of a rather rugged style of physiognomy—on the contrary, the eyes were decidedly contracted, the mouths expanded, and the lines and wrinkles intensified. Nevertheless we examined them with the keenest admiration, and felt that the spirit of Rembrandt had revived. Before that time little was the existence of a power, availing itself of the eye of the sun both to discern and to execute, suspected by the world—still less that it had long lain the unclaimed and unnamed legacy of our own Sir Humphry Davy.[1] Since then photography has become a household word and a household want; is used alike by art and science, by love, business, and justice; is found in the most sumptuous saloon, and in the dingiest attic—in the solitude of

---

1 Sir Humphry Davy (1778-1829), English chemist who gave popular lectures on scientific topics at the Royal Institution in London. Eastlake later cites Davy's practical application of silver nitrate, an important chemical in developing the photographic image.

the Highland cottage, and in the glare of the London gin-palace—in the pocket of the detective, in the cell of the convict, in the folio of the painter and architect, among the papers and patterns of the millowner and manufacturer, and on the cold brave breast on the battle-field.

★★★

And this brings us to the artistic part of our subject, and to those questions which sometimes puzzle the spectator, as to how far photography is really a picturesque agent, what are the causes of its successes and its failures, and what in the sense of art are its successes and failures? And these questions may be fairly asked now when the scientific processes on which the practice depends are brought to such perfection that, short of the coveted attainment of colour, no great improvement can be further expected....

But while ingenuity and industry—the efforts of hundreds working as one—have thus enlarged the scope of the new agent, and rendered it available for the most active, as well as for the merest still life, has it gained in an artistic sense in like proportion? Our answer is not in the affirmative, nor is it possible that it should be so. Far from holding up the mirror to nature, which is an assertion usually as triumphant as it is erroneous, it holds up that which, however beautiful, ingenious, and valuable in powers of reflection, is yet subject to certain distortions and deficiencies for which there is no remedy. The science therefore which has developed the resources of photography, has but more glaringly betrayed its defects. For the more perfect you render an imperfect machine the more must its imperfections come to light: it is superfluous therefore to ask whether Art has been benefited, where Nature, its only source and model, has been but more accurately falsified. If the photograph in its early and imperfect scientific state was more consonant to our feelings for art, it is because, as far as it went, it was more true to our experience of Nature. Mere broad light and shade, with the correctness of general forms and absence of all convention, which are the beautiful conditions of photography, will, when nothing further is attempted, give artistic pleasure of a very high kind; it is only when greater precision and detail are superadded that the eye misses the further truths which should accompany the further finish.

For these reasons it is almost needless to say that we sympathise cordially with Sir William Newton,[1] who at one time created no little scandal in the Photographic Society by propounding the heresy that pictures taken slightly out of focus, that is, with slightly uncertain and undefined forms, 'though less *chemically,* would be found more *artistically* beautiful.' Much as photography is supposed to inspire its votaries with aesthetic instincts, this excellent artist could hardly have chosen an audience less fitted to endure such a proposition. As soon could an accountant admit the morality of a false balance, or a sempstress the neatness of a puckered seam, as your merely scientific photographer be made to comprehend the possible beauty of 'a slight *burr.*' His mind proud science never taught to doubt the closest connexion between cause and effect, and the suggestion that the worse photography could be the better art was not only strange to him, but discordant. It was hard too to disturb his faith in his newly acquired powers. Holding, as he believed, the keys of imitation in his camera, he had tasted for once something of the intoxicating dreams of the artist; gloating over the pictures as they developed beneath his gaze, he had said in his heart 'anch' io son pittore.'[2] Indeed there is no lack of evidence in the Photographic Journal of his believing that art had hitherto been but a blundering groper after that truth which the cleanest and precisest photography in his hands was now destined to reveal.

★★★

Here, therefore, the debt to Science for additional clearness, precision, and size may be gratefully acknowledged. What photography can do, is now, with her help, better done than before; what she can but partially achieve is best not brought too elaborately to light. Thus the whole question of success and failure resolves itself into an investigation of the capacities of the machine, and well may we be satisfied with the rich gifts it bestows, without straining it into a competition with art. For everything for which Art, so-called, has hitherto been the means but not the end, photography is the allotted agent—for all that

---

1   Sir William Newton (1785-1869) claimed that photography was most valuable as a tool to assist the fine arts in "Upon Photography in an Artistic View, and in Its Relations to the Arts," *Journal of the Photographic Society of London* 1 (3 March 1853): 6-8.

2   "And me, I am a painter" (Italian).

requires mere manual correctness, and mere manual slavery, without any employment of the artistic feeling, she is the proper and therefore the perfect medium. She is made for the present age, in which the desire for art resides in a small minority, but the craving, or rather necessity, for cheap, prompt, and correct facts in the public at large. Photography is the purveyor of such knowledge to the world. She is the sworn witness of everything presented to her view. What are her unerring records in the service of mechanics, engineering, geology, and natural history, but facts of the most sterling and stubborn kind? What are her studies of the various stages of insanity—pictures of life unsurpassable in pathetic truth—but facts as well as lessons of the deepest physiological interest? What are her representations of the bed of the ocean, and the surface of the moon—of the launch of the Marlborough,[1] and of the contents of the Great Exhibition[2]—of Charles Kean's now destroyed scenery of the 'Winter's Tale,'[3] and of Prince Albert's now slaughtered prize ox[4]—but facts which are neither the province of art nor of description, but of that new form of communication between man and man—neither letter, message, nor picture—which now happily fills up the space between them? What indeed are nine-tenths of those facial maps called photographic portraits, but accurate landmarks and measurements for loving eyes and memories to deck with beauty and animate with expression, in perfect certainty, that the ground-plan is founded upon fact?

In this sense no photographic picture that ever was taken, in heaven, or earth, or in the waters underneath the earth, of any thing, or scene, however defective when measured by an artistic scale, is destitute of a special, and what we may call an historic interest. Every form which is traced by light is the impress of one

---

1 Marlborough House, Pall Mall, London, was under renovations at the time; it became the home of the Prince and Princess of Wales in 1863.

2 The Great Exhibition of 1851 was held in the Crystal Palace in Hyde Park, London, and consisted of 13,000 displays from all over the world to advertise the industrial, economic, and military power of the British Empire.

3 Charles Kean (1811-68), British actor and theatre manager. Kean staged his 1856 production of Shakespeare's play set in ancient Greece with an extravagant set of Greek columns, elaborate costumes, and lavishly painted backdrops.

4 Landowners exhibited their finest livestock, and many times these were the subject of paintings, drawings, and photographs. Prince Albert garnered a string of prizes at the Smithfield Club Cattle Show in London.

moment, or one hour, or one age in the great passage of time. Though the faces of our children may not be modelled and rounded with that truth and beauty which art attains, yet minor things—the very shoes of the one, the inseparable toy of the other—are given with a strength of identity which art does not even seek. Though the view of a city be deficient in those niceties of reflected lights and harmonious gradations which belong to the facts of which Art takes account, yet the facts of the age and of the hour are there, for we count the lines in that keen perspective of telegraphic wire, and read the characters on that playbill or manifesto, destined to be torn down on the morrow.

Here, therefore, the much-lauded and much-abused agent called Photography takes her legitimate stand. Her business is to give evidence of facts, as minutely and as impartially as, to our shame, only an unreasoning machine can give. In this vocation we can as little overwork her as we can tamper with her. The millions and millions of hieroglyphics mentioned by M. Arago[1] may be multiplied by millions and millions more,—she will render all as easily and as accurately as one. When people, therefore, talk of photography as being intended to supersede art, they utter what, if true, is not so in the sense they mean. Photography *is* intended to supersede much that art has hitherto done, but only that which it was both a misappropriation and a deterioration of Art to do. The field of delineation, having two distinct spheres, requires two distinct labourers; but though hitherto the free-woman has done the work of the bondwoman, there is no fear that the position should be in future reversed. Correctness of drawing, truth of detail, and absence of convention, the best artistic characteristics of photography, are qualities of no common kind, but the student who issues from the academy with these in his grasp stands, nevertheless, but on the threshold of art. The power of selection and rejection, the living application of that language which lies dead in his paint-box, the marriage of his own mind with the object before him, and the offspring, half stamped with his own features, half with those of Nature, which is born of the union—whatever appertains to the free-will of the intelligent being, as opposed to the obedience of the machine,—this, and much more than this, constitutes that

---

1   Dominique François Jean Arago (1786-1853), French astronomer and physicist, requested that Louis Daguerre make a photograph (called a "Daguerrotype") of the moon in 1838, and so launched the field of photography.

mystery called Art, in the elucidation of which photography can give valuable help, simply by showing what it is not. There is, in truth, nothing in that power of literal, unreasoning imitation, which she claims as her own, in which, rightly viewed, she does not relieve the artist of a burden rather than supplant him in an office. We do not even except her most pictorial feats—those splendid architectural representations—from this rule. Exquisite as they are, and fitted to teach the young, and assist the experienced in art, yet the hand of the artist is but ignobly employed in closely imitating the texture of stone, or in servilely following the intricacies of the zigzag ornament. And it is not only in what she can do to relieve the sphere of art, but in what she can sweep away from it altogether, that we have reason to congratulate ourselves. Henceforth it may be hoped that we shall hear nothing further of that miserable contradiction in terms 'bad art'—and see nothing more of that still more miserable mistake in life 'a bad artist.' Photography at once does away with anomalies with which the good sense of society has always been more or less at variance. As what she does best is beneath the doing of a real artist at all, so even in what she does worst she is a better machine than the man who is nothing but a machine.

2. Levy at Newnham College: Norwich House, 1880

[Amy Levy lived in Norwich House with other students while attending Newnham College, Cambridge University. She appears in this photograph in the top row, fourth from the right, approximately above her signed initials "A.L." at the bottom. In 1877 Newnham College leased Norwich House for three years when Newnham Hall, the original housing facility for the College, ran out of space. The building still exists in Cambridge near the present University Botanic Gardens. Miss Torry, who appears in the center of the photograph, was in charge of Norwich House from January 1879. For an example of Victorian art photography, see cover image, from an 1862 photograph by Clementine Hawarden.]

Norwich House, Cambridge, 1880.
Reproduced by permission of Newnham College Archives, Cambridge University.

Appendix F: Map of Levy's London from Bacon's New Map of London (1885)

Locations from Levy's Life:

1. 11 Sussex Place, Regent's Park (residence 1872-84)
2. 26 Ulster Place, Regent's Park (residence 1884-85)
3. 7 Endsleigh Gardens, Bloomsbury (residence 1885-89)
4. British Museum
5. University Club for Ladies, 31 New Bond Street
6. West London Synagogue, Upper Berkeley Street

Locations in *The Romance of a Shop*:

Select Bibliography

Works by Amy Levy

Novels

The Romance of a Shop. London: T. Fisher Unwin, 1888;
  Boston: Cupples and Herd ("The Algonquin Press"), 1889.
Reuben Sachs: A Sketch. London and New York: Macmillan and
  Co., 1888; Peterborough, ON: Broadview Press, 2006.
Miss Meredith. London: Hodder and Stoughton, 1889, serialized
  in *British Weekly* (April-June 1889).

Poetry [Collections]

Xantippe and Other Verse. Cambridge: E. Johnson and Co., 1881.
A Minor Poet and Other Verse. London: T. Fisher Unwin, 1884.
A London Plane-Tree, and Other Verse. London: T. Fisher Unwin,
  1889.

Short Fiction [A partial list]

"Mrs. Pierrepoint: A Sketch in Two Parts." *Temple Bar* 59 (June
  1880): 226-36.
"Euphemia: A Sketch." *Victoria Magazine* 36 (August-September 1880): 129-41, 199-203.
"Between Two Stools." *Temple Bar* 69 (1883): 337-50.
"The Diary of a Plain Girl." *London Society* 44 (September
  1883): 295-304.
"Sokratics in the Strand." *The Cambridge Review* (6 February
  1884): 163-64.
"Another Morning in Florence (Dedicated to Mr. Ruskin)."
  London Society 49 (May 1886): 386-90.
"The Recent Telepathic Occurrence at the British Museum."
  The Woman's World 1 (1888): 31-32.
"Cohen of Trinity." *The Gentleman's Magazine* 266 (1889): 417-24.
"Addenbrooke." *Belgravia* 68 (March 1889): 24-34.
"A Slip of the Pen." *Temple Bar* 86 (1889): 371-77.
"Eldorado at Islington." *The Woman's World* 2 (1889): 488-89.
"Wise in Her Generation." *The Woman's World* 3 (1890): 20-23.

Essays [A partial list]

"James Thomson: A Minor Poet." *The Cambridge Review* 21, 28 (February 1883): 240-41, 257-58.

"The New School of American Fiction." *Temple Bar* 70 (March 1884): 383-89.

"The Ghetto at Florence." *The Jewish Chronicle* (26 March 1886): 9.

"The Jew in Fiction." *The Jewish Chronicle* (4 June 1886): 13.

"Middle-Class Jewish Women of To-Day." *The Jewish Chronicle* (17 September 1886): 7.

"The Poetry of Christina Rossetti." *The Woman's World* 1 (1888): 31-32.

"Women and Club Life." *The Woman's World* 1 (1888): 364-367.

"Readers at the British Museum." *Atalanta: Every Girl's Magazine* (April 1889): 449-454.

Collected Edition

New, Melvyn, ed. *The Complete Novels and Selected Writings of Amy Levy, 1861-1889*. Gainesville: UP of Florida, 1993.

Late-Victorian Periodical Press on Modern Women

"How I Drove an Omnibus" ("by a Girl"). *English Illustrated Magazine* 18 (1898): 155-61.

Billington, Mary Frances. "How Can I Earn My Living?—In Journalism, Art, or Photography." *The Young Woman* 2 (June 1894): 307-10.

Black, Clementina. "The Grievances of Barmaids." *The Woman's World* 3 (1890): 383-85.

Crawford, Emily. "Women Wearers of Men's Clothes." *The Woman's World* 2 (1889):283-86.

Eliot-James, A.E.F. "Shopping in London." *The Woman's World* 2 (1889): 5-8.

Hawksley, Julia M.A. "The Influence of the Woman's Club." *The Westminster Review* 153 (1900): 454-57.

Hetherington, Annie. "Type-Writing and Shorthand for Women." *The Woman's World* 2 (1889): 326-29.

Hughes, Jabez. "Photography as an Industrial Occupation for Women." *Victoria Magazine* 21 (May 1873): 1-8.

Innes, E. Robertson. "On Married Women's Surnames." *London Society* 49 (May 1886): 516-19.

Jones, Dora M. "The Life of a Bachelor Girl in a Big City." *The Young Woman* 8 (1899-1900): 131-33.

Marshall, M.D., Mary A. "Medicine As a Profession for Women," *The Woman's World* 1 (1888): 105-10.

Secondary Reading on Levy

Beckman, Linda Hunt. *Amy Levy: Her Life and Letters.* Athens: Ohio UP, 2000.

Francis, Emma. "Amy Levy: Contradictions?—Feminism and Semitic Discourse." *Women's Poetry, Late Romantic to Late Victorian: Gender and Genre.* Eds. Isobel Armstrong and Virginia Blain. Basingstroke: Macmillan, 1999. 183-206.

Jusová, Iveta. "Amy Levy: The Anglo-Jewish New Woman." *The New Woman and the Empire* (Columbus: Ohio State UP, 2005) 131-77.

Nord, Deborah Epstein. "'Neither Pairs Nor Odd': Women, Urban Community, and Writing in the 1880s." *Walking the Victorian Streets: Women, Representation and the City.* By Deborah Epstein Nord. Ithaca: Cornell UP, 1995. 183-206.

Parsons, Deborah L. "The New Woman and the Wandering Jew." *Streetwalking the Metropolis: Women, the City, and Modernity.* By Deborah L. Parsons. Oxford: Oxford UP, 2000. 82-122.

Scheinberg, Cynthia. "Amy Levy and the Accents of Minor(ity) Poetry." *Women's Poetry and Religion in Victorian England.* By Cynthia Scheinberg. Cambridge: Cambridge UP, 2002. 190-237.

Vadillo, Ana Parejo. "New Woman Poets and the Culture of the *Salon* at the *Fin de Siècle.*" *Women: A Cultural Review* 10.1. London: Routledge, 1999: 22-34.

Vadillo, Ana Parejo. "Amy Levy in Bloomsbury." *Women Poets and Urban Aestheticism: Passengers of Modernity* (London and New York: Palgrave Macmillan, 2005) 38-77.

Wagenknecht, Edward. *Daughters of the Covenant: Portraits of Six Jewish Women.* Amherst: U of Massachusetts P, 1983.

Weisman, Karen. "Playing with Figures: Amy Levy and the Forms of Cancellation." *Criticism* 42.1 (Winter 2001): 59-79.

Secondary Reading on "New Woman" Fiction

Ardis, Ann. *New Women, New Novels: Feminism and Early Modernism.* New Brunswick, NJ, and London: Rutgers UP, 1990.

Brake, Laurel. *Subjugated Knowledges: Journalism, Gender and Literature in the Nineteenth-Century.* Basingstoke: Macmillan, 1994.

Brandon, Ruth. *The New Women and the Old Men.* London: Secker and Warburg, 1990.

Cunningham, Gail. *The New Woman in the Victorian Novel.* London and New York: Harper & Row, 1978.

Flint, Kate. *The Woman Reader 1837-1914.* Oxford and New York: Oxford UP, 1993.

Heilman, Ann. *New Woman Fiction: Women Writing First-Wave Feminism.* London: Macmillan, 2000.

Heilman, Ann, and Margaret Beetham, eds. *New Woman Hybridities: Femininity, Feminism, and International Consumer Culture, 1880-1930.* London and New York: Routledge, 2004.

Ledger, Sally. *The New Woman: Fiction and Feminism at the Fin de Siècle.* Manchester and New York: Manchester UP, 1997.

Nelson, Carolyn Christensen, ed. *A New Woman Reader: Fiction, Articles and Drama of the 1890s.* Peterborough, ON: Broadview Press, 2001.

Pykett, Lyn. *The "Improper" Feminine: The Women's Sensation Novel and the New Woman Writing.* London and New York: Routledge, 1992.

Richardson, Angelique. *Love and Eugenics in the Late Nineteenth Century: Rational Reproductions and the New Woman.* Oxford and New York: Oxford UP, 2003.

Richardson, Angelique, and Chris Willis, eds. *The New Woman in Fiction and Fact:* Fin-de-Siècle *Feminisms.* London: Palgrave, 2001.

Secondary Reading on Victorian Photography

Armstrong, Nancy. *Fiction in the Age of Photography: The Legacy of British Realism.* Cambridge: Harvard UP, 1999.

Green-Lewis, Jennifer. *Framing the Victorians: Photography and the Culture of Realism.* Ithaca: Cornell UP, 1996.

Groth, Helen. *Victorian Photography and Literary Nostalgia.* Oxford and New York: Oxford UP, 2004.